HOUSE FULL OF
STRINGS

HOUSE FULL OF
STRINGS

Emmi Kolosov

I'd like to dedicate this book to my cats, Enzi and Luna.

There are many people who've supported and guided me throughout my life—more people than I can count, really. People like my parents, my friends, and so many others that bring color to my life and, by extension, the stories I create. I wouldn't be who I am today without them.

Anyway, getting back to the cats, 80% of actually writing this book was spent with you furry little gremlins on my lap, so you two are practically my co-writers.

Chapter 1

Levi Learns to Weaponize Makeup

On a cloudy December day, a young boy made his way down the damp streets of the little town he called home, doing an excessive number of cartwheels as he went and somehow not slipping on muddy snow in the process. He passed a building with a bright neon sign hanging from it that said *Maine's Best Pasta!* in flashing colors.

The boy scowled. That sign had been taunting him for ages. It looked like it'd be a perfect addition to his room, yet he could never jump high enough to reach it. Not to mention the size of it; there was no way he could drag it all the way back to the run-down rambler house he'd made his abode. And while his friend who provided him with housing and food—otherwise known as Kearney, as that was much quicker—was taller than him, the boy knew Kearney would never approve of such thievery, so it seemed the sign would get to live another day.

The boy went back to his cartwheels, nearly sending the contents of his giant backpack flying everywhere in the process. His gloves were muddy, and his fingers freezing, but it'd be well worth it. Because he was on a mission—a mission to show off his sheer awesomeness to the world and all who inhabited it. A mission to get a tattoo.

He dove behind a dumpster when he recognized the curly brown hair and worn black hoodie of the person coming his way. Kearney.

Kearney raced up to a woman who'd been minding her business up to this point and said, "Have you seen my little brother?" The urgency in his voice faded as his nervousness took over. "H-His name is Levi. He has b-blue eyes, and...." He trailed off, awkwardly staring at her. Then he hurried away with his gaze fixed on the ground.

Befuddled, the woman went back to her personal business, which happened to be staring intently at a cold bowl of soup and pondering her existence.

Still as scared of grown-ups as ever. Levi smirked. *Well, I'm not. I'm not scared of anything. You'll see that soon enough.* He slipped down an alleyway, chuckling mischievously under his breath. He shoved his nose into his faded pink scarf as he ran. *Gotta keep the cold air from freezing my insides,* he noted. Not all of Kearney's pearls of wisdom had been ignored.

Levi was soon out of the alley and back in the sun's pale light. The noise of pedestrians filled the street, which pleased him greatly. *That should make things easier.* He fixed his attention on what was waiting for him on the other side of the road: the tattoo parlor. His eyes scanned left and right. *All clear.* He beelined for the parlor, his muddy sneakers splashing through puddles as he ran. *Nothing can stop me now!*

2

On the subject of things stopping Levi, his path just so happened to cross Kearney's at that very moment. They froze and stared at each other. Kearney inched between Levi and the tattoo parlor. "Levi, no."

Levi inched forward in response. He had no intention of giving up now.

"Levi, *no*," Kearney repeated, as if putting enough emphasis on the word no would convince Levi to stop like it would a well-trained dog.

Unfortunately, Levi was neither a dog nor well-trained. He sped past Kearney, only to swiftly get himself caught in an aggressive bear hug.

"What is wrong with you?" Kearney yelled. He sounded angry, which was rare. "Do you *want* to throw your future out the window?"

"You're being dramatic!" Levi barely managed to squeak out as he kicked his legs.

"No, I'm not. Too many things can go wrong!"

"Like what?"

"You could get an infection and die, for one!"

"Oh, *brother!*" He wriggled out of Kearney's grip and darted away. He raced across the road, narrowly avoiding a car in the process.

"Levi!" Kearney shrieked as he chased him, almost becoming roadkill in the process as well before he started gaining on Levi at a rapid pace.

Levi looked over his shoulder, screamed, and dove into the nearest store he could find. It looked like the tattoo would have to wait. Kearney marched after him without hesitation even though Levi had just barged into a makeup shop, meaning whatever damage they were about to cause was bound to be expensive.

To the shoppers' confusion, Levi yelped and dove behind a shelf. He started grabbing cosmetics at random and throwing them. In response, Kearney yanked a mirror off its stand and held it up as a shield. The mirror shattered in seconds, and, unfortunately for the now-screaming customers, Levi turned into a machine gun, his bullets being flying makeup.

Kearney flinched as bottles shattered against the broken mirror but continued his approach. "Levi, stop it!"

Levi tossed another sampler in response. The sampler somehow managed to ricochet off the mirror and slam right back into his face. He now deeply regretted throwing that sampler.

Kearney took the opportunity to charge forward, slamming the mirror into Levi and sandwiching him between it and the wall. Levi's arms flailed as he desperately tried to wiggle free. He managed to grab a hairbrush and started smacking Kearney over the head with it. It got stuck in Kearney's hair seconds later.

"See?" he yelled while trying to pull the hairbrush out. "This is why you should brush your hair!"

Kearney winced as he fought to hold his ground. "Oh, *what*, so you can smack me over the head better?"

Levi growled in dismay as he struggled to free himself from Kearney's trap. Soon, exhaustion was the victor of their battle, and his arms were waving in defeat. "Truce. Truce!"

"Only once you give up your obsession."

"It's not an obsession!"

"Give it up!"

"Fine!"

With a huff of satisfaction, Kearney dropped the mirror and collapsed on the ground. "Thank you," he sighed.

Levi didn't bother hiding how tired he was. He fell over right next to Kearney. The two were now panting and a complete mess. They lay in silence for another minute while onlookers stared at them.

Kearney groaned. "I'm a terrible role model." He ran a hand over his face, smearing all the colorful makeup on it.

Levi shook his head patronizingly. "You're just the worst."

"But at least you're not getting that tattoo."

"Not *today*."

"Not ever."

Levi rolled his eyes, still panting and struggling not to show it. "I'll put it off for…a bit. But only if we get doughnuts."

"Levi…."

"Think about it."

Kearney bit his lip as he stared at the ceiling, considering Levi's proposition. "We haven't gotten them for a while, have we? Okay. But only if I tie you to a lamppost when we get there."

Levi frowned. "Only if you get me the ones with jam inside."

"Sounds like a plan."

Ten minutes after the attack on the salon, a man standing behind the counter of a drugstore stared as his most
infamous customer strode in. The oversized backpack
the boy always wore bounced up and down with his
steps as he walked up to the counter. A little something
that made this time different from all their other interac-
tions was that the eleven-year-old's normally white hair
was now dyed rose pink. Either he was going through
another phase, or this was a result of a plan gone spec-
tacularly wrong.

"Hi, Rob," the boy, Levi, greeted him.

"Hey."

Levi started admiring his lighter display. He then
grabbed an engraved wooden lighter and looked Rob in
the eye, challenging him.

"No." Rob shook his head, exhausted already. "Put it
back."

"Make me," Levi said as he grinned. "I dare you."

"I doubt you'd be talking like this if Kearney was
around." Rob's tired gray eyes scanned the store. It was
somewhat concerning that Kearney wasn't here to hold
Levi back from destroying the place. "Speaking of
which, where is he?"

"Getting doughnuts." Levi ran a finger along the counter and shriveled his nose in disgust when he saw all the dust he'd collected on his fingertip. "He told me to stay here until he's back."

Rob sighed. In truth, Kearney was probably trying to find a way to compensate for whatever damage Levi had just caused. "You did something, didn't you?"

"I sure did, Robby."

"Don't call me that." His hand was on Levi's desired lighter now, keeping it hidden under his palm.

Levi frowned indignantly. "I'll fight you for it."

"We both know you can't fight."

He paused in thought. "I'll have Kearney fight you for it."

"Kearney won't want to fight me."

"Well, maybe Kearney needs to man up." Levi's face scrunched up as he tried to pry the lighter from between Rob's fingers.

After a moment of silence, Rob spoke again, "A lady walked in a minute ago. She was a mess. Said something about two kids starting a fight in a makeup store." His eyes drifted to Levi's hair. "You didn't happen to be around when that happened, did you?"

Levi's smirk returned. "I'm honored, truly. After all, only the best criminals are recognized for their work. And I didn't even *mean* to trash that store. See how much I can do on accident? That's pretty legendary, isn't it?"

"I wish you'd try to become a legend in more productive ways."

"I tried to before we trashed the store!"

"Really?" Rob sounded incredulous.

"Yeah, I wanted to get this awesome tattoo of a fire chicken." Levi made a dramatic gesture with his hands that somehow meant *fire chicken*. "But Kearney stopped me! Can you believe him?"

"Hardly."

Levi leaned against the counter with a sigh. "Whatever. I'll find another way to get one. After the terms of our agreement end, of course. That's what the doughnuts are for."

"I didn't realize you could be bribed so easily." Rob tilted his head curiously. "*How* would a tattoo have made you legendary, exactly?"

"Because you don't see other kids my age doing it. Imagine all the adults I'd impress if I had a tattoo!"

"Why are you interested in something like that?"

Levi's smile faded, and a guarded look came over his face. "None of your business, Robby."

Rob let out a heavy sigh. "If you want people to like you, stop terrorizing them. Being a criminal and getting a tattoo won't magically draw parents toward you."

"Who said anything about parents?" Color flushed Levi's face as he frowned. "Anyway, nothing else seems to work," he muttered.

Rob had known Levi and Kearney for years now. It was the 21st century, and yet, CPS still hadn't scooped these two up. How that was the case was beyond him.

He lifted his gaze then sighed with relief. Rescue had come. "Hey, Kearney."

Kearney had just walked through the door with a bag of doughnuts in hand. That was the least interesting thing about him, given his face was practically a makeup rainbow. "Hi."

Rob chuckled. "I don't think you know how to use a hairbrush, kid." He pointed at the hairbrush still sticking out of Kearney's hair.

Kearney didn't reply. Instead, he grabbed Levi and walked away. "Thanks," was all he said before leaving.

Once they were outside, he let Levi go and put his free hand in his pocket, his eyes looking ahead and fixed on nothing in particular. Meanwhile, Levi was focused on the bag of doughnuts. *The bag's steaming. They're warm!* His mouth watering, he reached for them, but Kearney quickly whisked them away.

"These are for when we get back."

Levi frowned. "Fine."

They walked through the streets, which were a lot more packed than before. Kearney was subconsciously trying to keep as far away from the crowds as possible. Levi could tell because he was practically pressed against the buildings as they passed the clusters of pedestrians.

"Don't you think this is a little much?"

Kearney glanced at him. "What's much?"

Levi opened his mouth to say more, then realized it'd be pointless. After all, there was no changing Kearney's strange little habits. They continued walking in silence, which bored Levi to tears, so he shrugged his backpack off his shoulders and started sifting through it. He pulled out a pair of slap wristbands and started slapping Kearney with them.

Kearney struggled to keep a straight face as he kept his gaze fixed ahead. Then, in a dramatic twist, he yanked one of the bands out of Levi's hand and started fighting back. Their battle went on until they stopped at a wooden fence.

Kearney pulled a loose plank out of the fence, and they walked through the gap. They walked down the wobbly path and up to the worn-down brick house they called home. Kearney pulled out a rusty key, stuck it into the door's keyhole, and twisted it.

A bit of peeling brown paint fell off the door as if to say, "Welcome back." The door squeaked open, and they headed inside.

Kearney shut the door behind them, locked it, unlocked it, then locked it again.

Levi raced up to the tiny heater humming at the opposite end of the room and thrust his hands at it, sighing in delight as feeling came back to his frigid fingers. Meanwhile, Kearney was pulling out two worn diner chairs from the pantry and dragging them over to the little table in the center of the room. Once the table was set, Levi raced over only to get dragged off to the bathroom.

"We have to clean up first," Kearney chastised.

Levi groaned but didn't protest as Kearney dunked his face into the water-filled sink before rubbing it dry with an old towel. Once all the traces of pink were gone, Levi was dismissed.

"You can go eat. I'll join you when I'm done," Kearney said as he began cleaning his own face. He seemed to kick up a storm of vibrant powder every time he moved, not to mention the hairbrush still sticking out of the side of his head was quite the fashion statement. He'd probably be cleaning himself up for a while.

Levi watched him for a second then walked away. He sat at the kitchen table and studied the bag of doughnuts with a frown. The guilt had finally begun to set in. There was no way he could eat those doughnuts now that his conscience was dirty. He sat there for a solid ten minutes, staring them down until Kearney reappeared, now completely makeup-free.

He sat down beside Levi. "You didn't start yet?"

"I wanted to wait," Levi said with a shrug.

Kearney grabbed a doughnut, but even then, Levi continued to stare at the tantalizing rings of fried dough. He shifted awkwardly as he glanced at Kearney. "Sorry about earlier," he blurted.

"It's alright." Kearney pushed the box toward him. "Now, you'd better hurry up before I eat them all," he said with a grin.

Levi smiled back and grabbed a doughnut, but nothing could shake that feeling in his gut.

Kearney always said the same thing: *It's alright.* Even when it wasn't, he said that, and at this point, hearing it made Levi feel icky. Because instead of saying all the things he could and probably *should* have been saying, Kearney just let things go.

Levi sighed and decided to eat the guilt away. He shoved a doughnut into his mouth, and Kearney was about to do the same but paused.

His doughnut was hovering just before his lips. "Did I lock the door earlier?"

Levi nodded absently. "You did. You walked in, closed it, and locked it." He started gesturing with his hands to match Kearney's previous actions. He'd done it so often at this point he hardly had to think about it anymore.

Kearney watched the movements closely. "Okay. Thanks."

Levi leaned threateningly far back in his diner chair as he ate. He loved having dessert before dinner. Something about it made him feel like he was breaking divine law, and that lifted his spirits.

He glanced at Kearney. "Do you think we'll see a lot of stars tonight?"

"We might."

After a couple more minutes, Levi hopped out of his seat. "I'm going to my room."

"Okay," Kearney replied through a mouthful of doughnut. "I'll get dinner in about half an hour."

"Sounds good." Levi walked into the hall and through a door that had his name sloppily written on it in blue paint. He dropped his backpack at his feet and tossed himself onto the mattress on the floor. He stared up at the ceiling, which was covered in even more splatters of paint left by him. It was his personal little Sistine Chapel, one that he believed rivaled Michelangelo's.

He let his eyes trail over the rest of his room, which was filled to the brim with random things he'd gathered over the years. Feeling pleased with himself and his little bedroom kingdom, he reached into his coat pocket and pulled out the wooden lighter from earlier. His smile grew as he recalled how he had slipped it out of Rob's hand when the guy had looked up to greet Kearney. The whole operation was seamless. *That'll teach him to underestimate me.*

He paused, fidgeting it between his fingers. *What would Kearney think if he saw it?* He shook his head with a groan. He tried to distract himself from that thought by imagining where he'd put his new trophy, which didn't help much. He continued doing so for about ten minutes before Kearney, ever-inconvenient at the most perfect of times, walked in.

They stared at each other.

"Why didn't you knock?" Levi demanded.

"I wanted to check on you," Kearney replied. He noticed the lighter. "Is that from Rob's?"

"Maybe." Levi gripped the lighter defensively.

"You have to put it back," Kearney said urgently.

Levi balled his fists. *Of course, you only reprimand me when it comes to Rob. You just loooooove Rob.* "It's fine!"

"We're on good terms with him. Why do you want to change that so badly?"

"Cut out this 'we' talk. *You're* the one who's besties with him, not me!"

Kearney sighed as he rubbed his temples. "Give me the lighter."

One side of Levi wanted to be civil and listen. After all, Kearney was right. But the other, much louder side of him was screeching about how pretty and special the lighter was and how much he wanted to keep it. "No."

"Levi..."

"It'll be *fine*. Rob didn't even notice!"

"I can't just break his trust—"

"I don't care about his trust, and you shouldn't either!" Levi couldn't understand why Kearney respected the guy so much. The only thing Rob was to Levi was annoying. To be fair, the feeling was probably mutual.

Kearney opened his mouth to say more but stopped himself. He let out a heavy sigh. "I'm going to get dinner now."

Stop changing the subject! "Can I tag along today?" Levi asked, his teeth gritted with annoyance. He forced himself to relax and crossed his arms.

Kearney shook his head.

"Come on!"

"I have to do something today. I'll take you tomorrow, promise."

Levi scrunched his nose. "I'll let it slide this time. Since you promised and all," he said reluctantly.

Kearney nodded gratefully. "I might be gone for longer than usual, so don't worry about me." After that, he left Levi's room, closing the door behind him.

Levi felt that familiar knot twist in his stomach as he heard the sound of receding footsteps, followed by the front door slamming shut. He let out a huff as he fell back onto his mattress. His thoughts went back to their conversation, specifically to what he could've said better. He already had a list, and he wasn't too eager to go over it. He tugged his hair and groaned. He hardly knew what it was he really wanted. The only thing he *did* know was whenever he'd see Kearney react to something, he'd imagine what his own parents would've done differently.

Levi bit his lip as he clung to that word. *Parents.* He and Kearney hardly talked about those. Kearney had never mentioned his parents, and Levi had only been four when his own had died, yet the image he had of them in his mind was crystal clear. How they talked, how they laughed…the whole world had made sense when he'd had them. Now, nothing made sense.

He thought back to Kearney and cringed because he knew exactly what that 'something' Kearney had to do was.

You don't have to clean up my messes. Make me do it, for once.

Chapter 2

Kearney Has a Chat with the Most Terrifying Being on Earth

Kearney had spent at least an hour at the salon scooping up broken glass and restocking the shelves while trying his hardest to dodge the manager's repetitive, "Who are your parents?" and "Learn to manage your bratty brother better." Now, he was completely drained and felt thankful that all he had left to do was get dinner and go home. Now, he stood outside Rob's drugstore, unable to move an inch, no matter how hard he tried.

The truth was, he and Levi didn't have a lot of money; given Kearney didn't have a job, that made sense. That meant things like doughnuts were a luxury. The two of them were only able to have dinner every night because of Rob.

Rob, a guy in his late twenties struggling to pay off both his apartment and store's rent, worked two jobs: one at his drugstore and one at a Chinese takeout place a few blocks away. Every night, he'd grab some leftovers for them, and Kearney would come by Rob's drugstore to pick them up. Once in a while, Rob would even come by their place and leave a small envelope of cash in their mailbox.

Things like that meant the world to Kearney, so he tried his hardest to cause Rob as little trouble as possible. All of that went right out the window whenever Levi got one of his bright ideas. And with how things had gone earlier that day, this was one of those dreaded evenings where Kearney would get an earful.

Kearney peered through the window and saw Rob talking to a woman inside the store. He tensed up a little. *There's someone else in there. That's even worse.* He shook his head. *Come on, loosen up. It'll be fine. Probably.*

With a jolt of determination, he headed inside, moving the door so slightly he didn't even ring the bell overhead when he entered. He'd gotten good at doing that. He slipped behind a shelf and watched the interaction curiously. He rested his hands at his sides and told himself to relax, but that didn't help much.

The woman Rob was talking to looked to be middle-aged, with long, unkempt brown hair and bags under her eyes.

"...It's been three months already, and there's still nothing?" Rob asked wearily, running a hand over his stubble with a long sigh.

The woman nodded and rubbed her reddened eyes. "I don't know what to do anymore," she whispered. "What if that's just it? What if all this is for nothing?"

"Don't talk like that." He held her hand, his eyes full of resolve. "You know how resourceful that kid is. We'll find her." He glanced at the poster she was holding. "Tell you what, I'll run and print some more right now, and we'll walk around and hand them out. Okay?"

The woman nodded. Rob disappeared through a door behind the counter, leaving the woman staring at the face on the poster in her shaking hand.

Kearney continued watching her in silence. He'd been seeing papers like those everywhere lately. It was interesting to see where they were all coming from. Sobering, even.

He glanced back at the money in his hand, his objective now his prime focus again. *This is perfect. I'll walk over there and leave the money on the counter with a note. No interaction required.* He slid up to the counter, grabbed a sticky note and pen, and started writing as quickly as possible. However, his note wouldn't do much since his handwriting was just as indecipherable as an ancient script. He paused. *Wait, this won't work. I'd still have to talk to Rob to get dinner—*

"What are you doing?"

He snapped out of his thoughts and looked at the woman, who seemed to have been watching him for a bit now. His mouth opened, but only a stutter came out. He stared at her as she stared back and felt himself begin to shake. Save for Rob, Kearney tried his hardest to avoid interacting with any and all adults, but no matter how careful he was, it seemed moments like this were inevitable. *Say something.* "Nothing."

The woman furrowed her brow. "You're out late, aren't you? Where are your parents?"

"Th-They're outside."

The woman glanced out the window and saw no one there.

He winced a little. *Well, if she didn't think I was suspicious before, she definitely will now.*

"I didn't realize they're invisible." Her eyes floated back to him.

I have to hurry before Rob comes back. He felt his heart beat faster and his breath quicken. *But, what if I bolt out and that lady thinks I'm doing something shady and tells Rob, then* he *thinks I'm doing something shady and gets even madder?*

"You should be careful, you know."

He snapped out of his thoughts. "Huh?"

"I said you should be careful." Her grip on the poster tightened. "It might not be as safe around here as it used to be."

He stared at the girl on the paper. "Do you know her?"

"She's my daughter."

"Oh." His eyes widened. "I'm sorry she's missing."

"Don't be. It's not like you had anything to do with it." Her gaze wandered away, not fixed on anything in particular.

Kearney watched the lady. In a normal situation, he would've been terrified of her, but he didn't feel afraid at all right now. Maybe it was the unnaturally calm air that seemed to float around her. It brought him comfort, like a fluffy cloud he wanted to hug and never let go of. "If it makes you feel better, I'll keep an eye out for her. And if I ever find her, I'll bring her straight here."

"Thank you. I really appreciate that." The woman's eyes drifted back to him, and she smiled. "I'm Isma."

He smiled back. "Kearney." They stood in silence as they waited for Rob. This was the first time Kearney had ever felt truly relaxed standing next to an adult, and he kept standing by her because he wanted to savor that feeling for as long as possible. He didn't even realize he was still smiling.

Sadly, that smile faded moments later when Rob reappeared. Kearney's anxiety immediately returned when he remembered Levi's crimes.

Rob glanced at him. "I'll be with you in a minute." He turned back to Isma, and they continued their conversation. He handed her a stack of papers, and she headed outside with them, but not before saying bye to Kearney, which made him very happy. Rob leaned on the counter, his eyes back on Kearney. "What are you doing here, kid?"

Kearney stiffened. He glanced at the money on the counter and started shoving it toward Rob. "I'm r-really sorry about Levi." He felt his hands shaking. "I-I wish he wasn't so r-r-rebellious...."

"Deep breaths, Kearney. Calm down." Rob looked at the money on the counter. "This is for the lighter?"

Kearney nodded.

"It's alright, you can keep it."

Kearney watched Rob, trying to figure out what his underlying motive could've been.

"You've got something else you want to say?" Rob met his stare. "My sister's waiting for me outside, and I still have to close up shop, so you'd better say it now."

Kearney looked over his shoulder. *Isma is his sister?* That made sense, given they have the same brown hair. Kearney found himself staring at the door as his mind wandered. He didn't think he had anything more to say to Rob, and yet he still felt so conflicted. "How did Levi look earlier when he was talking about impressing people?"

"The same as he always does."

Kearney shoved his hands into his pockets. "Do you think he hates me?" he asked quietly.

"What led you to that conclusion?"

"His whole scene today, mainly."

Rob sighed. "He's impulsive, Kearney. He doesn't hate you, but whether he admits it or not, he needs parents."

But I can't let that happen. What kind of brother would ever do something so reckless? He's my responsibility, after all.

Rob's expression softened. "You're only fifteen. No one expects you to be the perfect caretaker. You know, there are always going to be families out there willing to take him in—"

Kearney's head shot up. "No!"

Rob watched him for a moment. Then he smiled. "For what it's worth, I think you're doing just fine. I doubt that kid would even be in one piece if he didn't have you looking out for him. I think he knows it, too."

Kearney's shoulders gradually relaxed. "Really?"

"Really. But I want you to think about what I said, alright?"

Kearney's smile faded. "Okay. Thanks, Rob." *I appreciate the advice, but it's never happening.* He cleared his throat. "I should probably head back soon. It'd be a shame if Levi starved while I was away."

Rob chuckled, pulling out a bag from under the counter. "Right. We can't have that, can we?" He handed it to Kearney.

Kearney opened it and smiled when he saw the takeout boxes inside. He let out a content sigh as the warm air wafted out of the bag and up his nose. "Thanks."

"No problem, kid," Rob replied with a nod. "Have a good night."

Kearney stepped outside. He held the bag close to his chest and watched as steam swelled from it and into the air. He smiled as all his worries melted away. *It looks cool.*

He jumped when something shifted in the corner of his eye. He then heard the sound of someone struggling to climb a chain-link fence. He turned to the fence beside Rob's shop and saw a short boy with an absurdly large backpack struggling to scale it.

He sighed. "Levi."

Levi froze, one leg already over the fence. "Who?"

"What are you doing?"

Levi looked over his shoulder with a hint of guilt in his eyes. "What are *you* doing? You said you were getting dinner, but now I catch you working your butt off and trying to pay for my lighter! And did you get that food from *Rob?*"

Kearney rubbed his temples. "It was just a couple of little errands, that's all."

"Little," Levi spat. "Stop hiding things already. You know I hate it when you do that."

"Can you get down?" Kearney asked, tired of arguing.

"You bet I can." Levi jumped off the fence and landed on the other side with a grunt. "Do you want to eat by the cool house?" he asked hopefully. He had that awkward look on his face that said, *I really don't want to spend the rest of the night mad at you, so I'll let this go in the quietest way possible.*

Kearney was exhausted. He wanted to go home, collapse on the floor, and wake up in the next century. But he couldn't bring himself to say no. "I don't see why not."

Levi beamed. "Let's go, then!"

Kearney forced a smile. *After all, there's no real harm in it.* He climbed over the fence and joined Levi, who grabbed his hand and started leading him down the alley. The two walked together and enjoyed the quiet that came with the frosty night. Kearney finally felt himself beginning to relax.

"So, what's going on with that lady you were talking to?" Levi asked.

Kearney shrugged. "She's just looking for her daughter. I think she's the one who's been putting up those posters."

Levi's eyes were fixed on a rock he was kicking around. "It's nice that her mom's looking out for her, but let's be real. She probably just ran away."

"That's not very polite."

He rolled his eyes. "I'm sure she's fine. We live in the most boring town humanly possible."

"Wasn't there a shooting last spring?"

"That was miles from here," Levi said with a dismissive wave.

Kearney bit his lip in thought. "Why would she run away, though? Her mom doesn't seem that bad."

"Maybe she just decided she didn't want parents anymore. That's why you ran away, wasn't it?" Levi looked back at him, searching for a response.

Kearney paused. That was the story he'd always told Levi. *That I ran away. That I ran away because I wanted to.* It wasn't the full truth, and he preferred it that way. Some things were best left unsaid. "Right."

Levi continued skipping along. "You know, you're the one telling me adults are scary and all, but you looked real cozy with that lady."

"I wasn't cozy," Kearney protested.

Levi stared up at the sky. "She reminded me of my mom." His eyes darted back to Kearney. "Don't get me wrong, I don't care about her at all!"

"That's what a person who really cares says," Kearney teased with a smirk. "If you like her so much, why don't you run back to Rob's and ask her to adopt you?"

"No way," he snorted. "You're overprotective enough as is. I don't need another one of you. I want my parents to be fun, like me." He suddenly pointed up, his finger fixed on a star. "I think that one's new! It's your turn to name it."

Kearney looked up to where Levi was pointing. He furrowed his brow, feigning deep thought. "How about Isma?"

Levi snickered. "I wonder where you got that from."

"It's a nice name!"

They were near an old, dark gray brick house now. It stood nestled between the alley's walls with an almost welcoming air. Levi smiled as he sat down on the house's cement steps and glanced at the giant arched crimson-red doors. They were engraved with all kinds of intricate swirling patterns like they had once been part of a Romanesque church. If he could yank them right off their hinges and put them in his bedroom, he would have. He gestured for Kearney to sit beside him.

Kearney settled down and started handing takeout boxes to Levi. "I never got why you like this house so much. It's pretty, sure, but that's about it for me."

"Because it definitely has some cool treasure inside," Levi replied as he opened one of the boxes, letting steam and the delicious smell of orange chicken float through the air.

"Maybe." Kearney's tone was thoughtful.

Levi handed him a box of yakisoba. They sat there for a long while, eating and talking until nearly every box was empty.

Kearney closed up a box half-filled with white rice. "This will be for tomorrow."

Levi set a small plastic container on top. "Don't forget the sauce."

"Of course."

They got to their feet and began walking away, and Levi paused to glance back at the house one last time.

"I'll get your secrets someday," he promised as he pointed a finger gun at it, "and whatever treasures you're hiding, too." His smile faded. The house's doors were beautiful, with lovely silver loops for handles, but there wasn't a single keyhole to be seen. "It'd be a lot easier if you had a lock to pick," he muttered before following after Kearney, leaving the house in the stillness of the alley.

House Full of Strings

Chapter 3

Levi Breaks His Back

Kearney watched with a small smile as Levi gawked at the thin sheet of snow on the sidewalk. Although it had barely snowed overnight, it was enough to get him hurrying outside the moment he woke up. Kearney didn't fully get it, but there were many things Levi got excited about that he didn't understand. Snow, lighters, used bottle caps—Kearney just assumed they were all "normal kid things."

Levi held a ball of dirty sleet over his head, ready to fling it at Kearney, and his disappointment could be read all over his face when Kearney sidestepped the attack. He grabbed Kearney's arm and pulled him toward the snow. "Come on!"

"No, thanks." Kearney slipped his wrist out of Levi's hand and stayed stationed in place.

Levi groaned. "Just act like a kid for once!"

"I'm fine." Kearney smiled. "Go have fun, okay?"

"But I want to have fun with *you*."

"I'm having fun."

Levi glared at him, unconvinced. "Your definition of fun is sad to watch."

"What sounds fun to you, then?"

Levi paused in thought then snapped his fingers. Or, rather, he tried to, but his gloves prevented him from doing so. "Hot cocoa."

Kearney's smile warmed. "From that place by Rob's?"

"Definitely."

"We can go now if you want." He started adjusting Levi's scarf. It was old and worn, but its flower pattern was still visible enough.

"I'm not six anymore," Levi protested.

"But I like doing it." Kearney scanned him. *Gloves, boots....* "Where's your hat?"

Levi frowned. "In the house."

"Why aren't you wearing it?"

Levi shrugged.

"Go get it. I'll wait for you."

"Why are you making me dress up like we're going to Antarctica when you're only wearing a coat?"

"I don't want you to get frostbite."

"Well, you don't seem to mind losing all your fingers," Levi sulked as he went inside. Not even a minute later, he raced back out. His backpack and the ear flaps on his wool hat swayed as he ran. "Alright, let's go!"

The two held hands and strolled away from their house and down the street, Levi's cozy hand warming Kearney's. Snow started drifting down, floating around them as they went, and Kearney couldn't help but chuckle as Levi tried catching snowflakes with his tongue.

Soon, they were walking alongside a river, and they both stared at it as they passed it, not in awe but wariness. They knew how cold the river was in the spring, and they could only imagine what temperature it must have dropped to now that its surface had frozen over.

They quickly reached the town square and headed for their desired hot cocoa. Kearney felt incredibly grateful Rob had let him keep his money the day before. Rob had always been good to the two of them, even if he seemed a little icy at first. In truth, he was the only person other than Levi that Kearney felt truly comfortable around. The only *adult* was a better way to put it.

They sat on a bench in the square, sipping their hot cocoa. Kearney only became aware of how cold and stiff his fingers were when he had the warm cup in his hands.

Levi noticed him staring at his hands. "How do you feel about losing your fingers now?"

"I like having my fingers," Kearney admitted.

"This Christmas, I'm getting you a pair."

Kearney's smile became strained. "You don't have to."

"Kearney," Levi said as he raised an eyebrow, "you deserve a pair of gloves."

He sighed. "If you insist."

Levi drank more hot cocoa, leaving a chocolatey mustache above his lip. "Anyway, if you want to keep fixing my scarf for me, you'll need all your fingers to do it."

Kearney chuckled with a defeated nod. "That's a good point."

Levi took another big sip before rising to his feet. "Let's go see the cool house."

"We just saw it yesterday."

"I know, I know. But it'll just be a minute, I promise. Anyway, it's right over there." He gestured to the chain-link fence beside Rob's store.

Kearney stared at his cup before shrugging. "As long as you're quick." A few minutes later, he was still sipping away, only now, he was holding Levi's hot chocolate as well as he watched Levi clamber over the fence.

Levi's plan started to go awry when one of his backpack's straps got caught on the fence. He struggled to tug it free.

"You need a hand?" Kearney asked.

"I'm fine," Levi replied. He kept fighting with the strap until it ripped, giving way for him to fly over the fence and fall flat on his back.

Kearney jumped when he heard the sound of shattering coming from Levi's backpack. "Levi!" He dropped the cups of cocoa and started hurrying over the fence. He was horrified, thinking Levi's spine had made that noise even though the sound of spines breaking was nothing like shattering china. *How could I allow this? He'll never walk again!*

"I'm fine." Levi winced as he sat up and looked in his backpack. "But my stuff isn't!" he screamed in horror.

Kearney let out a shaky sigh of relief, comforted by Levi's apparent wellness. He got to the other side of the fence and helped Levi up. Then he glanced down the alley where the house was waiting. "Why do you keep coming back here?" Kearney asked. "I know there's something you're not telling me."

"Why would I hide anything?"

"I know you well enough to know when you're not telling me things."

Levi huffed. "Fine. It's because I keep having a dream. Happy now?"

"You keep coming back because of a dream?" Kearney tilted his head. "What makes this dream so special?"

Levi frowned as he glared. "It's my dream. Why would I tell you?"

"Because it's making you break your back while falling off fences."

Levi let out his frustration with a groan. The lines on his face relaxed when he gave up on arguing, and his lip quickly bent into a smirk. As much as he seemed to not want to share the details of his dream, it was clear he even enjoyed just thinking about it. "I'd always dream about a giant room filled with treasures: little trinkets, gold, whatever you can think of. And then I'd hear a voice telling me they were all mine."

Kearney stared at him in disbelief. "That's why you're obsessed with it?"

Levi nodded, his brow knit with resolve.

"How did you even manage to correlate some random dream about your greed to that old house?"

"I had a hunch. And since when are my hunches wrong?"

"Since when have they been right?" Kearney suddenly became aware of the fact that Levi was slowly backing away from him with a wry grin. "Hang on!"

Levi raced off.

"Levi!" Kearney laughed as he hurried after him. "Slow down!" He raced down the alley, and as soon as he was able to make out those red doors amidst the shadows, he could see Levi tugging at their handles with all his might. He watched Levi struggling and then, with a small grin, decided to play along. *Fine, I'll indulge your greediness this time.* He grabbed Levi by the waist and lifted him up as he tugged with him.

Levi glanced down at his dangling feet. "Pull harder!" he ordered.

The doors creaked in annoyance as the two boys tugged it.

"Harder!"

Kearney strained with all his might. *Come on. You can't let Levi down, can you?*

"Harder!"

With an angry rumble, the doors gave way, sending the boys flying back. They tumbled down the stairs, and Kearney barely managed to stay on his feet while Levi landed on his backpack once again, breaking something else in the process.

Levi quickly sat up and stared at the house, his mouth gaping open in awe. "It's open!" he cried as he jumped to his feet. "It's really open!" He raced toward it, only to be grabbed by Kearney.

Kearney pulled him back. "Levi, no!"

Levi turned to glare at him while trying to wrench his arm free. "It's open, Kearney! Do you really not want to know what's in there?"

"I really don't!"

"But you just helped!"

"I didn't think it'd work!"

Levi looked back at the house, admiring the room that had been hidden behind those doors all this time. Even with his limited view, he could see the room was decorated with crimson carpets and couches, which were perfectly complemented by the rich, dark color of the oak furniture. Crimson curtains draped all the walls, and in the center of the room was a marble statue of a tall figure with antlers, practically beckoning Levi forward with an outstretched hand and a smile on its face.

"It looks so cool!" he exclaimed.

"It looks like any other house!"

"No, it doesn't. Don't you see that weird statue?" Levi successfully managed to free his arm and raced up the steps. He stopped at the door and glanced back at Kearney. "Come on, or I'm going in myself," he taunted.

Kearney's feet were frozen to the ground. "I have a really bad feeling about this place," he whispered.

"What? You have a hunch?"

"I do," he said with a vehement nod.

Levi frowned. "So, my hunches are wrong, but yours are law."

"Please, Levi," Kearney quietly begged.

Levi looked away with a sigh. Then he extended a hand toward Kearney. "It'll be fine."

Kearney's eyes fixed on Levi's hand. *Okay. Just take his hand, then pull him away as quickly as you can.* He carefully slipped his hand into Levi's. Levi suddenly surged toward the door, his grip tightening on Kearney's hand in a heartbeat, pulling Kearney with him. Kearney's mouth opened in a scream. *He saw it coming!*

Every inch of him was tense in anticipation of the absolute worst, but when they entered the house, nothing changed. He let out a shaky breath as he looked at Levi, who was laughing with a giant grin on his face. Kearney then looked over his shoulder at the doors they'd come through. They hung open for a moment, then swung shut with a loud *bang* that shook every bone in Kearney's body.

"L-Levi," he stammered as he ran back to them. He slammed his palms against the doors and leaned his full weight on them, but they wouldn't budge. "Levi, they closed."

Levi was too busy racing around the room, admiring every bit of it. "This place looks so vintage!" He hopped up to the statue. "This guy looks so weird. He's got deer antlers! And look at all these little doors!"

"Levi, we're t-trapped here...."

"I bet all they all have treasure behind them!"

"This is what you get for not listening to me." Kearney had fallen to the floor in defeat.

"You need to learn to calm down," Levi snapped, as if Kearney was being the most dramatic person in the world.

"Why didn't I stop you…?" Kearney pressed his face against the doors, too bewildered to do anything but sit there. *I'm supposed to be the responsible one!*

Levi started walking around and twisting each door's handle, his excitement turning into bitter disappointment when door after door ended up being locked. He frowned but stayed hopeful as he kept trying. After all, there were at least twenty doors in this room alone; surely, one of them would open.

Kearney had finally gotten to his feet and was watching Levi in increasing horror. "They're all locked?" he asked quietly. *We're trapped in a tiny room with no way out.*

"I'll only know once I've tried them all," Levi said as he tested another.

Kearney rushed over to him and started frantically twisting the doorknob. He glanced back at Levi. "Th-This isn't a problem. We'll just check them all and find our way out. It's just a tiny house, after all." He let out a strained laugh as he raced around the room, twisting every doorknob he passed. "It's just a t-tiny house," he muttered, trying to comfort himself.

Levi smiled. "Yeah, you *are* making a big deal of nothing." He swung his arms as he sauntered up to another door. "It's just a tiny house!" He grabbed its handle and turned it. And, luckily for him and Kearney's sanity, it opened.

Instead of amazing treasures, Levi was met with a bunch of branches to the face. They sent him flying backward then swayed gently back into a resting position as he lay dazed on the ground. Kearney screamed as he rushed to help him, but Levi jumped back to his feet just as quickly as he'd fallen.

"I'm fine!" He fixed his attention on the branches that had humiliated him, but the annoyance in his eyes quickly turned into curiosity. He reached out and touched one of them. The leaves were made of cut strawberries, and the wood was white chocolate. "Woah!" With a big smile on his face, he looked back at Kearney. He took a step toward the door.

Kearney tensed. "Levi, don't be rash." *Please don't. Please don't.*

"I think I'll be rash," was the last thing Levi said before he rushed into the strange branches and through the door.

But instead of finding solid ground on the other side, his foot was met with nothing but empty air. With a yelp, he plummeted straight down.

Chapter 4

Levi Fights Some Kindergarteners

Levi screamed wildly as he plunged straight down, ramming into branch after branch. *I can't die here. That'll mean Kearney was right! He can't be right!*

His shrieks finally ended when he crashed into a thick branch stomach-first. He struggled to suck in a breath as he lay dazed, his limbs dangling limply from his body. He stared down, trying to figure out just how much longer he could've fallen. Fortunately, he could see the ground. He wrapped his arms tightly around the branch. That wouldn't have been very fortunate if this branch hadn't broken his fall.

"Levi, I'm coming!" Kearney's voice came from overhead.

Levi looked up and spotted Kearney sliding down the tree trunk. He stopped his descent on the same branch as Levi, albeit much more smoothly, before hurrying along the branch to help him up.

"I'm fine," he snapped as Kearney lifted him to his feet. He scrambled to the tree's trunk and wrapped his arms around it in an attempt to copy Kearney's slide down the trunk, but his results were much sloppier. With another scream, he plummeted straight down as chocolate cut into his palms, and before he knew it, he'd slammed into the ground at the base of the tree. He rubbed his sore behind as he stumbled to his feet and looked up, only to be met by Kearney's brown eyes staring down at him.

"Don't you dare say anything!" Levi yelled up at him.

Kearney's head disappeared from view. Levi could've sworn he heard a chuckle. Seconds later, he saw Kearney gliding down the trunk. He landed very smoothly before giving Levi that look again. Levi looked away in annoyance but got over it fairly quickly once he'd spotted what was waiting beyond the tree. He rushed ahead, awe swelling in his chest. *There's no way that's real.*

The ground beneath him sank slightly under his weight, but he was still able to run just fine. He stopped and scooped up a handful of the soft earth. Then, to Kearney's disgust and horror, Levi bit into it. He grinned at Kearney, his mouth stuffed. "It's marshmallow!"

Kearney stiffened, nervously scanning the area. "Don't do that again, please."

Levi had already moved on from the marshmallow ground. He was now picking chocolate pinecones off the jelly pine trees that towered overhead and shoving them down his throat. He watched as rivers of melted chocolate lapped at their roots. He looked ready to jump in, but Kearney rushed to hold him back. A sickeningly sweet smell wafted around them, filling Levi with ecstasy. "This is the coolest forest *ever!*"

Kearney shivered as he stared up at the trees as if intimidated by them.

"Kearney!" Levi shook him. "Don't you know what this means?"

Kearney didn't reply, and Levi chose to believe it was because he was just so dumbfounded by all the possibilities that he was speechless. "Not only will we find this place's treasure, but we have an infinite source of delicious food, too! This is amazing!"

Kearney shook his head. "No. No, this is too weird." He yanked Levi's hands off his shoulders. "You should at least be a little suspicious!"

Levi snorted. "Whatever. You wouldn't know a good idea if it bit your nose off." He started yanking lollipop flowers out of the ground and shoving as many into his pockets as possible. His giant smile suddenly turned into a look of pure disgust when he noticed something in the distance. "Kearney," he hissed, "there are kids over there."

Kearney glanced at him. "What did you say?"

"Kids! There are kids!" Levi stared at them with what only could've been pure bloodlust. "I'm going to fight them."

"What?" Kearney looked up.

There *were* kids a few yards away. One of the kids was screaming orders to the others, who had chocolate sticks in their hands. It looked like they were trying to beat a cotton candy bush to death.

"Why would you *ever* want to do that?" Kearney sounded angry, probably because he'd hoped he'd raised Levi to be better than this.

Levi was already heading toward them. "Because they're obviously here for my treasure. I have to show them who's boss."

Kearney looked back at the group of children. They looked too busy abusing the bush to be interested in any treasure. "You've done plenty of questionable things, but I think wiping the floor with a bunch of kindergarteners would be a first."

Levi paused, conflicted. "I'll only fight them if they really drive me to it, then!" He marched toward them, leaving a very disappointed Kearney watching. Levi reached his opponents, who were about six kids, none of whom could've possibly been older than seven.

They all turned to face him, and one of them smiled. "Wow, Mr. Calder, you were right. We didn't even have to set up any traps!" she exclaimed. "That fleshy person came right to us!"

A boy with dark green hair and even darker brown skin nodded. "'Course I was right. Fleshy peoples are stupid!" he said with a wave of his hand. He took a step toward Levi. "What do you think yer doin' on my turf? Did you lose yer mama?" he jeered, and his companions started to snicker.

Levi's face scrunched up in resentment. "You're one to talk, vomit-hair."

"That's the best you could come up with?" Kearney yelled from behind him.

Levi decided to act like he hadn't heard that comment. He focused his attention back on the little green-haired brat.

The green-haired boy named Calder chuckled as he cracked his neck and balled his fists. "I wasn't plannin' on beatin' you up that badly, but you're beggin' for it now, fleshy person."

"*You?* Beat *me* up?" Levi squared his shoulders with a confident grin. "I'd like to see you try!"

And to Levi's embarrassment, Calder did a lot more than try. He rushed forward, but instead of fighting up-front, he began running circles around Levi, poking and kicking his shins.

Levi spun around in an attempt to push him away. "Stop fighting dirty!" The soft marshmallow ground tripped him up, and fell back with a shriek.

Seeing Levi's predicament, Kearney joined the fight. Three kids jumped at him, and he politely grabbed them and set them aside, which left them feeling very disappointed. He then caught Levi's opponent by the arm and lifted him into the air.

"You're really light." Kearney's eyebrows knit into a line then rose in shock. "Why's your arm...wooden?"

"All of me is, fleshy person!" Calder shouted as he swung his legs and kicked Kearney in the stomach, effectively winding him. Calder landed on his feet with an eager grin, hopping around and raring for round two. "Yer pretty tough, huh?"

Kearney's eyes were skipping between Levi and the terrifyingly unpredictable boy. "He's made of wood!"

Levi's eyes widened. "He's *what?*"

"We're all made o' wood, dummy," Calder snapped. "Now cut out your blabbin' an' fight me!"

"I don't want to fight you!" Kearney screamed.

A blonde girl standing to the side held up a little book made of two waffles. "You have to. For honor and stuff!" She pointed to the book. "It's in the rulebook."

"That's two waffles stapled together!"

"It was the best we had, fleshy person!" she retorted. She stuck out her tongue and joined the rest of the kids in chanting, "Calder! Calder!"

Calder tossed himself at Kearney with a battle cry. Purely by instinct, Kearney caught him again, but all that did was expose him to Round Two of Calder's relentless stomach-kicking.

"Get off him, you little punk!" Levi dove in and grabbed Calder by the arm. Calder, being made of wood, simply popped it off and continued pestering Kearney, leaving Levi staring at the dismembered arm dangling in his hands. He shrieked, causing all of the dolls to stop and stare at him in bewilderment. With how he'd screamed, they probably thought they'd done something that was causing him, a fragile fleshy person, to actively die on the spot.

Kearney seized the moment to shove Calder off of him and grab Levi. He attempted to bolt away, but they were quickly surrounded. Calder picked up his arm and popped it back into its socket while cackling with excitement. He stomped his foot with a triumphant laugh.

Strangely enough, the marshmallow ground beneath him sounded hollow.

"We got 'em. Let's head out!" he barked.

The ground started to shake, and something began rising out of it. Kearney hugged Levi in terror, and while Levi tried to shove him away, the lack of stability beneath them was of greater priority at the moment. The rumbling only got louder and more violent. Trees around them were being unearthed by the giant object that was rising from the ground. The sound of chocolate wood snapping clean in two flooded the air.

Then the noise stopped altogether. Once the dust settled, Kearney and Levi could see that they were all standing on top of a giant candy tank so big it peeked above the trees. The tank honked as the dolls on top of it hollered. Kearney spun around, his eyes on the ground, which was at least twelve feet below them at this point. He kept holding onto Levi as tightly as possible as he tried to figure out what to do next.

"'Ey, Freckles!"

They turned to look at Calder, who was rolling up his sleeves and staring Kearney down.

Kearney stiffened. "Me?"

"Yeah, you!" Calder yelled. "Either yer lettin' us lock you up now, or I'll beat you to a pulp first!"

"But I don't want to fight!" Kearney stumbled back while trying to keep Levi safely behind him.

"I don't care!" Calder pointed a finger at him. "We're takin' the both of you to the Mister, whether ya'll are bruised up or not!"

"Mister?" Levi peered around Kearney. "Who...?"

"Make up yer minds!"

"Stop yelling already!" Kearney cried. He glanced over his shoulder before shoving Levi over the edge of the tank and jumping off after him. He slid down the side of the tank, grabbed Levi with one hand and a branch with the other, and swung them through the air. Then he let go of the branch, sending them flying to the ground.

Levi barely managed to land on his feet and yelped when Kearney grabbed his arm and yanked him up. Before he could fully register it, they were both running. He kept looking over his shoulder as the tank rolled after them. *If we get away from these psychos, I'll never bully a kid ever again! I swear!*

Branches slapped them as they ran. The marshmallow ground posed a much larger issue now, as it made running exhausting. Low-hanging gummy vines threatened to grab them. But none of these things fazed the giant tank behind them one bit. Tears of fatigue streamed down Levi's cheeks. He deeply regretted never having taken Kearney's advice to empty his backpack at least a little.

Meanwhile, Calder's tank swerved wildly behind the pair, threatening to pancake them the same way it was the trees. "Stop runnin', fleshy people, and I promise the Candy Crusher won't kill you!" Calder hollered as he swung around at the top of the giant candy tank.

Levi sobbed in distress as his backpack bounced up and down with his body, further draining him. He rubbed his dry eyes and looked forward. The clearing suddenly opened, and before he knew it, the forest was behind them. Now, they were faced with a dusty desert and a giant brick castle.

He looked at Kearney excitedly. "Kearney!"

A big grin came over Kearney's face. "Sweet refuge!" he gasped.

The clamor from the dolls behind them grew more hectic, and the pair could hear Calder frantically shouting to his peers, "They're gettin' to Jolly! We gotta stop 'em!"

Levi looked at Kearney. "Jolly?"

"If *they* don't like him, then I'm sure we'll get along pretty well!"

Levi forced himself to run even faster, his legs screaming in protest. *That castle must have so much treasure!* How he could think like that in situations like this was beyond even him.

The Candy Crusher continued to accelerate, getting menacingly close. Dozens of little candy corn machine guns popped out of its sides and fired at them, stinging as they hit their legs. When Levi slowed down even slightly, Kearney pushed him ahead.

"Keep going!"

He nodded and kept running, only to look back in horror when he realized Kearney wasn't at his side anymore. As a matter of fact, Kearney had stopped dead in his tracks and was facing the Candy Crusher head-on. He ripped a candy cane out of the ground and rushed at it, and with a shocking and frankly scary display of agility, he jumped from the Crusher's bumper and leaped his way up the side of the tank in seconds. Shocked by his nemesis's frightening power, Calder shrieked and jumped back, only for the crook of the cane to hook around his neck and lift him, leaving him hanging helplessly in midair. As invincible as the wooden boy was, he was very light. The tank skidded to a halt, and Calder's crew went dead quiet, staring and wondering what their leader would do next.

Calder thrashed, scratched, and screamed but, after a minute, gave up. He glared at Kearney. "You got a lotta nerve thinkin' you can come onto my turf an' treat me like this."

Kearney glared back as he hopped down the Candy Crusher, but his glare vanished once he was back at Levi's side. Levi stared at him in astonishment, hardly able to comprehend what his boring brother had just done. Kearney stuck the candy cane back in the ground, leaving Calder stranded for his underlings to collect. He then grabbed Levi and hurried toward the castle's yawning doors.

Relief flooded over them as they made it inside, and Levi practically collapsed. The doors slammed shut behind them, making Kearney jump. He looked back at them in apprehension. Levi patted his back. "It's alright. We got away from those little freaks, that's what matters!"

"Did you already forget the last time a door slammed shut behind us?"

Levi started strolling away with a laugh, and Kearney nervously trailed behind. Kearney studied the castle's adorned halls closely, still trying to piece together the strangeness of everything they'd encountered in the last ten minutes. *Ten minutes. Ten minutes, and I already want to go home.*

Meanwhile, Levi was opening every door as he went, once again letting his lust for treasure fuel him. "This can work, right?" He looked over his shoulder. "I mean, sure, the locals aren't the best, but now we have a whole castle to ourselves. We don't even need to leave!"

"Levi...."

"I'm going to scope everything out!" He raced off, the knickknacks in his bag clanking against each other as he went. Then, he stopped in his tracks. "Didn't those wooden kids say something about a guy named Jolly here?"

Kearney stiffened. He'd had enough fighting to last him a year, and he really hoped this Jolly guy would be kinder than the wooden brats had been. He squeezed his eyes shut as he tried to force himself to relax then opened them again when he heard the incessant sound of rattling doorknobs. It was Levi, who was racing around and scouring for a room that looked interesting to him. He soon opened a door and gasped in excitement when he saw what was inside. He raced out of sight, and what followed was silence.

Kearney waited for him to come racing back out, but he never did. Kearney walked up to the door and peeked inside only to see Levi sprawled out on a couch and soaking in the warmth of a fire burning in a hearth by his feet.

Kearney felt himself relax just a little. *Maybe everything will be alright. For now.* "I'm going to look around."

Levi absently mumbled something in reply.

With a curt nod, mostly to himself, Kearney left him and started walking down the hall. The hall was massive, and its doors looked like they were made for mice in comparison. The whole castle gave off an air of ancientness as if it was a piece of history. *I wonder who made this place. I don't think those dolls are smart enough to do it.*

Briiiing!

He spun around and saw an old purple payphone standing in the middle of the hall. It rang again, seemingly beckoning him to it. He stared at it, then tentatively took a step toward it. He kept inching closer to it as it rang. He rolled back his shoulders in an attempt to calm himself. After all, it was just a phone. What would it do, bite him? He let his fingers graze it, then felt goosebumps and pulled his hand away with a shudder.

The payphone felt…fleshy. Maybe it *would* bite him.

He stared at it as it continued to ring. After another moment, he braced himself, grabbed the phone, and held it to his ear, cringing as its strange texture brushed against his skin.

"*Hey-a, Kearney!*" a voice yelled at him through the phone, causing him to flinch away. The voice had a youthful playfulness to it, one that was completely drowned out by the raspy bite it carried. It was very loud, too, which only made it sound raspier thanks to the static coming from the phone itself.

"H-How do you know my name?" he nervously asked as he wrapped the phone's cord around a finger, already forgetting about the fleshy feel.

"*I know lots of things about you, Kearney. **Lots of things.**"* The voice became deeper and distorted, to the point where it almost sounded inhuman. "*I also know you're in a pickle.*" It went back to sounding somewhat normal.

Kearney bit down on his tongue, partly due to the terror of being in a strange world and partly in response to the questionable mental stability of this stranger who knew his name. "What do you mean?"

"*The castle you're in's a nasty one. I think it gets it from its host, personally.*"

"Do you mean Jolly?"

"*Jolly who? Nah, there's nothing jolly about him. Anyway, the first thing you should worry about is this castle looooves moving around.*" The line went dead.

"Wait! Who is he? What do you mean?" Kearney cried in vain, but he knew it was hopeless. After a minute of staring at the receiver in his hands, he dropped it, leaving it hanging by its cord as he raced back to where he'd left Levi.

"Levi, get up!" he snapped as he skidded into the room.

Levi rolled his head back to look at him. "Why?"

"We're leaving. Right now!"

He groaned. "We're in a giant castle. Those stupid kids aren't coming after us again."

"We're going to die if we stay!"

"Being constantly worried about everything must be exhausting for you," Levi replied as his eyes fluttered shut again.

"A voice told me!"

"A voice?" Levi opened his eyes with an incredulous look. "I thought you told me not to talk to strangers."

"This is different!"

A rumble disrupted their argument, and everything around them gently quaked. Levi sat up. "What's that?"

Before Kearney could answer, the room jerked and threw the pair against the wall. Kearney yelped before wrapping his arms around Levi. The tremors ended as quickly as they'd started.

Levi rubbed his sore head as he looked up at Kearney anxiously. "Was that an earthquake?"

Kearney let him go and stumbled to the window, only to look out and realize they were hundreds of feet in the air and climbing higher at a rapid pace. He saw tiny dolls running around far below them and firing at the castle. *Calder's fighting the castle. And the castle's...fighting back?*

The castle was stomping, kicking, and swinging its arms as if Calder and his gang were nothing more than a bunch of mildly irritating ants. But every motion, no matter how little effort the castle made it with, tossed around everything inside. Realization hit Kearney like a brick.

He hurried to Levi and helped him to his feet. "W-We have to get out of here. Now!"

Levi was a complete mess. "What's happening out there?"

Kearney didn't reply. He grabbed Levi by the hand and rushed out of the room and down the castle's quaking halls. *This is bad. This is really bad.*

Levi tried to wiggle his hand out of Kearney's grip. "Tell me what's going on!" he cried.

He can't know. He can't know.

"Kearney!"

The castle rumbled and jerked forward, propelling them into another room. The door swung shut behind them, and they were tossed around like vegetables being sautéed in a frying pan. Kearney screamed in terror, and that terror was only heightened when he realized Levi wasn't making a sound. *Is he okay? Did he hit his head?* The violent shakes soon reduced to angry little rumbles, and Kearney could sit up again. He brushed himself off and glanced at Levi, who was lying on his back and desperately fighting back tears of pain.

"Levi, are you alright? Please tell me you're alright!" Kearney was at his side in seconds.

Levi nodded while trying to keep himself from shaking in agony. "I'm awesome," he whispered through gritted teeth.

Kearney gently grabbed his arm and tried to lift him to his feet, but Levi slapped him away. "Tell me what's going on!"

He stiffened. "Well," he began slowly, "we've seen sentient dolls, right?"

"Right."

"So, sentient castles aren't too big of a stretch, right?"

Levi's eyes widened. "The castle's *alive?*"

"Yeah, I know, b-but it's not *that* scary once—"

"I have a living castle!" Levi jumped to his feet, wincing in pain as he did. "We have to find the control center and use it to beat up those kids!"

Kearney grabbed his arm again. "Levi, there's no control center. This is a *living being.*"

"Wait. It's *alive*-alive?"

"It is!" Kearney grabbed him and started running again, looking around in panic, only just noticing the hundreds of silver strings hanging from the ceiling and draped all over the floor. They pulsed with crimson-red energy and quivered as the boys ran past them.

"What are those?" Levi asked nervously.

"I don't know—" Kearney's reply was cut off by a short gasp as a string lunged for his foot and wrapped itself around it. He tripped with a yelp and slammed into the ground, wincing as his chin took the full force of his fall.

The string quickly snaked down the hall, dragging him with it. He clawed at the ground that was slipping past him at a terrifying speed while kicking and writhing in the hopes of shaking off the string. He looked up and saw Levi screaming while chasing after him.

Levi pulled his wooden lighter out of his pocket as he lunged forward, barely managing to grab Kearney's arm. The string continued to slither along, now dragging both of them with it. Levi reached forward as far as he could, struggling to keep the lighter lit as he held it close to the string. Soon, it snapped from the heat of the lighter, and the boys slid to a halt. They gasped for breath as they lay motionless on the ground. Kearney lifted himself to a sitting position before glancing at Levi, who'd done the same.

He hugged Levi as tightly as he could, his heart beating wildly. "I'll g-get you out of here. I p-promise." *I promise. I promise....*

Levi stiffened for a moment before relaxing and hugging him, patting him on the back, likely in an attempt at comfort. "I trust you, Kearney." He gave Kearney a reassuring smile. "After all, you always keep your promises, don't you?"

Kearney let out a shuddering sigh as he slowly nodded. *I do...I'll keep this one, too. I'll protect him.*

They got to their feet then searched for where the string had gone. When they spotted it, it was slipping under a giant pale blue door, quickly vanishing. They shared a glance before Levi reached forward and grabbed the handle, and Kearney did the same. They pushed the door open, and dust flew out of the room and into their faces like they were entering a sandstorm. Kearney coughed wildly as he tried to wave it all away. When the air cleared, he froze in shock and felt Levi hug his arm in fear.

It looked like they were in some type of throne room, but it was in complete disarray, with those strange strings scattered in every nook and cranny of the room and converging around a wooden box dangling in mid-air. The box itself almost looked like a coffin. Beneath it, slumped on a broken throne, was an old, lanky doll, although it looked more like a mummy, which was just as tightly wrapped in string as the box overhead. And it had deep blue eyes; Kearney knew that because it was looking right at them.

It suddenly twitched. *"You didn't knock."*

The boys staggered back, unable to comprehend that the wooden being had just spoken. Kearney's breath hitched as he remembered what the voice had said to him over the phone. *This must be the host.*

The mummy twitched again. *"Get out."*

The castle jerked back, sending the boys flying away from the creature and across the room. Kearney barely had time to process the fact that his back was now hitting a window because moments later, the glass had shattered, and he and Levi were sent flying. His eyes darted around wildly, quickly drying from the sheer force of the wind blowing into them, and his stomach tightened as he plummeted. He looked back at the giant castle, which was getting farther away by the second. He barely managed to spot Levi, who was screaming wildly and flailing his arms. He was too far away to reach.

"Levi!"

"I don't want to die!" Levi sobbed.

Before Kearney could say another word, his back slammed into water. His eyes darted around as a river of tea flowed around him, its sweet taste flooding his mouth and nose. He found himself trapped in a haze of panic, one he swiftly snapped out of when his head

broke the surface. He immediately heard Levi screaming his name.

"Levi, I'm coming!" His head was spinning as the
river's current carried him along. He narrowly avoided
a jagged rock in his path, yelping as it caught his leg and
cut clean through his jeans and into skin. Terror
screamed in his mind as he searched for Levi. He remembered the last time the two of them had ended up
in a river as merciless as this one.

He quickly spotted Levi, who was scrambling to get
on top of a giant peppermint candy bobbing in the water. Once he'd done it, he started frantically rowing with
his hands toward Kearney, who was barely managing a
doggy paddle at this point.

Levi grabbed Kearney's hoodie and strained to pull
him onto the makeshift boat, which they both quickly
realized he was too weak to do. Kearney clawed at the
candy and pulled himself up, collapsing and gasping for
breath once he was safely on it. They looked at the chaotic scene behind them. Calder's tank was pursuing
them on land, and the giant castle monster was hot on
their tail.

Kearney's eyes fixed on the castle's face; he couldn't
understand how he hadn't noticed it sooner. Jolly wore
a giant drama mask that boasted a huge smile and a pair
of eyes squinted in mocking mischief. *So, that's why he's
called Jolly.*

Jolly was on all fours like an enraged toddler. He
reached forward, slamming his hand into the river. The

river was fast, sure, but the rabid castle monster was definitely faster.

"Kearney...." Levi was shaking. "The castle wants us, too, doesn't it?"

Kearney's eyes were darting every which way. "Find something to row with!"

They just barely managed to grab a pair of cinnamon stick reeds and used them to start frantically rowing.

Calder fired at them from the tank, raining down chaos on the pair as they rowed as best they could. Jolly slammed a foot into the water as it reached for them. The river water surged forward, rushing even faster, and the boys soared along with it. The peppermint candy flew into the air.

"I'm sorry!" Levi screamed as he clutched his cinnamon stick, his voice barely audible over the roaring of the water. "I'm sorry I was rash! I'm sorry! *I'm sorry!*"

Their makeshift raft slammed back into the water, flipping in the process and sending the boys flying. Kearney cried out as the hungry river gulped him up again. He spun around aimlessly, his lungs screaming for air.

Where's Levi? He slammed into a rock pillar, the impact winding him. Fatigue started to overtake him. He did all he could to fight it off, but it was too powerful. He watched as the bubbles he'd just coughed up went floating to the surface, leaving him behind. *Levi....*

He felt something grab his hoodie and pull him out of the water. He dangled limply as he was lifted into the air and dropped onto a hard surface.

Air rushed into his lungs as his chest jerked uncontrollably. He heard the sounds of clanking machinery, rumbling engines, and frantic shouting, but they were all drowned out by the sound of his own violent coughs. He struggled to open his eyes but still saw nothing. He banged on his chest to clear his lungs and finally managed to sit himself up. He leaned against something cold and hard, exhaustion making his chest sore. There were countless hazy voices screaming around him, but the only voice he could recognize was Calder's.

"We got one o' 'em. That's good enough! Let's get out o' 'ere!"

"N-No," Kearney choked out. "Y-You have to g-get Levi." He collapsed with another shudder as the world ebbed into darkness. *You have to get Levi. He's still in the water...he'll drown....* He crumpled under his weight every time he tried to get up. *I promised him...I promised him he'd be okay.... You have to go back....*

Exhaustion swallowed him up, wrapping around him tightly like a heavy blanket.

House Full of Strings

Chapter 5

Calder Explodes

Kearney blinked awake. His cheeks felt crusted and icky. He realized it was because of the tear streaks that had long since dried on his skin.

He's dead. That was the first thought in his mind, and it hurt more than anything. There was no way Levi could've survived. Between the raging torrents and the psychopathic castle, it had been nearly impossible for Kearney to keep his head above the water, and Levi barely even knew how to swim.

I promised. He's gone. Kearney stared at the ceiling. It didn't feel right. It didn't feel *possible*. How could he lose Levi in such a brief moment? He curled up on the floor. Thinking about it made his stomach hurt.

Levi was counting on me, and I failed. Sleep was only a brief escape from that painful reality, and he spent every waking moment ruminating on that fact. It'd been three days already, and he still felt the same as he had the first time he'd woken up without Levi by his side.

Kearney didn't move. He didn't think of much. He just sat on the floor in empty silence.

He heard yelling nearby, which was probably what had woken him to begin with. He slowly lifted his head as his gaze strayed to the barred window, which was his only source of light. He stared blankly outside, hoping to distract himself from the pain.

He wasn't in the Candy Crusher anymore. Instead, he was in a tower carved out of a giant piece of hard candy. It was impressive that a bunch of tiny dolls could create something so resilient. What wasn't impressive, though, was their soundproofing skills because Kearney could hear *everything*. He mainly overheard the two guards stationed outside his door constantly arguing with a different hostage. There was only one other prisoner, and from the sound of her voice, Kearney concluded she was around his age. Luckily, her cell wasn't too close to his, so he wasn't at the forefront of the daily arguing sessions, but he was a victim of them nonetheless.

It felt like the only time those three stopped bickering was when Calder himself came down there. Unfortunately, Calder only ever came down to ramble and gloat to Kearney for hours on end, so even then, there wasn't any peace. Kearney didn't remember half of what that kid said, nor did he have the energy to figure out how Calder managed to think up the other half.

Kearney stared at his fingers. They were sore and stiff. One thing he'd realized about living in a world of candy was that candy was sticky. Very sticky. It got all over his skin and only added to his misery.

But no matter how much he told himself he hated all the commotion and inconveniences, deep down, he knew that he wouldn't have it any other way. If there had been silence, there'd be nothing to keep him from thinking about Levi.

He looked out the window again. The sky was a cloudy blue, like it was about to cry. It looked like a watercolor painting. That blue was starkly different from the bright pink color of the candy desert beneath it. The blanket of sand spread out seemingly endlessly, uncaring and unchanging. And resting on that sandy blanket was the most uncaring of them all: Jolly.

Kearney watched the terrifying giant sitting not too far away. *I wonder what he's waiting for. Does he want me, too?* He wasn't interested in fighting the castle. He wasn't interested in anything, really. All he wanted was to sit in silence and try to remember how good life had been before he had let his little brother die.

The sound of a door rolling open behind him snapped him out of his thoughts. He looked over his shoulder and saw a blonde doll watching him—the same doll who'd had that waffle book.

"Hey there, hot stuff!" She waltzed up to him with a tray of food in her hands. "How's my favorite prisoner doing?"

He went back to looking out the window without replying, which deeply upset her.

"You know, you're lucky I'm making an effort to be nice to you, so cheer up already!"

He squinted. Just out of the corner of his vision, he could see a bright flashing light. It almost seemed like it coming from a window near his. He groaned as the light reflected off the vivid sand and back into his eyes. All he wanted was to be sad, and it seemed like the whole world was personally offended by that and decided to bother him all at once.

"Just take your stupid food," the doll snapped. She held out the tray to him, not even looking at him out of what seemed to be indignation.

Kearney felt his breath quicken. It seemed he wasn't the only one who'd noticed the flashing. "Jolly's coming."

"What?" The doll stared at him.

"J-Jolly's coming." He backed away from the window, chills rippling down his spine. It seemed the castle had decided it *did* want him to die. With every step the brick giant made, the ground trembled in fear.

The doll's face had gone pale. "We have to go now. Now!" She grabbed his sleeve and started shaking him. "We have to go now!"

"Jolly's comin'! Ev'ryone, to your stations!" Calder's muffled voice hollered overhead. Kearney could hear dolls racing in panic, but he himself couldn't move an inch. He was scared, but he didn't know why. Was he scared because Jolly was huge? Was he scared because he was defenseless and small? Was he scared because he wasn't ready to die?

He realized the doll who'd been with him must have run out of the room and locked the door behind her. So much for having to go.

"Hey!" He started banging on it. "Hey, come back!" He looked back at the tiny window as he pressed against the door. He couldn't see any blue skies or pink sand anymore. Only Jolly.

Another rumble shook Kearney's cell. He slid to the floor and stayed frozen in place while the world screamed around him. *This is it.* Helplessness was a horrible feeling, one he'd only felt in his nightmares anymore. He'd hoped—*yearned*—that it would never come back, but it was real again.

The door opened behind him, but he still didn't move.

"Freckles!" It was Calder. He started shaking Kearney. "Freckles, move!"

What will happen when I die?

"Freckles!"

Will I be okay?

Jolly was just outside the window now. He already had the tower in his grip. It started shaking and, in moments, was ripped in two, sending everyone inside flying. Kearney clutched onto whatever he could, but once his grip slipped, he was falling through the air. He squeezed his eyes shut in anticipation of the pain of slamming into the ground, but it never came. Instead, he felt a strong jerk on his clothes and let out a choked *urk!* as his hoodie tightened around his throat.

He opened his eyes and realized he was dangling in the air. He craned his sore neck to look up, only to see a girl no older than he was clutching onto his hoodie, just barely keeping her own feet on the ground as she did. She squirmed as she struggled to keep him from plummeting, and he took the opportunity to grab one of the tower's broken beams and pull himself up.

Out of breath but determined, the girl grabbed his hand and pulled him with her as she hurried through what was left of the devastated tower. Kearney's head swiveled as he looked for Jolly in the dusty haze. The sounds of the gang's struggle against the giant were loud but eerily out of sight.

He looked back at the girl. Her hand felt soft in his. Fleshy. "Who—?"

She jumped off the platform, catching him off guard and plunging him with her into the lake of tea below. He sank deep into the warm water and quickly scrambled upward, not skipping a beat. Once his head broke the surface, he was relieved to see she was still beside him. She smiled as she bobbed up and down, seemingly completely oblivious to the debris raining down around them. "So, it *is* true." Her smile widened. "You're really real!"

"You're a normal person, too?" he asked breathlessly as he kept most of his attention on the tower's broken structure leaning over the lake, threatening to crush them if—or rather, when—it fell.

She nodded. "My name's Gabi. What's yours?"

"Kearney. We have to move."

She didn't seem to acknowledge his comment. Her eyes, one green and the other blue, were studying him keenly. "I only ever heard Calder call you 'Freckles.' I can see why now." She laughed. "They look kind of cute on you!"

He opened his mouth to continue elaborating on the immense danger they were in but only managed a gasp of panic when a couch-sized piece of candy fell into the lake a few feet away. That seemed to be warning enough. He scrambled through the water, his new ally right behind him, as more debris rained down on them. Relief flooded over him once his feet reached solid ground, and he paused to catch his breath.

That would prove to be a mistake.

"Watch out!" Gabi rammed into him from behind, sending him stumbling out of the way. He looked at her right before a broken piece of wood smashed into the back of her head.

He screamed as he caught her.

"I-It's okay," she stammered as she struggled and failed to get to her feet. She brushed her short and now very wet brown hair out of her face. When she looked at the hand she'd brushed her hair with, she saw it was covered in blood. She groaned. "That sucks."

He hugged her, holding her tightly while shaking. If she was dying, hugging her wouldn't do much to prevent that, so he didn't know why he kept hugging. *She's going to die.*

She shoved him away. "Let me go. I'm not going to die!" It seemed she had the ability to read minds.

He shook his head frantically as he lifted her to her feet. *I have to get her somewhere safe. Her wound might get infected. The infection might reach her brain, and then—!*

She shoved her way out of his arms and started stumbling away from him, likely in an attempt to prove her physical well-being, but it only made him more terrified at the prospect of her potential death. "Don't move around so much! It'll make the infected blood spread faster!"

"That's for snake bites!" she snapped.

He grabbed her arm in an attempt to calm her down, but that only made her madder, as she then tried to wriggle out of his grip. Their struggle only ended when a threatening piece of debris landed inches away, helpfully reminding them of their current situation.

His hand still firmly holding Gabi's, Kearney raced off. More bits and pieces of wood and candy pelted them as they fled, but as far as he was concerned, they were safe as long as Jolly didn't spot them. Once they'd gotten far enough, they stopped to catch their breath, but Kearney didn't relax for a minute. He kept his eyes fixed on the chaos, even as he was hunched over trying to slow his heartbeat.

Jolly was jumping on the tower's remains, stomping it into dust while dancing like a maddened jester. Given the mask, that lined up pretty well.

Kearney glanced at Gabi and spotted a smug grin painted over her face. It only got bigger when her eyes met his. "Those kids were in for a big surprise, weren't they?" she asked.

"We're lucky we even made it out."

She pulled a golf-ball-sized pearl candy out of her pants pocket and waved it around, showing off its bright luster. "It turns out Jolly loves shiny things."

He stared at her, shocked. *So, it was you.*

She looked back at the chaos Jolly was wreaking. "I have a place not far from here," she said. Then she scoffed. "What am I saying? It's a cave, hardly a place to call home."

Kearney nodded absently, continuing to watch as the infuriated castle dug out the ground beneath the tower, sending debris flying hundreds of feet into the air. He watched with great interest as a small chunk of wood flew in their direction. He wasn't sure if his ears were tricking him or not, but he could've sworn he heard a scream steadily getting louder as the wood got closer. He squinted, struggling to make out its shape, and then realization hit him. *It's Calder.*

Calder flailed his arms as he soared through the air. Luckily for Kearney and Gabi, he landed a couple yards away from them, meaning they weren't in any danger of getting hit. Unluckily, Calder's wooden body splintered into a million pieces once he landed, and those pieces went *everywhere.*

Kearney screamed as he hunched over again, desperately trying to rub sawdust out of his eyes. Gabi fell over because of how hard she was trying to hack out the splinters she'd inhaled. After a minute of maddened coughing and crying, they barely managed to get back to their feet. Kearney stared at where Calder had landed, eyes red from rubbing. Other than the impressive dent in the ground, there was no evidence that Calder had ever been there, probably because he'd practically disintegrated on landing.

Kearney glanced at Gabi; she was staring at the same spot as she coughed out more wood. Her expression said *good riddance.*

"You said there's a cave?" he asked.

She nodded with another cough.

"I'd like to go there now."

"Me, too," she croaked.

What followed was a solid hour of them limping through what seemed to be endless desert, complaining and snapping all the way about how one had it worse than the other.

The sandy ground was different from that of the forest's. While the forest's marshmallow ground liked to suck in Kearney's feet, the dust in the desert stuck to the bottoms of his shoes, causing them to stick to the floor with every step he took. He'd occasionally cast Gabi a glance. She was sweaty, and the dust took that opportunity to cling to every inch of her face, making her look even more miserable. Her hair was practically pink at this point.

Eventually, they made it to a group of gummy caves. Gabi headed into one of the smaller caves, and Kearney followed. Although Gabi hardly seemed to notice them, Kearney was thoroughly off-put by the tiny gummy bear faces that were in the caves' walls, as if they'd committed some horrible crimes against their people and had been melted into the walls as punishment.

His eyes continued exploring the fairly empty cave until they landed back on Gabi, who'd removed her light blue sweater and was now left in a tank top. She shook her sweater violently, sending candy bits and sawdust flying everywhere. Once the sweater was clean enough, she started using it to rub her face clean.

He watched her. *I could've sworn I've seen her somewhere before.*

She furrowed her brow when she noticed him. "You stare a lot, don't you?" She glanced back at the sweater awkwardly.

He lowered his gaze to his shoes. "Sorry." Then he gasped. "Your mom's looking for you!"

She jumped in shock. "M-My mom? What?" Her eyes narrowed. "How would you even know my mom?"

"She's been putting up posters of your face everywhere," he explained.

"Really?" She chewed her lip anxiously. "I-I wasn't planning on being here that long. And I left my parents a note and everything, so they shouldn't be *this* worried."

"They've been putting those posters up for months now."

"Months?" She paced back and forth as she hugged her sweater. "I've been here for *months?* I have to hurry up, then!"

"Hurry up?"

"Hurry up with getting to the end of this crazy place. My sister's there!"

"Your sister?" Kearney furrowed his brow. "What else is at the end?"

"I'm not sure. But I know she's there."

"How do you know?"

"I just do, okay?" Her glare was intimidating enough to make him look away. She glanced at her sweater momentarily before her eyes trailed to the stick of taffy leaning against the wall. "Is it alright if you sleep on that? I've got nothing better," she mumbled.

"It's okay," he said with a curt nod. He watched as she gave him one last glance before picking up a make-shift bag and heading outside.

Her eyes were still wide and worried. She looked like she wanted to say more. Ask more questions, maybe. But all she wound up saying was, "I'm going to make some dinner. As much as I hate that there's nothing decent to eat in this place, I've gotten used to it. I mean, you have to, you know?" She slipped her sweater back on and headed outside.

Kearney nodded, watching as she left. He slowly sat down on his taffy bed and all the tension in him out with a long, long sigh. After a short while of having staring contests with the gummy bears in the walls, he heard Gabi calling him. When he went outside, he found her sitting by a small campfire, eating what she liked to call *melted marshmallows à la grande*. They ate for a short while but quickly got sick of the marshmallows. When they were done, they continued to sit around the fire.

At night, the sad blue sky became nearly black. It looked like a child's bedroom ceiling with glow-in-the-dark stars plastered all over it. Kearney stared up at it and reminisced. He wished he could name them with Levi again. With a small sigh, he lowered his gaze to Gabi, who was looking up as well.

She pointed at random clusters of stars. "Those look like real constellations. Funny, isn't it?"

He nodded, but he wasn't looking at the stars any-more. Instead, he was staring at his shoes, which was definitely better than staring at her, as she seemed to hate it when he did that. *I should be on my way already. Her head seems better, so she'll be fine without me.*

Even though he wasn't staring at her anymore, she still sensed he was staring at something and that he was looking very conflicted while doing it. She watched as his eyes trailed to a bit of hardened caramel beside him, standing upright in a coral-like shape. He gently ran his fingers over it before breaking off a piece and eating it, possibly in another attempt to make himself relax.

"You like caramel?" she asked.

"It's nice," he explained. His shoulders were rigid even though he was telling himself over and over to re-lax.

"It is." She smiled, but it faded after a moment and was replaced with a look of concern. "Something you want to talk about?"

He shook his head. "I'm just tired."

"Alright." She looked up again. "So, how'd you end up here? You walked through a red door, right?"

He nodded, but when he realized she wasn't looking at him, he said, "Yeah."

They sat in silence for a minute before she let out a long sigh. "You're a great conversationalist."

He stiffened. It probably wasn't right to let her do all the talking. He stared at his shoes in thought again. "Do you know how to leave?" *A great choice of topic. Doesn't imply you want to be rid of her at all.*

"Not exactly. All I know is that there's some type of exit past a big thing called the Wall," she replied. "It's up north. The dolls talk about it all the time, specifically who's hiding behind it. I'm sure you heard Calder mention the Mister at least a million times?"

Kearney nodded.

"Yeah, me, too. I don't know much about the guy other than that he made the dolls, and they all seem to love him," she said.

"That's interesting."

After that, they quietly stared at the sky. Kearney felt uneasy. He looked at Gabi again. *I shouldn't stick around.*

She was watching the sparkling dust as it blew across the desert. "You know, the dolls have this myth about how the desert used to be full of grass. Apparently, there were even mountains made of rock candy that were filled with beautiful caverns."

"Really?"

"Yeah." She said, lying on the ground and causing a cloud of sand to swell around her. "They say Jolly stomped it all into dust."

Kearney laid down beside her. "Sounds like him."

"It does."

They lay in silence a little longer.

"I'm heading to bed."

She glanced at him. "You sure you don't want to stay up?"

"Yeah." He got to his feet and headed into the cave, but not before looking over his shoulder and saying, "Good night." In the cave, he dropped onto his stiff bed and stared at the gummy bear faces overhead as he tried to fall asleep. *Gabi wants to get to the end. Maybe I should get there, too.*

He paused, wincing at the sick feeling swelling in his stomach. *That's it, huh? I'm going to get out of here and forget this ever happened.* It didn't feel right. Like he'd be leaving Levi behind if he did that. If he were to get out, would he forget this place ever existed? Would he forget how he'd lost his little brother? It felt like a disgrace to Levi's memory.

Kearney rolled onto his stomach and buried his face in his arms. He kept trying to quiet his thoughts, but when that proved unsuccessful, he went back outside to talk with Gabi. She seemed happy he'd come back, but the whole time they were together, he only had one thought playing on repeat in his head.

Tonight, I'm leaving. It'll be better for both of us. Take care, Gabi.

House Full of Strings

Chapter 6

Levi Joins a Circus

Ring, ring, ring.

Levi groaned as he was pulled out of sleep. That stupid triangle had woken him up again. He sat up, hitting his head on the roof of his cage in the process. Then he looked at the dolls surrounding him. They were straining as they pulled the cart his little wooden prison was on, and yet, they still had the strength to sing "Ninety-Nine Bottles of Beer on the Wall" for the twelfth time in a row. A shorter doll marched in front of them, waving a broken candy cane around like a glowstick at a concert while singing especially loudly.

Levi leaned against his cage's wall and pressed his palms against his ears. He knew Kearney would come and save him. But if he didn't do it soon, Levi would probably lose his mind first. He paused. *Now that I think about it, I shouldn't assume he'll save me. I bet he needs me to save him.* He smirked to himself, imagining rescuing the damsel-in-distress of a brother his imagination had created. *Yeah, he definitely needs me to save him.*

Diverting his attention from his daydreams of saving Kearney, Levi observed his new surroundings. He wasn't in candy land anymore. The dolls had marched under a giant gate and into some type of amusement park city. The city was colored with soft purples, grays, and pinks. It looked beautiful, sure, but it also felt faded. Levi frowned as he studied the broken rollercoaster he was passing by. It was strangely depressing. The rides were dead, but the streets were filled to the brim with crowds of dolls that flowed like a never-ending brook. Somehow, they only added to the lifeless feeling. The buzz of their chatter sounded like the low hum of a running machine. The buildings themselves were square and felt flat. It was like this once lively place was now trapped in monotony.

Levi growled when random observers kept running up to his cage to poke him. His captors hardly seemed to care about his distress and kept marching. Eventually, they stopped in what must've been the town's plaza. The short doll with the candy cane set a bucket down in front of Levi's cage, jumped onto it, and started yelling to the masses, "Come one, come all, to see the one and only White-Haired Freak of Nature!"

Levi's mouth gaped open. "The *what?*"

The doll ignored him and continued, "If you give him enough money, he might do a backflip!"

This marketing strategy seemed to be pretty effective, as a crowd soon gathered. The short doll glanced at his companions, and they rushed Levi out of his cage. They put him in front of the crowd and tied his hands with red licorice, but he could tell they were struggling to do so, so he quietly tied it for them.

"This thing is a wild beast," the short doll continued, "easily more dangerous than Eye Stealer. No! More dangerous than the Purple-Eyed Monster!"

The dolls admiring Levi gasped in astonishment. Someone in the crowd looked Levi in the eye and was so terrified by whatever it was they saw in him that they screamed and ran away. Levi frowned. *Really?*

The short doll's companions started yanking the rope around, jerking Levi with it.

"Look at that!" The short doll's eyes were huge as he pointed at Levi. "He's rabid!"

Everyone in the crowd cheered as they threw money at Levi, which hurt a good amount.

The short doll, who Levi decided to refer to as the ringleader, smiled with satisfaction as he turned to pull out Levi's backpack. "One of the many habits of this elusive being is hoarding. This is a pouch that grew on the monster's back, surgically removed by yours truly!" The ringleader struggled to stand as he shook Levi's backpack, as it was at least twice as heavy as he was. "Help us make enough money, and we might just open a museum to show off all of this creature's findings!"

More money flew at Levi. He was getting ready to tear the licorice rope off his hands and stuff that stupid doll into his backpack. *That'd be a show.*

The ringleader unzipped his backpack. "Since you've given us such a warm welcome, how about a sneak peek?"

Levi's eyes went wide as the tiny doll pulled out a broken snow globe. The ringleader proceeded to show it off to the crowd. "This thing was broken by the creature when it went into a murderous rage!" He held it high above his head. "Starting price is two hundred nyxies!"

The crowd got louder as each prospector yelled their price over the other, and Levi stared at his snow globe in anger. *No one messes with my snow globe. No one.* He bit at the licorice rope until it snapped and rushed at the ringleader.

The ringleader yelped as Levi wrenched the snow globe from him and shoved him off the bucket, sending him flying to the ground. The crowd stared in shock before scattering like ants, and Levi smirked as he put his snow globe back in its place and slipped his backpack over his shoulders. *That'll teach them.* He raced through the frenzied crowd and away from the chaos before diving behind a crate, hiding patiently as his captors ran past him in their hunt.

After a tense minute of waiting, he crept out from behind the crate. He looked around at all of the dolls strolling through the streets. A few were eyeing him suspiciously. None of them were his pursuers from before, so he assumed that meant he was safe. He let out a small sigh of relief and looked over his shoulder. Behind him was a small brick office with a torn pink flag hanging over its front window. His gaze traveled down from the fluttering flag to the window, where a peach-haired doll was staring at him.

She looked disappointed in him, which he thought was a weird emotion to have toward someone you'd only just seen for the first time. She watched him for another second before backing away from the window and disappearing.

Immediately after, the old PA machine overhead wheezed awake, and a young girl's voice boomed through the town: "*My little friends, there appears to be a fleshy person in my town! White hair, blue eyes, fairly short. The first of you to bring him to my office will get a delightful reward.*"

Levi froze and slowly spun around. Everywhere he looked, eyes were on him, and they all looked hostile. He felt his heart trying to leap out of his chest. Now, he had an entire town of tiny psychos after him. He raced off again, this time from a much larger crowd.

"There's our cash cow!" The ringleader and his little troupe rejoined the chase. "Get him! Get him!"

Levi screamed in terror as he ran as quickly as possible, but the dolls were faster by a long shot. Before he could do anything about it, they had their little arms wrapped around his heels, and one somehow managed to land on his back. His assailants tripped him, and he face-planted into the ground as they collectively jumped on him and cheered their victory.

"Wait!" The ringleader and his troupe struggled to catch up. "He's mine!"

One of the dolls on top of Levi squared his shoulders with a resolute shake of his head. "No, *we* caught him fair and square!"

"I caught him first!"

"Finders keepers, losers weepers!"

Levi groaned as the dolls on top of him jumped and stomped in excitement.

"Hey, kid! Over here!" a high-pitched voice rang out.

Me? Levi lifted his head and spotted, to his confusion, a hand puppet sticking out of a window and aggressively waving its tiny arms at him. He paused and stared at it for a moment before looking back at his celebrating captors. He didn't know if anything could top today. Without a second thought, he scrambled to his feet, causing the dolls to tumble off of him, and raced for the window as he heard shouts of distress behind him. These dolls just weren't good at keeping prisoners.

He leaped through the window and slammed it shut behind him, leaving tiny hands clawing on the other side. He leaned against the wall and let out a sigh of relief. Unfortunately, that relief was cut short by the sound of footsteps approaching him.

Whump. Whump. Whump.

Who's there? Levi jerked his head around and frantically searched for the source of the footsteps. It had only just hit him how dark the room was. He pressed against the wall and stifled a fearful gasp as he heard the footsteps getting closer. They stopped, and he froze in anticipation of what was to come.

An enthusiastic voice suddenly rang out: "Well, hello there, friend! I think it'd be quite nice if you joined our little clique. Do you approve, Anais?"

A second and higher-pitched version of the first voice trilled in reply, "I think he'll fit in our group perfectly!"

Dread shot through Levi like a jolt of electricity. He pressed so tightly against the wall he could've been part of it.

There was a clap, a light bulb dangling above him lit up. The red-haired puppet from before was now right in his face. "Hello!"

Levi shrieked and waved his hands wildly in an attempt to slap the puppet away.

The puppet didn't have a mouth. It only had two teal beads for eyes, giving it a strangely lifeless look. It held its tiny stubs for hands to its face. "Oh! Don't be scared! Don't be scared! I'm just a puppet!" It was pulled to the side, revealing the cheery face of the crimson-haired man behind it. "See?"

Levi shrieked even louder and attempted to dart away, only to be caught up in the man's arms.

"Anais doesn't bite, promise!" the strange man said as he held the hand puppet close to Levi's face again to demonstrate.

Levi wiggled out of the man's grip and raced into the darkness. "Stay away from me!" he cried. *I hate this place. I want Kearney! Where's Kearney?*

"Little boy!" The man was running after him and frantically waving his arms as if that would help him catch Levi's attention. "Come back!" He hardly seemed to notice when his little puppet flew off his hand and vanished into the darkness behind him.

Levi slammed into a wall, which was to be expected when running around in the dark. He collapsed, completely winded. The man stopped at his side before clapping again, and another dangling bulb lit up, revealing Levi's nemesis, the wall.

The man grabbed Levi by the collar of his shirt, lifted him to his feet, and knocked on his head. "Are you alright, little one? No damage to the skull?"

Levi snapped back to reality and shoved the man away, sliding to the floor in the process. He backed up against the wall and scanned the man up and down, and the man looked *strange.*

He had soft gray skin with two cranberry-red stripes that started at the base of his cheeks and reached his eyes. His hair was that deep red as well; most of it draped over the back of his neck but for two small, neat braids dangling in front of his pointed ears. And antlers. He had deer antlers. As one did.

Levi froze. *Just like the statue.* "D-Don't touch me again."

The man drew away, eyeing him carefully. "You don't need to be afraid, boy," he said gently.

Levi paused and stared at him in bewilderment. "Who are you? *What* are you? And what do you want from me?"

The man placed a hand on his chest. "My name is Phantasos."

Levi brushed his messy hair out of his face. "…That's a weird name."

"It's quite an uncommon one." The man named Phantasos shrugged and smiled. "As for the whats, well, that can be explained later."

"Later?"

"If you don't mind there being a later." Excitement flickered in Phantasos's crimson eyes as he jumped to his feet. "As for your last question, I've come to notice you look positively famished. And, not to mention, in desperate need of a bath!" He tried to take Levi's hand, but Levi yanked it away.

Phantasos's expression softened. "I'm sorry. I get ahead of myself quite often." He kneeled down to Levi's level. "You seem a little lost. And afraid. But don't worry, I can help you, little one."

Levi studied him carefully. *I don't think I can get away from him. And he did just save me—kind of.* He was strange, no doubt, but at least he seemed nice. That was a first so far. "Yeah, I'm lost," he blurted, "but I'm waiting for my friend to find me. I know he will."

Phantasos cocked his head to the side, his braids swaying as he did. "Well, when?"

"Soon."

"Soon," he echoed. "Well, while you wait for that *soon* of your friend's, I can offer you a warm meal and shelter *now*."

Levi bit his lip in thought. He had no idea where Kearney was or how long it'd take for him to reach this town. And would Kearney be so mad if he made a new friend? He looked up at Phantasos again and put a hand to his stomach. A meal sounded great right about now. "I wouldn't mind that too much, I guess."

Phantasos smiled with satisfaction, reached out, and took his hand. Levi didn't resist as he helped him to his feet.

"Oh!" Phantasos's eyes widened. "But first, you *must* help me find poor Anais!" He looked over his shoulder. "I suppose I dropped her somewhere back there." In his own world, he began walking off and rambling about Anais with Levi's hand still in his own.

Levi tried to free his hand, but it was no use. Phantasos had an impressive grip, that was for sure. So, Levi gave up and started rambling along with him. After a bit of wandering around in what was mostly darkness, they found Anais, and Phantasos fitted her snugly back onto his hand. Then he snapped his fingers, and the floor gave way, plunging them into complete darkness.

Levi pulled his hands away from his face and nervously looked around. He wasn't falling anymore. Instead, he was in the halls of a mansion. And in Phantasos's arms. He tentatively asked Phantasos to put him down, and once his own feet were on the ground, his fear was completely forgotten.

"This place is your home?"

Phantasos beamed. "Indeed, it is."

"How is it right under that weird doll town?"

"Oh." Phantasos laughed. "We're not under the town, little one. We fell through a portal, in a sense."

"A portal?" Levi was spinning around as he admired the halls. "Huh. Kearney and I found a castle that looked like this place. Except that one had a lot more blue."

Phantasos smiled as he started walking down the hall. "Is it the one in the Happy Place?"

Levi followed him. "The Happy Place?"

"Yes. The place with the candy and skies made of paintings."

"It has a name?"

"Every area in this world does." Phantasos leaned closer to Levi and smiled. "The Happy Place is my favorite, by far. It has the most *delicious* chocolates."

Levi smiled. "And marshmallows, too!" He suddenly stopped in his tracks. "Hang on." *I almost forgot.*

"Yes?"

"The statue from the entrance looked just like you!"

"I'm well aware."

"But why?"

"Because I made it. I was sure to capture my good side as well," he said with a proud grin.

Levi stared at him, waiting for him to elaborate further, but Phantasos just gave Anais a confused glance before staring back.

"This is the part where you explain," Levi finally said.

Phantasos's eyes lit up. "I see!" He continued walking down the hall. "In simple terms, I am the creator of this place. This castle, the Happy Place, and everything in between."

Levi followed him. "All of this? How?"

"I'm not quite as human as you are, little one." He tapped his antlers and winked.

Levi watched him curiously. "If you're not a human, what are you, then?"

"It's quite complicated."

"There's no way to dumb it down?"

"It's not very easy to do so."

"We'll come back to it, then. So, where are we going?"

Phantasos stopped walking again, causing Levi to run into him. He spun around and pointed at a door to their right. "There!" He opened it and made a grandiose gesture. "After you."

Levi stepped through the door and looked around the room waiting on the other side. His mouth gaped open.

The room easily could've been the size of a football field. There were countless paintings and shelves filled with treasures spread out all over the red walls. In the middle of the room was a long, rectangular dining table, the comically long kind you'd see in the movies. He stared at the food spread out on the gigantic table and felt his mouth water. *I didn't even know it was possible to have so much food in one place.*

Phantasos took Anais off his hand and sat her in front of a plate, as she was way too small to sit in a chair. He then grabbed Levi by the shoulders and led him to a chair. "Don't be a stranger, boy. Have something!"

Levi sat down, his eyes wide as he scanned the table. "Can I have the mashed potatoes? And some gravy, too?"

"Yes, you may!" Phantasos clapped his hands and looked expectantly at the bowl of potatoes and jug of gravy.

Levi stared at him, brow furrowed in befuddlement. "Why did you—?"

The bowl suddenly jumped to life, fumbling around on its tiny legs. The jug did the same and, seemingly unable to balance itself, tripped and dumped gravy all over the mashed potatoes, as well as the tablecloth. It twitched and fell still as Levi gasped in terror and astonishment. The bowl wobbled over to him and dumped its contents onto his plate, tipping over in the process.

Phantasos smiled. "Enjoy!"

Levi gawked at the bowl, which had stopped moving. He poked it, but it didn't do anything else. "What was...how did you...*did* you?"

"Oh, don't worry your little head about it. I do that all the time!"

"*How?*"

"Would you like something to drink as well?"

"Wait, you didn't answer! How did you—?" His question broke off into a shriek when a teapot skipped over to them, fell off the table, and shattered on the floor, spilling scalding tea all over Phantasos's foot.

Phantasos winced. "It's much easier to control it when I'm not focused on something else."

Levi gasped. "Are you okay?"

"Yes, yes, quite alright." He gloomily lifted the broken shards and dropped them on the table. "But I always loved that teapot."

"No, I meant that." Levi pointed at Phantasos's wet shoe. "That tea looked hot."

Phantasos glanced at it. "So it was. I believe it was my favorite blueberry tea. Most unfortunate to let it go to waste."

"No, I wasn't...." Levi sighed. "Never mind." He scooped up a spoonful of mashed potatoes and shoved it in his mouth.

Phantasos sat beside Levi and watched him. "You were referring to pain?"

Levi looked at him. "Well, yeah."

"That makes sense." Phantasos slowly nodded. "Pain isn't something I've experienced for quite a long time. It seems I'd forgotten about it entirely."

Levi furrowed his brow. "What do you mean you don't feel it? What about when you stub a toe?"

Phantasos sighed. "There are things a young boy like you may not yet comprehend entirely, but simply put, my search for immortality led me to make a great sacrifice, that being giving up my 'true' physical form."

I guess he does look a little...stiff. "Are you a doll, too?"

"If you mean possessing a body of wood, then, yes."

"Are the dolls related to you, then?"

Phantasos smiled. "So, you've met them? I grew rather bored of dwelling here alone, so I created them." He lowered his head. "Unfortunately, my little ones began to go through a rebellious phase, and I was forced to send them all away."

"That's sad." Levi furrowed his brow. "What if they want to come back?"

"Then I would greet them with open arms!" Phantasos's eyes sparkled with excitement. "All this talk of my little ones reminds me of a certain someone I wanted to introduce you to. You see, I'm not completely alone here." He glided out of his seat and clapped his hands.

A few seconds later, a doll in a maid's dress strolled into the room, her shiny black hair swaying. She stopped at Phantasos's side, her half-closed eyes fixed on Levi.

Phantasos patted her on the head. He opened his mouth to say something, but the maid cut him off, likely without even realizing it.

"Are you Master's new toy?" Her voice was airy. Her gaze had already drifted off to look at something more interesting.

"*Friend,* Annette." Phantasos groaned before glancing back at Levi. "She's a bit dull at times, but she gets the job done. Occasionally."

"I'm not dull." Annette's smile widened. "*You're* dull."

He cleared his throat, ignoring her comment. "Annette here will be your personal assistant. She'll help you to your room, treat you to meals and whatever else you desire. All you need to do is ask!"

Levi grinned with excitement. He jumped out of his seat and ran up to her. "Annette, get me the biggest bedroom with the softest blankets you can find!" he ordered.

Annette's green eyes were shut now as if she was absorbed in a daydream. "Whatever you say, stud." She waddled out of the room.

Once she'd gone, Levi turned his attention back to his host. "She's funny," he said with a smile.

"And quite adorable," Phantasos added. He sat back down. "So, tell me about this Kearney fellow. I assume he's your friend? Have the two of you known each other for long?"

Levi sat down as well. "I've known him ever since I was four, just about."

Phantasos spooned some mashed potatoes and attempted to feed them to Anais, who was slumping over. "Are your families well-acquainted? I've found that's how most long-lasting friendships among youth tend to happen."

Levi stared at his plate "We're both orphans, actually."

Phantasos's eyes widened. The spoon fell out of his hand. "I'm so terribly sorry! I-I didn't mean to bring up such an upsetting subject!"

Levi held his hands up in reassurance as he chuckled. "Don't worry about it! I know I called Kearney my friend earlier, but the truth is, he's more like my big brother. And he's all the family I need."

"But nothing can ever *truly* replace a parent." Phantasos's eyes drifted away. "Did you at least know them?"

"Yeah, I did," Levi replied with a sad smile. "I loved them more than anything. Still do."

"That's wonderful." He nodded. "Well, regardless, let's change the tune. I won't have you have that dreary look on your face any longer!"

Levi laughed. "Okay, okay. What about you? Any family?"

"Oh," Phantasos rolled his eyes, "don't get me *started*. If anything, I had too much family! A terrifying mother and thousands of quarreling siblings all fighting for her love!"

"That sounds like a bit of an exaggeration."

Phantasos threw his head back dramatically. "Just be thankful you only have one brother. I assure you, thousands is a nightmare."

Levi chuckled. "Well, were you at least close with some of them?"

Phantasos shrugged. "Somewhat. I was on good terms with two. But the first was an arrogant brat, and the other," he bit his lip as he leaned farther back in his seat, "well, the other was just plain scary. We all parted ways eventually, and I'm happy for that."

Levi nodded before rubbing his eyes, which Phantasos immediately noticed.

"It's getting quite late, isn't it?"

Levi stared at him. "Is it? I thought it was just daytime."

"It's not."

"Oh. What time is it, then?"

"I don't know."

Levi paused. "Aren't there any clocks here?"

"No clocks."

"At all?"

"At all."

"How do you know what time it is, then?"

Phantasos kicked his feet up and rested them on the table. "Call it my intuition. But don't worry, time isn't incredibly important here. If anything, Annette will let you know of any time-sensitive occurrences, such as dinner, bedtime, and petteia game nights."

"Pit...aiya? What's that?"

Phantasos clapped excitedly. "Only the most amazing board game created by your kind! Don't fret. I'm sure Annette won't mind sitting out the next time we play to let you have a go." He leaned a little closer and winked. "Though I must warn you, I am the undisputed petteia champion in this house. I suppose that isn't much of a surprise, though. A grape has more brains than Annette does."

Levi heard the sound of shuffling coming from the doorway. He glanced over his shoulder to see a blonde-haired doll wearing a tan trench coat over a white sweater. He was staring at Levi, brow wrinkled in what seemed to be confusion.

"Who's that?" Levi asked.

Phantasos's head swiveled to look at the doll. "It seems I forgot to mention: that's Henry. He's like Annette but smarter, although not by much."

"Good evening to you, too, Master," Henry curtly replied. He continued eyeing Levi closely. Levi could've sworn he saw annoyance briefly flash in the doll's brown eyes. "Your room's ready," Henry said.

"Where's Annette?" Levi slowly asked.

"She got tired, so she decided to take a nap on your bed."

"Well then, you'll just have to wake her up." Phantasos waved his hand. "How's about you lead our guest there now?"

Henry promptly nodded before spinning around and leaving the room. He stopped and waited for Levi to follow. Levi glanced back at Phantasos, who smiled encouragingly. "Don't worry. You can spend the rest of the night getting comfortable there. I'll see you tomorrow, friend!"

With a smile, Levi marched out of the room and followed Henry. Levi found himself wondering what was going on behind that little doll's big brown eyes. Now that he thought of it, they reminded him of Kearney's. His attention quickly shifted to his surroundings, and he bounced excitedly through the halls of Phantasos's home while spouting question after question. "What's that thing? What's in that room? What's that?"

"Shut up."

Levi stopped and stared at Henry, who kept walking as if nothing had happened. *What did he say?* "Are you alright?"

"You should be asking yourself that."

"I-I just...." Levi felt words getting caught in his throat. "You're so...."

"Well, get over it." Henry twirled around, revealing the glower on his face. "I'm Master's servant. Not yours. Your room is just around the corner, so I'll be out of your hair soon enough. I just hope your precious ego can survive until then."

Levi glared at the little doll. Henry's eyes weren't like Kearney's at all. His eyes were narrowed and hostile like a cat's. And if cats were one thing, it was pure evil. Levi shoved his fists into his pockets as he trailed behind Henry, still trying to process half of the venom the tiny doll had just spat at him.

Henry soon stopped and pointed at a door. "That's your room."

Levi stared at it. "Alright."

The two stood in place before Henry looked at him again. "What? Go inside already!"

"I thought you were going to lead me in. You know, give me a tour or something."

Henry pointed at it more vigorously. "Your bedroom. Right there. Furniture, bathroom, and blankets inside. *Go.*"

Levi glared at him. "You're the worst butler I've ever met."

"In the state you're in, I doubt you've ever had the leisure of ever meeting one, let alone becoming pals with their boss." He spun around and walked away without giving Levi another glance. "And you haven't seen the worst of anything until you've seen Annette in action."

Levi scoffed and marched into the bedroom, slamming the door behind him. He then pressed himself against the wall and sighed. *Just brush it off, Levi. On the bright side, Phantasos is really nice.* He started looking around his new bedroom, and his gripes with Henry were immediately forgotten. The room was nice. The bed looked to be king-size, with soft scarlet blankets layered over it. The furniture—the bed, dressers, and everything else—was all made of dark cherry wood. And those curtains he and Kearney saw when they first entered the House were there, too. He ran over to the window and skimmed the curtains out of the way, ready to admire the view, but found disappointment instead. At the moment, all he could see were gray skies and a massive chasm between Phantasos's manor and whatever was on the other side. *I wonder how far that doll town is from here.*

He turned his attention to the bed and slumped onto it, only to hit his shoulder against something hard under the blankets. He jumped back with a yelp.

Annette's head poked out from under the crimson comforter. "You need something, stud?" she mumbled.

"I'd like my bed, please."

"It's right here."

"I'd like to have it to *myself.*"

She rolled off the bed and slammed onto the ground, although she hardly seemed to notice or care. She got to her feet and wandered out the door without another word, leaving Levi watching in befuddlement.

Everyone's so weird here. He shuffled under the blankets, his eyelids growing heavy. He eyed a door at the other end of the room, which was probably the bathroom. *Here I am, a sweaty mess, getting under a stack of clean sheets.* He smiled to himself and got even cozier. *Henry will handle it.*

After a minute of lying there, he opened his eyes. His smile faded. Things were so quiet. No random chattering, no sirens or cars, and no Kearney. It wasn't right. *Kearney will come soon. He always does!* He rolled onto his side and sniffed. *But how soon?*

A loud crash suddenly sounded on the floor above, making him flinch. He stayed frozen in place, trying to figure out what it was. It sounded like something fragile had broken.

"*Henry!*" Phantasos's muffled voice shrieked overhead. "*Henryyyyy! There's glass everywhere!*"

"*I'm coming, Master!*" Levi listened to Henry's tiny footsteps, followed by, "*Master, get down from there! You'll fall!*"

"*But then I'll get glass on my shoes—!*" There was another shriek, followed by a giant *thud* that shook Levi's bedroom, which was probably the sound of Phantasos falling.

"*Master!*"

A smile crept across Levi's face, and he let out a giggle. He probably shouldn't have, but it made him feel just a little better.

Chapter 7

Levi Realizes Glitter Is Just as Weaponizable as Makeup

Levi yawned and hugged the now-messy blankets. *Did I sleep in again?* "Kearney," he mumbled, half awake and slowly sitting up. "You here? Don't worry about breakfast. We can go…together." Feeling his heart sink, he lowered his head and brushed his hair out of his face. *Right. He's not here.*

He got out of bed and made his way to the door. It didn't feel right to wake up alone. Even when he used to, he always knew Kearney would be back in a matter of minutes, but now, he wasn't even sure if Kearney knew where he was.

Levi opened the door and began dragging himself down the hallway, hardly discernable from a zombie.

Henry happened to be walking by with a stack of folded towels in hand. He paused and scanned Levi from head to toe. "Did you even shower last night?"

Levi shook his head.

Henry rolled his eyes before guiding him back to his room. "Whenever pigs are invited to feasts, they're usually the main course. So at least *try* to make yourself presentable for Master."

Levi didn't reply. He was too busy trying to understand what Henry's words even meant. It seemed that would be a recurring theme. Henry prepared to drop the towels onto Levi's bed but almost gagged upon seeing what had become of his previously clean sheets. "I think I might've offended those pigs by comparing you to them." He put the towels on the floor and began shoving Levi toward the bathroom.

"Can't I do it after I eat?" Levi snapped, now fully awake.

"You still have the gall to eat with Master while looking like *that?*" Henry resumed shoving. "I won't allow it!"

Levi grudgingly submitted and waited as the tub filled with water. "I can do it on my own," he commented.

"I doubt it." Henry turned off the water. "The bath's ready. Clothes off."

Levi gripped his shirt defensively. "You're not going to leave?"

"If I leave now, you'll probably hurt yourself by strangling yourself with the shower hose or in some other dumb way. Now take them off, or I'll do it myself."

After an awkward moment, Levi got into the tub, uneasily sitting in place as Henry aggressively rubbed shampoo into his hair for the next few minutes. After that, Henry washed him off, ushered him out, and wrapped him in a towel, pulling out a neat pile of clothes and leaving it on the sink.

"These should be your size. Put them on and brush your hair and teeth." He spun on his heel and glided out of the room without another word, leaving Levi sitting on the tub lip, still wrapped like a burrito.

A few minutes later, Levi was out in the halls again, this time warily keeping an eye out for Henry and his nasty comments. He walked into the dining room and looked around. Henry wasn't anywhere to be seen, but neither was Phantasos.

Levi noticed a plate of pancakes sitting on the table and walked up to it, chuckling when he spotted the smiley face made of berries on top of the stack. He sat down and, after a few minutes of voracious eating, found a thin box wedged between the bottommost two pancakes. He pulled it free and opened it to find a note waiting inside.

Come to the library for a surprise! -Your best friend, Phantasos.

Best friend already, huh? Levi jumped out of his seat and started wandering around in search of the library. *Guess I shouldn't keep him waiting.* Though he'd been worried he'd get lost in Phantasos's massive home since Phantasos had forgotten to give him a tour, he was lucky enough to find the library behind the first door he opened. He stepped inside and looked around. The library was massive, that was for sure, but it was one giant room in which you could see everything from anywhere you stood. So where could Phantasos and his surprise possibly be hiding? His eyes fixed on a table in the center of the room. It was covered in books, but there was something there that looked out of place.

"...My snow globe?"

"That it is."

Levi jumped in surprise, but the frightened look on his face turned to excitement once he looked up and spotted Phantasos hanging from the chandelier over-head. "How'd you get up there?"

"With relative ease." Phantasos smiled proudly. "Would you like to join?"

"No, thanks."

Phantasos shrugged. "Suit yourself." Then, he stepped off the chandelier. Levi jumped, biting back a scream as Phantasos fell. He was thoroughly relieved when Phantasos landed perfectly on his feet and even did a fancy bow.

Levi let out the breath he'd been holding. "Sorry, I-I forgot about the whole...being-wood thing."

"There's no need for apologies." Phantasos smiled as he led him to the table with the snow globe. "Now, what do you think?"

Levi studied the snow globe. "You fixed it?" There was a mix of emotion in his voice.

"I did." Phantasos's smile faded when he saw the conflicted look on Levi's face. "Do you not like it? We can break it again if you'd like."

"No, that's alright!" Levi smiled. "I've just gotten used to it, that's all." He picked it up and admired it. "After all, I was four when it first broke." *On the night they died, too.*

Phantasos's smile was back and bigger than ever. "I added a little something to it. Would you like to see?"

"Sure."

Phantasos rested his hand on the snow globe before running his fingers along it. When he did, it expanded like a balloon. It kept growing and growing until the pair were both surrounded by its little world. Levi took a panicky step back. "What's going on?" He shook his head. "This has to be a dream...."

Phantasos scooped up a handful of glittery snow and tossed it, hitting Levi in the face. "Did that feel like a dream?" he teased.

Levi's bewilderment vanished, and he cackled as he patted down a ball of glitter to fight back with. "You'll wish it did in a minute!" He hurled it at Phantasos, who nimbly dodged it.

"Come on, snowflake," he taunted. "I can't wait all day!"

"*Snowflake?* What's that supposed to be?"

"Your new nickname!"

"Don't you dare!" Levi threw another one, half amused and half annoyed.

Phantasos snickered as he dodged again. "With those throws of yours, I don't even have to dare!"

Levi grabbed another handful of glitter and ran after him, zipping everywhere while trying to nail his target. With a cry, he tossed it as hard as he could, and it hit Phantasos right in the face. As soon as Phantasos fell in defeat, the world twirled around them as it shrank, and soon, it was back in the snow globe.

Levi laughed as he shook glitter out of his hair. "Done already? You're such a sore loser!"

Phantasos chuckled as he brushed himself off. "Maybe I am."

Levi sighed with contentment as he wiped his brow. "That was amazing. How did you do it?"

"A magician never reveals his secrets." Phantasos smiled as he tapped the snow globe. He pushed it toward Levi. "Let this be a keepsake for you. To our friendship!"

Levi studied his snow globe again. After giving a reluctant chuckle, his apprehension faded away, and he smiled proudly as he held it up. "To our friendship!"

House Full of Strings

Chapter 8

Levi Gets Assaulted by the Local Plantlife

Levi and Phantasos were standing in a room full of treasures, ranging from old antiques to novelties created by Phantasos himself. They'd gotten into a brief argument about Levi wanting to go outside despite being repeatedly told it was dangerous. The result of that argument was the tantalizing treasure room, which was essentially Phantasos's quiet attempt at distracting Levi to keep him from wandering off.

As Levi's greatest weakness, greed, rapidly overtook him, Phantasos was running his hand over his chin in feigned thought. "I've had this place boarded up for quite a while now. Full of souvenirs from my past travels. Now, they do nothing but collect dust." Phantasos cast Levi a sideways glance. "Would you like them? I'd prefer it if you stayed here rather than go out there."

It's just like my dream. Levi hopped with joy. "Yes. Yes!" He took off so quickly that he sent dust flying up behind him. With maddened cackles of delight, he scooped up whatever looked interesting and shoved it into the depths of his already full backpack.

Phantasos stared in shock. "Am I giving gifts to a friend or being robbed?"

Levi paused, his hand firmly grasping a small silver abacus he knew he'd never use, and stared back. "...But you gave them to me."

"Yes, but you're not leaving already, are you?"

"No." He couldn't see where Phantasos was going with this.

"Exactly. So, you can leave all these here, and this will be another room of yours."

Leave it, huh? Levi's eyes narrowed. *Just like that? No way. I've gotta keep an eye on this stuff.* "I'm sleeping here now."

"It's very dusty." Phantasos laughed as he awkwardly scratched the back of his head. "You don't have to—"

Levi pointed at Henry, who was hiding behind Phantasos and watching in disgust. "Move my bed here!"

Henry's face scrunched up in a scowl before he walked away. Phantasos, seeing there was no more conversation to be had, left shortly after, leaving Levi to slink around his new den of treasures like a greedy dragon. He eyed a fancy hourglass just out of reach and spun around to grab the armchair in the middle of the room. He pushed it to the shelf before jumping onto it, which he immediately realized was a mistake when he sent at least centuries' worth of dust into the air. He shrieked with dismay and jumped off, hastily brushing the dust off his pants.

He grabbed a very expensive-looking rod and repeatedly smacked the chair with it, making dust puff up into the air. After a few minutes, the chair was dust-free and beaten to a pulp, and Levi was now content to use it. Once he finally got his fancy hourglass, he sat in the chair and leaned back, grinning as he soaked in the quiet. But the smile on his face faded as he ran his fingers through the faded pink scarf around his neck. Strangely enough, this giant gift from his new friend reminded him of the little gift from his old one.

All Phantasos had to do was snap his fingers or open a door to give Levi what he wanted. As wonderful as that was, it only made Levi miss Kearney more. After all, Kearney would disappear, sometimes for hours on end, only to return with a pair of gloves or an old scarf. But even though Levi had a taste for the expensive, it was those little things that were the most precious to him. He rubbed the old scarf again. He wouldn't trade it for anything in the world.

His moment of silence was interrupted by the sound of a dull scraping that was steadily getting louder. He leaned forward as he watched the door, and soon, the foot of his bed crept into sight. He could hear Henry grunting as the bed inched forward. With a nonchalant shrug, he looked away and leaned back in his armchair. He stretched his legs and looked out the window.

"I can't fit the bed through the door," Henry called from behind the bed. The bed hit the door frame, refusing to budge any further.

Levi paid him no attention. *I want to go outside. That'd be fun.* He sighed as he threw his head back in disappointment. *But Phantasos says it's dangerous. I wonder what's out there.*

"Levi. The bed. Help."

He jumped to his feet in realization. *Hang on, he's right. I'm Levi. I don't take orders from anyone. I can go find what's out there myself!* He beamed with pride. He'd almost forgotten how awesome he was. He spun around and marched to the door, climbing over the bed while Henry continued to struggle.

He glanced at Henry. "What does the door that leads outside look like?"

Henry frowned. "Big and red," he seethed.

With a satisfied nod, Levi hurried off again, studying each door he passed. Soon, he'd gotten pretty far and realized that getting lost in Phantasos' home was still a very big threat. So, he decided to pull an enamel pin off of his coat and stick it into the carpet as a marker. He went back to walking and stuck another pin into the carpet after a little while. *This should keep me on track.*

He did that for about ten minutes, walking down countless twists and turns and sticking pins into the carpet until the lapels of his coat had no more to give. He stared at them as he sighed.

Suddenly, something creaked behind him.

He spun around to see what the sound was, but there was nothing. Feeling uneasy, he looked away and found himself teetering off balance, like the floor was twisting beneath him. He stared at his feet but found he hadn't moved an inch, and the carpet hadn't gained a single crease. He let out an tense huff. *Was that just me?* He started walking faster. *Just get over it. You're fine.* He felt the house twisting around him again and froze in his tracks, but as soon as he stopped running, anything he thought he'd seen was gone.

"Snowflake, why are you littering?"

Levi gasped and spun around to see Phantasos with a pile of pins in his hands and an annoyed look on his face. Levi let out a small groan. *Still calling me that, huh?* "Sorry, I didn't mean to make a mess." He crossed his arms. "I'm trying to find the door outside, and the pins are for tracking, which you've just ruined. So, thanks for that."

"What? Why?" Phantasos furrowed his brow. "It's dangerous outside."

"Yeah, I know." Levi tried to keep the confident glint in his eye for Phantasos to see. "But I can fend for myself."

Phantasos stared at the pile of pins he was holding with a dejected look on his face. "Don't you trust me?"

"Stop being such a victim. I trust you just fine! If I want to go outside, I'll go outside."

"There's nothing out there but danger, snowflake...." Phantasos shook his head as he thrust his pin-full hands forward, not even looking at Levi anymore.

Levi squinted as he stared at Phantasos. Physically, he looked upset—slumped shoulders, lowered head, and so on—but there was something in his eyes, something Levi just couldn't read.

"Here are these," Phantasos muttered. "Do whatever you like, I suppose."

Levi took the pins before looking back at Phantasos, who'd already begun sulking away. "Phantasos, wait!"

He spun around excitedly. "Yes?"

"Where's the door?"

That unreadable look was back as his shoulders went back to slumping. "Take a left here, then two rights." His voice sounded as deflated as he looked.

"Alright, cool."

Phantasos resumed his sulking, but Levi didn't pay him much attention. He started following Phantasos's directions without skipping a beat. *I wonder what that was about. Anyway, I'll be fine!* Another genius idea came to him. *I'll just have to do something crazy dangerous today to prove myself capable to him. It didn't work on Kearney at all, but you never know. It might just work on Phantasos!* A short while later, he found the door and made it outside. He took a deep, satisfied breath before looking around. *Time to find something dangerous.*

He started racing around in search of anything interesting, but his search wasn't fruitful. There was nothing around the mansion but rocky ground and the occasional dead plant. Compared to the Happy Place, it was incredibly depressing. Admittedly, Levi thought the mansion's location could be deemed pretty dangerous, given that it was right next to a giant gorge that seemed to be filled only with darkness. Not the best place to put a house, but who was he to judge?

He squinted as he tried to see the other side of the gorge. It was incredibly far away, but he could just make out a large gray object way off on the horizon. It almost looked like a wall. He let out a thoughtful hum. *I wonder what's there.* He kicked a pebble into the gorge before going back to looking for more dangerous things around the mansion. The deadliest thing he could find seemed to be the weeds in Phantasos's tiny garden, which looked like it hadn't been touched in ages.

He groaned. *So, he's a liar, too. There's nothing even remotely exciting around here for miles!*

As if hearing his thoughts, the weeds around him began to tremble. He looked down at them. "What? Are you going to do something?"

As it turned out, they were. They sprung out of the ground, reaching for a beat-up scarecrow and wrapping around it. They slithered up every inch of the scarecrow, then began moving its limbs.

Levi gasped in amazement when he saw the weeds piloting the scarecrow. "This is perfect!" he cried moments before the weed-riddled scarecrow sucker punched him in the face. He fell back but jumped to his feet seconds later. "Bring it on!"

The scarecrow most definitely did. Its upper half leaned back as its legs scrambled at Levi. Then its upper half swung forward in a smooth motion that ended with it smacking its head into his. And even though it was fairly soft, the sheer force of the hit was enough to knock Levi back yet again. He fell as the scarecrow tackled him, and the two tussled in the mud. He barely managed to yank a stake out of the dirt before scrambling to his feet and stabbing the scarecrow through the head, sending cotton flying everywhere. Its arms scrabbled wildly for a moment, and then it gave up and accepted defeat.

Covered in mud and scratches, Levi cackled victori-ously as his foe lay on the ground. His eyes flicked to Phantasos's manor, specifically a window. There, he spotted Henry staring back at him in utter confusion and repulsion. He crept away from the window and out of Levi's view. Levi stood in place, his cheeks hot. Who knew what Henry would do with the strange but frankly useless information that Levi had just beaten up a scarecrow?

Levi then realized just how muddy he'd gotten, gath-ered his bearings, and headed back inside. After a few minutes of searching for his room and failing, he spotted Henry, who was now in the middle of talking to Annette beside a closet. He seemed to be trying to show her something inside of it.

She smiled. "That's cool, Henry."

"Yeah, yeah." He nodded a little too enthusiastically. "Now, since you're my friend, I'll let you get a close look at it."

"Can I touch it?"

"Sure, you can touch it." He threw open the closet door and scanned the halls, probably making sure there'd be no witnesses. As he did, Annette ambled into the closest without hesitation. She didn't even make a sound when he slammed the door shut on her and locked it. He snickered as he raced away, leaving Levi staring in shock at the closet Annette was trapped in, trying to figure out whatever it was that had just played out before him.

After a minute of silence, he walked up to the closet and knocked on the door. "Annette?"

"Yeah?" her muffled voice hummed from the other side, completely unperturbed by her current situation.

He opened the door and spotted her sitting on the floor with a ribbon in her hands. "Are you alright?"

"Why wouldn't I be, stud?" she replied as she gently stroked the ribbon.

Would everyone please stop with the nicknames? "Because you just got locked in a closet."

"Henry was showing me his snake." She shrugged, her smile as big as ever. "Anyway, I'm his friend. He said so."

"I know I haven't known him for as long as you have, but I'm pretty sure I can tell when he's lying."

"Nah." She shuffled out of the closet with the ribbon still in her hands.

"You know that's not a snake, right?"

"Of course, it's a snake. It's long like one." She didn't even look at him. "I used to see them all the time, so I think I'd know."

He opened his mouth to further argue but shut it once he realized quarreling with an airhead was pointless. "Do you know where my room is?"

"You'll find it."

"That doesn't help."

"Then ask Master where it is."

Levi frowned. "He got upset at me earlier, so finding him will probably be tough. I bet he's crying in a corner like a baby or something."

"He just likes keeping an eye on you," she replied with a grin.

He paused. "What's that supposed to mean?"

"Exactly how it sounds."

"He can watch me when I'm outside, too."

"Nah, he's stuck in here."

Levi stiffened as his eyes fixed on her. "…Stuck?"

"He's got a string. Around his neck." She gestured to her neck as if to demonstrate. "Keeps him tied to the mansion so he'll be okay. Because he's safe in this house. We're all safe in this house."

His head tilted. "What's any of that even supposed to mean?" *And if he can't leave this place, how did he find me all the way in Toy Town, then?*

Instead of answering his question, she drifted around the corner and disappeared, lighter than a cloud.

He groaned as he threw his head back. "Why is everyone so *annoying* around here?" he yelled into the air. He went back to marching around in search of his room and soon spotted his bedroom door down the hall. He ran for it, but to his astonishment and horror, the halls around him twisted, and the door to his room was replaced with the one to the library.

He kicked it. "I knew it! I knew I wasn't seeing things earlier! This *house* is annoying, too!" At the sound of footsteps approaching, he spun around so quickly and violently that he almost sent himself careening into Phantasos.

Phantasos frowned as he passed Levi with a plate in hand, showing no interest in talking with him. The asparagus on his plate quivered as if it was also angry with Levi. It seemed Phantasos's food really liked to voice its opinions.

"Hey, Phantasos." Levi had the kind of look on his face that said he'd commit murder if this conversation didn't go the right way. "Guess what I did outside today," he said in a strained voice.

Phantasos stopped to glare at him over his shoulder.

Levi felt a chill run over him like a block of ice had just been shoved down his shirt. "I-I fought a scarecrow," he explained.

"How lovely for you." Phantasos's voice was thick with sarcasm.

"It would've killed me," he continued.

"I'm sure it would've."

He balled his fists in annoyance. "If only you could go outside and watch me do it." That sentence came out with more poison than he'd meant.

"Unlike you, I rather *like* being indoors." Phantasos's eyes narrowed. "If you'd like, I can watch from a window next time you go out. I'll be sure to clap when you stomp down the killer grass that's terrorized me for so long."

Levi's face was red now. "Killer grass is nowhere near as cool as killer scarecrows."

Phantasos didn't reply. The coldness remained as he continued walking away without a word.

Levi searched for something more to say that could pique his interest. "Henry shoved Annette into a closet."

"Now, *that's* believable."

Levi didn't realize how tense he was until after Phantasos had gone. He stared at his shoes in silence, still trying to comprehend what exactly he'd done to make things so suddenly hostile between them.

He'd never felt it before — that iciness.

Chapter 9

Kearney Helps a Duck

Kearney never thought he'd use the word "wasteland" to describe an endless field of candy, but that summed it up pretty well. Candy dust blew along the ground and stuck to his skin, occasionally making him suffer by getting in his eyes. He'd seen cacti made of spiky blue candy, little oases of tea surrounded by banana trees, and many other strange things that he was too tired to remember. He wiped his sweaty brow and kept walking, as he had been for the last few days. Maybe it'd been more than a few. He hadn't been keeping track.

He tried to avoid thinking about anything, but that was hard to do when nothing interesting was happening. He felt guilt creep in every time Gabi came to mind. He thought of how happy she'd been when she'd found out she wasn't alone in this strange and scary place. As much as he'd wanted to stay with her to avoid the somber loneliness he found himself trapped in now, a restless anxiety in him wouldn't allow him to. After all, what if he got too attached and things went horribly wrong? He shook his head. *This is easier.*

He wasn't sure if he was going to the Wall. He decided he still wanted to go home. Even if that home would never be the same, it'd at least be better than whatever this place had in store for him. He wasn't interested in feuding with dolls and castles for the rest of his life.

He slowed to a stop, his head lowered as he started nodding off. His eyelids felt heavier than bricks. Night never came in this place. That, combined with just how bright the sand was, made it hard to get much, if any, sleep.

Briiiing!

His head shot up. A purple payphone had materialized right in front of him. The same one as before. How it had gotten there in the two seconds his eyes had been shut, he had no clue. But what he did know was that he wasn't in the mood to pick up the call. He walked past it. When the ringing ceased, he looked over his shoulder, only to find that the phone had vanished. He shook his head in confusion as he focused back on what was ahead of him. Somehow, the payphone had appeared in front of him once again. With a groan, he sped past it, but once he blinked, it was in front of him again.

Briiiing! it taunted.

He yanked the phone off its receiver and held it to his ear. "What now?" he snapped.

"Hey-a, Kearney." It was the same voice as before. *"I've got a riddle for you. Wanna hear it?"*

"No."

"It's a pretty easy one. I think you'll get it," the voice continued, ignoring his reply. *"What's white at the tip, is very annoying, and used to be alive?"*

118

He stared at the ground, his mind too blank to even bother thinking up an answer.

"Levi!" the voice screamed, causing Kearney's ear to ring.

He shoved the phone back onto its stand with a yell. He blinked again, and it vanished. His breaths became shorter, mixed with little sobs as he desperately tried to keep his volcano of emotions from erupting. He stared at the ground and kept walking as his cheeks burned with anger and shame.

Then his head rammed into something hard. He looked up. It was the payphone.

He grabbed it again. "Leave me alone!" he yelled into it. He left it hanging by its cord and marched away.

"I didn't realize you were such a baby," the voice called after him from the dangling phone. *"Just get over it. That's what I did, and I turned out great."*

He didn't bother looking back at it, and he had no intention of listening to anything else the voice had to say.

"C'mon, Kearney."

He kept walking.

"Keeeearneeeey."

He was tempted to go back and punch that phone until his knuckles bled.

*"**Pick up the damn phone, you little idiot.**"*

He stopped with a wince. The first time, the voice had done that, he hadn't really seemed angry. This time, he definitely did. Kearney reluctantly went back and picked it up. "What?" he asked quietly, trying to keep his fear from being heard.

"*Took you long enough,*" the voice snorted. "*Listen, kid, I only care about your safety. I'm the one who told you about the castle, wasn't I? It's not my fault you were so slow to react.*"

Kearney bit his tongue.

"*There's a town not far from here. A stupid town, but a town. They have a little triangle sound they love to play all the time, and it's hella annoying. Anyway, start walking to the left of this phone, and you'll get there soon enough.*"

"Why would I do that?" he asked, voice hollow. "Because the creepy stranger on the phone told me to?"

There was a brief silence before the voice replied, "***Because I only care about your safety, Kearney.***"

There was a click, and the call was over. Out of the wasteland's silence came another ring, this time from the sound of a triangle far off in the distance. *Ring, ring, ring.*

Kearney stared in the direction the voice had told him to go, his dusty shoes scraping against the ground as the ringing echoed in his ears. *What else is there for me to do, really?* He dragged his feet along as he obeyed the voice's order, and even though he could see nothing in the distance, he kept walking.

The town's gates towered high overhead, their twisted bars bent in such strange ways that Kearney would have no way of squeezing through them. On each side of the gates were giant brick walls that wrapped around the entire town, meaning walking around the gates would be useless.

He studied the words spelled out in the gates' bars: *Toy Town.* His eyes continued to trail up the gates until they were fixed on the very top. He let out a huff, brushed his hair out of his face, and gripped the bars. He started climbing up, which to some would have seemed like a death wish, but that thought hadn't and wouldn't cross his mind. He didn't look down or pause once, which probably helped keep his fear at bay.

After a few strenuous minutes, he made it all the way up and sat atop the gates, scanning the town below for any signs of activity, but he saw nothing. After his climb down, during which he was much more careful than he was on the way up, he made it to the ground on the other side of the gates. He slowly spun around and admired the strange little city, the words in the twisted bars etched in his mind. *Toy Town.*

He started walking through the town and admiring the scenery, although he was more alert than before. After all, silence could be a façade, and in a place with as many twists and turns as this, threats could be hiding anywhere.

The town itself was beautiful in an almost haunting way. He felt like he was walking through a painting. There were not only houses but rollercoasters, carousels, and tilt-a-whirls. He watched the rides closely. It looked like they were sleeping.

Other than the jingle of the triangle playing on repeat over the old PA system, everything seemed so quiet that he thought he was in a ghost town, which, now that he thought about it, didn't seem impossible. Soon, he found himself before a giant Ferris wheel, sitting peacefully in what looked like the town square. He sat down, still staring at it as if in a trance.

Something about this place felt unnatural to him. The dark reds and pinks painted across the evening sky, the town's empty yet eerily welcoming atmosphere, even that repetitive little jingle—it all came together to give him a strangely lonely feeling, but unlike before, it wasn't a bad feeling. He felt a tear slide down his cheek and wiped it away.

I wish Levi were here. He hugged his knees and took in the silence. Even though there was still a dull ache in his heart, for once, it almost felt like everything would be okay.

Maybe this is peace.

He paused, mulling over that thought, then chuckled to himself. He was all alone, stuck in a strange, dangerous world, and he felt peace.

There was a loud bang in the distance, and with a gasp, Kearney jumped to his feet. The bang was immediately followed by cheering. His eyes darted around, his prior relaxation immediately forgotten. The noise sounded far away, but he still couldn't risk being found.

On instinct, he slipped into the nearest alleyway, warily creeping closer to the source of the uproar. *The quiet was too good to be true.* Soon, he was able to make out words.

"She's so big!"

"Are we sure she's a fleshy person?"

"No. That's why we have to burn her!"

He peeked around the corner and spotted a large crowd of dolls gathered around a person tied to a pole on top of an impressive pile of broken sticks. He frowned. *So, this place belongs to them. Great.* He glanced at the pyre, specifically at the poor person the mob had stuck on top of it.

Lo and behold, it was the one and only Gabi.

She tried to squirm out of her bonds, but it was no use. "You can't burn me!" she shrieked.

The crowd stared at her. One of the dolls, who was holding a very threatening-looking match, asked, "Why not?"

"Well, if I'm a fleshy person, then that'll kill me!"

"No, it won't. Wood burns, flesh doesn't."

"Nothing could be further from the truth!"

"...But how else can we tell if you're made of wood or not?"

She paused in thought. "You guys have a lake nearby, right?"

The dolls all looked up at her and nodded.

"Alright, then there's your other way of telling! Wood floats in water, right?"

"Right!" they all shouted in unison.

"And guess what? Flesh doesn't!"

The crowd started cheering again.

"W-Wait! I forgot to mention. If I'm tied up, then I'll float whether I'm wood or not, so you have to throw me into the water *untied*."

The doll with the match, which had long since gone out, nodded. "That makes sense."

The crowd started shouting with excitement, but their joy was interrupted yet again, this time by a different doll. "Hang on. What if she's lying?" He pointed an accusing finger at her.

The other dolls stared at him. "Why would she do that? Flesh doesn't float."

"That's what *she* says. We should ask The Tailor. She'd know for sure!"

The crowd started cheering one last time, and the little dolls lifted Gabi's pole off the ground and carried her away as she screamed in protest. Kearney chuckled as he followed the fanatic crowd from a distance. They marched down the cobblestone road until they reached a small white house. Outside of it, a torn pink flag hung on a pole. One of the dolls crept up to the door and knocked.

A peach-haired doll in a white dress appeared on the other side. "What do you want? Did you get my fleshy person?" she asked.

"No, but we got a different one. We think."

A different one? Kearney furrowed his brow.

The Tailor looked past the doll standing in front of her and studied Gabi. "What do you mean, 'you think'?"

"Well, we were *going* to test to see if she's really fleshy, but now we're not sure how to."

Another doll added, "We wanted to burn her, but she told us to toss her untied into the lake instead."

A look of perplexity came across The Tailor's face for a brief second, but her previous cool visage quickly replaced it. "Why did she say that?"

"She told us flesh doesn't float in water but will if it's tied up. So, that's why we can't."

The Tailor nodded slowly. "And what if she floats away and escapes?"

The doll cocked her head to the side. "Why would she do that? If she's a doll like the rest of us, then she won't need to escape."

The Tailor shook her head slowly. "See how easy you are to deceive? Wood isn't the only thing that floats in water, my dear. Do you know what else does?"

The crowd collectively pondered.

After watching them come up with nothing for a few minutes, The Tailor gave her answer: "A duck."

The crowd gasped. "Do you really think she's a duck?"

The doll standing in front of The Tailor blinked, clearly still puzzled. "But, I thought ducks were small and had feathers."

The Tailor rolled her eyes with a scoff. "Honestly, it's like you've never even seen one before!" She waved her finger. "Ducks, my little friends, are quite deceitful creatures. And what are ducks good at other than floating?"

The doll furrowed her brow. "...Lying?"

"No. They're good at *swimming*. And do you know what could've happened if you tossed her into the lake untied?"

"She would've floated and swum away!"

"Exactly. So, what will you do with this new information?"

"Not throw her in a lake, that's for sure!" The doll turned back to the rest of the crowd. "We'll burn her, after all!" She paused and glanced back. "Ms. The Tailor, does flesh burn?"

The Tailor saw Gabi's panic-filled face and smiled. "No."

The crowd began cheering, and Gabi was carried off yet again. Kearney couldn't help but snicker. Gabi seemed to be as good at getting herself out of sticky situations as she was at getting into them, but she'd probably need his help for this one.

It didn't seem like he'd be able to help her without being seen, and he didn't know the strange town well enough to create an effective diversion, so he opted to be quick instead.

Soon, the dolls had propped Gabi back up on the pyre as she bawled and were preparing to light it again. One of them, a lit match in hand, danced up to the pile of sticks and held the match over it. "Let's count down from ten!"

The dolls all started hopping in excitement and chanting like it was New Year's Eve. "Ten! Nine! Eight!"

Gabi flailed her legs wildly in an attempt to kick the match away. "Stop it!" she hissed.

"Seven! Six! Five!"

Kearney seized his moment and darted through the crowd, making a beeline for Gabi as bystanders gasped in surprise. He was bolting up the pyre in seconds.

"Four! Three! Two!"

As soon as Gabi noticed him, her face scrunched up in anger. "Oh, so *now* you show up!" Her voice was thick with sarcasm, and she no longer seemed concerned about the imminent threat of being burned to a crisp.

"What's that supposed to mean?" He started working with the rope but was a little lost, as all Gabi's captors had really done was make a bunch of knots.

"Oh, I don't know, maybe the way you up and left in the middle of the night? That hurt, you know!"

"Alright, I'm sorry!" It didn't take long for him to sort out the rope, and she was soon free from the knotty mess. The two stood in silence on top of the pyre and looked at the crowd, which was now watching Kearney with fascination.

"Is he a fleshy person, too?" one doll asked.

The doll holding the match shrugged. "Only one way to find out!" She tossed the match onto the pyre and set it ablaze.

Gabi shrieked, and Kearney wrapped his arms around her and jumped off the pyre. But since it was a pile of unstable sticks, he twisted his ankle while trying to take off, and the two tumbled their way down as the crowd watched in awe.

Once he landed, he clutched his ankle while stifling a cry of pain.

Gabi rubbed her sore head and looked at him. When she saw his miserable state, she frowned. "You got hurt, didn't you?"

He shook his head with his eyes squeezed shut and barely managed to whisper, *"I'm fine."*

She sighed, ignoring his comment and studying his ankle. "On a scale of one to ten..."

"Zero."

"...how bad is it?"

"Zero!"

Meanwhile, the dolls were watching closely. One of them dropped to the ground and started mimicking Kearney. They started chattering amongst themselves.

"We still don't know if they're fleshy or not."

"Should we still toss them into the fire?"

"Maybe we could just stick an arm in or something."

A voice spoke above the rest. "My little friends! I know exactly how to address this situation." The Tailor sauntered out of the crowd and up to the pair as the crowd watched her. She scanned the pair up and down before spinning around to face the crowd. "Thanks to my expertise, I have confirmed these are indeed fleshy people! Thank you all for your assistance, but now, Sheriff Dakota and I shall take over."

As The Tailor gave her speech, a doll with shoulder-length black hair in a makeshift uniform and oversized police cap hopped over to Kearney and Gabi. "Hi, mister and missus, I'm Dakota." He excitedly showed them a pair of handcuffs. "You have to come with me, please."

Still in immense pain, Kearney glared at Dakota, who was completely unperturbed.

"I can get you a smoothie if you're really nice," the little doll added excitedly.

Gabi was in The Tailor's office with The Tailor, waiting for Dakota to bring in Kearney. The Tailor was too busy sewing a dress to bother looking at her, so the two sat in silence—at least, until Gabi asked, "Care to talk about earlier?" Her lip pinched in a frown.

"Not in particular."

Gabi resumed her glaring. "I'm sure you *loved* watching me almost get crisped into a French fry, didn't you?"

The door flew open, and Dakota wheeled Kearney into the room in a wheelbarrow. Even though Kearney insisted he was well enough to walk, Dakota insisted harder that he give Kearney a ride, which was very polite. What wasn't very polite was him dumping Kearney onto the floor once they entered the office.

The Tailor rubbed her temples as she groaned. "There's dirt on my carpet, Dakota."

Dakota winced and hid behind the wheelbarrow. "Sorry, Ms. The Tailor."

"Whatever. I'll have you clean it later."

After Dakota left, Kearney managed to lift himself off the floor and crawl into the chair beside Gabi. The Tailor put her project aside. Kearney glanced at Gabi and was taken aback by how livid she still looked.

"What's going on?" he asked, inching his seat away from her.

"What's going on is your friend here has never heard of loosening up before. Anyway, it's about time we got down to business." The Tailor folded her hands on her lap. "You may call me The Tailor and nothing else. I'm the founder of this town, and what I say goes. Any questions?"

"Why was almost turning me into a churro something you felt the need to do?" Gabi snapped.

The Tailor sighed. "I had a hunch there was more than one of you, so that little show was mainly to draw him out." She pointed to Kearney. "And I had a good laugh, I'll admit that much."

Kearney stifled a laugh. Gabi looked ready to murder him, so he decided to get serious and asked, "What's the point of keeping us here?"

The Tailor's green eyes studied him closely as she spoke. "The point is for me to know and for you to possibly find out. I think you two will come to realize that I have some special little skills. I know things no one else knows, and I can do things no one else can do."

Gabi continued glaring. "Like what?"

"Like convince a whole town that a girl is a duck." She grinned. "You're in my town now, so you follow my rules. And the rules are such: fulfill a handful of tasks for the good of Toy Town, and you'll be free as birds."

Kearney shifted uneasily. The more The Tailor talked, the more nervous he felt. She seemed so dignified, like she really did deserve respect. And while Gabi seemed perfectly content to argue back and forth with her all day long, Kearney was following a very different thought process. *Adults are scary. The Tailor talks like an adult. The Tailor is scary. Therefore, listen to The Tailor.*

Gabi crossed her arms, eyeing The Tailor carefully. "A few tasks? That's it?"

"It is." She grinned. "If you're not one for chores, don't worry. Work around here tends to be very, shall we say, eccentric. Dakota!"

The door creaked open, and Dakota peeked into the room. "Yes, please?"

"Escort these two to their new residence. They start tomorrow."

"Yes, ma'am!" He skipped to Gabi's side and held her hand while trying to get her out of her seat. She glared at the little doll and stayed in place as he struggled. "Get up, please," he strained as he kept tugging.

She glanced at Kearney, who had already wobbled out of his chair and collapsed into his wheelbarrow without a word; he seemed perfectly content with being a prisoner yet again. She groaned and rose to her feet. "Whatever you're really planning, you'd better watch yourself." She pointed a finger at The Tailor.

The Tailor winked. "Whatever you say, little friend."

Once that interaction had ended, Dakota took Kearney and Gabi to a run-down building that once housed a ride, which seemed to serve as the town's makeshift jail. He smiled proudly. "Welcome to jail, please!" Once his blue eyes trailed to Gabi, his smile became much more strained, likely from fear.

Is she that scary to him? Kearney wondered. "It looks nice," he commented with a smile.

That seemed to put Dakota at ease. Gabi was too busy looking mad to care about what they had to say, so she ignored them while having a very serious staring contest with a crowbar on the floor.

Luckily, Dakota no longer seemed to notice her attitude. He pointed at a group of tilt-a-whirl booths that had been taken off their tracks and neatly arranged in a row. "You'll be staying in those. Do you want me to put you in the same one?"

Gabi ignored him again while Kearney vigorously shook his head. Those booths looked tiny, and he had no interest in sharing what little space he'd have.

Dakota looked at Gabi, and his smile faded. His eyes widened sympathetically. "It's okay, ma'am."

Her eyes snapped to him. "Huh?"

"I said it's okay. I'll get you the softest blankets I can find." He held her hands, his blue pools of eyes staring into hers as if he were making the most important promise of his life. "I'll get you yummy food every day, and if you ever get lonely or have a really scary nightmare, you can call me, and I'll give you a big hug!" He wrapped his arms around her to demonstrate.

Gabi's hands fell to her sides as his hug melted her very being. "Th-That sounds great," she stammered.

He gave her one last squeeze before letting go. "Do you want to choose a cell, please?"

"O-Okay!"

Kearney grinned to himself as he watched Dakota hold Gabi's arm and lead her over to the cells to get a closer look. Her shift had been shockingly quick, but Dakota did seem pretty lovable, so it wasn't too surprising. Kearney's eyes drifted to another cell, one that was closer to him. There was a doll lying in it. They didn't have any hair and were only wearing a tattered green sweater that reached their knees.

Kearney walked up to the doll as Gabi very loudly praised Dakota and his 'adorable little jail' in the background. *Best if I'm on good terms with everyone here.* He tentatively forced a smile. "Hi."

The doll didn't respond. Kearney got a little closer, hoping to get a better look while remaining unnoticed. *Are they sleeping? Do dolls sleep?* He jumped when the doll twitched and lifted their head to look at him, and there was nothing but scratched wood where a face should've been. He stumbled back, alarm rippling through his body. He hardly even noticed Dakota, who'd skipped to his side.

"Are you okay, mister?" Dakota watched him worriedly.

"W-Why doesn't it have a face?" he stuttered.

Dakota looked at the doll and smiled. "It's not polite to call her 'it,' mister. Her name is No-Face!"

"No-Face." Kearney stared at him. "Tell me how that's any better."

Dakota's smile faded as he fidgeted his thumbs. "I'm really bad at picking names. But no one else was going to give her one." His eyes drifted to No-Face, who'd sat up and seemed to be listening intently. "I found her in a dumpster. It looked like she fell in and got stuck. Ms. The Tailor told me to get rid of her, but that felt like a bad thing to do."

Kearney forced himself to ease up a little. "You think she appreciates it?" He was still watching No-Face reluctantly. "Being here, I mean."

"I hope so. I try to be the best friend I can!" Dakota's eyes flicked back to Gabi, who'd chosen a cell for herself. "I gave you a cell right next to the nice lady. Is that okay, please?"

"Huh? Sure," Kearney replied absentmindedly. He was caught off-guard when Dakota grabbed him by the hand and started leading him away from No-Face, but he quickly regained his composure.

Once Kearney was snug inside his new cell, Dakota put a giant marshmallow in his hands. "This is for sleeping on, not eating. Okay, mister?" He was talking to Kearney slowly, like one would a toddler.

Kearney nodded as he squeezed the pillow, immediately taken aback by its softness. He set it on his lap and began squishing it, feeling all his worries melt away as he did.

Dakota watched him with a smile. "I'm glad it makes you happy, mister!"

Kearney nodded again and closed his eyes as he breathed its sweet scent. He suddenly became aware that the waves of tiredness from before were washing over him again. Maybe they had never really left to begin with, but with something soft to lean his head on now, he found the allure of sleep too tempting to ignore.

House Full of Strings

Chapter 10

Gabi Gets Attacked and Barely Survives

A gunshot crackled through the silence like thunder.

Kearney opened his eyes. He was in a bedroom. A tight bedroom with nothing but a bed. Like every other dream he'd had of this room, he was alone. Not planning on wasting any time, he got up and made his way to the door. He peeked into the hall, only to be met by walls with peeling beige paint and an eerie silence. He held his breath as he stepped into the hall and quickly tiptoed to the stairwell. He flinched as each step whined in complaint while he made his way down.

Halfway down the stairs, he spotted the door out, and he felt his heart beat faster as he hurried toward it. Heavy footsteps sounded behind him, but he refused to stop.

"Kearney," a man's voice boomed, coming from everywhere and nowhere all at once.

He started walking faster, letting out a panicked squeak as he held his breath.

"Kearney."

Kearney was running for the door. His lungs begged for air, but fear refused to let him breathe.

"Kearney."

He slammed into the door and grabbed its doorknob, panic freezing his fingers as he desperately tried to twist it and be free from this nightmare.

"Kearney!" Rage seeped into the voice, shaking everything like an earthquake.

The door finally gave way, and he flew out of it, gasping for breath as he ran.

*"**Kearney**."*

"Kearney."

Kearney blinked awake and looked up to see Gabi staring down at him.

She cleared her throat as she shifted awkwardly. "Dakota sent me to wake you. He said we have work to do." She kept staring. "Also, I don't know how you managed to fall asleep like that, but it looks really painful."

Kearney glanced at himself. Admittedly, she had a point. He had his back on his booth's seat cushion, but his lower half was propped up against its tiny curved wall, meaning his feet were hanging right above his head. He glanced back at her, trying to hide his own confusion as to how he'd gotten into that position to begin with. "It's comfier than it looks."

She nodded skeptically before walking off, her hair bobbing up and down as she went. He got to his feet, wincing in pain as he stretched. He was sore all over. He paused when he heard the sound of something moving and looked around. It was No-Face, in her own booth; she'd probably sat up because she heard their voices. Kearney watched her without moving an inch, which he quickly realized was probably confusing her, so he opted to talk instead. "Good morning, No-Face."

She swiveled her head as if trying to figure out which way she should be facing, but she quickly gave up. There was no response after that.

He put his hands in his pockets and watched her curiously. "So, what do you normally do around here?"

She lowered her head, and he started to worry he'd upset her. But she started feeling around for something inside her booth. A few seconds later, she scooped up a wooden toy that'd been sitting on the floor of her booth. She held it up in the hopes that Kearney could see it, and luckily for her, he could. He squinted and tried to make out its shape as best he could. It was a xylophone, but it was very old and only had a few keys attached to it.

She paused before tapping a key and ringing a note. She then threw her hands in the air, expecting Kearney to be just as amazed as she was. He smiled and clapped, feeling like he was praising a toddler. "That's awesome!" He glanced at Dakota, who'd just popped into view and was heading over to No-Face.

"I'm happy you guys are friends now," he said with a smile as he opened the door to her cell. He held her hand and led her out. "I wanted to take her with us today. She needs to stretch her legs."

Kearney kept watching her. "She can't see, right?"

"No. But she can hear really well." He fixed his over-sized hat on his head with his free hand, and a grave look crossed his face. "So, don't say anything mean to her, or I'll have to lock you up for disturbing the peace."

No-Face perked up when she heard that.

"Don't worry, you won't hear anything from me," Kearney replied.

Dakota grinned. "Thank you, please." He glanced back at No-Face. "I need to help her out really quick. Can you wait outside with Ms. Gabi, please?"

Kearney nodded and left them to it. *No-Face sure is something,* he thought to himself as he walked out of the building. He paused and looked around. *Where's Gabi?* He picked up on the sound of angry grunting coming from around the building's corner. He furrowed his brow as he got closer to the sound, and his suspicions were confirmed when he spotted Gabi frantically trying to toss a rope over the giant brick wall that kept her from freedom.

"What are you doing?" he asked.

She jumped with a yelp and spun around. "Don't sneak up on me like that!" she hissed. She sighed and turned her attention back to the wall. "I'm getting out of here, that's what." She tossed the rope again, but it slapped the side of the wall before sliding down to the ground.

Her aim's all wrong. "Can I try?"

She looked back at him. "Sure." She tossed him the rope and leaned back as she stared at the top of the wall. "Alright, give it your best shot!"

He let out a huff of determination before bunching up the rope and flinging it, but it didn't fly very far when he did.

She watched in disappointment as it fell to the ground. "Can you try being a little more...coordinated?"

He frowned, his jaw clenched in annoyance and embarrassment as he scooped up the rope. *I got farther than you did.* He quickly whirled his arm in circles to gain as much momentum as possible. He tossed the rope again, but it slammed into the wall before slinking to the ground once more.

She glared at him. "You're ridiculous."

"Just be glad I didn't say anything about *your* tries," he snapped. "It's not easy to throw this thing."

"Try throwing it like a lasso," she snapped back. "Actually, just give it to me!" She yanked it out of his hands. She raised her hand high above her head and started whirling the rope around. She flung it up, but her aim was off by a long shot.

Kearney stared up at her, his eyes unreadable. If he said something now, she'd most likely hurt him. But it'd be absolutely worth it.

She met his stare. "Don't you dare."

He clamped his teeth shut.

"What are you doing, missus?"

They yelped in alarm. Gabi dropped the rope. They spun around and realized Dakota was standing right beside them. Kearney's mouth gaped open in hopes of replying, but he found it hard to think up an excuse on the spot.

Dakota stared at the rope for a second. "Let me try, please." Without waiting for a reply, he scooped it up, squatted down until his chest touched his knees, and sprung up, throwing the rope into the air as he did. It didn't go very far. His head dropped in defeat. "Sorry, please."

Kearney patted him on the head. "You did good."

He let out a huff then glanced over his shoulder. "No-Face walked away."

He and Kearney both started looking around before staring at Gabi, who stared back. Her confusion was cleared when her eyes trailed down to the faceless doll clinging to her leg. Gabi let out a scream of absolute terror as she began to kick her leg around wildly. No-Face hardly seemed perturbed by this reaction, but Dakota was crying out in panic. "Stop, please! Stop, please!"

Gabi shot him a panicked look. "Get it off!"

"She's friendly, missus! Promise!"

"She's not friendly, she's creepy!" She continued swinging her leg around.

"Gabi, stop!" Kearney yelled. "You're going to hurt her!"

"I will unless someone gets her off me!"

"Stop moving, then!" He grabbed No-Face as Gabi stayed perfectly still with one leg in the air like a flamingo. He tried to pull them apart, but No-Face didn't budge. He started pulling harder, which made Gabi lose her balance and fall on her back. Even then, No-Face continued to hang on. Kearney shook her with the still-extended leg she continued to cling onto, which also yielded no results. Gabi was lying on the ground, her arms splayed out in defeat.

Kearney glanced back at Dakota. "Help."

Dakota gently patted No-Face's shoulders. "You have to let go, please."

She shook her head.

"Why not?"

She gave Gabi's leg a gentle squeeze.

"You like her?"

Neither Kearney nor Gabi had any idea how Dakota knew what No-Face was trying to communicate, so they both stayed quiet as they watched. Dakota gently wiggled his hand into No-Face's. "If you like her, then you have to be nice to her, okay?"

After seemingly mulling over what Dakota said, No-Face let Gabi's leg slip away. Or, more accurately, let it get yanked away, as Gabi pulled it back the instant she saw the faceless doll's grip had loosened ever so slightly. After that, Gabi jumped to her feet and dove behind Kearney, her eyes warily fixed on No-Face.

Dakota cleared his throat as he helped No-Face to her feet. "Ms. The Tailor said we have to go, please. Your first job is really close to here, so that's nice!"

Kearney nodded while Gabi tried hiding her irritation over her failed escape plan and the fact that a freak without a face had just violated her personal space bubble and basically attacked her.

Kearney glanced at her. "Let's get moving, then?"

Her glare started to soften. "Fine."

Dakota held No-Face's hand as they walked off, and Kearney and Gabi followed close behind. While Gabi paused once or twice to debate running away, Kearney stopped her each time. He wasn't interested in getting on The Tailor's bad side, and he definitely didn't want to ruin Dakota's sunny mood.

Soon, they were near an old building, and Dakota rushed to scoop up the burlap sack sitting just outside its door. He opened it and pulled out two claw sticks for Kearney and Gabi to admire. "These are my stickies, and I put a sticker on each one just for you! I hope you like them, please." He handed one to each of them.

Kearney carefully observed his "stickie" and noticed a little dinosaur sticker on its handle. He looked at Gabi, who smiled just slightly as she saw a fox on hers.

Dakota grinned from ear to ear. "Foxes are my favorite. That's why I gave you one, missus!" He glanced at Kearney fretfully. "Dinosaurs scare me a little, but I only had a dino sticker left for you. Sorry, please."

Kearney shrugged. "It's fine. So, what are we doing here?"

Dakota's attention snapped back to his objective. "Look over there, please." He pointed to the old building, and the pair obediently looked at it. No-Face wound up staring eagerly at a lamppost while trying to follow Dakota's command. "Ms. The Tailor wants you to go into that factory and clean up. But you have to be super careful because there are boxes that used to revive dolls but don't work that well anymore and aren't very safe," Dakota continued.

"Those are what we're supposed to clean up?" Gabi asked.

He nodded. "That's why you need stickies. If you poke them enough, the boxes blow up, so hide once they start shaking, please. There's some other stuff, too, but the boxes are the most important part."

"Other stuff?"

"Well, stray dolls, mainly. You'll see one or two, or maybe even none at all."

"Here I was thinking you were all stray dolls," Gabi muttered under her breath. "That begs the question: why didn't The Tailor just hire dolls to handle this to begin with?"

"Well...when boxes break, they make our brains act a little funny until we get away. That's what I mean by stray dolls." Dakota shuddered. "It's really bad." He glanced at the factory nervously before looking back at them. "I'll be waiting right here with No-Face, so if you get hurt, let me know right away, please."

Kearney replied with a nod and a smile. He exchanged a glance with Gabi, then they headed for the factory. He studied it carefully as they got closer. If he didn't know better, he would've thought it was a church. Its roof was tall and pointed, and it had numerous stained-glass windows that, if they hadn't been shattered, might've been beautiful. He wondered what images those windows used to display.

It seemed the strange factory church had been un-touched for decades because inside it was *dusty*. As soon as they opened the front door, a literal dust storm flew out to greet them. After an intense few minutes of coughing and eye-rubbing, which wouldn't have been the first time for them, the dust finally settled enough to allow the pair to enter without racing back out to cough up dust bunnies.

Inside, an incredibly dusty royal blue carpet ran through a long hallway; at least ten doorways stood on each side of it. The spaces of wall in between the doors boasted torn paintings, all of the same person. All of them had the same white-skinned woman on them. Even through the wear and tear of the canvases, the woman's pink eyes still seemed so vibrant and alive. They looked like they were watching Kearney.

He glanced back at Gabi. The two shared a weary glance when they realized just how much work they had to do and agreed to divide and conquer, dreading the long day ahead. Kearney walked into the room closest to him and started poking every box in his path, flinch-ing each time one would shudder and pop. Soon, he'd gone through them all and was on his way back to the hall, but doubt caused him to stop in his tracks.

He glanced back. *I got them all, right?* He stared at the boxes, but even the perfect stillness that met him wasn't enough to satisfy his gnawing worry. He felt his stickie slipping in his sweaty palms as he poked each box once again.

Then, he heard a yelp that made him jump. "Gabi?" he called.

"I'm okay," she replied. "Some dumb string got my leg, that's all."

String? "Are you sure you're okay?" He wanted to rush over to her but held himself back.

"Yeah, it's gone now."

After another brief moment of silence, he felt himself relax a little and went back to work. Back to poking boxes, then poking them again and again, never sure which one would....

"You're still not done?"

He jumped and spun around, only to see Gabi staring at him. He shook his head. "I-I was just double-checking, that's all."

She nodded. "That's a good idea. I should do that, too." She walked away and checked the rooms she'd gone through, which took roughly five minutes. Once she'd returned, she found Kearney poking the same box she'd left him with. "Is there a problem?" she asked.

He glanced at her. "No problem. Just double-checking."

"But I thought you double-checked it already."

"I just want to be sure."

She sighed as she walked up to him, grabbing his sleeve. "You did a good job here. Now, let's move on."

He stared back at her with wide eyes as she led him out of the room. "What if I missed one?"

"I highly doubt that."

"But—"

"Come on!" She was using all her strength to drag him away, as he'd stopped walking and looked ready to race back into the room.

He took a step toward it. "I'm just going to check one more time."

"It's fine!" she insisted, her voice strained.

"You don't know that," he replied.

She had her arms wrapped around him and leaned back with her full weight, but her attempts to hold him back hardly had any effect. "All you're doing is wasting time!"

"I'd rather be safe than sorry." Kearney marched back into the room, dragging an unrelenting Gabi with him. He started poking all the boxes in the room a third—or possibly fourth—time, the only difference now being that Gabi was hanging off of him and yelling. He was relieved when she let go of him but jumped in fear when he saw what she was doing next.

She jumped onto a box, landing on it in a sitting position. She grinned at him.

He gasped. "Get off that thing!"

"Why?" She kicked the back of her heel against it. "You've already checked it, haven't you?"

"I have. B-But it's not safe!"

"But you already checked it. More than once, too."

"But I'm not sure!"

"How come?"

"I don't know!"

She sighed. "Do you want to know why I'm sitting on this thing right now?"

Kearney shook his head.

"It's because I trust you, and I trust that you did a good job. It's about time you trusted yourself, too." She scooted over and patted the spot next to her, and after a short moment, he reluctantly sat down beside her.

"You don't have to be so tense. We're still alive, aren't we?" she said.

He nodded but was so scared of provoking the box that he hardly moved his head at all.

She smiled. "See? You did good."

He found himself staring at her, her words ringing in his mind. *You did good.* "Really?"

"Really."

"Huh." After that, he contentedly folded his hands on his lap, and his lips bent into a smile. *I did good.* He'd never really heard that before.

They sat in contented silence for another minute before she gently punched his arm. "You ready to go now?"

He nodded. They both got to their feet and moved to the next room. "Gabi?"

She looked over her shoulder. "Yeah?"

"Thanks."

She smiled. "Sure." Her smile morphed into a sly grin as she grabbed his hand. "Let's go mess around in the next room!"

He froze, immediately getting nervous as he looked at their intertwined fingers. He didn't want to recoil when she touched him, but he was only just getting used to her. Clinging to each other while jumping off a burning pyre and escaping murderous castles was one thing, but holding hands was different. It was quiet. It felt strangely intimate. He'd only ever held Levi's hand before.

Before he could react, she'd pulled him into the next room and let him go. The moment was over just as quickly as it had started. He stared down at his clammy hand as he reminded himself to breathe. He looked up to see that they were now in a room full of unchecked boxes.

Gabi was racing toward them, brandishing her stickie. She looked back at him expectantly. "You coming?"

He smiled and ran after her. They laughed wildly as they poked the boxes and, soon, each other. Kearney quickly gained the upper hand and repeatedly poked Gabi in the stomach, which made her fall to the ground in a fit of tickle-induced giggles.

"Stop it!" she squealed as she blindly waved her stickie at him. Unfortunately, her attempts did nothing to stop his vicious attacks. Soon, they called for a truce, and Kearney sat beside her, still trying to stifle his laughter.

"This doesn't feel like a chore at all!" she exclaimed.

He threw his head back with a laugh. *It really doesn't.*

Once she'd managed to sit up, her eyes fixed on a red box sitting in the opposite corner of the room. "Did we check that one?"

"I don't think so."

"I'll be quick, then." She scooped up her stickie and marched over to it. It was slightly bigger than the others, maybe a foot taller than she was, but otherwise, it was nothing out of the ordinary. She poked it, and it responded. It quivered excitedly before going still again, which was something none of the other boxes had done. "I'm not sure if it'll do anything," she commented.

Kearney's grip on his stickie tightened. "It might. Just come back."

She looked back at the box again before poking it. It quivered, this time lighting up a little. "I'm going to poke it again." And she did, but the box still did nothing more than quiver.

Kearney winced. "Gabi, get back!" *What is she thinking?*

She poked it again. It responded with another little tremble.

"That's enough. You're going to hurt yourself!"

She stared at it for a moment before grabbing it and shaking it.

"Gabi!" he hissed, jumping to his feet.

She backed away from it and glanced at him. "Don't worry, this one's all bark and no bite."

Kearney's face shifted from annoyance to fear as the box, unbeknownst to Gabi, quivered again. Except now, it was more of a rumble, and it looked like it would do more than shake this time. He rushed forward and tugged her away as her arms flailed around.

"Stop panicking already!" She wrenched herself away from him and turned her attention to the box, which was now ominously rocking back and forth. Her eyes widened. "It's doing the thing!"

"I noticed!"

They dove for cover and watched it anxiously. The box kept rumbling, its flaps trembling with energy until it let out a loud *pop!* Smoke seeped out of its cracks, and it fell apart, leaving a green-haired doll in its debris.

The doll spasmed to life, shrieking and kicking his legs as if waking up from a nightmare. He let out a shaky breath and looked around before fixing his dark green eyes on Kearney and Gabi. "Weird-Eyes an' Freckles?"

They both groaned before they could even think. Of the hundreds of dolls in this place, why did it have to be Calder?

Calder jumped to his feet and brushed himself off, looking a little embarrassed. He straightened himself out with a huff and, to the pair's dismay, started marching toward them.

Gabi pointed her stickie at him menacingly, probably still trying to process how he was even standing in front of her. "Back off unless you want a beating, you little jerk!"

He ignored her threat and pointed at her. "It was you. You made Jolly come an' beat up my gang, witch!" He continued his menacing approach while rolling up his sleeves. "When I get my hands on you, yer gonna regret crossin' me!"

"Oh, like I *wanted* to be mixed up with you little gremlins to begin with." Spite edged her voice. She rushed at Calder with her stickie in hand, yelling at the top of her lungs. And Calder, despite being unarmed, ran at her with the same ferocity. As exciting as this battle had been shaping up to be, all Kearney ended up witnessing was Gabi smacking Calder over the head with her stickie as he fastened himself onto her leg, possibly trying to tip her off balance, but the only flaw in that strategy was his lack of weight.

Kearney stared for a minute, contemplating what he should do. *Those two have baggage. Probably best to let them get it out of their systems now.* He saw no need to risk hurting himself by getting in the middle of the struggle, not that either of the fighters presented any real capability of hurting anything at the moment. But after another minute, he got tired of watching their fruitless battle and went to pry them off of each other. He dragged Gabi away from the fight, causing her to drop her stickie and squeak in what was either annoyance or distress.

She started kicking her legs wildly. "I can handle this myself!"

While he struggled with her, Calder decided to make the situation worse by clawing at Kearney's legs. "Let 'er go, Freckles! It's unruly to interrupt a duel of rivals!"

Kearney tried to kick him away. "Stop it, you little psycho!" He realized the error of his approach when he lost balance mid-kick and fell backward with Gabi.

Calder cackled with excitement and tossed himself on top of the pair, leaving all three of them piled on the floor. He then got to his feet and stood victoriously on top of them as if they were a mountain he'd just conquered.

"No more games. I gotta finish my job, an' I can do it with or without my gang!" He pointed down at the pair. "Now, on yer feet, pris'ners! We're marchin' straight to the Mister from 'ere!" He froze at the sound of boots pitter-pattering their way up the stairs.

Everyone went quiet and stared in the direction of the sound.

"Missus and mister, are you okay? I heard exploding and screaming and stuff," Dakota called. He reached the top of the stairs and gasped when he saw Calder. His eyes widened in what looked like joy. "You came back?"

"What?" Calder sputtered as he jumped off the duo, backing away from Dakota. "N-No! I came out of the box, that's all. I didn't *wanna* come back 'ere."

"But if the box really brought you here, maybe it's a sign that you should stay!"

"I already told you I don't care about you or this stupid town!"

Kearney had no intention of getting involved in whatever this was, but Gabi was tensing beside him. "Hey, don't talk to him like that!" she snapped at Calder.

Dakota didn't look her way. He kept trying to reason with Calder. "But—!"

"Cut it out, D'kota!"

Dakota's lip quivered, but he quickly bit it still. He hurriedly pulled out a pair of makeshift handcuffs and rushed toward Calder. "Then, by the laws made by Ms. The Tailor, I can't allow a trespasser running around in Toy Town causing trouble. Calder, you are under arrest! Put your hands up where I can see them, please!"

"Are you crazy, D'kota?" Calder balled his fists. "Bein' here's makin' you act all weird!"

"Hands where I can see them, *please!*"

Kearney and Gabi flinched, and seconds later, Gabi tried to make a move toward Dakota, but Kearney put a hand on her shoulder to stop her. Whatever this was, it wasn't their place to intervene.

Calder stared at Dakota in shock. He then slowly raised his hands. "A-Alright. Just stop yellin'."

Dakota let out a huff and cuffed him. He glanced at Kearney and Gabi, who were watching in silence. "Sorry, please," he muttered, lowering his head.

Kearney opened his mouth to say something, but the words were lodged in his throat. He glanced at Gabi, who only nodded while trying to mentally sort out everything that had happened. Calder was staring at his feet and had fallen silent.

"We can go now, please." Dakota forced a smile. "You two did a really good job cleaning up."

Gabi looked away and crossed her arms, and Kearney nodded as he watched Dakota lead Calder out of the room. Kearney and Gabi trailed behind them. Kearney watched Dakota closely.

Dakota didn't seem like one to act up like that, not over nothing, at least.

Chapter 11

Calder Gets Taken to Court

After their incident in the factory, Dakota rushed the pair back to the tilt-a-whirl jail before leaving with Calder. He said something about a court but didn't pause to elaborate. Once they were left in peace, Kearney glanced at Gabi, who Dakota had mistakenly crammed into the same cell as him. "So...."

"So," she repeated, her lips flattened into a white line. Things seemed just a tad awkward.

"Earlier was fun."

She grinned. "It was."

That seemed to ease things up a little, and they both got comfortable. Or rather, as comfortable as they could get in such a tight space.

"What do you think they'll do with Calder?" she asked.

"I'm not sure. What I do know is that it'd be a nightmare if they made him stay here with us."

She snorted. "That'd be the worst."

After another pause, he looked at her again. "Speaking of Calder, do you know how the boxes work? I get they revive dolls and all, and we got to see that firsthand, but how?"

"Calder told me all about it back when I was his prisoner. How did it go...?" Gabi pursed her lips as she fidgeted with a strand of her hair. "Oh! It's the strings. They hold memories or something, and when those memories go into boxes, they can be used to bring dolls back to life."

"So, dolls don't really die?"

"Technically, no. Their bodies just break." She paused. "But...Calder also mentioned that 'dying' can be really scary. It's unpredictable, and everything that happens before you end up in a box can feel like you're trapped in a nightmare. Dolls don't know which box they'll come out of or how long it'll take for them to be revived. It could be right here in Toy Town, or it could be way on the other side of the Wall. It could be a day, or it could be ten years. Kind of scary to think about, huh?"

"It is." Kearney stared at his shoes. He almost felt bad for Calder.

A regretful look came into Gabi's eyes. "I should've done more to help Dakota with Calder earlier," she blurted.

"I think it was better you didn't."

"But I wanted a chance to make things right with him." She shook her head. "Everything that's been happening lately has been really getting to me. I've been saying lots of things I regret. I wanted to at least make up for how I treated Dakota before. After all, he seems like a good kid."

"I don't think you have to worry about that. You'll get your chance."

"I guess." She furrowed her brow with a small smile. "It's kind of funny that I called Dakota a kid. I guess that's exactly what he seems like, huh?"

"What do you mean, 'seems like'?" Kearney hadn't really thought too hard about it before. The dolls looked and sounded like kids, so he thought of them as kids. The idea that they were anything but kids was actually a bit disturbing to him. "How old are they?"

"The dolls? Ancient."

"You're kidding."

She shook her head, grinning at his surprise. "The House has been around for a long, long time, and so have they."

"So, Dakota…"

"…could be hundreds of years old, for all we know."

His mouth gaped open. *Oh.*

"It's weird to think about at first, but you get used to it over time."

Kearney's fingers rubbed against each other as he processed that Dakota was possibly older than the Statue of Liberty. For all he knew, Calder might've been around since before the pyramids were built. It must've been strange, being stuck in the body of a child while time kept moving just beyond the House's doors. He wondered why the Mister had made them that way.

He felt Gabi nudge his arm. "Don't think too hard about it. I doubt the way they behave is an act, so, in a sense, they are kids. Just really old ones."

"You know, they kind of are." Kearney nodded thoughtfully. He forced a smile, hoping that would get rid of his unease. "They're loud, annoying," he turned to poke her nose, "and think you're a duck."

She let out a sound that was half scoff, half laugh. "We don't talk about that!"

After a minute of their snickering, the silence returned, but Kearney felt perfectly comfortable in it. It was as if he didn't need to say anything at all and that things were fine just as they were. When he looked at her and saw the smile still on her face, he knew she felt the same.

"You know, you should be a tour guide around here. You seem to be a natural at it."

She laughed. "Honestly, I might as well be." Her smile faded. "I've been here that long, haven't I? And now I'm stuck here. It's just setback after setback in this crazy place."

"You'll get home soon," he said. "I'll make sure you do."

She cast him a sidelong glance and smiled. "You're pretty great, you know that?"

He smiled back.

Her head tilted as she pursed her lips. "So, what do you think The Tailor's going to make us do next? Clean out chocolate syrup swamps?"

"No, thank you. That sounds too messy." He rested the back of his head on the cell wall. "Maybe she'll have us start a circus."

"That makes more sense than a syrup swamp?" she teased.

He shrugged. "Or maybe she'll just lower us into a lava-cake volcano to fish out candy gems."

Her eyes lit up. "I wish!"

"...Or maybe she'll have us do the most boring thing in the world."

The excited gleam in her eyes was replaced by annoyance. "Well, looks like someone's an optimist."

"I am." He smirked. "Because I know, whatever it is, we'll find a way to make it fun." His gaze trailed away from her to a cell nearby. He studied it carefully. "Do you know where No-Face is?"

Calder fidgeted his hands in an attempt to get out of his wooden handcuffs but stopped every time Dakota glanced his way. After all, it'd be a bad look to slip out of his bonds in front of a cop in the middle of a courtroom, especially when his judge was The Tailor.

She curled the hair from the giant white wig she was wearing around her finger. "If I recall correctly, Calder, you were banished. What gave you the guts to come back and face me?"

His eyes blazed with indignation. "I didn't! That stupid box tossed me 'ere!"

"Really?" The Tailor glanced at Dakota. "You didn't put that in the report!" she hissed.

"Sorry, Ms. The Tailor," he replied as he lowered his head.

She rubbed her temples in annoyance before continuing with Calder. "So, you didn't have any control over where you ended up, but you *did* attack my new workers." She pulled out a small gavel and pointed it at him. "That's two accounts of assault."

"No, I didn't!"

"You're not supposed to lie in court, Calder," Dakota whispered.

"Shut it!" he snapped. He looked back at The Tailor. "You can take your stupid laws an' toss 'em into the Dark Place!"

"I'm charging you with ten accounts of disrespecting me for that one," she replied, scribbling it down on paper.

His face was turning red. "You better put that pen down, or I'm shovin' it into your skull in a hot minute!"

"...And twenty accounts of threatening me."

"That's not ev'n how that works!"

The Tailor ignored him and stood up, her paper in one hand and gavel in the other. "Adding all these charges up amounts to roughly two hundred tasks for Toy Town." She banged her desk with the gavel at least eight times. "That's your verdict. Now leave me alone."

"Two 'undred? Yer crazy!" Calder spun around to yell at Dakota, who was trying to lead him away. "An' yer crazy, too!"

"I was rounding down for you, Calder," The Tailor curtly replied.

Dakota grabbed him by the handcuffs. "And don't yell, please, Calder. It's not polite."

Calder only got louder as he was led away, spitting curses at The Tailor and Dakota as he did. He continued to yell the whole walk back to jail, which would be a lovely surprise for Kearney and Gabi, who'd spent the last hour in what would look like complete bliss compared to the storm Calder was bringing with him.

House Full of Strings

Chapter 12

A Random Voice Drives Levi Insane

"I'm sorry…. Take me back…."

Levi's panicking heart jerked him out of his sleep, leaving him in a cold sweat in his bed. He clutched his chest and took a deep breath in an attempt to calm himself down. He didn't know who the voice belonged to, but she sounded so lonely. And it didn't help that she just wouldn't leave him alone.

He crawled out of bed and made his way out of his room. He had no idea what time it was, but even without the presence of clocks, he knew it must've been astoundingly late. He kept walking, probably in an attempt to find the source of the voice, but he was too drained to have any specific goals voiced in his mind.

"It's so dark…. So dark…."

He was walking faster now. The voice was closer. He knew it.

"Can't see…. Want to see him again…."

He stopped in his tracks and spun around, finding himself face-to-face with an old tattered door. He stared at it for another minute, too tired to function.

Meanwhile, the distant voice kept sobbing. *"So lonely…."*

He slowly reached for the handle but was afraid to find what was on the other side.

"*So lonely….*"

"Snowflake?"

He gasped and whipped his head around to see Phantasos standing behind him. In truth, he and Phantasos had been avoiding each other for the past few days, so Phantasos willingly speaking with him befuddled his tired brain at first.

"What are you doing out of bed at this hour?" Phantasos asked, his eyes wide with concern. "I heard crying. That scarecrow didn't scare you that badly, did it?"

"It didn't scare me." Levi huffed and quickly pulled his hand away from the doorknob. "And I don't cry. I thought I heard something, just like you."

"That's interesting." Phantasos's eyes trailed to the door for a brief moment before they snapped back to Levi. "I wonder why there'd be crying in your dreams."

Levi furrowed his brow. "I'm not dreaming."

"You are, snowflake."

He stared at Phantasos in confusion. "Then…are you part of the dream, too?"

"Not quite." Phantasos winked. "I told you I'm not human, didn't I?"

"Are you finally going to tell me what you are?" *He'd better.*

"I suppose I might as well." He started walking and beckoned Levi to his side, and they strolled through the halls together.

Levi studied the walls as they walked. Crimson energy flowed through them in snaking patterns like blood through veins. "Why do they look like that?"

"Now that you're dreaming, you get to see a bit of how this place looks behind the scenes."

"This house isn't alive, is it?" He thought back to the castle from before, Jolly, or whatever that stupid thing was called. He felt himself tense as he watched the energy pulsing through the walls.

"In a sense, it is, but it doesn't have a mind of its own. It gets its 'aliveness' from me. Everything in this world does."

"So, why can I only see it now?"

"Because you're dreaming. It's only natural that the stretch of a dream god's power be made visible through, well, a dream."

"A what?" Levi was completely taken aback. "*You?*"

"It's true." Phantasos laughed sheepishly as if embarrassed. "It doesn't matter that much, I don't think."

"It matters!" Levi exclaimed, his eyes brimming with awe. Then that awe was replaced with annoyance. "Hang on. You can control this place?"

"Yes."

"So you were keeping me from my room on purpose!"

"I was just teasing." Phantasos chuckled light-heartedly. "You found it eventually, didn't you?"

Levi opened his mouth to protest, but when he heard Phantasos's laugh, he felt like that'd be a dumb thing to do. *Just teasing. Take a joke, Levi.* He then realized how relaxed he'd become when Phantasos had laughed. How every muscle in him had collectively sighed at that moment. It was like the ice from before had thawed, and now only warmth was left. He smiled before laughing along, although a little more awkwardly.

A small grin crept across Phantasos's face. "How's about I give you a bit of a show? You are my guest, after all."

Levi nodded excitedly, and Phantasos lightly tapped his foot on the ground, making dull thuds against the carpet. Little ripples traveled through the carpet in response, like when a pebble hits the water. The farther the ripples got, the more they grew until they became rolling waves. The carpet turned from a deep crimson to a deeper blue, and it swallowed them up.

Levi sucked in a deep breath, expecting to be whisked down into some watery abyss, but instead, he found himself sitting on solid ground. He tentatively looked around, and he noticed he and Phantasos were on a ship in the middle of a swirling ocean of carpet.

Levi squinted as he studied the ship's flowing purple sails, and then it hit him. "I know this ship. It was in my room." A smile grew across his face as he glanced at Phantasos. "In the bottle!"

Phantasos nodded excitedly. "You catch on quickly, don't you?" With a whisk of his hand, he conjured a fancy pirate hat and dropped it on his head. "So, where to, lieutenant?"

"Can I wear the hat?" Levi impatiently asked.

Phantasos chuckled in response. "No. It's mine." He marched forward and grabbed the steering wheel, and instead of gently steering like a normal person, he jerked it to the left and let it spin freely. The ship turned with it, causing its two passengers to slide along the deck. Levi shrieked in terror as he reached for Phantasos, who was already skidding along the deck. He successfully managed to grab Phantasos's cloak, but that didn't wind up being any help whatsoever, as they both just kept sliding until they hit the rails. Levi squeezed his eyes shut as he waited to get flung overboard and plunged into the icy water below, but instead, he felt a hand wrap around him and hold him steady. He opened his eyes and saw Phantasos.

Phantasos smiled as he pulled his hand away. "Don't be nervous, now. Everything's quite alright."

Levi nodded shakily as he gripped the handrails and stared up. The sky was dark and empty, like the bottom of the ocean.

Phantasos's expression softened. "Try looking down, snowflake."

Levi lowered his head and was met with another dark sea below. But this one was full of glowing starfish. He let out a small gasp of awe. "I'd watch the stars with Kearney all the time. But this...."

Phantasos chuckled. "This is far more beautiful, yes?"

"It really is."

Phantasos leaned against the rails as he watched the sea. "Maybe it was in the stars that we'd meet."

Levi furrowed his brow. "What makes you say that?"

"Well, I think we're quite a great pair, that's all." He smiled as he draped some of his cloak over Levi's shoulder as if they were sharing a blanket. "It's almost like we're meant for each other."

Levi looked at him thoughtfully. "Really?"

"Of course!" He was grinning from ear to ear now. "I'm quite lucky to have met you."

I was worried he hated me. Levi quickly turned his head, trying to make it look like he was distracted by the stars, but nothing could hide the smile on his face. *I didn't realize he thought of me like that.* He became aware of the fact that Phantasos was getting closer.

Phantasos stretched an arm out and pulled Levi into a hug as they continued to watch the sky.

Levi didn't realize it, but he was leaning toward Phantasos, holding Phantasos's cloak around him a little too tightly, trying to soak in as much of the hug as he could. He closed his eyes as he breathed in Phantasos's scent. *He smells like a spiced candle. He makes me feel warm and cozy.*

Kearney couldn't make him feel half as warm in a lifetime as Phantasos could in a minute.

Phantasos gave Levi an affectionate squeeze as he rubbed Levi's arm. "It's about time we got our rest, isn't it? How's about you head back to bed, and I'll have Henry make us the most delicious breakfast tomorrow?" he asked softly.

Levi cracked a smile. "I like that plan." He blinked, expecting to still be on that ship under a blanket of stars.

But instead, he was back in the hallway. He looked up at Phantasos. "Are you going already?"

"Do you want me to?"

Levi hugged him tighter. "Not yet."

As they hugged in silence, Levi suddenly felt unhappy. And he felt angry that he was unhappy. After all, he was hugging the person who *made* him happy. But that unease was like a parasite, eating away at him as that voice whispered in some unreachable corner of his mind.

"Can't move.... Can't see...."

He hugged even tighter as he hid his face in Phantasos's cloak, quietly begging the voice to leave him alone.

"Something bothering you?" Phantasos asked.

Levi shook his head. "I'm fine."

Phantasos watched him for a minute, then began leading him back to his room. As Levi got in bed, Phantasos sat beside him.

Levi squinted as he studied something wispy and glittery floating near Phantasos's neck. Phantasos seemed to notice it, too. He waved at the wispy tendril, and it vanished.

Even when it was gone, Levi kept staring, thinking it might come back. *Is that the string around his neck? The one Annette was talking about?*

Phantasos glanced at him. "There was a song my mother would sing to me when I was little. Would you like me to sing it to you? It might help calm your nerves."

Levi was pulled out of his thoughts. "Huh? O-Oh."
He felt a bit self-conscious at the idea of being sung a
lullaby, but it didn't feel right to turn down the offer. He
lay down, his head hitting the fluffy pillow. "Sure."

Phantasos smiled. "Very well." He leaned back, his
eyes wistfully fixed on the ceiling as he sang.

"Three kings are sleeping,
Each in his bed.
Three kings are sleeping,
Mother tucked them in.
Three kings are dreaming.
The first dreams of dreams,
The second dreams of monsters,
The third dreams of strings."

The next morning, the first thing Levi did was jump out
of bed and race down the hall, not even bothering to
change. He replayed the memory of his dream as he
tried to remember where that old door had been. *It
should be right next to my room.* But it wasn't. His eyes
narrowed as he studied every door he passed. *Is it possible the door isn't real? Maybe it was just part of my dream....*

"...I'm sorry...."

Levi jumped as the voice echoed through his mind.
He stood frozen in place, trying to decipher whether

he'd really heard it or not. But now there was only silence. He swallowed nervously as his eyes trailed over every door around him. He hurried down the hall as he continued his search, and he was so focused that he didn't even notice Annette until he'd rammed into her, knocking her to the ground.

He gasped with horror as he rushed to help her to her feet. "Annette, I'm so sorry!"

Once she was standing again, she grinned at him. "It's cool. I heard people are rough with you when they really love you."

"W-What?" He furrowed his brow. Nothing she said made the slightest bit of sense to him. "Anyway, can you help me with something?"

"What do you need, stud?"

"I'm looking for a closet door."

"There are tons of those."

"The one I'm looking for is really old."

She paused, her face scrunched up, and her fists balled. Levi stumbled back in shock. *Did I upset her? Why would she get upset about a closet?* But as she stayed frozen in that state, her gaze focused straight ahead on nothing in particular, it hit him. *She's actually thinking.*

She made a small squirming sound, which made him wonder if he should intervene, but he did nothing but watch the strange spectacle that was Annette thinking. She let out a hum that rapidly got higher in pitch, like a computer starting up, and then her eyes went back to their typical dull look as she relaxed. "It comes and goes sometimes. It started popping up a lot more lately."

"So, I'm not crazy?" Levi asked with a relieved laugh. "The door's out there?"

"Yeah, but I don't like it much," she replied with a shrug.

"Why not?"

"Because there's a voice. It talks sometimes, but not to me, so I don't talk back."

And there's a voice! Either Annette's crazy, too, or I'm perfectly sane! Levi exhaled as joy washed over him. "Do you have any idea where I can find it?"

"I dunno." She shrugged again. "Just walk around until you hear a weird voice."

His bliss vanished. "That's the best you have?"

"If you want," Annette said, "you can walk around with me. We can do stuff. Maybe the voice will start talking then."

"This sounds like an excuse to get me to help you with your chores."

She grinned. "Yeah."

He stood still for what could've been a minute before finally groaning in defeat. "Why not?"

A few minutes later, he was in a room decorated with tons of shelves filled to the brim with cups of all shapes, sizes, and colors. The only thing the cups had in common was that they were all made of glass. Annette had him roll in a small cart with more cups. She said they'd been used and cleaned and had to go back where they belonged. While Levi hadn't expected such a simple task to get so frightening, his heart practically leaped out of his chest when he saw Annette scoop all of the cups off the cart and into her arms at once.

She swayed back and forth, threateningly close to dropping all the cups at once. Levi stretched his hands toward her, ready to jump in at any second to save the cups from her incompetence. His mind was put at ease when she finally stood still, and the cups stopped rattling in fear for their fragile lives.

He sighed. *Thank goodness.*

"Think fast." She tossed one at him. With a yelp, he rushed to catch it but just missed, and it went careening to the ground and shattering.

His mouth gaped open in horror. "What are you doing?" he cried.

She tossed another without warning, but luckily, he had enough sense to focus this time and catch it. By the time he caught it, she'd already tossed another and another, resulting in an absolutely terrifying game of catch that he had no way of escaping.

"Annette, stop!" he cried as he kept catching cups. "Please!"

She leaned back extra far before throwing the next cup, which hit him square on the nose. He stumbled back as his nose ached in complaint, and the cups cradled in his arms all slipped out and crashed onto the floor, making a sound loud enough to be mistaken for a chandelier falling five stories before slamming onto a dinner table and brutally crushing whoever was in its vicinity.

Levi stared at the glassy massacre at his feet. *Phantasos is going to kill me.*

Annette grinned again. "That was great."

"No, it wasn't!"

She studied his expression. "Why?"

"Because you broke all these cups!"

"So?"

"Phantasos will be mad!"

"I don't care."

"Well, I do!"

"Why?"

He opened his mouth to reply, but only an angry sputter came out. He closed his mouth again, now staring at his glass-covered shoes. *Because...because of the cold. I don't want the ice to come back.* "Because he's my friend, obviously."

Annette's dull green eyes narrowed slightly. "I don't believe you," she replied plainly.

He glared. "I don't care if you do or not."

She didn't hold his stare. Instead, she spun around and floated away, leaving him with a mess of glass at his feet. "Thanks for the help, stud."

He watched helplessly as she disappeared around the corner before looking back at the floor. He let out a sigh that didn't relieve his stress at all. *I'll just have to clean it up before he finds out. It'll be fine.* He started walking around in search of a broom, dustpan, or anything else that could help him effectively get rid of the glass. He had a hunch Phantasos didn't have a vacuum cleaner waiting around the corner, so manual would be the way to go. *Where's a closet when you need it?* He walked faster. *Come on....* He froze.

He'd finally found a closet, but it had an old, tattered door. He stared at it before taking a dazed step forward. He let out a shaky breath. *Here it is. I...I found it. Because of Annette, of all things.* He reached out and rested his hand on the knob. The voice was long gone now, but he still wanted to find it, wanted to know why it cried. He looked around before kneeling down to the keyhole's level, slipping a lock pick out of his backpack pocket. He shoved the lock pick into the lock and started fidgeting it, his eyes darting every which way as he did.

In truth, he'd been picking locks for so long at this point that he didn't even need to look anymore. It was just second nature to him. He heard a little *click* and quickly twisted the doorknob and opened the door, letting light pour into the room, which was full of dusty bookshelves and boxes. He took a deep breath and stepped inside.

"Alright, where are you?" he muttered.

"*...Light?*"

He focused on the other end of the room. *That way.* He started walking toward it. Surprisingly, the closet was much longer than he'd thought, as he couldn't seem to reach the other end of it no matter how much he walked. But the voice kept getting louder, so that meant he was making progress.

"*...Footsteps? Phantasos?*"

"Hello?" Levi called out.

"*...Oh. I think I know you,*" the voice replied, sounding disappointed. "*You're the cute one with the white hair, aren't you?*"

He shifted self-consciously. "I-I guess. Where are you?"

"*Don't bother.*"

"What do you mean?"

"*Give up while you're ahead. I'm not interested.*"

"Not interested? But I came to help you!" he yelled into the darkness.

"*So?*"

"You sound like you're in trouble!"

"*I'm not. You can leave now.*"

"I'm not leaving!"

Silence followed.

Panic started to set in. "Please, let me help you!"

There was still no reply.

Levi started looking everywhere for the voice. He was moving shelves and checking under boxes to no avail, and he was seething with anger now. *Where is she?* He spotted something that was a striking orange color in the corner.

It was Phantasos's fleece puppet, Anais. Her teal beads for eyes greeted him as kindly as the eyes of any inanimate object could.

He picked her up, brushing dirt out of her red hair. "How'd you get here?" he asked, mostly to himself. He held her in his hands as he continued his search, but it was ultimately fruitless, and he was left wondering yet again if the voice had ever been real to begin with. Soon, he found himself standing back in the doorway and staring helplessly into the darkness of the closet, hoping that the voice would call out one last time. But he was met with only silence.

He sighed and glanced down at Anais, who was still in his hand. "At least you won't be gathering dust anymore." He chuckled as he tried to lessen the sinking feeling in his chest. He looked back one last time before shutting the closet door.

House Full of Strings

Chapter 13

Levi Encounters a Hysterical Puppet

Levi observed the ship in the bottle as he rested snugly in his armchair, wrapped in a blanket. When the ship had been giant, it'd been easy to notice the flowing patterns etched onto its purple sails, but now that it was in the palm of his hand, it was much harder to make out those patterns. All the same, something about holding a tiny version of the ship he'd ridden on was so captivating. He glanced at Anais, who was cozied up in his shirt pocket.

"I know it doesn't look like much," he began, "but this thing is so cool scaled up."

She didn't reply, which was bound to be expected, but he was still a little disappointed. He went back to holding the bottle at different angles to study the ship's details.

"I don't know how he did it, but Phantasos made the water look so beautiful. I've always been scared of it since...." He shook his head. "Anyway, it looked amazing." He continued to admire the ship. "Do you like Phantasos? I mean, I don't see why you wouldn't, but I'm curious." The idea of ending his one-sided conversation with Anais didn't occur to him. There was something comforting in talking to her. "I think he's great.

Other than Henry, I don't really have a problem with being here. Although I still miss Kearney. But being with Phantasos made that a lot easier, and—"

"Do you ever stop talking?"

He jumped in his seat and anxiously looked around, his head swiveling left and right. *The voice!* It had been so strangely distant before, but now it sounded like it was right next to him. He glanced back at Anais. "Was that you?"

"Who else?" she retorted.

"B-But you're a puppet," he stammered, baffled.

"I noticed."

"Then why have you been giving me the silent treatment this whole time?" He felt annoyance creep in. *Here I was, worried sick about a tiny puppet who didn't even care enough to let me know when I finally found what I was looking for.*

"Because I was waiting for you to put me back in the closet, but since it looks like you aren't planning on it, I thought I'd just tell you to."

"You want to go back there?" He stared at her like she was insane, which was definitely the case in his mind. "Why?"

"Because that was part of our agreement."

"Our?"

"Phantasos and mine. We had an argument and needed time apart, that's all."

"He put you in there because you had an *argument*?"

"I asked him to."

"Why would you ask for that?"

"Because I deserve it."

"What kind of pity party were you having in there?"

"It wasn't a pity party!" she snapped. "Stop shoving your nose into other people's business and listen up. I know what I'm doing!"

"No!" He clenched his fists in irritation, squeezing her in the process. "You can spend time apart from him somewhere less depressing!"

"But that was the point of me being there!"

"Well, that's dumb! *You're* dumb!" He set her on his desk, propping her up against his snow globe with a determined frown.

"Stop it!" she hissed.

"No, I'm going to make sure you have a *good* time here. Now suck it up and deal with it!"

She scoffed before becoming completely quiet.

Levi watched her closely. "Anais?"

She didn't reply.

He cleared his throat as he looked over his shoulder. It'd definitely look bad if Henry walked in right now. He stiffened. *What would Phantasos think?* "Anais, please talk to me."

She still didn't make a sound.

He felt himself growing more antsy by the moment. *I have to think of something she'd be interested in talking about....* "So, the first time we met, when Phantasos was wearing you...were you alive then, too?"

"I've always been," she muttered.

"Right." He stared at his shoes. "I just—"

"Put me back from where you got me, or I'll scream."

He winced. "P-Please don't." *She's a ticking time bomb. I have to get out of here.*

Annette slammed open the door, causing Levi to jump with a scream. She grinned. "Lunch time."

Anais had gone quiet.

Levi stared at Annette. "Already?" *That's some freakishly good timing.* He raced after Annette without hesitation. "Y-Yes. Yes! I'm starving!" He hurried down the hall, a giant grin plastered on his face. "I'm absolutely starving! Yes!" It was probably safe to drop the act at this point, but he was genuinely scared to.

Levi toyed with an olive between his fingers, debating whether or not to bring up Anais. He glanced at Phantasos, who was downing his fourth lamb shank in five minutes. The other shanks he hadn't touched yet were actively trembling on the plate, watching as their brethren got devoured before their very eyes.

It took Levi a bit to get used to, but it turned out it was perfectly normal for everything to be alive at the table when Phantasos sat down to eat. Apparently, it was one of the only times he "let loose," and his magical powers spread into the room. Therefore, things like rebellious cups of juice trying to escape the dining room and bowls of salads that took naps on Levi's lap were perfectly normal.

Levi picked olives from the bowl getting comfy on his lap, using its little stubby ceramic legs to knead his pants. He popped an olive into his mouth before he said, "I thought you're made of wood. So, how come you need to eat? And so much, too?" *And how are you still so skinny?*

Phantasos looked up, still swallowing down the last shank as he reached for the next, which was inching away from him. He paused to finish swallowing before answering. "Well, there's quite a lot on the inside that must be fed."

"Really?" Levi cocked his head curiously.

"Yes, but that's only me. That's why you'll never see Henry or Annette eat." The shank sprung off the table, but Phantasos quickly caught it. With a satisfied hum, he got ready to take a big bite out of it.

"You got any plans after we eat?" Levi asked.

Phantasos grunted as he struggled to hold the shank in place. "I was thinking we could play a game of petteia."

Levi poked at his food. "That sounds nice." As nonchalant as he seemed, he really just wanted an excuse to avoid going back to his room. Specifically, he wanted to avoid the whiny toy sitting on his desk. Phantasos grinned and rushed to finish his meal. Levi's plan was a go.

Once Phantasos was done, he summoned Henry and ordered him to make tea before leading Levi to the tea room. Once they got there, he hopped over to a table and gestured to the board game set up on it. "Don't be shy, snowflake. Have a seat!"

Levi smiled and sat himself on the couch facing the table, observing the board game carefully. There were about sixteen circle-shaped pawns, half of them painted crimson red and the rest emerald green, sitting on an eight-inch-by-eight-inch board.

Phantasos dropped himself on the couch opposite Levi. "Shall I explain the rules?"

Levi nodded eagerly, and Phantasos cleared his throat. "Starting with the pawns! As you can see, we each have eight. And you'll be green because I'm always red. Continuing, taking turns, each player can move one pawn vertically or horizontally, and they can only put their beads on empty spaces. The way a pawn can be defeated is if it's surrounded by two of the other team's pawns on opposite sides...."

He soon finished explaining, and the two started their game. Phantasos waved his hand, and one of his pawns moved a space forward.

"So, Levi," he began, "tell me more about this Kearney fellow. You told me he'd be here soon, but I have yet to see him. It's been how long at this point?"

"It hasn't even been a week yet," Levi snapped. He moved a pawn. "To be honest, I have no idea where he is right now. The last I saw him was in that castle, and I hardly know anything about this place."

"Well, he couldn't have gotten that far. Perhaps he's reached Toy Town."

"Toy Town?"

"Yes." Phantasos beamed. "It's a quaint little town my dolls have made for themselves. It used to be an amusement park, but it stopped working. Due to lack of use, I assume."

Levi moved one of his pawns behind another. "It must look pretty cool."

"Why, you were there earlier!"

Levi looked up at him. "*That* was Toy Town?"

"Indeed. Quite adorable, wasn't it?"

"I guess." He moved another pawn forward without much thought. Then he thought back to Kearney. He nodded as if to reassure himself. "Kearney will be here. He always comes through."

Phantasos nodded back, his expression concerned. "Do you often have to wait alone for him to…come through?"

"Not that often. Or, not for this long, I guess."

Phantasos waved his hand, and another pawn moved. "So, it's just been the two of you, yes?"

Levi nodded. "He raised me, pretty much."

"One child hardly seems capable of raising another," Phantasos commented.

"Well," Levi searched for the right words, "he doesn't like grown-ups that much, so that's probably why he took me under his wing."

Phantasos looked away. His eyes were wide with worry. "Is that why you've been an orphan this whole time? He's been *gatekeeping* you?"

It was at this point that it became obvious Levi and Phantasos were riding on completely different trains of thought. Levi's train was on a simple path from New York up to Vermont, while Phantasos's train had jumped the track somewhere between those two points and was now doing loop-de-loops in Canada, with the intended destination being Japan.

"What? No!" Levi glared at him. "He just wants to protect me, that's all!"

"It doesn't sound like that to me." Phantasos crossed his arms. "All I've been hearing is that your 'friend' likes keeping you cooped up inside while he disappears for extended periods of time, tells you not to interact with well-meaning adults, and is borderline obsessed with your wellbeing."

Levi's face was red with anger. "You're twisting my words. It's not like that!"

"I'm not *twisting* anything. I'm merely *repeating* what you've already said!" Phantasos thrust his hands forward in a dramatic gesture. He aggressively waved his hand right, sending a pawn flying at Levi's and knocking it off the board. "Try to take better care of them, snowflake."

Levi frowned and thrust another pawn ahead. "I told you to stop calling me that," he mumbled.

"But it suits you."

"No, it doesn't!"

"Yes, it does! You have white hair, and you're small. Snowflake fits perfectly."

"But I hate it," Levi groaned as he moved another pawn.

"I, for one, think it's quite cute." Phantasos rolled his eyes. "You're making a big deal out of nothing. It's just a nickname." He waved his hand again, and another of Levi's pawns went flying. "Are you even trying?"

"I am."

That icy atmosphere seemed to creep back into the room as Phantasos looked away, his arms crossed. "Perhaps we should change the conversation before you blow the *roof* off this place."

Levi let out a huff. "Agreed."

Despite this agreement, no new conversation was picked up, and the two aggressively continued their game with faces so scrunched up it looked like they'd just sucked on lemons. Levi fought to keep himself relaxed, but he was tense all over and didn't know why. He was sitting more awkwardly, trying not to lean forward when he reached to move a piece.

Soon, he forced himself to look at Phantasos and immediately thought of Anais when he did. *Maybe a quarrel like this got them so mad at each other. After all, they both seem pretty petty.* He swallowed back his worry. *The same thing won't happen to us, right?* "I haven't seen Anais in a while. Where's she at?" He tried to ask tactfully, but his tone was a little shaky.

The irritation in Phantasos's eyes began to fade, but only slightly. "I've been rather occupied with you lately, so I haven't had as much time with her. As of now, she's having a vacation in my bedroom."

"I miss her," Levi continued.

He frowned. "If you love her so much, why don't you marry her?" he muttered under his breath. "Anyway, why do you need her so badly when you already have me?"

I can have more than one friend, you know, Levi thought begrudgingly. *Why did you lie about where you put her?* His hand hovered above a pawn as he froze in thought. *What are you hiding? You don't have to hide from me.*

Phantasos watched his hand with cold amusement. "Don't worry too much about that one, snowflake. It's going to get taken out in the next move, no matter what you do."

Levi looked up and scowled. "It's my first time. You can at least pretend to go easy on me."

Phantasos nodded with mock determination. "Of course!" He moved one of his pawns away, giving Levi's pawn another chance at life. He then watched Levi with wide and encouraging eyes. "Go on, snowflake. You've got this!"

Levi cracked a smile before moving a pawn to the side, closer to one of Phantasos's.

Phantasos waved his hand and moved said pawn away before smiling at Levi again. "You are truly a master among masters! I'm shaking in my boots from your sheer skill!"

Levi laughed. "Stop it!"

"But I can't!" Phantasos fell back on the couch in a mock faint, dramatically throwing his hand over his eyes. "You're just too good!"

The ice was melting. Levi felt himself drawing closer to Phantasos again. He moved his pawn toward Phantasos's, and Phantasos moved his away once more, and the two dedicated the rest of their game to this strange game of chase. After doing that for a while longer, it ended in a tie, and the pair decided to finish the evening with a nice cup of tea.

Levi smugly grinned at Henry, who was filling his cup while scowling at him. He then looked at Phantasos, who hadn't noticed Henry's sour face due to his intense focus on the cookies in front of him. The cookies were inching toward him, clearly just as excited as he was that they were about to be eaten.

Levi felt his smile fade, and a different ice than before crept in. *You lied to me,* he thought as he stared at Phantasos. *You knew Anais was in that closet. You put her there. Why?*

House Full of Strings

Chapter 14

Levi and the Annoying Piece of Fleece Learn to Get Along

Levi woke up on the floor just outside his bedroom, which must've thoroughly perplexed Phantasos and made Henry's day. He woke up because Annette had tripped over him.

She wobbled away, unknowingly abandoning her lace headpiece, which had flown off her head when she'd fallen.

Levi glared at her then went back to hugging his backpack on the cold floor, only now, angrily. Apparently, he'd been hugging it the whole night, but he didn't remember that. He only remembered dreaming about the terrifying toy that was now commandeering his bedroom.

He eventually managed to drag himself to his feet and brush his messy hair out of his eyes as best he could. He knew he wanted to avoid Anais, but he didn't think he wanted to so badly he'd be willing to spend a whole night on hardwood. He stared at his bedroom door, half in dread and half in exhaustion. *If I want answers about anything, I have to start with her. No more being afraid. After all, it's not like she'll hurt me or anything.*

He opened the door and looked around. Anais was propped up against his snow globe where he'd left her, not making a sound. He walked up to her and scooped her up before dropping onto his bed and setting her beside him.

"If I could move, I would've thrown your precious snow globe on the floor ten times over already," she muttered.

He let out a heavy sigh. "Good morning to you, too. I don't think you got my name yet. It's Levi."

"I don't care."

And the dynamic grows from here. "I don't either." He didn't skip a beat before resuming the conversation. "You got any hobbies?" *If I want to get answers, I'll have to gain her trust first.* He smiled to himself. *Chances are, I'll be the next Sherlock Holmes.*

Anais sighed. She seemed to finally accept she had no escape from Levi's dreaded small talk. "I guess."

"Care to name one?"

"Well, reading."

"I like reading, too." He paused. "Or...I collect books. Sometimes."

"And you don't even read them?"

"I read them." He paused again. "Sometimes."

"Sometimes isn't a hobby."

He mumbled something rude under his breath then resumed the conversation. "So, what books do you read?"

"You mean what genre?"

She knows Italian. That'll probably never be useful.
"That's what I meant, obviously."

She huffed. "Well, I really like—"

A knocking came from the door, and Levi practically flew off the bed. It seemed he was still a little tense from his night on the uncaring floor.

"Quick, hide me!" she whispered.

"What, why?" he whispered back.

"Just do it!"

He grabbed her and shoved her into a drawer without a second thought as she squeaked in complaint. He then raced to the door and opened it to be greeted by Phantasos on the other side.

"Good morning, snowflake," he said with a smile. His antlers thumped against the doorframe as he peeked through.

Levi felt his grip on the door handle tighten slightly. *He's still calling me that?* "What's up?"

"Well, after the state I found you in a bit ago, I just wanted to check on you."

"I'm doing alright. So, thanks!" He slammed the door shut, largely by accident, leaving a confused Phantasos on the other side.

Meanwhile, he could hear Anais's muffled screaming: *"What do you mean 'checking on him'? I thought you only checked on me!"*

"S-Snowflake?" Phantasos's voice came from the other side of the door. *"Do you want breakfast? I can have Annette bring it to you if you'd like."*

"Yeah, sure, thanks. Now go away." Levi tried to keep the panic out of his voice, praying Phantasos wouldn't hear Anais's shrieking.

"Okay...."

As the sound of Phantasos's footsteps receded, Levi braced himself and opened the drawer. Anais's screaming became ten times louder.

"Why are you yelling?" he hissed through his teeth.

"Because he told me *I* was special! Why are you getting all the attention now?" Her voice only escalated in volume from there.

He winced as he shut her back into the drawer. Her shrieking became more erratic. "Please, calm down."

"Shut up!"

He jumped away from the drawer, continuously being impressed by Anais's never-ending increase in volume.

"Shut up! Shut up! He said I was his favorite! He told me he loved me!" She started breaking down into tears. *"After what I've done, n-no wonder he doesn't anymore...."* She quieted down until all that was left were tiny whimpers.

Levi tentatively opened the drawer and pulled her back out. "Don't say that, Anais. I'm sure he still cares about you."

"But it's true. After everything he's done for me, I hurt him."

"Alright, how bad was it?"

"It's too horrible for me to tell anyone!" she bawled.

He let out an exasperated sigh. "Anais."

She started crying louder.

"Anais, please."

It didn't look like she would be stopping anytime soon.

Levi found himself staring at the hysterical plushie in his hand. He wasn't used to girls or girl feelings. All he knew was that Kearney had told him to avoid them. But Kearney told him to avoid everything, so he hadn't really paid attention to that advice in particular.

"H-Hey, Anais." He started awkwardly stroking her yarn hair. "Don't cry. Please." *Please let this work.*

She got a little quieter, but that was likely from fatigue rather than his words. Although he wasn't sure if plushies could even experience fatigue.

Luckily for him, an idea popped into his head. "Let's head to the library! Maybe we'll find some nice books there."

She continued to sob, but he was determined that this would lift her spirits. He put her in his backpack and marched through the halls, trying to get to the library as quickly as possible. As he walked, she got quieter and quieter until her crying had gone completely silent. Levi sighed as his ears knew peace again. Soon, they were at the library.

He propped her up against a stack of books and grinned encouragingly. "So, anything interesting you want to read here?"

"Not really," she said quietly.

"Come on, I'm sure there's something here for you!"

"Levi, stop."

"Come on!" His smile got bigger. "Something tells me you really want to," he sang.

"…Well, there is something."

He smiled. "What's it called?"

"It should be somewhere on this table. I didn't read it that long ago. Just point around, and I'll tell you when you're there, I guess."

"Okay." Levi started sifting through books. He pointed to one. "Is it this one?"

"No," she muttered.

"What about that one?"

"No."

He returned to searching, and soon, he heard her gasp and spun around to face her. "What is it?"

"I see it!"

His eyes lit up. After another minute of pointing around with Anais guiding him, he pulled out a book with a leathery black cover titled *Double-Edged Kisses*. He furrowed his brow. "This is it?"

"Yeah, that's the book!" she exclaimed. "Go to page fifty-four. There's a really steamy scene there."

"Steamy?"

"Don't worry, you'll love it!"

He nodded and glanced back at the book. It couldn't hurt, especially if it made her feel better. He flipped to the page and cleared his throat. He held the book incredibly close to his face as he squinted his eyes to read.

"Why are you holding it like that? Do you need glasses or something?"

"I'm fine!" In truth, the words were very blurry, but he could tell where one word ended and another started, so as far as he was concerned, his vision was as sharp as an eagle's.

He started reading, "*Sophie leaned against Grayson's bleeding chest and stared into his fierce, dominating eyes. He fastened his grizzly arms around her and pulled her close, his lips hovering above hers as he breathed ragged breaths.*" The unease in his voice grew as he realized what 'steamy' meant. "'*The mafia is coming,*' *she whispered, her legs shaking as she leaned her weight against him.* '*I won't let them hurt you,*' *he replied, holding her tighter. His hands slid down her waist*—Th-That's enough of that!" He slammed the book shut and let it fall to the floor, feeling a strong urge to wash his hands. He'd promised himself he'd never interact with *girl stuff*, and he felt more disgusted with himself for breaking such a sacred pact than with the book itself.

"What happened? Does any form of physical romance make you *that* queasy?"

"No, I just don't read stupid stuff!" *Is that really what she calls fun? It's more like torture. Girl stuff torture.*

"Stupid?" She let out a huff. "Whatever. You're not as cultured as I am, I guess."

He fell into a chair beside her. "Not my fault you have nothing better to do with your life."

There was a tense silence between them for the next few seconds before Anais spoke again. "...It was nice of you to try to cheer me up. So, thanks for that." Her voice was slightly bitter but with less of an edge than before.

He shrugged. "If it makes my friend feel better, it's a win for me." *Except that I just read girl stuff.*

"You think of me as a friend?"

He stared at her, confused, then quickly caught on. As much as he hated lying, it had to be done. Deceit was a necessary part of detective work. "Sure." He grinned before asking, "Why did you get so upset earlier? With Phantasos?"

"Oh. I was hoping you forgot about that." She laughed awkwardly. "It's nothing."

"You sure?"

"Yeah...." Her voice trailed off. "It's just...Phantasos only checks on people he really cares about, and I thought he cared about me. I guess I got jealous."

Finally, a start. Levi smiled. "I'm sure he still cares about you. He's nice like that."

"No, Levi, he was really hurt by what I said."

"What did you say, then?"

"I...I told him—"

There was a series of thuds behind the pair, and Levi spun around, letting out the breath he was holding once he realized it was just some books that had fallen off their shelf. He rushed to pick them up and returned to Anais's side just as quickly.

"Sorry. You were saying?"

"N-Never mind." She sounded a little shaken. "It's nothing important."

This nice guy act isn't working. He slammed his hands onto the table. "It's very important! I need you to tell me what you know!"

"Know about what?"

"About Phantasos and you. Tell me why you were in that closet!"

"Well, now I'm definitely not doing it!" she snapped.

His mouth gaped open in shock. *I got sloppy. She's onto me.* "I-I...I didn't mean it that way, just—"

"Don't you 'just' me," she hissed. "Get out!"

He stumbled back in shock. He had no idea how he should've been reacting in this situation, but his first instinct told him to do whatever he could to keep the little piece of fleece from hysteria.

"Get out, *get out!*"

He hurried out the door and slammed it shut behind him, letting out shaky breaths as he pressed his back against it. *I'm terrible at this.*

About an hour later, Levi snuck back into the library and started scouring the shelves for books, trying to be as quiet as he could to ensure Anais wasn't made aware of his presence. Soon, he'd mustered up the courage to go back to her. He sucked in a deep breath. He'd stepped too far last time; now, he had to go back to square one and take it as slow as needed.

He hurried over to where he'd left her. "I'm back!" *Please don't scream at me.*

"What now?" she asked, sounding exhausted.

He dropped the books on the desk. "I brought you these." *Please like them. Please.*

"Is this an apology or something? You can't bribe me." She went quiet for a moment. "How about we just talk?"

"Oh." He tried to hide the surprise in his voice. *That works.* "Sure." He settled down beside her, still unsure as to whether or not he was fully safe from another sudden fit of girly mania. "What do you want to talk about?" he asked.

"I don't know," she muttered. "Just something. Silence is the worst. So, if you really insist on holding me hostage, at least make it more bearable for me."

He bit his lip as he stared up at the ceiling. "Maybe we should start with some icebreakers."

"Icebreakers are boring. Truth or dare, on the other hand, that's how you get the juicy stuff fast."

"Alright then, truth or dare?"

"I can't move. How can you dare me to do anything?"

"I can dare you to tell the truth." He leaned closer with a grin.

"You're not funny," she grumbled. "Let's cut out the middle man. Truth."

"Alright." Levi plunged deep into the hundreds of questions he had for her but winced when he remembered he had to turn off his investigator brain. He stifled a groan as he tried to think up the simplest question he could. "What's one thing you wish you could change in your life?"

Anais was quiet for a moment. Then, she let out a *hmm* as she thought. "Probably my hair color. I always thought I'd look nicer as a blonde."

"Really?" Levi tilted his head. "You wouldn't even wish to move on your own?"

"No," she replied nonchalantly. "It's not like I've ever known anything else. And I don't mind it for the most part, either."

"For the most part?"

"Well, when people like you get their hands on me...."

Levi chuckled with embarrassment. "I see your point."

"Alright, my turn. Would you date someone shorter than you?"

"I wouldn't have it any other way," he replied with a smirk. "I like the idea of having a partner who looks up to me."

"Given how tall you are, that'd mean your date would have to be...at most, seven years old." She was so gloomy that she didn't even laugh at her own joke.

He scoffed at her comment but swiftly picked up the mantle to continue their game of Truth and Truth. "What's something you pretend to like but actually hate?"

"I-I don't know if I can say," she muttered.

"My lips are sealed. Promise."

She paused a little longer before answering, "I don't like reading at all. It bores me to tears."

He furrowed his brow. "Why'd you say you did, then?"

She sighed. "I lied because...because it's my role."

He tilted his head, having absolutely no clue what that meant or how to respond to it.

"What's your problem?"

"I don't know what that means," he replied with a shrug.

"What's not to get? It's the role I was made for!"

"I still don't know what that's supposed to mean."

She let out an annoyed huff. "When Phantasos made me, he gave me a role—a character I'm meant to play. He gave me my name, hobbies, personality, everything, and told me to always stick to it."

Levi studied her tiny fleece face in an attempt to clear his confusion. "Do you know why he gave you that role?"

"All he said was that I'm part of his 'special plan,' but I don't even know the first thing about that."

"Huh." He leaned back in his chair. "That's interesting."

"Interesting is the kind of word you use when something's weird to you, but you want to sound polite when expressing how you feel about it," Anais retorted.

"Interesting's the word you use when you want to sound polite and *honest*," he bit back.

"I guess honest is nice," she sighed. "Phantasos talks a lot, but I feel like there are so many things he still doesn't tell me. So...stay honest, okay?" That last sentence was very quiet. Hesitant, almost.

Levi studied her tiny face thoughtfully. "Okay." *I will.*

After another minute of silence, he got bored and sat back up, grabbing one of the books he'd brought for her before. "These books are dumb."

She snorted out a laugh. "Tell me about it."

He grabbed a book and read its back while squinting. "This one's about some chick named Wendy."

"And what's her horrendous dilemma?"

"Choosing between the love of her life and being herself."

"Can't the lady have both?"

"Not when you have sucky taste in men."

There was a short silence after that. "Her story's not the worst," Anais commented. "And she's got a cute name."

"I guess." Levi found himself staring at the ceiling. "Wendy."

"*Wendy.*"

"Weeeeendy."

"Wennnnsdy."

"Wednesday!"

Their raucous laughter filled the room, and once it quieted, Levi smiled. "You don't need to worry about any roles when you're with me, okay?"

"Thanks, Levi." Her voice was filled with warmth. "Maybe you're not as bad as I thought."

"Are we still friends?"

She chuckled. "We weren't really friends to begin with. If anything, this is the starting point."

He scoffed but couldn't hide his grin. *Friend. No matter what, I'm her friend.*

After a brief pause, Anais chuckled mischievously. "Do you want to go snoop?"

"I like how you think." He got up and grabbed her. "But we'll have to keep you hidden."

"Shouldn't be that hard."

He shot her a glare.

She groaned. "I won't start screaming again."

"You'd better promise me," he teased.

"Fine," she hissed.

With that, Levi walked through the hall, his chin lifted dramatically. "Where shall we snoop first, Lady Anais?"

She giggled. "I say we look behind the red door."

"The red doors seem to be the most exciting ones around here." With a vigorous nod, he skipped over to it. "Your wish is my command." He opened it, curiosity flaring in his eyes.

Said curiosity was most definitely satiated when he realized he was in a workshop. There were no tools of any kind in it; instead, there was only a soft red couch and dark oak table in the middle of the room. And while those things didn't scream *workshop*, what definitely gave Levi that impression were the unfinished blocks of wood scattered everywhere in small piles, the wood chips all over the floor, and the myriad of anatomical sketches and graphs plastered on the walls. His eyes fixed back on the middle of the room. Something was sitting on the couch, and he would've assumed it was another person if only it'd moved at all. He took a series of tentative steps toward the figure, which stared at him with an unchanging expression. He gently tapped its cheek once he was close enough only to realize it was hard. It was a doll, one with short brown hair and a big, stupid smile on its face.

"Is it supposed to move?" he asked.

"I don't know. Maybe she is, and she's just sleeping," Anais replied.

"Do dolls even sleep?" He studied the doll's face. The left eye was green while the right one was blue. *I wonder what Phantasos does in this room. Is this how he makes dolls or something?*

"I don't think they do." Anais paused. "She looks really familiar."

"Really?" He nudged the doll, causing its head to roll to the side. In size, it was a little taller than he was, but he was willing to bet it was much lighter. His foot kicked against something, and he looked down. There was another doll on the floor, although this one was a blank canvas compared to the completed one sitting on the couch.

He squinted as he studied the shape of its face. For some reason, it looked vaguely familiar to him.

"What are you doing here?"

Levi spun around and spotted Henry, whose mouth was gaped open in horror. "You can't go snooping through Master's things! Get out!" He rushed at them with a feather duster held threateningly above his head.

"We won't get in trouble or anything!" Levi said while scrambling out of the way.

"We?"

"Y-You and me." *Saved it*, he proudly thought to himself as he ensured Anais was held far enough behind his back to be out of view.

Henry rubbed his temples. "You'll be just fine. *I'll* be lucky if the most I get is a slap on the wrist." His eyes narrowed. "What do you have behind your back?"

"Nothing."

"Show me." He put his hands on his hips as he glared.

Levi shoved Anais into his back pocket under his coat before showing Henry his hands. "See? Nothing, Mr. Paranoia."

He scowled. "If you did take something, Master will be very angry if he finds out."

Levi sauntered past Henry with a smirk. "He'll be angry at *you*."

Henry groaned. "You just love this, don't you? Being able to do whatever you want and walk off scot-free. You'd better watch your step, *snowflake*. It won't always be that way."

Levi rolled his eyes as he left the workshop, and as soon as Henry was out of sight, he hurried down the hall with a chuckle as he pulled Anais out of hiding. "Where to next?"

Chapter 15

Gabi Meets Her Reflection

Kearney was running. He didn't know where; all he knew was that he had to keep going. Even though he was in a crowded street, he felt completely alone. He wasn't surrounded by people but by towering shadows that looked down at him with unreadable glowing eyes. They weren't even touching him, but they made him feel claustrophobic.

He swerved onto the road and stopped dead in his tracks, his hand on his chest helpless to slow down the beating of his panicked heart. The honking of cars and the chatter of the shadows flooded his ears, and he swayed back and forth, hardly able to focus on anything as his shaky legs struggled to hold him. He stared at the gravel under his feet, his mind clouded and desperate for something to focus on. Then he lifted his head, and dread set in. He was on a bridge.

He knew he had to get off as soon as he could, but by the time he fully registered the thought, it was already too late. He turned and saw a white car speeding toward him. To his utter horror, the car swerved, just inches away from him, and flew off the bridge.

Kearney woke up, his heart still throbbing in his chest. He brushed his hair out of his face and sat up. He stared at the ceiling of his cell and sighed.

"It's just another nightmare," he muttered to himself. He took a deep breath and quickly became aware of a sweet smell wafting into the room. He looked around.

Dakota was sitting on the floor by the jail's entrance with a little toy octopus in hand. Calder, sitting beside him, had a pirate figurine and was making *kachew* noises as he pretended to slash Dakota's octopus. This made Dakota very upset.

What confused Kearney, though, was the looks on their faces. It seemed like they were strangely distant, as if they were trying to reenact some old memory. They looked like a pair of estranged exes trying to make up.

Kearney's eyes drifted from them to Gabi's cell, which was empty. And that sweet smell kept getting stronger, so strong it made his stomach growl. "Dakota?"

They paused their game to look at him. "Yes, please?" Dakota asked.

"Where's Gabi?"

"Makin' breakf'st," Calder replied, still focused on the epic battle between the pirate and octopus. "She said she's makin' it just for you. Which makes sense since we can't eat it."

For me? Kearney wasn't used to having things be specifically for him. He felt his cheeks warm up. Luckily, Calder and Dakota had already gone back to their game, so if there was any color on his face, they wouldn't notice. After a few minutes of watching Calder annihilate Dakota's poor octopus, Kearney noticed Gabi had glided into view.

"Good morning!" She waved to him. She was covered in batter and flour.

He walked up to her and smiled. "Good morning."

She led him into the neighboring kitchen area and gestured to a small table. "I made breakfast!"

He admired the food. *So, it's true.* For the first time in what felt like forever, he had an actual breakfast. *Crepes! She made crepes!* He'd had candy for so long at this point that the very thought of it made him sick. But crepes? Crepes were *real* food. He glanced at her, starting to feel sheepish. "You shouldn't have!"

She smiled back, practically radiating joy. "I remember you told me you like caramel, so I added some just for you." Her eyes trailed back to the table apprehensively. "They *might* be a little burnt. I'm not that good at cooking, so...."

He'd already sat down, Calder's words playing over and over in his mind. *Just for me. I'd better show her I appreciate it.* He cut the crepe and proceeded to shove half of it down his throat. He didn't like all the crunching he had to do. Some parts tasted great while others were horribly burnt. One might think this made the crepe unenjoyable, but Kearney, who had no clue that burnt food was bad food, assumed it was all part of Gabi's masterfully crafted recipe for the perfect crepe. Once he managed to swallow it down, he glanced back at her.

"Th-That looked like a big bite," she stammered, staring at him in shock.

He grinned. "It's really good." *This has got to be the best meal of my life. Nothing will ever top this.* The crepes weren't really anything special. If anything, they left him with a horrible taste in his mouth that made him incredibly thirsty. He'd most definitely tasted better food at some point, and yet, he'd never experienced so much joy eating something. *She made them for me. Me! She made something all on her own and thought, "This will be just for Kearney!"*

She smiled sheepishly. "You like it that much? You can tell me if they're...not really good."

"Nothing's wrong. I love it." He kept eating. It felt like the crepes were getting more delicious with every bite. The burnt flavor was something to savor now.

Gabi let out a triumphant laugh. "Take that, Mom! My food *is* edible!" She crossed her arms with a proud glint in her eyes. "You want me to make more?"

"Yes, please."

She raced off, humming to herself as she went. Kearney kept eating the deliciously burnt crepes, and all that was on his mind was how amazing they were and how cute Gabi looked when she smiled.

Kearney, Gabi, and a very grumpy Calder were tied by their hands as they followed Dakota through Toy Town. Kearney was still rubbing sleep out of his eyes, and yet he kept thinking it was already time for bed again. He wasn't used to how the town was in an endless sunset. It was pretty, sure, but it messed with his head a good amount.

Dakota explained their next assignment as they walked. "Today, you're going to the Mirror House. It used to be a fun place, but ever since a bunch of strings tied everything up inside, nobody's gone there."

"What's wrong with a bunch o' strings?" Calder muttered.

"I'm not sure." Dakota shrugged. "Ms. The Tailor decided they were special, so she told everyone not to touch the Mirror House, but now, she wants the strings taken out. But I'm not supposed to ask questions."

After that, there was silence before Kearney asked, "So, why are we tied up?"

"Ms. The Tailor told me to. It's probably to help everyone in town feel safe."

Gabi locked eyes with a random doll, who dropped whatever he was doing to stare back. "What do they think we're going to do? Bite them?"

Dakota gently tugged the rope to keep everyone moving. "Maybe it's to make me look super cool and tough. I am the sheriff, after all."

"Do you want to look cool and tough?" Kearney asked.

Dakota paused in thought. "A little."

Calder's head was low as he mocked them under his breath.

Kearney scanned the packed streets of Toy Town, his old habits getting the better of him, even if his chances of being ambushed by rabid dolls were marginally lower at this point. His eyes fixed on something peculiar at the other end of the street.

Briiiing!

He groaned. Luckily, he couldn't pick up the call right now, even if he wanted to. The phone continued to ring incessantly as the group walked past it. Nobody else even glanced at it. Kearney furrowed his brow. *I'm not crazy, right? They can see it?* Before he knew it, they were at their destination, so there was no need to think about it anymore.

Dakota pointed at the Mirror House. "I had a friend leave some scissors in there for you. All you have to do is snap the strings, and they'll shrivel up," he continued, talking as he untied them. "I can't help today because I have to look for No-Face. Sorry, please."

Kearney watched Dakota closely. The little doll had a strange look on his face. Every time he glanced at the Mirror House, something lit up in his eyes. It looked like fear. Maybe No-Face's absence wasn't the only reason he wasn't planning on going with them. "It's alright. Good luck with that," Kearney said.

Dakota looked up at him with a smile. "Thank you, please." He waved goodbye before going back to his search, leaving the three standing outside the Mirror House. Calder waited for the moment Dakota was out of view then quickly spun around to face Kearney and Gabi with a restless glint in his eyes. "Alright, we gotta go right now."

Gabi furrowed her brow. "Go where?"

"To the Mister! I'm not givin' up that easily. Now, let's go, maggots!"

Kearney ignored him and started walking toward the Mirror House, and Calder chased after him.

"Freckles!" he yelled as he clung onto Kearney's shirt. "Don't disrespect me like this!"

"Stop. Please." Kearney slapped him away, more tired than anything else.

Calder flushed with anger. "Stop actin' like a wuss! I'm gettin' you there if it's the last thing I do!"

"Good luck, then." Kearney continued toward the Mirror House with Gabi at his side as Calder screamed behind them. Kearney got to the door, only to find it completely and incredibly neatly boarded up. He and Gabi exchanged confused glances.

"What's this all about?" Gabi muttered as she knocked against the wood.

"I'm not sure." He tried to pry one of the boards off with his hands, but they were so tightly packed together that it was hard to even get a decent grip on one.

"I'll go check around the building. Maybe there's another way in." She grabbed Calder by the arm and very insistently dragged him with her around the corner, vanishing from Kearney's sight. Meanwhile, he continued his attempts to pry a board off, but soon, he was distracted by a sound he was quickly growing to hate.

Briiiing!

His head swung to the side, and he spotted the pay-phone standing a few feet away, watching him. *Stalking* him, practically. It rang again, but he didn't pay it any attention. He went back to his efforts with that one pesky board.

Briiiing!

"Shut up," he muttered.

Briiiing!

The ringing made him angry, which seemed to make him stronger, which helped with freeing the board. With a loud grunt that was completely drowned out by the phone's ringing, he tore it off. A smile cracked across his face as he grabbed another board. Now that he was able to grab the boards at different angles and with a better grip, removing them was much easier. Before he knew it, he'd taken out enough of them for him and the others to squeeze through.

He glanced back at the payphone with a smug grin. "What do you think of that?"

The payphone had gone silent. It seemed the voice didn't plan on congratulating him.

Kearney sat down, his back against the building as he waited for the others to return. Soon, he could hear their voices, talking in hushed tones.

"…The Mister is behind the Wall, right?" Gabi asked.

"Right," Calder replied.

"So, in a way, we're all trying to get to the same place, huh?"

They're pretty close. Kearney got to his feet and peeked around the corner of the Mirror House.

Gabi was kneeling, her head level with Calder's as she whispered to him. "How about we form an alliance? We'll work together to get out of here and get to the Wall, and once we're on the other side, we'll go our separate ways."

Calder's eyes narrowed. "You're givin' me the short end o' the stick! The whole point o' gettin' to the Mister is havin' a fleshy person to give to 'im!"

"Well, maybe you can work something out with Kearney! I have no clue what he's planning on doing next."

He bit his lip. "Maybe."

"I'll talk to him, alright?"

"Fine. But I don't plan on stickin' around if he ain't comin'."

"We leave whether he comes or not."

Kearney stared at his shoes. He felt upset, not about Calder, but about Gabi. He'd come to enjoy her company. The idea that she'd leave whether he went with her or not hurt. He heard footsteps and sprung back. He pretended to be incredibly focused on the doorway, clear of the boards he'd ripped free, as Gabi and Calder rounded the corner. They had big smiles on their faces, like they hadn't just been talking about abandoning him.

Gabi gasped with excitement when she saw the door. "Kearney, how did you do that?"

"It wasn't that hard." He shrugged.

Her excitement faded when she fixed her eyes on his hands. She grabbed them, studying them keenly.

Kearney tensed. Blood pounded in his ears. *What's she doing?*

"Your hands are covered in cuts," she commented. "You shouldn't push yourself so hard, you know."

He glanced at his hands. "Oh. I didn't notice."

"Well, it's about time you did." She continued to hold them as she led him to the doorway. "I guess I'll have to keep an eye on you to make sure you don't hurt yourself any more today."

Calder trailed behind them. "Why're you watchin' 'im like that? What is he, a baby?"

She rolled her eyes. "Let's go before he gets worse," she whispered to Kearney.

They headed inside while Calder glared at them from behind. Kearney's smile faded the moment he entered the Mirror House because he was greeted by hundreds of *hims* staring right back. He jumped back with a yelp, but the other two laughed.

Calder snickered. "It's called a *mirror* house, dummy."

Kearney shoved his hands into his pockets and marched forward. He spotted three oversized scissor blades leaning against a wall and grabbed one while handing Gabi another. He took the third blade, meant for Calder, and stabbed it into the wall just out of Calder's reach. After that, he started hacking away at the thousands of strings that had weaved a web in the hall.

Gabi followed suit as Calder jumped, reaching for his scissor blade but nowhere close to grabbing it. Soon, the hall was filled with chopped-up strings lying lifelessly at their feet. They continued down the hall, leaving Calder to struggle.

Kearney's hands were clammy. *When is she going to tell me about the plan? She doesn't plan on keeping me in the dark until the end, does she?* He didn't mind leaving Toy Town. He wanted to get to the end, just like she did. The difference between him and her, though, was that he wouldn't immediately up and leave her if she didn't want to tag along.

Gabi's brown hair bobbed as she jumped to slash the dangling strings. "So, Kearney," she began, "who's Levi?"

He sucked in a sharp gasp. His eyes snapped to her. "H-How do you know that name?"

"Because you mutter it in your sleep, that's how," she laughed. They had their backs turned to each other. If she'd seen the look on his face, she might've understood the weight of the question she'd just asked.

"I...." Kearney stared at the scissor blade in his clammy hands. His mouth opened slightly, and he looked up to stare absently at his own reflection. He'd tried so hard not to think of Levi. Why did Gabi have to do this to him? "He's gone. That's all."

It hurt to think that was all he could say. He could've started talking about Levi's bombastic personality. He could've mentioned Levi's obsessive hoarding habits. He could've told Gabi about how Levi could've picked every lock in the world if he wanted to. But all he could say about Levi now was the one thing Levi was. Gone. And that was what he always would be. *Because I let him down. It was all my fault. From the very beginning, it was all my fault.*

Gabi looked over her shoulder. Kearney didn't look back at her, but he could see her hundreds of reflections watching him. Every pair of those green and blue eyes of hers were watching him with concern.

"Gone?" she asked quietly.

He nodded.

Her eyes lowered to the floor. "I know how it feels," she choked out. "...Do you want to talk about it?"

"No."

She lowered her head. "That's fair. I never really wanted to, either."

They kept cutting at the strings in silence. Kearney would occasionally look in the mirrors' reflections and see Gabi. Her brow was knit, and she had her eyes fixed upward like she was trying not to cry. In a weird way, it was comforting to know they were in the same boat. He paused, still watching her expression. She was biting her lip with a different emotion. Determination. Like she was trying to will the grief away.

Soon, the hallway forked in two directions, and Kearney headed one way without a word while Gabi went the other. He hacked at low-hanging strings as he continued through the hall and soon entered a room full of little connecting walls of mirrors.

He frowned. *It's a little maze, isn't it?*

He just wanted to be alone. If he cried, at least no one would be there to see it. But even though he was technically by himself now, it didn't feel very comforting to see his dozens of reflections watching him. With a huff, he stepped into the maze and, in moments, was surrounded by himself. He spun around as he looked for the way out, and his reflections spun with him in search of the exit.

Everywhere Gabi looked, she only saw herself, which was to be expected in a room where the walls, floor, and ceiling were lined with mirrors, but that didn't mean she had to like it. She kept marching, her head held low as the tip of her scissor scraped against the floor. She was mad. Mad at herself. Mad because she just *had* to ask Kearney about Levi.

She frowned as she scanned the room for loose threads, but there was nothing but mirrors. *I don't want to think about it. I won't. It doesn't matter if talking to Kearney reminded me of her or not. I won't think about it.* She let out an exasperated sigh. Every inch of her was rigid. *She's alive, and I'm going to find her. She's alive, she's alive, she's alive.*

She snapped out of her thoughts as her eyes fixed on something peculiar. It was another reflection, but this one was different. It looked just like her, but it had two green eyes instead of her one blue eye and one green eye. And it didn't copy her actions either, let alone move an inch. It just stared.

She warily inched toward it.

The reflection kept staring.

That's definitely not a mirror. Whatever it was, it was standing right in front of her. She reached out with a shaky hand and touched it. It felt like it was made of wood.

She pulled her hand away with a startled gasp and stared at it, her breath shaky. "Hello? Can...Can you talk?"

The reflection smiled oddly. Then it reached out and grabbed her.

Kearney sighed in relief as he finally made it out of the maze, and although mirrors still surrounded him, at least now, all he had to do was walk straight.

A girly giggle bubbled through the air, causing the hairs on his neck to stand on end. His eyes darted to the mirrors. It wasn't his reflection in them anymore. Instead, there was a girl, probably a few years younger than he was, with red hair in a ponytail and a pair of teal eyes. And she was watching him. Every one of her was watching him.

Kearney swallowed back his fear as he spun around the room. No one was there but him. So, where was that reflection coming from? *What the heck...? I can't wait to get out of here.*

The giggling echoed through the hall again. He froze before slowly turning his head. But once again, there was no one there but him.

He kept walking, rubbing his arms in an attempt to get rid of his goosebumps. *Where's Gabi? Shouldn't I be able to hear her?* "Gabi?" He felt his grip on his scissor blade tighten when there was no reply. He started walking faster. *The sooner I find her, the sooner we can leave.*

Then there was a loud bang, and something came crashing through the wall, sending glass everywhere. Kearney jumped back and screamed, only to immediately cut off his voice when he saw Calder.

Calder stared at him while shaking glass out of his tan sweater. "Did I scare you?" A smile crept across his face.

"It wasn't you! It was...." Kearney pointed at the mirrors. The girl was gone.

"Was what?" Calder furrowed his brow.

"N-Nothing," Kearney replied. "It was nothing." He shook his head before resuming his walk down the hallway.

Calder followed him. "Where are we goin'?"

"I don't know," Kearney admitted. "I think I might follow the strings. Maybe we'll find Gabi at the other end. They're acting up and twitching, so there's that, too."

"I think yer wastin' time."

"Then why are you following me?"

"'Cause I've already looked ev'rywhere else. I'm bored."

The two paused at the end of the hall and looked at the door waiting before them. They exchanged glances before Kearney grabbed the handle and opened the door. They slowly walked through the room, warily eyeing the broken glass littering the floor. Kearney glanced at Calder, who looked nervous. *Very* nervous. He was also doing some weird swagger, which might've been his way of hiding said nervousness. His green eyes were darting every which way as if a monster was about to jump out at them.

"What could've done something like this?" Kearney asked.

"I dunno. Do you think it got Weird-Eyes?"

Kearney shook his head. "Maybe that mess was there before we even came."

The truth was, he was panicking deep down because he believed the exact opposite. Thousands of possibilities were swimming through his mind, and the ideas of what could've happened to Gabi—most of which were horrific—caused him to panic even more. *Something* must've caused this, and Gabi had probably been unfortunate enough to cross its path. His eyes fixed on a little trapdoor in the corner of the room, hidden behind a broken mirror, and he hurried over to it. It was cracked open, and he leaned close to listen to what was inside of it. It was almost silent except for a tiny, desperate gasp.

Kearney felt his chest tighten in dread as he yanked the door open and crawled through it without hesitation.

"Freckles? What's in there?" Calder called, not far behind.

Behind the trapdoor was a long crawlspace, so Kearney was on his knees with his head held low to avoid the hanging, loose threads that were brushing against his hair. "It has to be Gabi."

Calder's eyes widened. "All the way in there?" When he saw Kearney wasn't stopping, he hurried after him.

Kearney made it to the other end of the crawlspace and rushed out, brushing cobwebs and bits of string out of his hair and face. He looked around anxiously, finding himself in a room full of strings. There were at least thousands in this room alone, and he realized that the room's walls were full of holes, which must've been how the strings had managed to snake through the rest of the Mirror House. From the looks of it, this was the heart of it all.

His eyes followed the strings to the ceiling, where they were all wrapped around something. His breath caught in his throat. It was Gabi.

"'Kearney,' yeah?"

He stiffened as he focused on what was standing beneath Gabi, the thing that had said his name.

It was also Gabi.

House Full of Strings

Chapter 16

Gabi's Previously Mentioned Reflection Tries to Kill Her

Kearney took a step back, his attention darting between the Gabi dangling from the ceiling and the one staring at him and grinning.

Meanwhile, Calder had come out of the crawlspace and raced to his side. He noticed the grinning Gabi. "Weird-Eyes!" He took a step forward before pausing, noticing the strange Gabi's two green eyes. "You don't have weird eyes."

"I have Gabi's eyes, not weird eyes," she replied with a giggle.

Kearney's heart started beating faster. *Since when does Gabi talk like that?* "Calder, get back."

Calder stepped back beside Kearney then spotted the Gabi who was dangling ten feet in the air. He stammered in terror, "W-Weird-Eyes! What's goin' on? Why are there two o' 'em?"

"Gabi's" eyes widened, and she tilted her head. "Why are you scared, Calder?"

He started trembling, and Kearney took a step forward. "Is that the real Gabi up there?"

"She was the first Gabi, not the real one."

"That's not what I asked."

Annoyance crept into "Gabi's" voice. "She's the *first* Gabi," she repeated.

"What are you doing with her? Why are those strings tied to her?"

"The strings are important. They hold doll memories, but they can hold fleshy person memories, too. Like hers." She pointed up at the real Gabi. "The strings connect to everything. They connect to boxes, and that's how dolls can come back through them." She pointed to Calder. "Like you. And that's why I look like a Gabi now."

Calder hid behind Kearney, still watching "Gabi."

"Gabi touched a string. The string touched a box. I fell in the box. I came out looking like a Gabi." She stared up at the real Gabi wistfully. "And for the first time in a long time, I remembered something. But it wasn't my memory. It was hers." Her lips bent into an odd smile. "But that's okay. I'll just be her now."

Calder's eyes widened. "*Be her?* What does that even mean? You can't be her!"

"I can. I am."

"That's why you need her memories," Kearney said with dread in his voice. That would explain the laughter and images of the girl in the mirrors. They were Gabi's memories, connected to everything by the strings.

The strings suddenly tightened and tugged, causing Gabi to start twitching and muttering restlessly, tears streaming down her face as she gasped in pain.

Kearney's heart was beating in a frenzy. "You're hurting her!"

"Gabi" shrugged. "I know. It's easier to have just one Gabi anyway."

"*One* Gabi?"

"Yeah, me."

He shook his head before marching forward. "No. No, you're going to let her go right now!"

"Don't talk to your friend like that."

"You're not my friend. She is! Now let her go!" He lunged at her.

"Come closer, and I'll make the strings tighter. They'll hurt her more. She might even die."

He froze, his target's throat hovering just out of reach of his shaking hand. "You're going to kill her either way," he said slowly, his voice bone-chillingly low.

"But I'll make it hurt less if you're nice." She smiled.

There was no hesitation after that. He wrapped his hands around her throat with a roar and slammed her into the ground. "Let her go!"

Overhead, Gabi cried in pain as the strings tightened mercilessly around her, and Calder climbed onto a string and hurried towards her. He pulled out his scissor blade and started hacking away at the strings entangling her.

Meanwhile, Kearney's anxiety mixed with rage had him relentlessly punching Gabi's lookalike in the face as she squirmed in panic. His knuckles started bleeding from the sheer force he hit her with.

"Let! Her! Go!" he yelled with each punch. Then he froze with a gasp as his thoughts cleared, and he looked into the eyes of the person he was punching. *I'm...I'm hurting Gabi....* He let out a shuddering breath as the reality that he was punching wood and not flesh slipped away from him. He stared at her, and she stared back. *What's wrong with me...?*

"Freckles! You have to catch her!"

I'm a monster.... How could I have hurt her...?

"Freckles, hurry!"

Something slammed into him from above, leaving him lying dazed on the floor as his world plunged into darkness. He gasped for breath and fought the aching pain that had shot through his body, and as the black faded from his vision, he slowly lifted his head and saw "Gabi." Her scratched face was unreadable as she pulled herself to her feet and stumbled away.

He then looked at what had hit him: a person who was now lying unconscious on the ground beside him. It was the other Gabi. The real one.

He paused and stared at her before reality came crashing back in, and alarm rippled through his body as he rushed to her. "Gabi!" He held her close. She was breathing, but barely. He fought back tears as he cradled her. "I-I'm so s-s-sorry. You'll be okay. You'll b-be okay." *Calder told me to catch her. Why didn't I catch her? She could be dying, and it's all my fault. Why didn't I catch her?*

"Freckles! Is she okay?" Calder landed beside them.

"N-No, she's not," he whispered. "Why did you have t-to drop her...?"

"What did you want me to do? Let them strings get her?" Calder cried, panic seeping into his voice.

"K-Kearney."

He looked down at Gabi, whose eyes were barely open but looking at him. "Gabi," he choked out. "I'm s-so sorry."

She smiled, although the pain made her mouth twitch. "Why are you sorry? You saved me…." Her eyes fluttered shut, and she went limp in his arms again.

Kearney swallowed back his terror before glancing at Calder, who looked just as shaken as he felt. Now definitely wasn't the time to panic. He got to his feet, Gabi still in his arms.

He tried as best he could to keep his voice steady. "We need to get help."

Kearney sat by Gabi's bed, his bandaged hand gently holding hers. Every once in a while, he'd put a hand under her nose to make sure she was breathing, subconsciously holding his own breath in fear as he waited for her to exhale. Everything in the room was quiet, so quiet that he could hear Calder talking to Dakota behind the closed door behind him.

"*…An' she looked just like Weird-Eyes! But she didn't talk like her.*"

"*She mentioned she didn't have any memories before she became a Liar?*"

"I think so."

"A good place to start would be to find out if there are any missing Toy Town residents...."

The conversation slipped away from Kearney, and his mind became clouded with worry. *Why hasn't she woken up yet? Is she that hurt?* He pressed her hand against his forehead and groaned. Feeling so helpless made him sick.

The door opened, and he lifted his head to see Dakota holding a sheet of paper. "Mister Kearney," Dakota said as he walked toward him, "I made a sketch of what the culprit looks like." He turned the piece of paper around to show him.

Kearney frowned. It was essentially a drawing of Gabi, the only difference being that she had thick, angry brows scribbled over two green dots for eyes. "Everyone's just going to come after the real Gabi with a poster like that!"

Dakota lowered his head, his oversized police cap tipping as he did. "I thought it looked good."

Calder joined the conversation. "It *does* look good! Freckles don't know what he's talkin' about." He frowned at Kearney. "I'm gonna go help D'kota hang these around town, so you gotta stay here an' watch Weird-Eyes." Calder grabbed Dakota's hand and marched out of the room.

Even now, Kearney could tell Calder was trying to force something. Friendship, maybe. He wondered if he and Dakota used to be close. If they were, what could've made them end up the way they were now?

"Don't call her that," Kearney muttered.

Calder stopped and glanced over his shoulder. "What?"

"I said don't call her that. Her eyes aren't weird."

Calder stared at him, seemingly trying to decipher whatever was going on in Kearney's head. "Okay." He and Dakota left, leaving Kearney alone with his thoughts once more.

After a while of sitting in silence, his exhaustion started to set in. He leaned back in his chair, struggling to keep his eyes open, but he soon gave in and let them slide shut. The next time he opened them, it was because someone was talking to him.

"Kearney?"

He groaned. "What?"

"You look comfy and all, but you've been on my arm for so long it fell asleep."

He turned his head and saw Gabi, who had her head propped up against her pillow and was watching him. He then looked down at what he was lying on; it looked like he'd fallen sideways in his sleep and ended up with his head on her arm. He sat up, still groggy. "Sorry."

"It's okay." She smiled, but he could see her eyelids drooping.

He stared at her for a second, his mind still half asleep. Then he jumped with a start. "You're awake!"

She nodded. Her eyes were unfocused, and her brown hair was a mess.

He grabbed her by the shoulders in his excitement, his drowsy head spinning as he shouted questions in her face. "How are you feeling? How's your head? Are you bleeding anywhere? Does anything hurt? Are you—?"

She tried to push him away, clearly just as sleepy as he was and nowhere near as excited. "I'm okay. A little sore in some places, but otherwise, all good." She rubbed her arms, which were covered in cuts left by the strings.

He quickly pulled away from her. *What am I doing?* Blood was pounding in his ears as he tried to make sense of his own strange behavior. He stared at the scars on her arms, his cheeks turning red with shame. *If only I'd gotten to her sooner. If only we hadn't split up. If only I hadn't let her fall.* "I'm sorry."

"It's alright. I'd probably be reacting the same if I was in your shoes."

"No, I mean…earlier, when that *thing* had you tied up, I was supposed to catch you." He let out a tense sigh. "But I let you fall."

"You let me fall?" She stared at him in shock. "On purpose?"

"Of course not! It's just…." He lowered his head. "I wasn't focusing on the right thing at the time."

She still looked confused but seemed to better understand what he meant. "Well, don't worry about it anymore, okay? I forgive you." She smiled, trying to change the mood. She brushed her hair back and rubbed the sleep out of her eyes. "So, you saw her, right? I'm not crazy?"

He frowned. "I saw her."

She glanced at his bandaged hands. "Did she do that to you?"

"More like I did it to myself. While punching her."

"You *punched* her?"

"I did. A lot. And I hope she learned her lesson and stays away."

She shifted uneasily. "I think she'll probably be back. She seems pretty goal-oriented."

"Well, I'll take care of you. So, don't worry, okay?" He took her hand and squeezed it.

She closed her eyes, and her smile returned. "Thanks, Kearney."

He smiled back, but it started to fade when the image of the red-haired girl came back to him. "What does your sister look like?"

"My sister?" She furrowed her brow with a confused smile. "...I have one?"

Kearney stiffened. There was no way he was talking to that clone, was there? He started replaying the memory in his mind in an attempt to remember if he'd held the real Gabi or not earlier. "You do. You came here looking for her."

"*That's* why I came here?" She seemed fascinated by such an idea.

"Yes. You care about her a lot, you told me!"

"Help me remember her, then!" She started shaking. "What does she look like?"

He thought back to the girl in the mirror. "She...has red hair. And her eyes are kind of like...a teal color."

She nodded vigorously as if his descriptions were helping her remember. "What was her name?"

"I don't know, you never told me."

"Why wouldn't I tell you?" Her voice was quivering with anger, likely at herself.

"I don't know," he replied.

Her eyes fixed on the ceiling. Suddenly, they welled with tears. "It *feels* like I should remember her. So, why don't I?"

He wrapped his arms around her in the hopes of comforting her, but all he ended up with was a tear-soaked shoulder. "I remember the clone thing said the strings hold memories. Is it possible that it pulled some out of you?"

She stiffened. "What would've happened to me if that faker managed to pull all of them out?"

He hugged her tighter. "There's no need to think about that." It felt like he was saying those words more for himself than for her. "You should rest more. It might help."

She forced a smile, but it didn't hide the fear in her eyes. "I don't think it will." After another minute, her body stopped jerking from tears, and she was quietly resting in his arms. "...Kearney?"

"Yeah?"

"If those memories aren't with me, do you think they're with the faker?"

He fixed his gaze on the window. "Maybe." He remembered the exchange he'd overheard between Gabi and Calder. "I-I don't know if this is a bad time to ask, but…would you really leave Toy Town even if I didn't come with you?"

She looked up at him quizzically. "Why would you say that? You already know I want to leave, and I know you do, too. There's no reason for me to leave without you."

"I heard what you said to Calder. First, you told him he could take me to the Mister; then you told him you were perfectly fine leaving me altogether."

Her cheeks turned pink as she shoved him away. "I told him what he wanted to hear! I mean, honestly, did you really think I'd let him take you to the Mister?"

He stiffened. "I-I mean…I don't know."

"He's tiny, Kearney. All we'd have to do is walk away from him once we leave Toy Town, and he'd have no way of stopping us!"

He stared at her. "Why were you making a deal with him in the first place, then?"

"Because he knows this place like the back of his hand. Apparently, he used to be an officer before he got banished. He was Dakota's superior, even!"

Kearney's ears felt hot as blood pounded in them. "Oh." *I'm an idiot.* He cleared his throat with a shake of his head. "Well, this is embarrassing."

She nudged him with a smile. "I care about you, Kearney. I wouldn't leave you here, and I definitely wouldn't leave you with Calder." Her smile started to fade. "Speaking of all that…I'm not sure what I'll do now. I have to figure out how to get my memories back before I can go anywhere."

"We'll figure something out. If the faker could use strings to take your memories, you can probably get them back the same way."

She nodded. "That makes sense." She frowned when she saw the worried look on his face. "Why don't you go outside? You don't have to sit with me all day."

He shook his head. "No way. It's too soon."

She paused then gave him a sly grin. "Well, I was *going* to take your advice from before and nap, and I'd rather I slept here by myself."

"Fine, I'll leave you be." He sighed with a slight smile as he got to his feet and headed for the door. He rested the palm of his hand against the frame as he glanced back at her. "If you ever need anything, call me. And if the nurses don't let me in, I'll just climb through a window."

She chuckled. "Sounds like a plan."

After that, he left. He walked through the little hospital's waiting room, his hands in his pockets as he tried to block out the chatter of those around him, most of which were reckless—or just stupid—dolls who'd broken a limb or two and wanted to get them replaced.

Kearney overheard a conversation between two neighbors, both of whom were severely broken yet still had to be held back by nurses to ensure they didn't rip each other to shreds. Apparently, Neighbor #1 had kidnapped Neighbor #2 and turned her into a scarecrow to protect his crops. It was all fun and games until Neighbor #2 managed to escape and retaliated by stealing Neighbor #1's leg to use as a baseball bat. For his head.

Kearney marched past them all and soon made it outside. He leaned back against the building as he finally allowed himself to relax, taking in the silence that was just beyond the hospital's walls. He closed his eyes and told himself everything would be okay.

Briiiing!

Never mind. Nothing was okay.

He glanced to his right, where the payphone impatiently awaited him. He stared at it blankly as it continued to ring. *Why not?* He picked up the phone and held it to his ear.

"*You're lucky, y'know,*" the voice spat. "*If you'd picked up the first time, your friend wouldn't have as much as a scratch on her.*"

Guilt began to worm its way into Kearney's stomach, making him feel sick. The voice had helped him before; that much was true. So why hadn't he listened to what he had to say then? *Maybe nothing would've happened to Gabi if I had.* He shifted uneasily. "I still don't know why you're doing this. Why you care so much about...my safety."

The voice chuckled. "*The same reason a farmer cares about his prettiest, fattest cow. Sure, he'll have to chop it up at some point, but at least it might fetch him a few prizes before it croaks.*"

Kearney groaned when there was silence after that, and thrust the phone back into its place. It was creepy having the voice constantly pestering him, especially when he seemed to know so much. Too much.

He leaned against the wall as the voice's words echoed in his mind. *The same reason a farmer cares about his prettiest, fattest cow.*

That evening, Kearney went back to Gabi's room, but she was still asleep. He sat in the chair beside her bed as quietly as he could. He'd just come to say goodnight, and while he'd only planned on being there a few minutes, he wound up sitting there for a good while longer. During every minute he'd spent away from her that day, his mind had raced with all the possibilities of what could happen to her, and he finally felt peace seeing that she was safe. He decided to stay by her side for as long as he could before Dakota came to get him.

His eyes fixed on her face as he sank into his thoughts, and they soon trailed to a little cut on her cheek. He thought of Levi. When Levi was little, he hated getting cut, and whenever he did, he'd always ask Kearney to kiss it for him. He said it was something his mom used to do. Kearney smiled. *Levi would've hated being reminded of something like that.*

Soon, he found himself leaning forward until his face hovered over Gabi's. After a moment of hesitation, he cupped one of her cheeks in the palm of his hand. She shifted slightly, and her head tilted to the side, her cheek now resting more snugly in his hand. After a moment of stillness, he smiled. *She's so warm.*

He felt strange when he was around her. He felt things he'd never felt before. Things he didn't know how to fully explain. At first, he'd been nervous; her bursts of emotion had taken him aback, and her hand-holding had made him want to flinch away. Then she became his new Levi; everything she did made more sense to him. It was like he knew her well enough to expect it. Now, he *wanted* to hold her hand and keep her close. He loved the sound of her voice. Her warmth brought him peace. Her smile made him feel like everything would be okay.

He kept leaning closer. His fingers brushed against her cheek as he softly kissed the scar on the other.

Guilt jolted through him, and he pulled away with a shake of his head. *Don't do that again.* He'd somehow managed to scare himself by kissing a girl. *A girl!* He sat straighter, staring at the ceiling in horror. *Oh. No, no, no....* The problem wasn't that he'd kissed a girl. That wasn't the problem at all.

No...not her...not me...together...no....

His mind was flooded with a torrent of thoughts, and he was helpless to stop them. His saving grace came in the form of Dakota, who came into the room to let him know it was time to go back to the jail.

Kearney got to his feet and shot Gabi one last glance. *Give up now, Kearney. She deserves better than you.* Even when he was back in the jail, the torrent of thoughts didn't stop. They weren't about Gabi anymore, but that didn't matter. They kept pelting him as he lay in his cell.

Who's that faker? Where did it come from? He stared at the ceiling, rubbing his thumbs against each other as he fell deep into thought. Messy, disorganized thoughts, all questions without answers that brought him no comfort.

Who is the Mister, really? Why do the dolls love him so much? Why does he live behind the Wall? Is he hiding from something? The only thing here that's really dangerous is Jolly. Who was the mummy in Jolly, anyway?

In a heartbeat, his thoughts shifted to a completely new topic. *The voice on the phone. Who is he? How do his phones pop up everywhere? And why do they feel so weird?* His fingernails were digging into his skin without his notice. *How did the Mister make this weird place? Why make dolls? Is he even alive if nobody's seen him in forever? Is the voice on the phone related to him? Is Jolly?*

He shook his head before his eyes drifted to Gabi's empty cell. *I wish Gabi was here.*

Chapter 17

Everything Blows Up

Although Kearney didn't realize it, he was rubbing his thumb against the bar of chocolate in his hand so much that it had started to melt. He stared at the door to Gabi's room. He didn't know why, but the nurse wouldn't let him in, and the only reason he could think of was that something must've gone so horribly wrong last night that Gabi's life was now hanging on by a thread. That was the only reasonable explanation.

He snapped out of his thoughts when the door swung open, and the little nurse pitter-pattered her way out. When her eyes skipped to him, she nodded curtly then was on her way. He jumped to his feet and hurried to the room but stopped when he almost slammed into The Tailor, who'd just come out.

He stared at her. "What were you doing?"

"That doesn't matter to you." She brushed past him and marched away. Then she paused. "When you're done fawning over her, meet me outside. I'll be waiting."

Dumbfounded, Kearney watched as she left. Then he shook his head and headed into Gabi's room. As soon as he entered, she smiled, which put his mind at ease.

"Good morning," she said.

"Morning." He handed her the now-limp chocolate bar. "I got this for you."

She took it from him, staring as it flopped to the side in her grip. "What did you do to this poor thing?" she asked with a laugh.

He stared at it. "I…have no idea." He reached for it. *I'll get her another.*

"What are you doing?"

He paused awkwardly. "I just thought I'd get a new one."

"Oh, it's fine. Sorry if I came off as ungrateful at first. Also, thank you."

He nodded slowly, still trying to comprehend whether she was upset or not. "Of course."

He stared anxiously at his shoes. Since yesterday, all he'd been able to think about were *those* feelings. He felt ashamed. Worse yet, he felt hopeless. No matter what he did, there was nothing he could do to either affirm those feelings or deny them.

She watched him, her brow knitting with concern, before inviting him to sit. "So, The Tailor just left," she began.

Kearney felt himself ease up. Talking helped. It was distracting. "I noticed. What did you talk about?"

"Mainly stuff about the clone. She said she was going to get to the bottom of it." Her mouth twisted into a frown. "She talked about you a lot, too. I think you've impressed her."

"Huh." He stared at the ceiling. *And now she wants to talk to me. I wonder what's going on.* His attention shifted back to Gabi when he felt her take his hand. He felt his cheeks get hot.

"You okay?" she asked.

He nodded.

"I'm alright if that's what's bothering you." She grinned. "And I'll be perfectly safe here, so feel free to go about your day."

He squeezed her hand as a smile cracked across his lips. "I'll make sure not to pester you."

She laughed. "That's very considerate." She bit her lip. "Hey, Kearney...?" She shook her head anxiously. "Never mind."

"What is it?"

"It's nothing, really. I wouldn't want to bother you with dumb questions or anything."

He smiled. "You can bother me as much as you want."

She smiled back, although it didn't reach her eyes. "Well," she began, "I feel like you might've come back yesterday. When I was less awake."

He froze, and all those feelings came back like a gut punch to the stomach. At least she knew of his sins.

"And, I could've sworn you..." the fingers of her free hand were fidgeting with the blanket, "...kissed me." Her eyes darted to him. "On the cheek! I meant on the cheek!"

Kearney felt beads of sweat forming on his forehead. "I-It wasn't a weird thing or anything like that." *What was it, then?*

"Right!" She looked just as panicked as he was. "And don't get me wrong. I wasn't, like, *pretending* to be asleep or anything weird like that, just...."

"...I n-noticed a scar on your cheek, and...."

"...I was kind of half awake, and the only thing I really knew was that you were there...."

"...I felt bad right after...."

"...The moment I really came to was when my cheek felt warm, and I saw you, so I figured...."

They both paused and stared at each other, their faces red. She looked away with a small smile. "It was sweet of you."

Isn't this the part where she turns me down? "You're not mad?"

She shrugged. "Not really, I guess."

"I-I won't do it again."

"Kearney, I already told you I'm not mad."

"I won't." He shook his head with resolve.

She sighed then smiled. "Alright."

He cleared his throat and rose to his feet, his shoulders rigid. "I'll go now."

"You don't have to."

He stared at her. "Do...you want me to stay?"

She looked a bit anxious. "If you don't mind." She cleared her throat, trying to hide her apprehension. "It's really boring around here. I like talking to you."

He sat back down. "Okay."

They stared at each other. Gabi remembered the melted chocolate bar in her hand. "I'm sorry about yesterday. At the Mirror House," she said as she pulled away the wrapper and handed him a slightly melted piece. "I didn't mean to upset you or anything when I mentioned…you-know-who. I felt bad about it ever since. I promise I won't bring him up again."

Kearney stared at the little square of chocolate between his fingers. "I'm not mad. It wasn't your fault." If anything, he was glad she'd snapped him out of his strange funk. Forget about Levi? What was wrong with him? Why would he ever want to forget his little brother? It didn't matter how much it hurt; he'd always love Levi. "I can tell you a bit about him. If you want."

She looked stunned. "If you don't mind."

He nodded, still staring at the piece of chocolate. "He was my little brother. Or, he wasn't my *real* brother, but I always thought of him as one. He was…a lot of fun." Only half of his mouth curved upward when he smiled. That dull grief returned, and he tried to swallow it back. "He was a collector. And a bit of an actor. And also a thief."

Gabi smiled. "He sounds adorable."

"He was." There was a raging ocean of emotions in him—guilt, grief, shame. But in the midst of the darkness of the storm, there was a tiny rock, sitting in a patch of sunlight, where he could sit and feel safe. Sitting on that rock reminded him that he would always love Levi. And that Levi always loved him. But even then, his stomach still felt queasy. He stared at his shoes. *But…I never even got to tell him that I….*

"Thanks. For sharing that with me. He must've been so lucky to have you as his brother." She wrapped her arms around him as tears welled in her eyes. "I'm sorry. I feel like I should be able to say more than I am now to comfort you. After all, I've experienced it, too, since...." her voice trailed off.

He hugged her back as he lowered his head to see her face better. "You okay?"

She was frozen in place, still clinging to him. Her eyes were anxious as they studied the floorboards. "No." She looked up at him. "I thought I lost someone, but I don't really remember." She pulled away from him, her head lowered. "I'm sorry. I don't know what's going on in my head right now," she muttered.

He gave her a reassuring shoulder pat, now very much ready to end the hug. "It's probably just your memory messing with you again."

There was a knock at the door. They both glanced at it. *"Mr. Kearney,"* a voice called from the other side. *"The Tailor is waiting for you."*

Gabi's eyes narrowed. "What does she want?"

Kearney rose to his feet. "I guess I'll find out soon enough." He gave her a reassuring smile. "Focus on resting today, okay?"

She groaned dramatically. "Yes, Doctor Kearney."

He chuckled and headed for the door.

"And Kearney?"

He paused to look back at her.

"I hope you have a great day."

He smiled. "You, too." He closed the door behind him.

She...likes me back. He felt something swell in his chest. *I can tell. She likes me back.* Then he shrank. *Crap. She likes me back.* She was the last person on Earth he deserved. If anything, confessing his feelings would be a disservice to her. She could do much, much better than *him.*

He shoved his hands into his hoodie pockets and kept walking. He stared at his feet as he walked. As soon as he stepped out of the building, The Tailor headed over to him.

"Nice to see you finally wrapped up your little lovefest in there," she said. She raised a brow when she saw the dreary look on his face. "I assume somebody died?"

His ears turned pink as he cleared his throat. "You wanted to talk to me?"

"I did." She adjusted her cufflinks as she explained, "While Gabi is incapacitated, you're going to help me. Dakota provided me with some information on Gabi's doppelganger, so I've launched an investigation."

Kearney watched her carefully. It was fascinating how a tiny doll like her could carry such an air of dignity everywhere her little feet took her. She looked like she was barely scraping nine years old yet talked like she was nine hundred.

He straightened himself as he tried to focus on the task at hand. "Why do you want my help? You have plenty of officers."

"Truthfully, I'd like to see the full extent of your capabilities. And if you want a more viable reason, I'll have you know my men can hardly seem to handle her."

"Really?" His brow went up.

She nodded, her arms crossed in annoyance. "Some of them just happen to be at the center of Exhibit A. So, unless you plan on running back into your dear Gabi's arms until I inevitably drag you away, let's begin our investigation."

Kearney looked around him in bewilderment. He was standing in a warehouse full of those red boxes from the factory. They had been carefully put away and, according to The Tailor, were guarded at every hour of every day. However, there were no guards present when they came to the warehouse, mainly because all of the guards had been taken apart and strung up like toys inside the warehouse. The same sentence was painted on each of their empty husks, over and over in various clashing colors.

GABI'S A LIAR. GABI'S A LIAR.

"Quite a sight, isn't it?" The Tailor sounded annoyed at most.

"Do you know when she did this?" Kearney asked quietly, trying to remind himself that those were chunks of wood swinging from the ceiling, not actual body parts.

"Sometime after the bell tower rang last night. At least, that's when the report came in."

He furrowed his brow. "And after that?"

"Nothing except for the additional statement from the doll who made the report."

"Which was?"

"That he'd seen Gabi walking out of the factory."

"But she's been in bed."

"Case in point." The Tailor pulled a needle out of her pocket for her fingers to fidget with. "I've been given the doll's address, so we'll head there next. If anything, I have a picture to identify him with." She started walking and gestured for him to join her. Kearney nodded curtly and started walking at her side. They walked in complete silence, which seemed to annoy her. After a bit, she glanced at him with a playful look. "Awfully serious now, aren't you? I've heard you can be quiet at times, but you haven't made so much as a peep so far."

He glanced back at her. "Why shouldn't I be serious?"

"Well, I just think your reasons for wanting the clone neutralized are more...shall we say personal?"

"Personal," he echoed.

"Yes. Either you're not good at keeping secrets, or I'm just very good at reading people. Take your pick."

He knew exactly what she meant, and he was terrified of the idea that it was that obvious. "Secrets?"

"Well, it's obvious you like her. I'm sure she knows it, too."

She does. She definitely does. That's the problem. "I just care a lot about her," he quietly replied.

"Care a lot because you like her," she toyed.

He vehemently shook his head.

She looked away with a smile. "What was it that Gabi mentioned in her report about missing memories?"

He was caught off-guard by the shift in topic. "Her memories of her sister, mainly. She's already talking about getting them back."

"You both are awfully persistent. Maybe that's why you're so drawn to her." The Tailor chuckled. Then her amused look faded. "Keep in mind, persistence can be a flaw at times, and being too similar through your flaws can be more of a death sentence than a gift."

Kearney felt a knot twist in his stomach.

"...Or maybe that's just my personal experience talking." She raised her head to look at the buildings they were passing by. "We're heading to that purple one there. Third floor."

His attention snapped to the house, and they were quickly met by a little doll with curly red hair in a police suit. He saluted as The Tailor came up to him.

"Report," she ordered.

"The witness is gone, ma'am," he replied, still in his stiff pose.

"Gone?"

"He jumped out the window."

She sputtered with anger. "He fell three stories and still got away from you?" she snapped.

"He was really fast, ma'am." The officer's voice was shaky.

The Tailor balled her fists as she struggled to keep them from flying into the redhead's face. "Which way did he go?"

"He was headed toward the Ferris wheel, ma'am."

"At least you saw that. Now get out of my sight."

The officer kept anxiously playing with the cuffs of his sleeves. "Ma'am?"

She sighed as she crossed her arms. "Yes?"

"Please be nice to him. He's not acting like himself."

She seemed intrigued by that remark. "How so?"

"He's been missing work a lot. And...the two of us are friends, but he doesn't even seem to remember me."

"Alright, then." She nodded slowly. "Be on your way."

The officer shuffled off, and The Tailor started heading toward the Ferris wheel. "Follow me," she ordered to Kearney before vanishing into the hundreds of dolls in the streets.

Kearney quickly realized how difficult it was to keep up with her. She kept her pace and didn't look back at him once. Meanwhile, he struggled not to trip over the sea of little heads swimming around his waist. She weaved through the crowd like an eel in a reef while he was the bumbling scuba diver trying to keep track of her. Fortunately, they soon made it out the other side of the crowd and reached the Ferris wheel.

The Tailor put her hands on her hips as she looked around, dissatisfied when the doll they were searching for was nowhere to be seen. The place was already crawling with police, and it seemed they weren't having any luck.

After talking with them, she turned to face Kearney, her face knotted in a frown. "Search the Ferris wheel. There has to be some indicator he was here, and if we're lucky, a clue to where he's going next. Search every booth."

"All of them?"

"Yes. Now."

With a reluctant nod, Kearney went through all the booths until the Ferris wheel had done a full rotation, and the only clue he came back with was a small circle etched into one of the booth's windows.

That was more than enough for The Tailor. She hurried over to it, dragging Kearney with her. They entered the booth, and the Ferris wheel kept slowly turning. The Tailor peeked through the little circle etched into the window during the ride, waiting to see something of interest.

He watched her carefully. "This is the edge of Toy Town. There's nothing to see over there but an empty desert. Why would he leave a circle, anyway?"

"I know that," she hummed in reply. "And the reason I suspect he's left this circle is because it's a punishable offense to vandalize the Ferris wheel in any way. Like many things in this place, the Ferris wheel is a gift from my dearest, 'the Mister.' Liars aren't residents here, per se, so they hardly care about our laws." She gasped, tapping his arm to usher him closer. "Look."

He peered through the circle and spotted a small shed far in the distance. "You think he's there?"

"Going there, yes. It should take him at least half a day to get through security and out of town, so we still have a chance to catch him."

"Why would he leave a circle?"

"It might be a message to someone else, not that I have any clue who. Another Liar, perhaps. We seem to have a lot of those around here lately."

Kearney paused. He remembered Dakota saying that same word the other day as well. *Liar.* "What's a Liar?"

"Liars happen when dolls are beyond helping. Instead of coming out of the boxes as themselves, they come out with the faces and memories of others. Their minds have been shattered beyond repair, and it's best not to bother helping them at all."

"Oh." He could only imagine how horrible it must feel to be a Liar, to be stuck with a face that never belonged to you. Were all Liars as desperate as Gabi's clone was? "So, would the suspect be heading to those big gates?" he asked, shifting the conversation back on track.

"The ones you climbed over?" She smirked knowingly. "No. There's a post farther west where lost dolls can enter the city. It's heavily guarded, but dolls coming *in* are the guards' main concern. Dolls going out won't even be glanced at twice."

The booth reached the ground, and when its door swung open, the pair hurried out. The Tailor quickly commandeered a tiny car delivering textiles, leaving its driver watching helplessly as she and Kearney rode off. They both hopped out once they made it to the station, where The Tailor waved down a guard.

His eyes went wide when he recognized her. "Missus!"

She stared at him for a moment, almost looking confused. She quickly recollected herself. "Yes, yes. Have you seen a doll who looks like this?" She held up the photo for him.

"Eri?" The guard smiled. "Sure. He was just here today!"

"Really?" She mocked a smile in return before dropping it to reveal her annoyance. "Did he leave?"

"Not long ago, yeah." He shifted nervously. "Is he in trouble?"

"Perhaps," she replied curtly. She started walking past him.

He seemed to be more at ease now and turned to talk to her some more. "Missus—?"

The Tailor unsheathed the sword-sized needle that had been strapped onto her back. She swung it at the guard without hesitation, cutting his head clean in two. His body crumpled to the ground, and everyone in the station stopped what they were doing to stare at the unfortunate doll.

Kearney's mouth gaped open in horror. "Why did you—?"

"Believe it or not, that guard is mute. Or, at least, the *real* him is." She swung her needle around to point it at the other guards ahead of her. "I never expected this of all places to be crawling with Liars," she spat. She took a step toward them, and they all stepped back in response. "I have a strong feeling our little friend is still here, and his accomplices here are trying to keep us at bay until he escapes. Soon, we'll know why." Without another word, she rushed at them.

Shredded wood flew everywhere in her wake. It was like she'd become the woodchipper version of the Grim Reaper.

Kearney watched her in fascination and horror. When he managed to pry his attention away from the spectacle, he noticed a pair of eyes farther in the back watching the scene as well. The moment they met each other's gazes, the stranger hurried away. Kearney raced after the doll, almost feeling bad for the poor guy. But the face matched the picture, and he had a job to do.

He raced around the corner, and the doll started pushing boxes in his way in a panic, causing one of them to spill its contents: at least a hundred tiny metal birds. They all flew into the air while singing in excitement, and Kearney blocked his face to protect it from the flurry of metal swirling around him.

The doll yelped when he reached a dead end. He grabbed a bird and thrust it forward for Kearney to see. "S-Stay back, or I'll set it off!"

Set it off? Kearney stepped back and forced a smile, hoping that would put the anxious doll at ease. "Are you Eri?"

The doll backed away. "Stay back!" he shrieked as he held the bird close to his chest, his fingers hovering over the wind-up key on the bird's back. "I'm warning you!"

"He's not Eri," The Tailor cut in as she sauntered toward him with sawdust from her victims still in her hair, the tip of her needle now much more worn than it had been before. "And that's why he's protecting our little friend, the clone. Isn't it? The same way your friends back there were protecting you?"

"I-I'm not protecting her," he stammered. "She's insane! Everyone's scared of her! She's...she's *more* broken than any Liar I've ever seen!"

"Funny you knew who she was just by seeing her once," she commented. "Liars tend to sniff out other Liars pretty easily, don't they?"

Eri shifted uneasily.

Kearney squinted as he stared at Eri. "How did you know he's a Liar?"

"Because, according to my research and the previously seen praise of others, Eri is a very punctual person," she explained. "So punctual, in fact, that he even received a promotion at work thanks to his dependability. Meanwhile, *this* Eri hasn't been at work for the last two weeks. And while that can be explained in a number of ways, what can't be explained is how he doesn't even seem to recognize any of his coworkers anymore."

The Liar named Eri stared at her. "I didn't do any-thing," he quietly protested.

"I know you didn't." She took a step toward him. "I assure you, you'll be perfectly safe in Toy Town. Just put the keykatoo down. Slowly."

He shook his head. "I know how you are with Liars. Y-You can pretend all you want, but you won't trick me like you did the others! Even here, you hurt all of my friends without even blinking!" He looked down at the keykatoo in his hands and started winding it up. He squeezed his eyes shut. "I never asked to be Eri.... *I never asked to be Eri!*"

With a mechanical *cheep*, the keykatoo started unfurl-ing its wings as the key on its back twisted. The keyka-toos around them sang with excitement, riled up by the *cheeps* of their wound-up companion.

The Tailor grabbed Kearney's hand and started run-ning.

"I thought we needed him!" Kearney cried.

"I prefer to keep myself in one piece over being blown up by a Liar!" They raced out of the building, and she covered her ears. Kearney looked back as the sound of the keykatoos' singing flooded the air. Moments later, their song was followed by a giant *kaboom*. The station burst into flames, sending debris and wood soaring every which way, and Kearney flew back. He fell flat on his back and quickly scooted away from the blooming fire. The air around him had gotten so hot it felt like he was in an oven.

The Tailor had managed to stay on her feet. She brushed ash out of her braids, then offered her hand to pull Kearney back up. He could hear the sound of screams around him and could see dolls racing away from the fire while firemen hurried toward it. He glanced at The Tailor, whose brow was knit in a line. "This is going to be hard to clean up," she commented.

"That's all you're thinking about?" he asked in disbelief.

"What else is there? The victims will wind up back here eventually, but my reputation won't be an easy thing to restore if I'm not swift." She crossed her arms. "You humans think in such interesting terms. Death, pain, time.... We dolls have lost touch with those aspects of life." She stared at the fire, her eyes wistful. Then she cleared her throat. "You've been a helpful resource today. You may leave now."

Kearney was still in a haze. "But the investigation—"

"The investigation was a tremendous success."

He stared at her in befuddlement. "It was?"

"It was."

He stood beside her, utterly stupefied.

She glanced at him again. "Is there something more you want to ask?"

He fidgeted his fingers. The smell of smoke made the air feel even thicker. "H-How was it a success?"

"That's confidential."

"Oh." He looked back at the flowering flames. "I've been wondering...you mentioned something before about a personal experience you had. If Gabi and I were to…you know, do you think we'd end up like you did?" *Is there a chance it could work? Just the slightest chance?*

The Tailor clasped her hands as she stared at the crackling fire, her eyes unreadable as the fire's glint glowed in them. At first, it seemed like she wouldn't reply, which wouldn't have surprised him, but then she spoke. "I'm sure you two would fare much better than I ever could with Henry."

"Henry? Who's that?"

She paused before giving a half-chuckle. "He was my right hand for a while. We grew…quite fond of each other, and it helped that we had a shared love of who the lowlifes here call 'the Mister.' A crude name, I think. His real one suits him just fine." Her eyes trailed from the fire to Kearney. "I've been behind the Wall before, through every nook and cranny of the place. I went through it all with Henry. We were trying to reach Phantasos, and I truly believed we could get there together." She crossed her arms with a heavy sigh. "Henry abandoned me right at the end."

Kearney had forgotten about the Wall. It felt like no one around here really talked about it. "I'm…sorry to hear that," he said.

She shook her head. "I don't need your pity. That aside, if I were in his shoes back then, I probably would've done the same."

"Really?"

She nodded. "The only real difference between him and me was that he loved Phantasos in ways I have too much dignity to ever stoop to."

"Maybe it's better that you never reached Phantasos," he began slowly, "because now, you get to focus all your attention on Toy Town."

Suddenly, she laughed. "I've never heard anything more ridiculous!"

He flinched back in confusion and embarrassment. He didn't even know what he was supposed to feel embarrassed about.

Once her laughter died down, she gave him an amused smile. "You have some interesting ideas, don't you?" She crossed her arms as she regained her composure. "Today was a pleasant experience, little friend. I'll be sure to arrange something similar in the future."

"What's that supposed to mean? You're not planning on letting a felon loose for us to catch, are you?" he asked half-playfully. His other half genuinely believed she'd do it and was now worried he'd inspired her.

"What would be the point in that?" She smiled again. "I have a plan, Kearney. And the more time passes, the more sure I am that you'll have a grand part to play in it."

He tensed. Whatever she was planning, he wanted no part in it. Simply put, The Tailor wasn't the perfect picture of morality.

But he had one more question. "How did you know those other guards were Liars? Sure, you knew about that one who talked to you, but there was no way for you to know the rest were as well. Not on a whim like that."

She didn't reply but seemed intrigued by where he was going.

"…You said that Liars sniff out other Liars easily," he continued. Revelation slowly came over him as he spoke those words. He stared at her in bewilderment.

She smirked. "Without a doubt." She then sauntered away.

Past Toy Town's gates loomed the Wall, so tall that it blocked the sun's light and trapped the city in an eternal sunset. The smoke billowing from the fire turned that pretty peach sky an ugly soot black.

Chapter 18

Gabi Starts a Fan Club

Kearney was on that bridge again, but now, he was staring at the river beneath him — the river the white car had just disappeared into. He felt his heart leaping in his chest, almost as if it was begging him to do something. But he just kept staring. He had to do something; he knew he did. But that was the only thought he could think. He had to do something.

The fog in his mind started to clear, and he leaned against the crooked guardrails that the car had plowed through. He had to do something. He kept leaning forward.

Do something.

He squeezed his eyes shut, and the next time he opened them, he was falling. He looked up as the bridge got farther away then looked down as the unforgiving torrent of water got closer. He plunged into it, icy water stinging his skin and forcing him awake.

Kearney jumped, coughing up water as he looked around frantically, expecting to have just been pulled out of a lake and resuscitated or something along those lines. But that wasn't the case at all. In fact, he was in his cell, just wetter. He quickly spotted Calder, who had an empty bucket in his hands.

He grinned. "Rise an' shine, Freckles."

Kearney stared at him vacantly, too tired to yell and already being reclaimed by his sleepiness.

Calder frowned. "I got you wet so you don't go dozin' off again. Now, on yer feet! D'kota's waitin'."

Kearney dragged himself out of his cell and followed him. *Maybe Dakota can have me wake everyone up for a change, and Calder's rude awakening can be getting tossed off a cliff.* They headed outside the jail, where Dakota and Gabi were talking and waiting.

It had been four days since the clone had attacked Gabi, and The Tailor ordered Dakota to keep the prisoners—if you could really call them that anymore—in jail while the situation was further investigated. At this point, the clone had vanished without a trace, and The Tailor was comfortable letting Kearney and the others get back to work. Gabi had almost fully recovered, and she insisted on coming along.

"Good morning!" She skipped over, linking her elbow with Kearney's before he could react. When she realized how soggy he was, she could hardly stifle her laughter.

His frown only deepened. How she could be so cheery at what felt like such an ungodly hour was beyond him. As they walked and she talked, his annoyance subsided. He felt more relieved than anything else.

She was safe and back to her old self, and he couldn't ask for anything more.

They kept talking until the bell atop the giant tower they were headed toward started ringing. Dakota and Calder stopped dead in their tracks and stared up at it. Kearney and Gabi exchanged confused glances. Kearney looked around and noticed that the town's hustle and bustle had completely vanished. Everyone was staring at the bell. Kearney turned back to Gabi, whose eyes were wide.

"Are they part of a cult or something?" she whispered. "This is *freaky!*"

Even though she was being completely serious, he struggled to stifle a chuckle. The look on her face was priceless. The bell rang a few more times, its chimes echoing throughout the town until it finally stopped swaying. Once it had gone quiet, the dolls immediately went back to their business. Their chatter filled the streets once again. Dakota and Calder kept walking as if nothing had happened, and Kearney struggled to keep himself from bursting into laughter at the terrified look stuck on Gabi's face.

Calder seemed to notice, as well. "What's goin' on, Gabs? You swallow a slug?"

She stared at him in befuddlement. "*What* did you call me?" She shook her head, trying to refocus her thoughts. She looked at Kearney. "I'm not the only one wondering about what just happened, right?"

"That was weird," he reassured her.

Calder glared at them indignantly. "Well, it's not to *us*. The Bell Tower is a gift from the Mister 'imself! Toy Town's got people takin' care of that thing all the time!"

"Well, clearly, they're not doing a good job. It rang fourteen times. There's no fourteen o'clock," Kearney said.

"It's not supposed to tell the time, you idiot!"

"Anyway," Dakota interjected, pulling Calder away, "the people who work there are the reason we're going there."

Calder stared at him with disbelief. "Becca an' Bens?"

Dakota nodded. "They've been fighting a lot with Ms. The Tailor lately, so she wants them gone."

"So, we're just doin' her dirty work this time 'round?" Calder crossed his arms.

"I guess." Dakota swallowed uneasily. "I like them a lot, but I'm supposed to listen to Ms. The Tailor first. Promise you'll be nice to them, please?"

Gabi sighed as she patted Dakota on the head. "Don't worry, we will." She glanced at Kearney. "Won't we?"

He nodded with a smile.

Dakota's eyes lit up. "Thank you, please!" He spun around and resumed the journey to the Bell Tower, and the other three followed close behind. "Becca and Benny are really nice," Dakota explained as they arrived in front of the tower, "but Becca gets scared easily, so be careful, please." With a loud grunt, he kicked open the door, which seemed to have been locked prior to that point.

Kearney had never expected to see Dakota do something like that. He suddenly wasn't sure if he was in reality or still in his cell dreaming of being in an action movie. He looked over his shoulder, expecting a poorly edited CGI explosion to come next. When none came, he was very disappointed. Either this was a really exciting day where Dakota kicked down doors or a very boring action movie dream.

As he headed inside the Bell Tower, he looked around, studying the giant room carefully. Admittedly, it was a pretty cozy place, with a soft, blue carpet and shelves full of gadgets and toys, and the walls were covered in ticking clocks, which he hadn't seen anywhere else in this place so far. The clocks all seemed to be showing different times, so it seemed they were all useless. His eyes trailed to a set of bunk beds covered in stickers and drawings. One of the drawings was of three stick figures holding hands. While he didn't recognize the first two, he noticed the third one had the same black hair and blue eyes as Dakota.

He glanced back at everyone else. Dakota was heading up a ladder while calling the others to join. After everyone else had followed after Dakota, Kearney climbed up, and once he reached the next floor, he paused to look around. It almost felt like he was being watched. He looked over his shoulder and spotted a pair of blue eyes staring at him through a hanging trench coat in the corner.

He grabbed the coat and tore it away, exposing the rack it had been hanging on and a dismembered doll head sitting on top. He stared at the head while Gabi, who'd just noticed, jumped back with a shriek. To the head's dismay, Kearney proceeded to pick it up.

"Why'd you have to do that?" the head asked.

"Because you're a helpless head, and I couldn't resist."

"It wasn't very nice," the head replied, furrowing his brow.

"I guess it wasn't. Sorry." Kearney shrugged. "I'm Kearney, and the screaming one's Gabi. Are you Benny?"

"That I am, mister."

Silence followed before Gabi, after staring at Benny long enough, mustered the wits to ask, "Where's the rest of you?"

"I don't have it anymore. We broke it."

"*How?*" Her face was all eyes.

"You and your sister, right?" Kearney cut her off.

Benny glanced back at him. "Yep. Speaking of which, she's going to get really freaked out when she sees you. I can tell you guys are fleshy people."

"Everyone keeps saying that like we're monsters."

Dakota and Calder froze when footsteps sounded overhead, causing little dust clouds to rain down from the ceiling.

Kearney glanced back at them. "That's Becca?"

"Prob'bly." Calder looked up and spotted a doll with the same brown hair as Benny staring down at them from behind a railing that surrounded the floor above.

Her green eyes grew huge when they met his, and she quickly ducked behind the rails and out of his view.

"Hey, wait!" Gabi took off after her and was up the stairs in a heartbeat, leaving the others to watch. Becca turned on her heel and raced up the ladder that led to the roof, her pursuer hot on her tail. "Stop running!" Gabi yelled as she grabbed hold of the ladder. Becca only glanced at her once before reaching the top and racing out of her view.

Kearney groaned with embarrassment. "Sorry. Gabi's a little intense sometimes."

Benny frowned. "You have to keep her on a leash or something?"

Meanwhile, Gabi kept hurrying after Becca. "Nobody's going to hurt you! You saw your brother down there, didn't you?" she called out. "He can tell you himself!" She panted for breath as she scrambled to the Bell Tower's roof, where she spotted Becca jumping from the balcony's rails to the bell hanging in the middle. It looked like she was about to lose her grip on the bell and fall, but she managed to hang on and scramble her way up. She wrapped her arms around the rope the bell hung from, locked eyes with Gabi, then quickly began to climb up.

Gabi looked up at her helplessly. "At least listen to what I have to say!"

"I saw you with Dakota. I know why you're here!" Becca looked over her shoulder as she kept climbing. "You're a liar, and you took Benny. Why would I listen?"

"He's okay, really. If you just come down, I'll show you."

"I don't believe you," Becca whispered as she clung to the rope, her face hidden behind her quivering fingers. "Please, leave."

"I'm not a liar." Gabi's voice softened. "If you take my hand, I won't let anything bad happen to you or your brother, promise."

Becca finally looked squarely at her. "What about the others? There's more than one of you, you know."

"Kearney wouldn't hurt a fly, Calder's all bark and no bite, and Dakota really cares about you guys."

Becca looked doubtful. "He does?"

"Of course."

"And what about The Tailor?" There was indignation in Becca's eyes now. "Benny and I helped her build Toy Town, but now she hates us! She made everyone else hate us, too. There's no fixing that now!"

Gabi paused, her lips flattened in a white line. "That's a good point," she admitted. "But...don't forget the people that don't hate you. Those are your real friends."

"Like Dakota?"

"Exactly. If anyone can help you out, it's him, right?"

"Right, but...." Becca groaned with irritation. "But it's not that easy."

"You're right, it's not. But you should know that whatever you do, The Tailor will find you. The only difference if you run now would be that you'd be all alone. No Dakota or Benny."

Becca's brow furrowed with indignation as she shook.

"That's not a threat. Just a simple fact." Gabi extended her hand. "Take my hand, and you won't be alone. I promise."

Becca stared at her hand conflictedly. She started to reach for it.

They both flinched at the sudden sound of crashing coming from the floor beneath them, followed by yelling and chaos. Calder was screaming, as was Dakota, but the only person who was saying actual words was Kearney.

"Gabi!" he cried. "Gabi, get out of there!" The sound of heavy machinery cut off his shouting, and moments later, everything fell eerily silent. Then came the sound of someone slowly making their way up the ladder toward them.

Becca's shaking intensified. "It's The Tailor. I bet she came to kill me herself," she whispered.

Gabi slowly shook her head. "…That person sounds too big to be her."

Soon, the footsteps stopped, and a pair of hands crept into view and firmly set themselves on opposite sides of the gap in the floor. They pulled the rest of the body up, and once the stranger's feet were firmly planted on solid ground, they stood up and stared Gabi in the eye with a smile. "Hi, first Gabi."

Becca's eyes widened as she let out a small squeak of terror. "Sh-She looks just like you! Is she a Liar?"

"She's not a liar, Becca." Gabi stiffened as she stared back at the faker. "But she has her own set of problems, that's for sure."

"No, a *Liar*." Becca's eyes grew even wider. "A doll with a stolen face."

Gabi's eyes shifted from Becca back to the clone. "I guess I know what I'll call you now."

"I'm *Gabi*." The clone's face scrunched up in resentment. "You turned out to be pretty rude. I think I'll make a much nicer Gabi than you."

Gabi's amused expression faded. "What did you do to the others?"

"They're fine." The clone shrugged. "Now, let's talk about *you*."

"Me?"

"Yes!" The clone grinned as she took a step toward her. "Let's talk about *Gabi*. About what makes her so special."

Gabi stiffened uneasily. "What are you doing?"

"Trying to learn how to be the best Gabi possible." The clone grabbed her arm excitedly. "We…We can be a club! Think of how fun that'd be. A Gabi club, even!"

"Do you think I'm an idiot?" Gabi pushed her back. "Stop trying to be all buddy-buddy. You tried to kill me!"

The clone stared at her before dropping her cheery façade. All that remained was a terrifying hunger in her eyes. "I need more," she said quietly. "It's not enough to only have a few memories. I need more of them." She reached for Gabi again. "*All* of them."

Gabi slapped her hand away, taking a shaky step back. "You're not getting them. If anything, I'm getting *mine* back."

The clone stared. "I don't see why. They're not anything special."

Gabi rolled up her sleeves, wincing as she agitated the cuts on her arms. She seemed very ready to fight the person that had bested her before.

"Don't fight her!" Becca shrieked. "You're going to get hurt!"

The clone smirked. Then she rushed forward and grabbed Gabi. The two spun around, yelling as they tussled until Gabi had successfully pushed the clone up against the rails. The clone grinned, grabbed the collar of Gabi's shirt, and leaned back, falling over the rails and off the roof and taking Gabi with her.

Chapter 19

Gabi Punches Herself

Kearney thrashed wildly in an attempt to free himself from his strange cage as he heard the sounds of fighting overhead. *I have to get out. Gabi needs me. She needs me now!* He looked at Dakota and Calder, who were both completely incapacitated by the shelf that had been dropped on them. Then he fixed his gaze on Benny, who'd only just rolled to a stop. "Benny! What is this thing?"

Benny had the back of his head facing Kearney. "Describe the thing."

"It's big and weird...." He scrambled for words to describe the strange contraption. "A-And there's a giant metal spike looming over me."

"That must be the mallow-molder."

"The what?"

"There's a lever near the foot of the machine. It's narrow and kind of pointy."

Kearney scanned the part of the machine beneath him and quickly spotted the level. He hastily reached out with his left leg and tried to kick it, but he missed, and it grazed his ankle instead. He let out a cry of pain. *That's way more than "kind of" pointy!* He tried to kick it again, this time succeeding. It rolled forward with a groan, and the arm-like sticks that'd been holding him down fell back.

The machine growled again, and the giant spike suddenly started free-falling toward Kearney. He screamed as he dove out of the way, and it pierced right through the spot where he'd been sitting. He stared at the machine with a befuddled and terrified look on his face, hopped to his feet, and raced up the ladder, no longer giving any thought to what would've happened if he'd sat there for even a moment longer. "I'll be back!" he called over his shoulder. He hurried up as quickly as he could, but once he'd reached the roof, he was met with silence.

The bell was slowly swaying back and forth, and there was a doll sitting on it and crying. She looked at him, her eyes glassy from unshed tears. "She f-fell with the Liar," she said shakily.

Kearney stared at her briefly before racing to the rails and scanning the area below. Many of the roof's tiles were out of place. Some had even fallen all the way to the ground. He stared down at they'd landed.

No Gabi. She made it down. "I-I have to go," he muttered as he raced back down the steps. *Is she okay? Why's it so quiet? It's too quiet.* He was hardly aware of Calder and Dakota, who were calling to him for help. He shoved the door open, and the street's noises flooded over him. His breathing quickened as he scanned the crowds. *Where is she? Where is she?* He wanted that payphone to ring more than anything in the world and for the voice on the other side to tell him where she was or if she was even alright. But the ringing didn't come. He buried his face in his hands as he groaned in frustration.

"Mister fleshy person!"

He dropped his hands to see a doll looking up at him.

"Where's the sheriff?" She demanded with her arms crossed. "You're always with him, and I need him now."

"I'm s-sorry, I don't have time—"

"There are some people down the street, and I'm pretty sure one of them's a Liar," the doll continued, ignoring his reply, "because they both look the same."

He froze. *That must be....* "Which way did they go?"

The doll looked over her shoulder. "They're that way—"

He raced past her, kicking up dust as he went. *She'll be okay. I'll keep her safe. I won't fail this time.* He felt his heart drumming as he ran faster than he ever thought he could. *She'll be okay. I promise.* He hurried through the crowds of dolls. *I promise.* He spotted two people fighting on the other end of the street, taller than the rest, both with the same short brown hair. And even though they were a good distance away, he could already tell which one was which.

The real Gabi was swinging a long candleholder at her doppelganger, who was avoiding the attacks by swinging the upper half of her body back so far and unnaturally that she would've landed first place in a limbo competition without breaking a sweat.

Gabi was yelling angrily, "Stay still and let me hit you!"

The clone grinned as she kept dodging Gabi's hits, but her smile faded the second she saw Kearney racing toward them. Fear flashed in her green eyes as she spun around and raced off.

Gabi yelled after her. Worse yet, she started chasing her.

"Gabi!" Kearney cried. "Come back, please!"

She didn't listen. Instead, she kept chasing her doppelganger until they rounded a corner and disappeared from Kearney's view. Once he'd made it around the corner, he spotted Gabi diving into a building, still in pursuit of her target. He reached the building, grabbed the handle of the front door just after she'd closed it, and froze when he saw her turn to face him through the door's window. He felt his muscles relax as he sighed in relief. He watched as she glanced down at the door handle, looked him straight in the eye, and locked it.

"Gabi." He felt dread mounting in his chest as he banged against the door, but it wouldn't budge. "Gabi, wait!"

She shot him a fleeting glance before racing up the stairway inside, leaving him watching in horror. *That thing's going to kill her.* He banged against the door again. "Gabi, please!"

Meanwhile, she was racing up the dark staircase, her candleholder still firmly in hand. The smell of fresh marshmallow flooded her nostrils, leading her to assume she was in a sweets shop. It was strange to think that the dolls even needed one, given the Happy Place just beyond Toy Town was nothing but candy. She scanned the stairs ahead for any sign of the clone, but even as she did so, she knew the clone was already waiting for her at the top. Once she'd made it up the stairs, she was met with a door and opened it without hesitation. Light poured around her as she stumbled onto the roof, shielding her eyes. Once they'd adjusted, they fixed on the clone, who was there waiting for her.

The clone tilted her head with a smirk. "Kearney here?"

Gabi brandished her weapon. "Why? Does he scare you?"

She took a step toward Gabi. "He punches hard."

"So I've heard." Gabi pointed her weapon at the clone. "I'm getting my memories back," she snarled.

The clone grinned. "Don't be so sure you want to."

Gabi charged at her with a yell, swinging the candleholder once, then twice. The clone nimbly dodged each time with that smile still plastered on her face. In one quick motion, she kicked in Gabi's knee, sending it snapping back.

Gabi yelped in pain as she stumbled backward, only to be met with a fist slamming into her chin. She fell on her back as the clone rushed at her, reaching for her throat. She tried to roll out of the way, but the clone still managed to grab her by the collar and hold her in place with another fist, raring to go flying down.

Gabi winced. Pain seared in her knee, but she fought against it as she whisked up the candleholder still in her hand. The swing hit its mark and slammed into the clone's left eye, and the clone flinched back with a shriek.

"It hurts!" she screamed with a hand over the struck eye.

Gabi shrank away, shaken by the cry.

The clone stood up, swaying, her good eye wide with horror. She nervously pulled her hand away from her left eye with a shuddering sob and saw flakes of dry paint in the palm of her hand. "No...it doesn't hurt," she muttered, almost confused. "I thought it would.... But it *did*...no?" Ripped out of her thoughts, she glared at Gabi with her one good eye. She let out a shaky exhale as she struggled to regain her composure.

"Are you okay?" Gabi asked in such a haze that she was hardly aware she'd said anything.

"Fine. I'm fine." The clone shuddered again. "I just...don't like remembering."

"You remember something?" Gabi's arms dropped to her sides in disbelief.

The clone's face contorted in some indescribable emotion. She shook her head. "No. No!" She let out another sob as she put her hand over her eye again. "No, I don't remember. I'm Gabi. *I'm* Gabi!"

"Hey, calm down." Gabi dropped the candleholder at her feet and took a step toward the clone, who reeled away in panic.

"I'm Gabi!" she sobbed. "Gabi has a face! *I* have a face!"

Gabi took another step toward her and froze. "Did you not have one before?"

The clone paused, watching her shakily. "I-I have a face now," she replied defensively.

Gabi watched the clone carefully. *She didn't have a face. Face.... No face....* "No-Face?"

The clone's eye narrowed. "Don't call me that," she hissed through gritted teeth. She reeled back again, this time coming menacingly close to stepping off the building's edge.

"No-Face, you're going to fall!" Gabi took an urgent step toward her.

"I said *shut up!*" No-Face's head was lowered, but her gaze was on Gabi all the same. She raised a shaky finger and pointed it at Gabi. "Next time I see you, I'll scratch your eyes out and see how you like it." She took one last step back before falling out of sight.

Gabi let out a panicked gasp as she rushed forward, but once she glanced over the edge, No-Face was already gone.

The sound of glass shattering behind her shook her out of her haze, and when she looked back, she saw Kearney racing up the steps while he rubbed one of his hands, freshly bleeding yet again.

When his eyes met hers, he paused to study her, and once he was sure he was looking at the real Gabi, he wrapped his arms around her. "What were you thinking?"

She hugged him back. "I'm okay—"

"Did it hurt you?" He pushed her away just far enough to be able to scan her up and down once again.

When he saw her buckling left knee, he looked ready to rush her back to the nearest hospital.

"I'm fine, Kearney, I mean it. No-Face is gone."

He looked confused. "No-Face?"

"O-Oh, right. The clone's No-Face." Gabi gathered all of her composure to hide the pain her knee was putting her through. "Now that we know, maybe we can get Dakota to talk some sense into her."

Kearney took a long minute to process what she'd said. Then he cleared his throat with an uneasy nod. "Th-That's good to know, I think. But, please, next time you see it—I mean, her—"

"I won't take her on alone. Promise."

He nodded, seemingly satisfied, but his eyes were still cloudy with worry. Gabi glanced down at his bruised hands. He was fidgeting his fingers without knowing it. Her gaze drifted back up and fixed on his eyes.

They were soft and caring, but what always caught her attention was how they constantly darted around as if there was danger around every corner. And they were a shroud, too. Always hiding *something*, even when he was speaking his mind. But even with that shroud, she never doubted a word he said.

She leaned into him until they were hugging again. She felt him shrink away at first, but she wrapped her arms around him to keep him in place. She liked hugging him. And she knew he liked hugging her. It was about time he said it. After a moment, he relaxed. She closed her eyes as she listened to his heartbeat slow down. He hugged back, albeit more awkwardly, but they both seemed at peace.

After another moment, she pulled away with a grin. "So," she began, "should we check on the others?"

His brows went up in horror. "I think I left them."

"Let's give them a hand, then."

He nodded vigorously, and they headed back down the steps. As they got closer to the bell tower, they spotted Dakota hugging Becca, who was holding Benny and gently correcting his glasses. Meanwhile, Calder was glaring right at Kearney with his nose scrunched up in irritation. Kearney stiffened when his eyes met Calder's, but he started to relax when he saw Dakota was just as cheery as usual, meaning only Calder hated him, which was perfectly normal.

"Ms. The Tailor came, and she said Becca and Benny can stay with us in jail!" Dakota clapped excitedly. "I'm going to take you all to Toy Town's famous hot springs today as a reward for a hard day's work!"

Benny gasped and looked up at Becca. "That sounds awesome."

Becca slowly nodded, Dakota's words seeming to put her at ease. "Okay."

Dakota smiled, but it faded when he focused on Gabi. "Where did the Liar go?"

"She ran off," Gabi said with a sigh. "And it's not just any Liar. It's No-Face."

"What?" Dakota furrowed his brow. "But...she was always so sweet. Why would she want to hurt you?"

"She likes having a face, I guess. Anyway, I scratched one of her eyes out, so that's fun," she added. She seemed very proud of that last part.

They all stood in silence, trying to think of what they could possibly do with that information. Dakota cleared his throat and forced a smile. "I'll tell Ms. The Tailor about it, so don't worry. Okay? Let's go relax now, please."

The others seemed pretty content with that answer, but Kearney felt a knot twisting in his stomach. *It's too dangerous to be lowering our guard like this. Especially now.* He opened his mouth to say something but clamped it shut when Gabi wrapped her arms around him in a big hug.

"That sounds awesome!" she exclaimed, looking up at him. "Doesn't it?"

"I...." His eyes trailed to the ground. "I'm feeling a little tired." *Why did I say that? Now they'll send me back, and I won't be there if they need me.*

She studied his face before turning back to Dakota. "I think we'll head back for now. We'll meet you guys for dinner later."

"You don't have to stay because of me," Kearney whispered urgently to her.

She leaned close. "Don't worry about it."

"But—"

"I know, I know." Her fingers impatiently drummed his shoulder. "But we can do something with just the two of us."

Dakota nodded his approval. "There's a booth in the jail full of games. You can use them if you want!"

"Thanks." Her fingers slid down Kearney's arm and wrapped around his hand. She tugged him. "Let's go!"

"Shouldn't we tell him we won't really be at the jail?"

"It'll be fine."

He followed her apprehensively, his eyes scanning the area as they headed back to the heart of the town. "So, where will we go?"

She flattened her lips as she thought. "How about that giant Ferris wheel?"

He nodded. He couldn't imagine how an angry No-Face could possibly ambush them up there, so it seemed like a relatively safe idea. "That sounds nice."

Gabi gave him a quick grin. "It's a date, then."

He forced a chuckle. "A what...?"

Chapter 20

Kearney and Gabi Name Some Stars

It had been at least three hours since Calder, Dakota, Becca, and Benny had first gotten to the hot springs, but it only felt like minutes to them. The chamomile tea lapped at them as they talked quietly, and they were so calm that, from a distance, they looked like a group of elders having a soak. But upon getting closer, one could see Calder leaning close to Dakota and vehemently talking to him about the Mister.

"...I don't like him." Dakota shook his head and shrugged. "I don't see why you do, either."

Calder's mouth gaped open in shock. "The Mister's my ev'rythin'. 'Course I love 'im!"

"All he did was make your hair green and leave you here." Dakota glanced at Calder. "Anyway, I liked it better when it was black."

Calder's only response was an eye roll. "As if you'd know *half* o' the cool stuff he did. You only met 'im twice."

Dakota stiffened and looked away.

Meanwhile, Becca watched in silence, nervously playing with her long braid as Benny's eyes darted between the pair. "...You guys are so tense," he exclaimed. "Anyway, all that's in the past, isn't it?"

"Yeah, D'kota." Calder shot him a glare. "Get over it."

Dakota's face was slowly turning red. "The only thing that's in the past is *us*. I know our friendship means nothing to you now. You'll probably leave the first chance you get, and you'll try to take Ms. Gabi or Mr. Kearney with you. Because the Mister loves you *so much,* you need to bring him gifts to remind him you even exist," he spat. "And you call that friendship."

Calder flinched, if only slightly. He got up with a huff and left. Dakota didn't watch him leave; he kept his gaze lowered.

"Dakota," Becca began as she slowly shook her head, still bewildered, "you shouldn't talk about the Mister like that."

"It's not like he can hear me," he muttered. "He's too busy hiding behind the Wall."

Benny spoke up, "The only reason he's behind the Wall is because the Purple-Eyed Monster—"

"The monster hurt me worse. I got over it."

Calder froze as he walked away, his back turned to them. His lip twitched with regret.

The twins went quiet. After another minute, Dakota's dreary look faded away, and he forced a smile. "Anyway, I don't need Calder anymore because I have a purpose now."

"Thanks to The Tailor?" Benny mumbled.

Dakota nodded. "She was the only one who really looked after me. Now, I get to look after others. I don't need any Mister to do that."

"What if she tells you not to do your job one day?" Benny watched him closely. "What will you choose then? Her or the job?"

The dreary look returned. He let out a sigh. "I'll have to think about that one."

That heavy silence was back. Becca suddenly shook Benny, nearly sending his aviator hat flying off in the process. "Stop pestering him, Benny!" she snapped. "We're supposed to be having fun, remember?"

"Right," the other two muttered in unison.

Kearney and Gabi walked down Toy Town's main street, their elbows linked as they admired their surroundings. He grinned as he recounted the moment he first walked down this same street and saw Gabi tied to a pole and surrounded by a crowd. When she threw her head back and started laughing, he laughed too. The dolls around them stared at them as if they were insane. Soon, their conversation quieted again, and they walked in comfortable silence, perfectly content just being with each other.

Kearney sighed as he stared at the sky and thought about Gabi. Lately, the only times he'd thought about her was when he'd worried about her, but now, they were both perfectly safe and healthy, and all there was to think about when it came to her was, well, *her.*

His lips bent into a small smile. Gabi had so much energy bundled within her that it almost seemed like she was a whole different species of human. But the two of them had a good balance because of it, and being around her felt perfectly natural to him. He loved every minute he was with her. A better way of putting it was that he loved her.

He paused, stopping the train of thought chugging along in his mind. He'd tried to avoid thinking about it. He'd figured if he never fully processed the thought, maybe it'd go away at some point. But now, it was too late. He shook his head as if that would shake his feelings away. *Don't think like that. Stop it.* But no matter how much he chastised himself, he couldn't stop thinking of the way her hair bobbed up and down when she walked, or the way her two gems for eyes lit up when she got excited, or the way her face scrunched up in that adorable frown when she got upset. And he didn't want to stop thinking about it, either.

"What's wrong now?" she asked with a chuckle, pulling him out of his thoughts.

He looked at her. "Nothing."

She nudged him playfully. "You sure? You've got that look on your face again."

"Yeah."

"If you want, we can head back."

"That's alright." He smiled. "I'm having a great time."

She squinted as she studied his expression. "If you insist."

He watched the evening sky as they walked. "Does it ever mess with the dolls, I wonder? Not knowing what time it is?"

"I don't know."

"I wonder how they know when to sleep."

"Oh. Kearney, they don't sleep."

He looked at her. "They don't?"

"Nope." She pointed to all the shops around them. "That's why these guys never close. Dolls are always busy all the time."

Kearney remembered how chaotic things had been back when he'd been Calder's prisoner. It seemed like there had never been a moment's rest in that tower. Now, it all made sense. "That must be exhausting."

"I can only imagine. Having to find something to do *all* the time? I think I'd lose it." They walked a little longer before a playful look danced in her eyes. "Do you know how to man a Ferris wheel?"

He laughed. "No. Why?"

"Because I have no idea if anyone there even works it."

He furrowed his brow as he nodded thoughtfully. "I think we can do it. I'll just have you sit in one of the booths while I hit *all* the buttons...."

She punched his arm and laughed again. "Nothing wrong with a plan like that!"

They were at the Ferris wheel before they knew it, but fortunately for them, there *was* a doll manning the controls. They hopped into a booth and got comfortable as they waited for the ride to start. With a rumble, the wheel jerked forward, rocking the booths gently. After that, it slowly chugged and spun, the ride becoming much smoother. It paused when Kearney and Gabi's booth was right at the top, giving them a perfect view of the whole town.

She leaned back in her seat as they both looked out the window. "It's pretty here," she commented.

He let out a relaxed sigh. "It is." He paused before feigning a yawn and stretching, pulling Gabi into a surprise hug in the process. It didn't feel strange or awkward to hug her. He rather enjoyed it. *I'll tell her soon. That we can't be together. But for now, I want to enjoy this.*

She chuckled as she leaned her head on his shoulder. They sat in silence as they admired the view. Soon, he found himself staring up at the sky again. He was able to make out a couple of stars in the midst of the sea of colors. It was probably a force of habit, but even when the stars were fake, he was still so enamored with them.

"Kearney?"

He finally looked away. "Yeah?"

"Before I lost my memories, did I mention anything about the nickname 'Gabs'?"

"No, why?"

"I've been thinking ever since Calder said it that one time. I don't know where he got it from, but it made me feel funny. Like there was a memory in the fog, just out of reach."

He tilted his head in thought. "I'm not sure. Maybe he'd know."

"Maybe."

Kearney pulled away, ending the hug in what he hoped was a natural way. They sat in silence for a bit before he leaned back in, deciding he wanted to hug her again. She smiled and hugged him back.

He glanced at her. *What are things like for her back home?* "Can I ask you a question?"

"Sure."

He hesitated for a moment. "What are your parents like?" *I at least want to make sure I'll be leaving her with good people.* He paused. *What am I saying? They were there for her before we even met. I'm not "leaving" her with anyone if they were there before I was.*

"My parents?" A big smile spread across her face. "My dad's really fun and smart. We go on hikes together all the time, and whenever I have a question, he always seems to have the answer. And my mom is the sweetest person I know. And the greatest cook, too."

Kearney nodded as he listened, as if there was some hidden meaning to glean from her words.

A question from her yanked him out of his thoughts. "What are yours like?"

He replied without much thought. "Parents?"

"Yeah."

"O-Oh." He stiffened nervously. "They're...nothing special."

"Come on, I'm sure there's something more you can say," she teased as she gently elbowed him. But as playful as she was, he felt uneasy. He grasped desperately for something to say that was believable, but he didn't even have the slightest idea of what an admirable parent looked like.

He bit his lip. "Whenever I'd have a nightmare, all I'd have to do is yell my dad's name, and he'd come running and give me a hug. And my mom...." He felt himself begin to shiver as the fantasies of his youth were shattered by painful realities, and he did all he could to push them away. "M-My mom was really gentle."

He couldn't tell if Gabi noticed his change in behavior, but he was put at ease when she smiled again. "Kind of like you," she said.

He chuckled. "Kind of like me." *You have no idea, Gabi. No idea at all.*

She paused, and her eyes widened with worry. "Why did you say *was*? They're okay, right? First your brother, now this. I didn't mean to—"

"They're fine." He smiled reassuringly. *That's a lie.*

She sighed in relief.

He lifted his head and continued staring at the sky, trying to alleviate some of his nervousness. His heartbeat slowed as he studied the sky, and his thoughts became more pleasant. "When I leave this place, I want to spend every night I have left watching the stars. The real stars. I'd love to watch them with you one day." He glanced at her and smiled. "Or, maybe every day?"

Her eyes lit up. "Really?"

"Of course." He felt a desperation gnawing at him. *I don't want to lose this. I don't want to let you go.*

Her cheeks turned pink, and her gaze slowly trailed to the shimmering sky. She opened her mouth to speak but hesitated.

"You were going to say something?"

"I don't know if I should ask." She shrugged.

"It's alright, go for it."

She cleared her throat. "Did Levi watch the stars with you?"

That dull ache returned, and Kearney finally let it stay. "We'd name them."

"That's really sweet."

"Yeah." He smiled as he thought of all those nights he and Levi had spent on their roof together. How they would huddle up in a blanket as Levi would point at random stars he'd probably pointed at dozens of times before and scream names at them.

Kearney let out a small chuckle and wished he could go back to those times. He pointed at a cluster of stars. "You see that little one in the middle?"

After searching for a second, Gabi nodded.

"I'm going to name that one Gabi."

She laughed before pointing at one beside it. "And that one's Kearney!"

Their laughter grew and grew until it filled the air.

Once it quieted down, she sighed. "That morning, when I woke up after you first left, I was *so* mad. I thought you were one of those guys who thought he was too cool for friends." She looked up at him and smiled. "But you're pretty great."

"Hey, you're great, too. I appreciate that you didn't give up on me. It's nice having a friend."

She stared at her sneakers with a smile. "Just a friend?" she asked playfully.

He hugged a little tighter. "Not just a friend." It felt like everything he'd told himself before was going right out the window. He wanted to be selfish. He wanted to love her.

"A best friend?"

"Maybe a little more."

"Funny, I was thinking that, too."

He found his head resting on hers as he held her close, and they shared each other's warmth. *Wait.* He started to pull away. *What is wrong with me? Stop it! Don't do this to her!*

Gabi noticed his shift immediately. "What's wrong? Why are you upset?"

He looked away and brushed his hair back. "I'm not upset."

"Don't lie to me," she said. "Why do you always do that?"

"Do what?"

"The thing where you look guilty and back away! Do you think I don't notice? It's so...." She stared at her shoes. "It's not me, is it?"

"No, of course, it's not you!"

"Then what is it?"

"It's nothing."

"What is it?"

He let out a heavy sigh. "It's me, okay? Will you *please* back off?"

Her eyes pierced into him. "Well, what about you, then?"

His mouth gaped open as he searched for the right words. "I-I love you, really, I do. I just feel it's unfair to you."

"Unfair?"

"Because I'm the worst person you could be interested in."

"Why?"

"You wouldn't understand."

"Then help me understand!"

Kearney shook his head as he thought of Levi again. He thought of the promises he'd made, the ones he'd failed to keep. "Because I don't deserve you."

Silence hung between them. Kearney dreaded the moment she'd say, *You're right* and walk out on him right then and there. To say he didn't see it coming would be a lie. But that didn't make it hurt any less.

What he definitely didn't expect, though, was when Gabi cupped his cheek in her hand. "That's not true," she whispered.

He found himself leaning into her touch and hated himself for it. How could he have allowed them to reach this point? Why hadn't he nipped it in the bud when he'd had the chance? Selfishness, that was why. "What if it is?"

"Why would it be?"

"Because...." He was desperate to keep the torrent of emotion under the surface, knowing that if he didn't tame it now, it'd come out the moment he spoke. "I'm a nobody. I don't have anyone waiting for me to come home. No parents, nothing." He heard his voice break. "I made them up."

Pain flashed in her eyes. Pain for him, probably. Not that he deserved it. "Kearney...that doesn't change how I feel about you. Not one bit."

"No, you don't get it. It *should*." He pulled away from her. "M-My parents knew better than to love me. You should, too."

Her eyes were wide with shock. "Are you crazy? Why would you ever think that?"

"I t-tried to deny it for a long time, but I can't run from it anymore...."

"Don't say that, Kearney!" She was about to burst into tears. She was screaming out words. "Firstly, your parents must've been *horrible* people if they didn't love you! And *secondly—!*"

He was pressed up against the booth's wall in his attempt to distance himself from her. He stared at the floor. His chest felt heavy as he remembered Levi, the only person who loved him. The person he'd failed. "I'll let you down," he whispered hoarsely. "I'll never be enough. Find someone better than me, *please.*"

She practically threw herself at him, sobbing as she hugged him. "I don't want to! I love *you*, Kearney! Just listen already!"

He didn't argue after that. They sat there, Kearney with his head held low and his arms hanging uselessly at his sides, and Gabi hugging him and sniffling, silently pleading with him to hug her back. After a moment, he raised his hands and set them on her shoulders.

She melted with relief. A thankful tear slid down her cheek. She opened her mouth to say something, only to realize Kearney wasn't hugging her back. He was pushing her away.

In the brief moments they were apart, she watched him give her a sad smile as his hand searched for the door handle. He twisted it, opened the door, and stepped back, falling out of the booth in seconds.

"*Kearney!*" She ran to the door, scanning the ground below for any sign of him.

To her relief, he wasn't on the ground. Instead, he was standing on a beam a few yards away. He had his back turned to her with his head held low. "I'm sorry. J-Just go back without me, okay?" he said as he walked along the beam and away from her.

"Kearney, wait! Please!" she cried as she watched helplessly. "Come back!"

He shoved his hands in his pockets, his freckled cheeks red with shame. He shook his head as he tried to tune her out. *What was I thinking? I can't. I never can.* He got to the end of the beam and began climbing down another. *I'll drag her down. Like Levi. She deserves better than a kid who has to lie about being loved by his own parents. About what really happened to the only person who did love him.* Tears threatened to soak his cheeks, but he fought them back, refusing to let as much as a whimper slip past his lips. *She deserves better—someone who can actually take care of her.* He was on the ground now, still breathing shakily as he headed to who-knew-where.

Briiiing!

He covered his ears with a sob. "Please, not now," he whispered helplessly. But the ringing continued without remorse. He started running, tears now flowing freely. "Please, stop."

Briiiing!

He ran and ran, but the ringing followed him. "Stop!" he cried.

Briiiing!

He froze in his tracks with his hands still on his ears. "I said *stop!*" He stood in place as he sobbed, maddened by the fact he could still hear the phone's ringing. He lifted his head and saw the payphone waiting right in front of him. He stared a little longer before picking it up. "What do you want?" he asked, his voice quiet and dull.

"I just wanted to see how my bud's doing, that's all."

"We're not buds."

"Well, I think we're buds," the voice hissed back. *"And, as your bud, I thought I'd give you some news to cheer you up! After all, who needs ladies, am I right?"*

Kearney's hand began to shake. If he could strangle the voice, he would.

"Now, I, for one, am awfully excited. Do you want to know why?" The last sentence ended on a high note, indicating the voice was eager to hear his guess.

Kearney didn't reply.

His lack of participation didn't seem to perturb the voice. *"Because of the surprise coming up, of course!"*

Kearney wiped his eyes and fixed them absently on the sky. "Surprise," he echoed.

"Yep."

He sighed in defeat. "Good for you."

The voice chuckled. *"I'll be seeing you, Kearney."*

Those words ripped him out of his haze, but the voice hung up before he could react. He was left standing there, shaking slightly as he stared at the phone in his hands. In that moment, it felt like he could do nothing but stare.

Just go back, he tried to calm himself. *Go back and get some sleep. You just need sleep. Get some sleep.* With a half-nod, he left the payphone and started heading back to the jail, his clammy hands in his pockets. He hoped more than anything in the world that he'd wake up the next morning back home with Levi.

He stopped. *Levi...I can't let her end up like Levi.* He shook his head again as his lip quivered against his will. He told himself to keep walking. *You just need sleep. Go get some sleep.*

House Full of Strings

Chapter 21

Levi Gets Looped into a Very Quite Sinister Plot

Levi's room was a complete mess, which was a shame since Annette had done a thorough cleaning of it not even an hour ago. And the monster causing the chaos was none other than Levi himself, racing around the room and ripping drawers out of their shelves like a rabid animal. *Where did Annette put her...?*

Anais wasn't anywhere to be found, but he wouldn't accept it. He *never* lost his things. Everything had its perfect place, assigned to it by him. If something wasn't where it was meant to be one day, the only reasonable explanation was that thing had gained sentience, rebelled against his divine will, and taken a business trip to Jamaica. In general, that was the most logical answer, but the theory that Annette had haphazardly hung Anais on a rack while thinking she was a towel made worlds more sense here. But the moment Levi had gone to the bathroom and seen a terrifying lack of Anais where the towels were draped, things had spiraled into chaos.

He soon abandoned his fruitless ransacking and opted to look for Annette instead. Sure, there might only be a ten percent chance she'd even know what she'd done with poor Anais, but ten was better than zero. He sped down the halls, the doodads in his backpack clanking and jingling as he ran. He soon spotted her out of the corner of his eye.

"Annette!" He skidded on his heels as he tried to turn without losing momentum. He failed miserably and went crashing into a wall but quickly regained his composure and hurried over to her as she was pulling some fancy plates out of a cabinet. "There was a little plushie with red hair sitting on my nightstand."

"Oh, yeah." Seemingly forgetting about the dishes in her hands, she dropped them, not even flinching when they shattered on the floor. "I saw her when I was cleaning."

Levi seemed to care about the dishes just as much as she did because he didn't even glance at them once. "What did you do with her?"

"I took her."

"Where did you put her?" He was annoyed but partially relieved that his secret had only been discovered by her. *She'll be easy to fool, at least.*

"With Henry."

His relief was gone in a heartbeat. "Why's she with *him?*"

"Because he told me to hand her over, duh." Her smile wasn't disturbed by his dismay in the slightest.

"Where's he now?" he urgently asked.

"On his way to Master." Annette grinned again as she pointed in the direction he went. "Good luck."

With an infuriated groan, Levi raced off, letting out panicked breaths as his feet thundered against the floor. *What'll Phantasos do if he gets her? Or if he finds out I knew about her? I still don't know why he kept her a secret in the first place!* He quickly spotted Henry, who was dusting furniture. He seemed to be in no hurry to spill Levi's secret. Levi's attention fixed on the laundry basket sitting at Henry's feet. More specifically, what was sitting right on top of it. *Anais!* "I didn't let Annette touch my things, and I'm definitely not giving *you* a pass!"

Henry glanced at him apathetically before picking up the basket. "You're forgetting Anais isn't yours."

"She's not yours, either," Levi growled.

"If you're going to yell at me, then go shove yourself into the closet you found her in and do it from there. Speaking of which, I'm curious to know how you even got yourself in there to begin with, given it was locked."

Levi struggled to compose himself. "It was on accident, that's all." *I doubt even Annette would buy that one.*

"Sure." Henry nodded with a mockingly puckered lip before walking away. "And I guess I'll just stumble over to Phantasos and accidentally plop Anais onto his lap, then."

Levi watched, wide-eyed, as Henry sauntered off. He felt his stomach twist into a knot. He had to do something. He could easily overpower the little gremlin, but what would Henry do after that other than rat him out? He started warily following Henry. *It wouldn't be that hard to kidnap him, would it? Maybe remove his legs to keep him from running? Or would that be going too far?* He shook his head. *Definitely too far. Don't do that.* He hardly thought any further before crying, "Wait!"

Henry turned to face him, clearly enjoying the little power game that was playing out. "Yes, Levi?" he asked sweetly.

"About Anais." Levi stared at her, trying to think up an excuse. "I've grown really attached to her, and she helps me sleep!" He heard Anais let out a small groan of disgust at the very idea.

Henry ignored her. "I'm sure Master can help you with that. He's much better at handling dreams than some toy." He grinned with what could've only been pure evil. "If you want her that badly, how about we take things to the top and ask Master to resolve this little spat himself? We can start by telling him all about how you found her!"

Levi bit down on his tongue as he glared.

"So, how did you find her?" Henry asked as he cocked his head.

"I picked the lock," he slowly replied.

Henry chuckled. "I'm sure Master would love to find that out."

"Don't tell him," Levi begged; he'd tried to keep his voice as flat as possible, but that had completely failed.

Henry put a hand on his chin as he looked up thoughtfully. His grin grew. "I might, but it'd cost you." His brown eyes narrowed. "In return, you'd have to keep your mouth shut about how I am when he isn't around, and more importantly, you're going to help me get rid of Annette."

Levi stiffened nervously. "What's your problem with her?"

"My problem is that Master loves her so darn much. Meanwhile, I do all the heavy lifting around here, and what do I get? Nothing!"

"Maybe that's because no one likes a jerk."

"Deal or no Anais, *snowflake.*"

Levi was biting down on his tongue so hard he could taste blood. He stared daggers into the smug little doll. "Fine, deal!" He thrust his hand forward.

Henry smiled and shook his outstretched hand. "Deal." He spun around to pick up his basket, waving Anais over his shoulder as he went. "You'll get her back once Annette's out of the picture. Meet me here after tea tomorrow, and we'll go from there."

Levi watched as he sauntered away, and the knot in his stomach tightened as Anais stared back at him with the same helplessness he felt. Sure, Annette was a little annoying at times, but the idea of doing something that could hurt her made him feel sick. He sucked in a deep breath as he tried to form anything remotely close to a plan. He'd have to find a way to get Anais back without playing Henry's games. The only problem was he had no idea how. The one thing he did know was that this was going to throw a massive wrench in his investigation.

When his workday finally ended, Henry went to his room with Anais shoved into his coat pocket. Once Henry had entered his room, Levi, waiting in the hallway, peeked around the corner. He crept up to Henry's door. *Maybe I can still get her back. Maybe it's not too late.* He paused when he heard a voice coming from behind the door. Luckily, it was cracked open, so he could peer inside.

Henry was sitting at a little table with a teacup in hand. "Would you like some tea?" he asked someone.

Levi leaned to the side in an attempt to see who it was and could barely stifle a laugh when he spotted that someone. It was a pillow wearing a pair of glasses. Henry pretended to pour tea from the teapot into the pillow's cup. "I got lavender, your favorite."

The pillow didn't reply, but Henry laughed as if it'd just cracked the funniest joke he'd ever heard. "That's a good one!"

Levi's eyes narrowed as he studied the scene. *The heck is this?* He shifted his feet, and the sound was just loud enough for Henry's gaze to dart to the door, but Levi quickly slipped out of sight. Henry watched the door a little longer before quietly walking over to it and peeking into the hall. He then closed it and returned to his business.

Levi was pressed up against the wall around the corner. A smile tugged at the end of his lip. *A new development in my case! And even better, it's dirt.* His grin grew as he tiptoed away, a plan already forming in his mind. *Time to get Anais back.*

Henry stayed pressed against the door after he closed it, staring at his pillow companion with a scared look on his face.

"You...You don't think that was Master, do you?" he asked quietly. His cheeks turned pink as his gaze fixed on his shoes. "...I don't think I ever told you this, but...I like having you around. It'd be a shame if he got rid of you." After his eyes revisited the pillow, he rushed forward and hugged it. He pressed his face against it as if in some vain search of comfort. "I'm so tired, Mama," he whispered.

Chapter 22

Annette Gets Buried Alive (in Pillows)

Every evening, Henry would sneak into Phantasos' workshop. Levi had no clue why, but he made note of it, and that information became very, very useful when he was trying to figure out when to break into Henry's bedroom. So, one evening, Levi waited around the corner until he saw Henry leave, then raced into Henry's room, snagged his precious pillow, and bolted out the door.

After that, he raced off with it in search of Phantasos and quickly discovered how cumbersome it was to carry a giant pillow through a house so big and strange that he needed a map to get around. The original plan was to go straight to Phantasos and have some fun with the pillow, but there was no fun to be had in spending a decade of his life just trying to find the guy. But eventually, Levi made it to the tea room and froze in horror.

Phantasos was sitting on the couch with a book in hand. That was amazingly lucky, but the horrifying part was the fact that Henry was also there, collecting dirty dishes from the little table. Little cupcakes were jumping off the plates and trying to flee the scene, but he quickly caught them and stuffed them into a box.

Neither of them seemed to notice Levi, so he slipped behind the door while he had the chance, being extra careful to ensure that he was holding the pillow as closely as he could. Coupling the giant pillow in front of him with the even bigger backpack behind him, it was hard to keep every inch of himself out of sight. He stayed hidden as he tried to think of what to do next.

Meanwhile, Henry was blabbing seemingly endlessly to Phantasos. His eyes drifted from the game of petteia set on the table back to the dishes. "Watching you play the other day reminded me of just how clever you are, Master."

Phantasos's only reply was a grunt as his attention remained on his book.

"You know, I've been practicing," Henry excitedly continued. "Maybe you and I can spar sometime. Maybe even now?"

Phantasos shook his head. "This game is for snowflake, not you."

Had they agreed to a game this evening? Levi couldn't remember.

Henry frowned. "I don't know what you see in him. He doesn't even appreciate you *half* as much as I do." He watched Phantasos expectantly. When Phantasos didn't reply, he sulked out of the room.

Levi stayed still as a statue, trying to discern whether the coast was clear or not.

"You can come out now, snowflake."

He peeked around the corner and saw Phantasos smiling. "You noticed when I ran in, didn't you?"

Phantasos chuckled. He threw his book, and it fluttered around in circles in the air before landing on the tea table, neatly closed. "I noticed you when you first rounded the corner up the hall," he said with a wink.

That's pretty far. Levi stepped fully into view, dragging the giant pillow with him.

Phantasos eyed it with confusion. "What's all this about?"

"It's Henry's," he replied curtly as he closed the door and dragged the pillow across the room. "He took something of mine, so I'm getting back at him, that's all."

"With a pillow?" He cocked his head curiously.

"Yes, with a pillow. He seems to love this thing—"

"Quite a lot. Yes, I'm aware. He's even been rushing through some of his work just to get back to his room sooner." Phantasos rose to his feet and held the pillow in a scrutinizing manner. "Honestly, I'm just jealous he seems to love this bag of feathers more than he does me!" he chuckled jokingly, although, with how his brow was knit in a fine line, it seemed he really *was* mad at the pillow for stealing his butler's affection. "Getting back at him, you say?"

Levi nodded.

"How so?"

"Well," a smirk crept onto Levi's face, "I was going to ask for a room full of pillows. I thought if anyone were to have one, it'd be you."

Phantasos's eyes lit up. "But it'd be so cruel of me to use it against Henry," he protested, though his tone gave away that he wanted to do it more than anything.

"Oh, what the hey." He grabbed Levi with his free hand and hurried out of the room with a giggle. "Don't worry, it isn't far. I doubt we'll run into—"

They both froze at the sound of small footsteps getting closer, and Phantasos shoved the pillow into Levi's arms, who only just became aware of how hard it would be to spontaneously hide the giant thing if Henry were to come around the corner in the next few seconds. He glanced up at Phantasos, who winked before gliding ahead and stepping into the fork in the hallway. "Ah, Henry!" he exclaimed.

Levi's shoulders relaxed. *A diversion! Perfect.*

Henry sounded surprised to see him. "M-Master! Is there something you need?"

"Oh, nothing in particular. But now that you're here, how's about we talk?"

"Talk?" He sounded overjoyed but then paused. "...Why are you acting so happy, Master? You didn't care at all a minute ago."

Phantasos chuckled. "I was just engrossed in my book, that's all!"

"But you're never like this...." Henry's voice trailed off.

Phantasos started looking sideways in Levi's direction, and Levi quickly realized why: because Henry was, too.

"Something the matter, Henry?" Phantasos asked.

"He's there, isn't he?" Henry asked quietly.

The strain in Phantasos's voice grew. "Who is? Are you seeing things now?"

Henry let out a sigh of complacency. "The...plants look less dead today," he commented, his voice now flat. "That's nice, I guess."

"It is, isn't it?" Phantasos's grin returned at full strength. "And the keykatoos have just been *loving* it! Have you heard them singing?"

"I have." Henry's voice was quiet now. "Master?" he asked.

"Yes?"

"Could we play a game of petteia tonight? Just the two of us?"

Phantasos stiffened with an awkward laugh. "I'm afraid I'm a little busy then."

Henry paused again. "When was the last time we played it, Master?" Henry's footsteps receded right after as if he didn't even expect a reply.

Levi found himself staring at the pillow in his hands. In a way, maybe it made sense that Henry loved it so much. After all, he certainly wasn't getting any affection out of Phantasos that wasn't forced. He snapped back to reality when Phantasos grabbed him and dashed through the hall, opening a door with a snap of his fingers before they both disappeared inside.

Not long after the prolonged silence from Phantasos and Levi, Henry and Annette were called into a room that had long since been closed off. When they got there, Annette was immediately smacked with a pillow to the back of her head. She went soaring into a giant pillow fort ahead of her and stayed perfectly still after that, likely taking the attack as an opportunity to sneak a nap. Meanwhile, Henry was frantically running from his assailants, who were also attacking each other while trying to get him.

Levi cackled as he dodged a pillow while swinging his own pillow at Henry, who was screaming in panic. Henry dashed out of the way of Levi's attack only to get hit from behind by Phantasos. He went stumbling forward into a pile of pillows but didn't move an inch after he landed. Levi paused and stared at him before glancing at Phantasos, who'd already gone up to him.

"Henry?" Phantasos patted his head. "Everything alright, my little oaf?"

Henry slowly got to his feet with a dazed look on his face. "Y-Yes, Master."

Phantasos smiled before picking up the pillow he'd dropped. "Wonderful." He smacked Henry in the face with it.

Levi kept staring. Henry's face wasn't as unreadable as before. His eyes were full of anger and pain. Suddenly, they locked with Levi's, and the anger in them intensified. Levi didn't feel guilty. If anything, this was long overdue. He just felt a little bit scared of Henry.

313

"Think fast!" Another pillow slammed into Levi's face, knocking him off balance. He fell with a laugh and immediately swung his pillow at Phantasos in response. Henry stared in horror at him—specifically at his pillow, which Levi was holding.

Levi couldn't help but grin when he saw Henry's face. *That's what you get for taking Anais. Now, I'm getting her back.* There wasn't a single doubt in his mind that Henry had Anais on him right then and there, sitting in his coat pocket and ready to be used as blackmail at any moment. But now that Phantasos was here, chances were Henry wouldn't dare pull her out. If Levi had to beat her off him to get her back, he gladly would. And even if Henry didn't have her, this was just plain fun.

In moments, he and Phantasos had ganged up on Henry, sending feathers flying every which way. Henry immediately started screaming his surrender, and the two stopped. Levi and Phantasos exchanged sly glances before Phantasos dropped his pillow with a nonchalant shrug.

"I suppose Henry simply can't handle our game. An awful shame, but I suppose I must be on my way, any-way." He guided Levi out of the room, leaning close to talk to him. "I must say, I haven't had half as much fun in a century and a half as I had with you this past week," he chuckled in a giddy half-whisper.

Levi laughed. "This was pretty great!"

Phantasos started walking away with a bubbly gig-gle, but he paused. "And, snowflake?" He glanced over his shoulder and smiled. "It's always fun to bug some-one after they've kicked you around, isn't it?"

Levi's heart skipped a beat as he froze. "What do you mean?"

"Well, Henry, of course." Phantasos winked. "I see a lot more than you think." Instead of continuing walking away, he headed back to Levi, wrapped his arms around him, and squeezed him in a big hug.

Almost immediately, every part of Levi melted into Phantasos. If there was any ice left, it didn't melt, it *evaporated* in the one-hundred-degree heatwave that swallowed everything up. Levi's eyes fluttered shut as he let out a sigh. He'd do anything to put this warmth in a little bottle and hold onto it forever. After what felt like so long but not long enough, Phantasos pulled away and patted Levi's shoulders with an affectionate smile.

"Good night, Levi."

"Good night," he replied, still dazed. As he watched Phantasos walk away, his thoughts were entirely absorbed in that warmth. In truth, it was addicting, and he completely embraced that.

"Levi."

He turned around and saw Henry. The little butler's blonde hair was a mess. His brown eyes were boiling with rage. "You took her," he said, shaking.

With how quiet Henry was, Levi couldn't tell whether he was planning on scratching his eyes out or just glaring. Either one would be bad.

Henry's hands balled into fists, and he didn't bother to hide them. "You *took* her." It seemed to be all he could say.

Phantasos had noticed and rushed back over. He put a hand on Henry's shoulder and tried to draw him away from Levi. "Now, Henry, there's no need to be upset about anything. After all, it was just a game, wasn't it?"

"That's not it. He *took* her."

"Took who?" Phantasos asked in feigned innocence.

Henry quickly clamped his mouth shut, eyes wide, then opened his mouth again to stammer, "N-No one, Master."

"You're not lying to me about anything, are you, Henry?"

"No, Master!" He sounded horrified at the very thought.

Phantasos paused, deep in thought, and Levi couldn't shake the chill that had come over him on seeing that frightened look in Henry's eyes. He didn't know why, but it bothered him so much.

"How's about we go play that game of petteia you wanted?" Phantasos asked Henry sweetly.

Henry nodded slowly. "O-Okay."

At that moment, Annette emerged from the avalanche of pillows, which surprised everyone since they'd forgotten she was there to begin with. What was also surprising was the fact that she wasn't in her dress anymore. Instead, she was wearing a pillowcase with two sloppily made holes for her legs, as she held it up with her hands.

Phantasos tilted his head. "Annette," he began slowly, "where is your dress?"

"I lost it."

"Might I ask how?"

"Dunno." She shrugged before drifting down the hall as everyone stared at her.

Then Levi's eyes lit up. *Henry must've dropped Anais in there. This is my chance!* "How about you guys go play that game of yours, and I'll find Annette's dress?"

Phantasos smiled gratefully. "Why, thank you, snowflake!" He started leading Henry away, and Levi raced into the room in search of Anais—and Annette's dress. But even as he searched, he couldn't shake the unease that had overtaken him. The way Henry had looked at him was scary, but Levi wasn't unnerved by Henry's anger; rather, he was bothered by the feeling hiding beneath it. There was something down there in Henry's pitch-black soul that he had just seen, and it looked a lot like grief.

Levi jumped into the pillows and started digging through them, but after what felt like forever, he only found Annette's dress.

"Anais!" he called in as quiet of a voice as he could, but there was no reply. He stared at the dress in his clammy hands. *Henry still has her.* With a weary groan, he rose to his feet and left the room, but after only a few seconds of walking down the hallway, he paused, foot mid-swing in the step he hadn't completed. He glanced back at a door he'd just passed. It looked like the one that led to Phantasos's workshop. More importantly, there was a pair of familiar voices talking behind it. He quickly pressed his ear against it.

"*Honestly, Henry, I'm hurt to hear you've been acting like this.*" It was Phantasos.

"*I'm sorry, Master. I promise I won't do it ever again.*"

Is that Henry? Levi furrowed his brow. *He…actually sounds sorry for once. Wait. I thought Phantasos said they were going to play petteia.*

"*Well,*" Phantasos sounded cross, "*you can prove you won't by bringing me Anais.*"

"*But—!*"

"*But nothing. She belongs to me, and sure, Levi didn't know any better, but you most certainly do.*" There was a brief silence. "*Unless knowing better is too much to ask of you.*"

"*…I'll bring her, Master.*"

Levi bit his lip as he backed away from the door. *Why does Phantasos want her? I thought…. He doesn't know she's alive. That's the only answer.* He felt tempted to rush into the room at that very moment and explain everything, but instead, he backed away and hurried down the hall to his room, carefully ensuring his footsteps wouldn't be heard. *Tomorrow, I'm telling him. I'm telling him everything.*

House Full of Strings

Chapter 23

Levi Goes Bungee Jumping

Whenever Levi's mom hugged him, his figure fit perfectly into hers, like they were two puzzle pieces that had been made for each other. Her hugs made him warm, and that was all he needed to be happy. He looked up at her. She had blue eyes like he did, and so did his dad. Simply put, looking amazing ran in the family.

He closed his eyes again and rested his head snugly under her chin, hoping this hug would never end because it was never truly long enough.

But then, he felt cold. His eyes snapped open as the hairs on his neck stood on end, and he fell forward as if his mother had suddenly evaporated. He managed to catch himself, and when he looked back, she was still there. In fact, she hadn't moved an inch. He rushed forward, trying to get back into her warmth, but his outstretched hands went clean through her. Like she was nothing more than smoke.

That cold wrapped its long, bony fingers around him again, and he desperately tried to shake it off. He kept rushing at the figure of his mom as tears ran down his cheeks. He wanted her warmth, needed it. But he couldn't reach her. That cold kept crawling under his skin, and there was nothing he could do to stave it off.

After breakfast, Levi found himself sitting in that dusty armchair again, staring at his shelves full of treasure. But he wasn't reveling in all he had; he was thinking of the one thing he *didn't*. Anais. But he didn't have much time to focus on that since Phantasos was sitting across from him, eating floating macarons and twisting his dark red braids between his fingers while trying to strike up a conversation. The results were less than exemplary.

"I recall you said your friend has a grudge against adults," he suddenly said.

Levi clenched his jaw. "I didn't say it *that* way."

"How, then, do you think he'll react to me?" he continued as he watched Levi curiously.

Levi paused as he felt doubt creeping in. *Kearney would be fine, right? He wouldn't make me choose. I...I love it here. I love Phantasos. He loves me.* "I'm sure he'll be alright with you."

"And what would set me apart from the others?"

"Well," Levi stared at his plate, "I trust you. And he trusts me." He looked back at Phantasos and felt peace. There wasn't any ice anymore. No reason to be tense. Why would he ever want to leave this for anything? "And even if he doesn't like you at *first*, no matter what happens, I'll stay. Promise."

"Promise?" Phantasos looked bewildered, but Levi could tell he was happy with that answer. "And what if he doesn't stay? He wouldn't change the terms of said promise?"

"I don't think it'll be a problem." He pushed away any doubts that crept into his mind. *There's no way Kearney would leave without me. No way at all.* "I'm sure he'll want to stay if I'm staying. After all, this is my home now!"

Phantasos smiled. "You think of this as your home? That makes me so happy!" He clapped his hands with joy. "Then I'll have to work hard to make this Kearney's home as well, won't I?"

That warmth flooded over Levi again, and he couldn't help but grin from ear to ear. His gaze trailed to his teacup as he remembered he was supposed to be doing something around this time, after tea—but what was it again? *Henry!* He jumped to his feet. "Sorry, but I have to go."

"Go where?"

"It's just some private stuff I have to do."

"Come now, you can tell me!"

"It's not that important."

Phantasos's eyes dimmed, and he stared at his plate. "I thought we were friends," he muttered.

Levi winced. "Sorry," he muttered as he spun around and raced off, trying to shake off that ice before it could get a hold of him. *I know there's something you're not telling me. But don't worry, I'll figure it out, and then there'll be no reason to be upset about anything. No more ice.*

After a few minutes of walking, he found Henry leaning against the wall where they had planned on meeting. He was tossing Anais and catching her as he waited. "Took you long enough." He didn't even look Levi's way.

Levi frowned. He stared at the floor as he remembered the day before. "Let's just get this over with."

He shoved Anais head-first into his pocket and nodded. "Nice to see we're cutting to the chase." He started down the hall. "This way."

Levi followed closely behind without a word, but thanks to Anais's muffled yelling, it was all but quiet. He watched Henry closely. "So, what exactly are we going to be doing?"

"Cleaning," Henry replied curtly.

"I didn't realize you're so incompetent you need my help with that."

Henry didn't reply. All he did was wave Anais over his shoulder, and Levi couldn't hide his frown.

Soon, they came up to a door. Henry rapped on it for a few seconds, and it creaked open.

Annette's sleepy face appeared on the other side. "What's up?"

He cleared his throat, an actor ready to perform. "Did you forget about what Master told us to do today?" His voice was suddenly urgent and full of panic.

"No."

"He told us to clean out the attic! Do you have any idea how upset he'll get if he finds out you forgot?"

Her smile remained unaffected. "Yeah."

"Then, let's go!" He grabbed her arm, and she practically floated beside him as he pulled her into the hall.

Levi watched closely. *I doubt he had to act like that to convince her.* But truth be told, this was just another show of how easy it must've been for him to slip under Phantasos's radar undetected for so long.

Soon, they were walking up a staircase and then going through a small metal door. They entered a giant, empty, cylindrical room with one thin platform, on which they stood, running straight through it. The room seemed to be both topless and bottomless and was filled to the brim with strings.

Levi glanced over the edge of the platform. *That's a long drop.* "Maybe someone should put some guardrails here or something."

"No need," Henry replied, clearly enjoying Levi's apprehension. "This is more fun."

They continued down the narrow walkway as the millions of strings around them strummed in harmony with their footsteps.

"What's this place all about?" Levi asked.

"This is where all the strings in the House converge."

"There's this many strings in Phantasos's place?"

Henry rolled his eyes. "The House, meaning this whole *world*."

"Yeah, Levi," Annette added. "Catch up."

"Cut it out, Annette. We don't need two Henrys," Anais snapped.

Levi groaned. He glanced back at Annette, whose hand was firmly in his own, mainly to make sure she didn't walk off the platform's edge while daydreaming. *Henry would love it if something like that happened,* he thought with a frown. He studied her for another moment before his eyes went to her dress. He had never really noticed before, but if someone were to cut the thin cord that was tied in a pretty bow around her neck, the whole dress would slide right off. His eyes continued to trail down her as if he was making some type of evaluation of her physical capabilities, which, knowing her, were likely incredibly low. His gaze stopped at her legs. She always wore white, knee-high stockings, and the skirt of her dress was just short enough that a bit of her bare legs was visible. He noticed that they were covered in scratches, the kinds left from wood scraping against wood.

"Did you hurt yourself?" he asked slowly.

She glanced at him with her usual half-asleep expression. "What?"

"Your legs. They're all scratched up."

"Really?" She lifted her skirt slightly to look at them. "Oh."

"She must've run into something without realizing it. Wouldn't be a stretch," Henry muttered.

"That wasn't me." Her eyes drifted to Henry. "That was Master."

"Stop spouting nonsense," he snapped. Then he grabbed her hand and rushed forward.

Levi took off after them. "Hey. Hey!"

Annette didn't look over her shoulder. In fact, she was keeping pace with Henry pretty well.

"Annette, stop!" Levi yelled after them.

She giggled as she kept running, probably thinking she was the most rebellious little maid to ever live. Henry started climbing a ladder at the end of the platform, and she quickly followed behind. Once they reached the platform above, he slammed the little gate shut behind them.

"Annette!" Levi cried again as he grabbed onto the ladder. "Annette, stop!" His panic only heightened when she didn't reply. He hurried up the ladder, and once he made it to the top, he grabbed the gate and fought to open it, but it wouldn't budge. He raised his head and spotted Henry wrapping a string around Annette's neck as he positioned her near the edge of the platform, chuckling to himself as he did.

"Henry, don't you dare!" Levi screamed as he climbed over the gate, which rocked unsteadily under his weight.

"She'll be fine," Henry replied nonchalantly. "In case you forgot, she doesn't need air."

"That's not the point. It's just not right!"

Annette did nothing but smile, her eyelids shut as if she were dreaming. "It's okay. Henry thinks it's funny."

"It's not always about what Henry wants!" Levi paused. "Scratch that, it's *never* about what Henry wants!"

"Don't listen to Levi. He's an idiot, not unlike yourself," Henry said to her as he tightened the string. "You're going to fall *so* far when I push you!"

Annette's grin only grew as if that was something to be happy about. At that point, Levi had made it over the gate and rushed at the pair. He grabbed the rope and tried to wrench it out of Henry's hands, who refused to let go. Soon, Henry's feet were above the ground because Levi was holding the string high over his head, but even that wasn't enough to deter the little butler from holding on. And before Levi knew it, his own feet were barely skimming the ground as well. He paused the fight to try to make sense of that. *What's going on?* He felt something tug at his shoulders and looked up. Somehow, a string had wrapped around his backpack and waist without him noticing, and it was pulling him up. He grabbed the string and tried to yank it off himself, but it was stubborn. His brows went up as he realized the gravity of the situation.

"Henry? Can you give me a hand here?" His head turned back to Henry, only to realize he was still hanging on. They glanced at Annette, who still had the string around her neck and her feet on the ground. She was staring off into space again.

"Annette!" Henry shrieked, "Cut the string!"

She glanced at him. "What?"

"The string! Get the string!"

"Okay." She latched onto it, and it lifted her into the air, too, so that was the end of her usefulness. The string kept lifting them higher, and soon, they were all completely airborne.

"Why are you like this?" Henry yelled at her.

She smiled without reply.

"What do I do?" Levi cried in panic.

"I don't know. I don't end up in situations like this as often as you do!" Henry screamed as he hung on for dear life. They continued to climb higher, helpless to whatever fate the string had in store for them. Henry let out an enraged growl as his feet kicked wildly. "Why do you have to ruin everything, you idiot?"

"Ruin?" Levi glared down at him. "You're the one who tried to hurt Annette!"

"I do that all the time. The only thing that's different now is you!" Henry hissed back. He started climbing up Levi, and Levi cried in complaint as he got shoes to the face. Once Henry was sitting on Levi's back, he grabbed the string and started trying to tear it.

"What are you doing?" Anais screamed, and Levi started kicking his feet in panic, swinging the four of them back and forth as he struggled to make Henry stop.

"I'll cut it myself," Henry curtly replied, his fear completely gone.

"You can't! We're too high up!" Anais yelled.

"Annette and I will be just fine. So will you. And Levi…." Henry froze, and his smile faded. His eyes were full of thought. "It's not murder," he said abruptly. He wasn't afraid at all anymore. Maybe he never had been, to begin with.

"It's murder," Anais replied, her voice full of horror. "And don't you even think about it!"

Henry turned his attention back to the string and kept tugging and scratching at it. "It's totally not murder.

Master will never even need to know how this went down."

"Don't let me fall!" Levi screamed as he fought against Henry, but his hands stayed firmly on the string.

Henry chuckled with excitement as he kept tugging. "I've been waiting for his moment forever."

"W-What's that supposed to mean?" Levi glanced down at Annette, who looked just as nonchalant as before even though this had started off as an attempt on her life. As he stared at her, something hit him. Annette didn't seem to have a problem with anyone, not even Henry. As much as Henry mistreated her, he never had a real reason to want her gone. But Levi? Henry had many problems with him, and it dawned on Levi that he might have had Henry's intentions all wrong. "You...You were planning this?"

Henry paused to smirk at him. "This is what you get for making a fool out of me, snowflake."

"This is murder!" Levi shrieked wildly. "This is definitely murder!"

"Not murder. Just a happy accident."

"Henry!" Anais screamed.

"Don't! Please, don't!" Levi cried hysterically as he kept trying and failing to get Henry away from what had now become his lifeline. But there was nothing he could do and definitely nothing Anais could do, either. The only person left to stop Henry was....

Levi's screams were cut off as Annette clambered up him, grabbing his hair as she slipped. Soon, she'd successfully made it onto his giant backpack and grabbed the string, which had been thinned a terrifying amount by Henry. "Stop it."

Henry smacked her away, his attention hardly diverted. She slapped him back. He stared at her in perplexity.

"Stop it," she repeated, now more sternly.

He sent his fist flying at her, and she didn't move as much as an inch, so his punch hit her squarely in the face. She punched him back. Their punching turned to slapping, and their strange little battle went back and forth in that manner as he sputtered in anger. Levi and Anais watched in anxiety and immense interest.

Levi's eyes flicked away from them for a moment, and he saw something that finally put his terror at ease. There was a platform not far overhead. He practically melted with relief. *I'm saved!* He started swinging his legs back and forth in an attempt to gain momentum. "Annette!"

"What?" she asked calmly. Very calmly, given that Henry had her by the hair and was actively trying to toss her overboard.

"When I say 'now,' cut the string!"

She paused. "I thought that's not supposed to happen."

Henry noticed the platform, and he looked scared. "Oh, no, you don't!" he yelled as he pinned her down. Despite that, Annette kept her focus on the string as she reached for it.

"Come on, Annette!" Anais encouraged frantically. "You can do it!"

"I know," she replied as she kept scrabbling for it.

Thanks to Levi, the four of them were in full swing now. They had just passed the platform. "Now, Annette, now!" he cried as they swung forward.

Still pinned under Henry, she couldn't fulfill the order. Levi's excitement turned into terror as they went swinging back. "Not yet, not yet!"

Annette managed to kick Henry away. He stumbled back with a shriek and barely managed to grab Levi's coat to keep himself from falling. They swung forward again.

Anais and Levi screamed in unison, "Now, Annette!"

She scratched at the string, but it still didn't snap. They swung back again, and Levi returned to shrieking, "Don't!" as the platform got farther below them. When they swung forward again, Annette sunk her teeth into the string, and it finally snapped, sending the four of them flying for the platform. Levi screamed one last time as wind rushed around him, and a shudder ran through his whole body the second his feet hit the ground with a resounding *thud*. He fell over with a cry of pain as he clutched his leg. Both his feet hurt plenty, but the moment he'd landed on his left leg a little funny, he'd known it was all over. Annette and Henry ragdolled to the ground beside him while Anais seemed to drift, landing neatly on top of Levi as he suffered.

His eyes stayed squeezed shut as tears of agony slipped out of them against his will. His pain only heightened when Henry started kicking him in the stomach and yelling in fury while Annette watched, her mental battery completely depleted for at least the next century. Then Henry's kicking and yelling stopped, and the only sound that was left was of a door creaking open, followed by footsteps. They were heavier foot-steps, and Levi had grown well-acquainted with them. He groaned in pain as someone lifted him up and held him, and he opened his eyes just enough to see it was Phantasos. *How did he find me?* he wondered, mainly in relief.

"Whatever happened here?" Phantasos anxiously asked.

Annette opened her mouth to speak, but Henry quickly cut her off. "I told Levi not to come here, but he didn't listen. By the time I got here, a string already had him!"

"And why was Annette here?" he asked with a per-plexed tilt of his head.

"I don't know. I-I doubt even she knows!"

"Stop lying!" Anais, who'd fallen to the floor, snapped furiously. "You're the one who—!"

"Anais?" Phantasos picked her up with a shocked look on his face. "How are you here?"

"I-I...." she stammered.

Levi feebly grabbed her out of his hand and held her close. For once, he didn't care about what Phantasos thought, only that he finally had his friend back. Phan-tasos stared at them both, eyes round with confusion be-fore he quietly turned and walked out the door, leaving Henry and Annette alone.

Levi winced as Phantasos walked, mainly because his ankle burned with pain every time he moved, even slightly. Luckily, he was soon back in his bedroom, sitting on his bed and propped up by pillows. He held Anais close and watched Phantasos, who'd just finished checking up on Levi's ankle and sat on the bed. He stared off, his expression stolid. "Why did you hide Anais from me?" he asked quietly.

Levi's stomach twisted into a knot as he stared at her. "I…I didn't *mean* to hide her," he shakily began. "It just kind of…happened."

"But how could you keep me in the dark for so long?"

"I don't have to tell you everything," Levi muttered.

Phantasos let out a weary sigh. "…I've only ever known people to be liars. My family, even my little dolls, have lied to me. Every last one of them. That was why I sent them away, Levi." Phantasos turned his head slightly to look at him. "Trust was all I wanted. I hoped I'd at least have that with you. Trust."

"Well, I hoped for the same!" Irritation doused Levi's guilt. "Either you're not telling me something, or you're being cold or getting upset over nothing, or…." His voice trailed off, and he sighed. "It's exhausting."

Phantasos lowered his head. "Force of habit, I suppose."

"Then get over it!" Levi couldn't help but be angry at this point. "How about *you* be honest for a change? Why was Anais in that closet?"

"You wouldn't understand, snowflake."

"Why was she?"

He stiffened. "We agreed on it."

"But you knew it was wrong. You just left her there all alone in the dark!"

"It was her idea."

"And you supported it. What did she do that was *so* horrible?"

"I broke away from my role," she quietly interjected.

"*That's* what's caused all this drama? How did you break it?" Levi demanded. "And why's your 'role' such a big deal to begin with?"

Phantasos opened his mouth to speak, but Anais cut him off. "It doesn't matter."

"Yes, it does!" Levi retorted. His attention shifted back to Phantasos. "You expect me to be completely honest with you. Meanwhile, you can't even look me in the eye and answer my questions. Who's the liar now?"

Phantasos shook his head as he reached for Anais. "Just…give her to me."

"No!" Levi yanked her away. "Start telling me the truth, or…or I'll leave!"

Phantasos stared at him, his eyes narrowed. Then, he slowly rose to his feet. Levi suddenly became aware of how tall he was. "You're willing to sacrifice your promise for a cheap threat?" His voice was low.

Levi felt that knot in his stomach return. "Th-There's nothing cheap about it."

Phantasos's eyes bored into him. "Choose your words wisely, snowflake." He walked out of the room, leaving Levi and Anais in silence.

Levi lowered his gaze and stared at the blankets covering him as he struggled to keep his thoughts in order. He was in a warm bed wrapped in blankets but felt cold.

"...Levi?"

He looked down at her. "Yeah?"

"I just wanted to say it's okay. I know how it feels when he gets mad, and...I'm here if you want to take your mind off it."

Levi forced a smile. "Thanks." He fixed his eyes on his clammy hands and didn't say a word.

"So," she began, still trying to take his mind off it, "do you really think you'll leave?"

He was caught off-guard by that question, but what bothered him more was that the answer didn't seem so simple to him anymore. "Maybe. I don't know, really. I'm just...getting tired of Phantasos hiding things."

"Me, too."

He leaned back, his head hitting the pillow as he frowned indignantly. "Like about that string around his neck. I bet it's not even real. Just an excuse to stay inside."

"Oh. Levi, it *is* real."

He glanced at her. "Really? Then how did he get all the way to Toy Town to meet me, huh?"

"It's...a very long explanation, and I barely even get how it works myself. And it'll probably sound like something right out of sci-fi movie."

"I'm listening."

She let out a thoughtful hum as she searched for the right words. "So, you have reality and...non-reality.

And there are these things in between the two that connect them. I don't know their names, but I like to call them liminal spaces."

"Why's that?"

"Because I like the word liminal," she said with a huff. "Anyway, liminal spaces don't work according to the rules of logic. They normally act as portals. You know that room you saw when you first walked into the House?"

"The one with the statue and all the doors?"

"Yeah. That's a liminal space—a portal between the real world and the House."

"So, Phantasos found me in Toy Town …"

"…because he was using a liminal space, that dark room he pulled you into. And in that space, logic was different, so the string around his neck wasn't holding him back."

"Huh. That's something." Levi furrowed his brow, his mind utterly broken by that explanation. *That does sound like it's from a sci-fi movie.*

"It's best if you don't think too hard about it. All that matters is that they're really, really weird."

"Well," Levi said, "that aside, he lied about you."

"Fair enough." Anais went quiet for a long minute before she said, "You know, now that I'm thinking about it, when Phantasos and I were first waiting in Toy Town, he kept referring to the person we were waiting for as a she. I don't think he was even expecting you."

Levi stared at her. "Who could he have been waiting for, then?"

"I'm not sure."

He stared at the ceiling. He hadn't given it much thought, but he'd assumed Phantasos had been in that town specifically to find him. Had he and Phantasos really met entirely on accident?

"Do you have any family?" Anais asked. "Family's, like, people you're related to, right? To be honest, I've only ever read about them."

Levi felt himself relax when he thought of Kearney. He shook his head, as if that would help clear the confusion muddling his mind. "I have a brother. I'm waiting for him to find me."

"Are you going to leave when he does?"

Levi furrowed his brow. "It wouldn't be right to leave Phantasos here all alone. He's got his problems, but we all do, right?" His words were hardly enough to convince him. After all, how can you ever truly help a liar if they're too good at lying? Where does the truth end and the lie start?

"...Levi?"

"Yeah?"

"If...If you ever do end up leaving, can I come? There are so many cool things I've read about that I'd love to see."

He smiled. "Of course, I'll bring you."

"Thanks," she chuckled. "I can always count on you."

Even though Levi didn't realize it, he didn't feel as cold anymore.

House Full of Strings

Chapter 24

The Tailor Ruins Everyone's Day

Gabi rubbed her eyes as she followed the little doll in the police suit marching in front of her. Up until this point, she'd thought Dakota was the only officer in all of Toy Town. She didn't know why she'd thought that, as it hardly made any sense, but now she knew better.

Speaking of Dakota, she didn't even know where he was. She furrowed her brow. The officer had woken her up very early that morning, and he hadn't said a word since he'd gotten her out of bed. He'd taken extra care to ensure he hadn't roused Kearney, too.

Gabi and Kearney had hardly spoken to each other since the incident on the Ferris wheel. *I miss talking to him. I just…wish he'd stop thinking the way he does.* She let out a heavy sigh. Her gaze trailed back to the cop as she tried to distract herself. *This whole morning's been weird, and this guy's even weirder.*

His red curls bounced as he stopped and glanced over his shoulder, green eyes scanning her. Then they trailed to the fenced-off building before them. "The Tailor told you to go there," he explained curtly.

"Why?"

He had a stony look on his face. "There's a group in there. Pretty religious. The Tailor deems them a threat to Toy Town's safety. You have five minutes, under-stood?"

She eyed him carefully. "Okay."

He nodded. "Be on your way, then."

She nodded back as she uneasily glanced at the old wooden building and started walking toward it. Its win-dows were boarded up, and it was a miracle the fence surrounding it was still standing given just how rotted it'd become. She struggled to keep herself from gagging at the musty scent that flooded her nose as she headed up the steps, which bent under her weight. They seemed to be on the verge of snapping at any moment. Finally, she reached the door and pressed her fingers against it, sending it creaking open. She glanced back at the strange little officer. He was still staring. She headed in-side.

The floorboards announced her presence with a loud creak, and she winced. But whoever was here didn't seem to notice. Suddenly, she heard muffled shouting and froze. A minute later, it quieted down, and she ten-tatively continued. She soon approached a door that was cracked open; from the crack, warm yellow light poured into the dusty gray hall. She leaned closer and peeked through it.

Inside the room was a group of dolls sitting on the floor in a circle around a propped-up canvas. She squinted as she tried to see what was on it. It was a pair of stick figures holding hands, one in a dress and the other with a mustache. *What in the world...?*

One of the dolls grabbed the canvas and cuddled it. "Ma and Pa say we should play hide and seek," he announced politely.

Another doll put her hands on her hips in annoyance. "Don't speak for them. *I* know what they said. They said we should play tag!"

The doll holding the canvas hugged it even tighter. "Ma and Pa say we shouldn't argue," he chastised.

"Let's hold a vote, then. Everyone who wants to play tag, raise your hand!" She immediately thrust her hand into the air, waiting for others to join her. Her eyes expectantly skipped from person to person until they spotted Gabi watching in the background. She pointed with a shriek. "Stranger danger!"

Her friends all spun around to look at Gabi, and they stared for only a brief second before jumping to their feet and scrambling away.

The door flew open as Gabi came through it. "Wait! I'm not here to hurt anyone!"

But all the dolls had already scurried away, leaving their precious painting lying flat on the floor. Gabi stammered as her eyes darted around, searching for the dolls, but they'd all vanished. Clearly, they'd been ready for someone like her. She looked back at the painting, and curiosity led her to walk toward it. She could practically feel the dolls' stares bearing down on her as she got closer to the painting, although she had no clue where they were all watching from.

Maybe this will draw them out. Then we can talk. She reached for the painting.

A one-armed doll raced out of the shadows and dove in front of the portrait with a shriek. "Leave Ma and Pa alone!"

Gabi stumbled back, relieved and shaken at the same time. She opened her mouth to say something, but the trembling doll quickly cut her off.

"I know The Tailor sent you! She wants us to forget them, but I don't want to forget!" She grabbed the painting and raced off, stumbling down the hall and crying as she struggled to carry the canvas with one arm, which resulted in it being dragged along the floor.

Gabi started following her. "You don't have to be scared!"

The doll, realizing that Gabi was keeping pace with her just by walking, shrieked and ran even faster, her feet kicking against the bottom of the portrait as she struggled to escape. Unfortunately, the portrait slipped out of her hands and slumped to the ground, and she tripped and fell a few feet away from it. She looked back with wide eyes as Gabi leaned down and picked it up.

"Please, don't take them away!" she wailed.

Gabi studied the crude little sketch on the canvas then the girl who loved it so dearly, and a heavy silence hung over them like a shroud. "...I won't."

"W-Why did you come, then?" the doll asked shakily.

Gabi's eyes trailed back to the painting. "I guess I just wanted to see if The Tailor was bluffing or not. Calling you a cult and all," she chuckled.

The doll tilted her head as she slowly got to her feet. She glanced back at the painting. "Can I have them back?"

"Of course." Gabi gently handed her the canvas. "I noticed you call them your...parents?"

"Yeah, so?"

"Oh, nothing in particular. I just thought it was cute."

The doll eyed her suspiciously. "You have parents, right?"

"I do."

"So, you love them with all your heart, right?"

She paused, caught off-guard by the doll's sudden fervency. "I do."

"So, there's nothing *cute* about wanting to remember them," the doll snapped, the painting held close to her chest.

"Remember?" Gabi furrowed her brow. "But you're a doll."

"Wasn't always." She stared at her shoes. "Same as the rest of us."

Gabi suddenly became aware of the sounds of shifting around her, and when she looked back, she saw dozens of eyes peeking through the door and staring at her. She looked back at the doll. "Wasn't always...?"

The PA system outside blared to life, making everyone in the room flinch. *"My little friend, wrap it up in there."*

Gabi felt herself tensing as she looked back at the shivering dolls. *What are the odds this kid's lying? What if she's just trying to throw me off my game so she and her friends don't get caught?* She shook her head. *I don't have time for this.* She grabbed the painting in one hand and held the doll's hand in the other. "Let's get out of here," she whispered urgently.

The doll tilted her head. "You're not turning us in?"

"Not to The Tailor of all people." She spun around as she scanned the room for an exit. "Now, where to?"

"This way," one of the dolls behind her said before taking off, and the others followed him. Gabi and the one-armed doll followed close behind and watched as the dolls moved a small dresser, revealing a passage that'd been dug out of the wall behind it. They ducked and headed through it, but it was so small that Gabi had to crawl through it on her knees.

"My little friend," the strain in The Tailor's voice was growing, *"whatever this game is, it's not very funny."*

Gabi felt her breath quicken as she urged the dolls ahead of her to move faster.

"You have one minute to get out here before I send rein-forcements to…assist you."

"Hurry up!" she hissed. She heard the sound of the front door breaking down and little footsteps marching through the halls. She guessed the little cop with the red curls was with them. *I'll have to beat him up later.*

One of the dolls ahead of her paused to look back in-dignantly. "I thought she said she'd give you a minute."

She shoved him. "She says a lot of things!"

Soon, they made it to the other side of the passage and emerged out of a hole in the side of the building. Gabi stretched, straightening her aching back, then hastily did a head count. She didn't even know how many dolls there had been to begin with, so that didn't help.

"Where will you go now?" she asked.

The one-armed doll glanced at the others. "Out of town, probably." They all gathered around her as she glanced back at Gabi. "Thanks. For not ratting us out." They hurried off, leaving Gabi to wait for The Tailor's guards to find her.

Maybe I can find a way to make it look like the cult kids got the jump on me or something.... I doubt The Tailor would fall for that one.

"It's nice that they remember."

The voice made her jump. The reason it made her jump was because it was her voice, but it hadn't come from her mouth. Her eyes darted around, searching for the voice's source, and found it sitting on top of a tower of boxes. No-Face.

She was staring down at Gabi with a grin. "And it's nice that you have them. But I don't want them."

Gabi stepped back. Her first instinct was to plan an escape or find a weapon, but curiosity quickly overtook her. She thought of what the one-armed doll had said. "You said your eyes were scratched out."

No-Face's grin vanished in a heartbeat.

"You said it hurt a lot when they were."

Anger sparked in her one green eye.

"Were you...a fleshy person when it happened? A kid?"

No-Face stared at the ground. "It was a monster. A monster with purple eyes." She looked back at Gabi as she let out a long sigh. "Why are you like this?"

"Like what?"

"Annoying." She began sliding down the boxes, her gaze fixed on Gabi again, but now with rage. "Trying to hold onto your name all the time. You'll die soon. You might even die here." She was on the ground, rapidly closing the distance between the two of them. In moments, they were only inches away from each other. "But *I'll* be stuck here forever. So let me at least have a *name* to be stuck with."

Gabi balled her fists. "So, you're here to scratch my eyes out after all?" Her voice was a low whisper.

No-Face paused to stare at Gabi's fists before balling her own, likely in a further attempt to mimic her. "I've thought about it a little. Not sure if I will or not, but I do know one thing." She grabbed Gabi's arms and pulled her uncomfortably close. "You *will* die here. And I'll be the reason you do."

Kearney stretched with a yawn, hardly aware of his knuckles knocking against the walls of his cell as he did. He rubbed the sleep out of his eyes. *No nightmare, for*

once. He looked around. Save for him, the jail appeared empty.

"Gabi?" he called. But there was no reply. *Maybe she's asleep.* He opened the door of his cell and stepped out, still groggy. "Gabi? You up?" He stiffened a bit when he realized her cell was empty. *Probably with Dakota.* He headed outside and looked around. *Where's Dakota, then?*

"Freckles, what are you doin'?" Calder was sitting crisscrossed on the ground.

"Looking for Gabi. Have you seen her?"

He shook his head. "Do you know where D'kota is?"

"No clue." Kearney scanned the streets. "Maybe they're together."

Calder slowly got to his feet. "I've been waitin' around for a while. I'm reachin' the point where I might ask The Tailor where he is myself."

The Tailor. That's a place to start. He took off in the direction of her office.

"Where you goin'?" Calder called after him.

"To The Tailor. Like you said." He didn't look back.

"Yer a r'lly bad listen'r, Freckles." Calder frowned as he watched. Then he sat back down. "If you see D'kota, tell 'im I'm 'ere."

Kearney nodded distractedly as he kept walking. *The Tailor. She'll know. Gabi had better be okay.* He started walking faster. *No-Face is still out there.* In the haze of his thoughts, he was hardly conscious of when he made it to her office.

347

He shoved the door open and marched to her desk. "Tailor, where's Gabi?"

She was in the middle of a conversation with Dakota, who looked very distressed. He panickily shook his head. "Ms. The Tailor, you can't—!"

"Enough, Dakota," she snapped. She groaned when she saw Kearney. "Your friend's running an errand. Now leave."

"Did you send anyone with her?" Kearney's palms were firmly planted on the desk as he leaned over her. His eyes darted to Dakota. "She can't be by herself right now. You're supposed to protect her!"

Dakota lowered his head. "...I have to listen to Ms. The Tailor first," he whispered helplessly. "I'm sorry, mister."

The Tailor didn't seem bothered by Kearney in the slightest. "It doesn't matter what happens to her, truly."

"*It does.*" His hands balled into fists. "Why didn't you send me with her?"

She shrugged nonchalantly. "You've proven yourself perfectly capable. As for her, she's useless to me now. Following that logic, it doesn't matter what becomes of her."

"*Useless?*"

"Stop acting so surprised. You knew I had my reasons for putting the two of you to work, and now you're lucky enough to get to know what they are." She crossed her arms as she leaned back in her seat. "I'm sure you know enough about the Wall and the Mister at this point. What I doubt you've heard before is my numerous failures whilst trying to make it through." She frowned as if her past defeats were still upsetting her, but it vanished when she fixed her eyes on him again. "But you? You're *strong*. You can get me through. I'm sure of it!" Her voice was low, but there was a sudden fierceness to it.

His chest tightened as he took a step back. "I'm not going anywhere with you."

"I'm not asking." She got to her feet. "We're going to-day."

"No. No, I'm not!" He spun around and marched out of her office, and she ran after him.

He tried to slam the door shut behind him, but she quickly caught it. "Enough, Kearney. I'm not in the mood for nonsense."

He didn't bother stopping for her. What he did stop for, though, was the sudden quake that seized the town. Everyone around him froze, exchanging nervous glances. Then came another quake. A louder one. Kearney shook in horror. He was all too familiar with that sound. The dolls' eyes all went to The Tailor, who looked mildly annoyed at most.

"The Tailor," one of them began slowly. "He won't come here, will he? You'll keep him away?"

She didn't reply. She only watched Kearney.

He slowly shook his head. "You wouldn't," he barely managed to whisper.

"Everything is a means to an end," she whispered back, eyes widened with excitement. "Even a little town full of idiots."

There was another rumble, and this time, Kearney could see what was beyond the town's gates.

Jolly. It was Jolly.

She chuckled. "Give your final test a warm welcome."

He let out panicked breaths as he focused on Dakota. "You let this happen?"

Dakota was shaking. "I-I didn't want this," he blubbered. "But Ms. The Tailor said—"

"Enough about her! Look around, Dakota!" Kearney pointed back at the panicking citizens. "They're counting on you to do your job, not be her lapdog!"

He stood motionless, not replying as he stared at his shoes.

Kearney shook his head, brow furrowed in disbelief. "I...I'm disappointed in you, Dakota."

Hurt flashed in the little doll's eyes, and his lip quivered, but he quickly flattened it into a line to keep it still.

After another moment of silence, Kearney turned away. "If you won't stop him, I will." He walked up to The Tailor's office and grabbed the stickie leaning by it. It was the one with the little dinosaur sticker. Then he started running.

He had no idea where to go or what to do, but he knew one thing: if he wanted to get rid of Jolly, dealing with his "host" would be the way to do it. He quickly spotted the Bell Tower and raced for it. Screams echoed behind him as buildings toppled, but he refused to let himself look back. He got inside and hurried through it, racing past a very confused Becca and Benny and getting up to the bell as quickly as possible. He was already panting for breath when he reached the ladder but didn't give himself as much as a second to rest. Once he made it to the top, he scanned the horizon for Jolly.

Jolly was kicking Toy Town's gates to dust. He looked at Kearney, then twitched. He started lumbering toward the Bell Tower, decimating buildings with ease as he charged through the city.

Every inch of Kearney was tense. What would he do when Jolly reached him? How would he get inside? What if Jolly crushed him before he even had the chance? A brief but bright flash caught his eye. He looked past Jolly and squinted as he scanned the decimated landscape. He spotted a black-haired doll running away from Toy Town with a mirror held high above his head. Dakota.

Jolly swung his giant head around, focused on the mirror. He started turning after Dakota.

No, no, no. "Dakota, get out of there!" Kearney shouted as loudly as he could, but he already knew it was useless. He watched as Dakota, nothing more than a little black-and-blue dot among the sands, ran as quickly as he could while Jolly stomped behind him. *When I said do something, I didn't mean this!*

Calder had just come clambering up the ladder of the Bell Tower, clearly alarmed by the sound of his nemesis approaching. "Freckles! Becca an' Bens ran off already. Why are you still 'ere?" A panicked look came over him when he saw Kearney screaming. He quickly turned his head and spotted Dakota.

Dakota kept racing away as Jolly tried to stomp him down. Practically in a trance, Jolly's gaze followed the little doll and the erratic rights and lefts he took. At least, that was until Dakota tripped, and the mirror flew to the ground and shattered. The dream-like state broken, Jolly reeled back and swung his foot forward.

"D'kota!" Calder screamed. "D'kota, *no!*"

Kearney stopped yelling. Instead, he just watched in nauseating horror of what was inevitably coming. *There's nothing I can do.*

Jolly slammed his foot down with a sickening *crunch.* Once he lifted his foot back up, all that was left of Dakota was shards of glass and splintered wood.

Calder froze. "D-D'kota…." He dropped to his knees, bursting into tears. "D'kota!"

Kearney stood frozen in place, his eyes glued on what was left of Dakota. *He's gone. Jolly took him. Took him away.*

"I promised myself I'd protect 'im this time!" Calder screamed with his face buried in his hands. "I want 'im to know I'm sorry! I want 'im to know!"

Kearney could only hear his own racing heartbeat. His eyes lifted from Dakota's remains to his murderer: Jolly. *You took him. Just like you took Levi.*

Without as much as a thought, Kearney grabbed the bell's clapper and, with a powerful thrust, swung it forward. It banged the sides of the bell, letting out a series of resounding gongs. Jolly stared at it briefly before heading toward it. Kearney balled his fists as his rage engulfed his fear. He watched Jolly's approach in silence as Calder bawled in terror. Jolly swung forward, decimating the top of the Bell Tower as he grabbed Kearney by his jacket and dangled him in the air.

He stared at Kearney, seemingly studying him. Remembering, maybe. Then he thrust Kearney into his mask's slitted mouth.

Kearney yelped as he flew forward before slamming into the cold floor of the castle, shaking in pain as he slowly got to his feet. He looked around as he squared his sore shoulders. He was in the throne room again. He slowly turned to face the throne. Surely enough, the mummy was right where he'd left it.

He studied its features closely, which was something he realized he hadn't done before. It boasted long, cloud-like hair, which could've been deemed black save its dark blue hue. It looked like it was the night sky itself, nestling peacefully behind the mummy. Where the roots of its hair met its head were two horns, wavy like an antelope's. Then, once again, Kearney's eyes stared into the mummy's, which still looked as dark and mysterious as the bottom of the ocean. But now, he became aware of the glint of madness, of fallen glory, in them.

An epiphany slowly came over him. It was more than just a mummy; it was a pharaoh—bound and locked in a deep chamber full of treasures—whose own people had long forgotten him and who'd long forgotten himself. He shakily unslung his stickie from over his back and pointed it at the mummy that had haunted him for so long.

"What do you want?" he asked, his voice a low whisper.

It stared at him. *"Leave."*

He stepped forward as courage pounded in his chest like a heartbeat. "Only once *you* leave Toy Town for good."

The puppet twitched but didn't reply. Suddenly, it thrust a bony hand up in a jerky motion, and the strings surrounding it quivered to life. The energy in them flowed into the coffin-like box overhead, and it began to shake. The strings snapped, giving way for the box to come crashing to the ground. More green energy pulsed through the carvings on the box before it let out a *pop*, the door slid open, and a doll stumbled out.

But it wasn't just a doll. It was Kearney.

Chapter 25

No-Face Takes a Dive

Kearney took a step back, bewildered, as he studied the doll. *That's me.*

The doll took an awkward step forward before freezing, its eyes fixed on him, seemingly just as astounded by him as he was by it. The strings that had let go of the box suddenly rushed for the clone and wrapped around it, and it squirmed as the energy and memories in the strings poured into it.

How…? Kearney froze. He only vaguely remembered the string that had grabbed him the first time he'd been here. Was that all the mummy had needed? Was one time enough to create a Liar?

The strings around the clone drooped, allowing it to slip out of their grip. When it did, it stared at Kearney again, only now in horror. It then stared the ground, seemingly contemplating its own existence, before looking back at the mummy and asking, "Why?" in a voice that was very distinctly Kearney's.

The mummy leaned back without reply, and the clone turned back to Kearney, harrowed by the lack of answer. It started walking toward him with cloudy eyes. Walking and walking for what felt like forever. When it was right in front of him, it leaned close to get a better look. Kearney bent back, unsure what he was supposed to do. *It's not me,* he tried to reason as he shivered. *It's a Liar. Just a Liar. Not me.*

The clone slowly raised its hands, its stare fixed keenly on Kearney's face. Kearney didn't move; he seemed to have forgotten how to. But his senses all came rushing back to him when the clone wrapped its fingers around his neck and slammed him to the ground, sending his stickie flying out of his hand as his head hit the marble floor.

He gasped as it began lifting him up and slamming him down again. It opened its mouth and spoke.

"I never should've had you." It was a woman's voice, cutting and bitter. *"Can't have anything nice because of you."* Its brows were twisted in grief, and Kearney understood.

It remembered, and it seemed to hate remembering just as much as he did.

He desperately tried to kick it away, but its grip was too tight. It was speaking in a man's voice now, screaming in fury and on the verge of tears. *"You don't deserve to be happy. You never even deserved to be born! Look what you've done!"* It slammed Kearney down again.

He winced as he thought of that night and kicked against the clone as those words sank in, but it slammed his head down again and again.

"Look at it, you horrible little bastard!"

"I-I didn't mean t-to," Kearney helplessly choked out. "I'm s-sorry."

"Look at her!"

356

The clone's fingers quivered and pulled away, and Kearney gasped for breath. But the next moment, the clone had grabbed him by the collar of his shirt with one hand and was relentlessly punching him with the other.

It sounded like him now, but younger. *"I hate me."* It punched him. *"I wish I wasn't born. Then they'd be happy."* It punched him harder. *"I want to die."* It kept punching and punching, leaving his face a bloody pulp. *"I want to die. I want to die."*

He squirmed under its relentless fury as the metallic taste of blood bloomed in his mouth, and those words flooded his mind like a monsoon. His crazed eyes fixed on his stickie, which had slid away, and he desperately reached for it as blow after blow pummeled his face.

"Can't have anything nice."

"Don't deserve to be happy!"

"Wish I wasn't born."

His fingers grazed against the stickie's handle.

"Never should have had you."

"You horrible little bastard!"

"I want to die."

He flinched. He was still reaching for the stickie. But for a second, he could've sworn he was reaching for a gun. *No gun. It's a stickie.* Just a stickie. *Grab the stickie.*

"Look what you've done!"

"I'm s-s-sorry.... I didn't mean t-t-to...."

He had the stickie. He had it.

"Look at her!"

"P-Papa, don't—!"

A roar erupted from deep within him, and he plunged the stickie into the clone's chest. He shoved the clone off of him, ripped the stickie out, and stabbed the clone again and again as he screamed. The clone's wooden chest broke. Splinters flew everywhere. Tears streamed down Kearney's cheeks as he kept screaming and stabbing, his mind begging for the clone to die already so he could stop hurting it.

The mummy on the throne stared at him, studying his erratic behavior.

His screaming turned into sobbing. He wiped blood-mixed tears away as he stopped and stared down at his own motionless and disfigured wooden body, brown eyes forever fixed on him. "I'm sorry," he whispered hoarsely, leaning against his stickie as he begged himself to look away from the clone. He pressed his forehead against his arm as his chest jerked from his sobs. "I'm s-sorry.... I'm s-so sorry...."

"Why are you sorry?"

He slowly lifted his head as he locked eyes with the mummy. He'd forgotten it was even there. He stumbled to his feet, his mind drunk on the sorrow overwhelming it, before shakily pointing his now-broken stickie at the mummy. "I s-s-said leave," he whispered, sounding more like he was pleading than demanding.

It tilted its head sideways. *"Why do you want me gone?"* it asked in a toying voice.

"You took Dakota...." He started heading toward it, dragging his stickie behind him as he held his head low. "You took Levi," he choked out. "And now you made me remember...made me hurt myself." He was standing only inches away from the mummy now.

It was slanted so far back in its seat that it had to look up at him. *"I'm just the worst, aren't I?"* it teased again.

Kearney raised the broken stickie high above his head, its sharp and splintered end aimed to go plunging down. "You are." He thrust it into the mummy's chest.

Gabi gasped for breath as she dodged the flagpole that was swinging for her head. She stumbled to her feet as her assailant whipped the pole out of the ground and swung it again, almost lopping her shoulder off in the process. She turned on her heel and started running as quickly as she could. She wasn't running from the fight; she had more honor than that. But No-Face had a habit of playing dirty.

Gabi raced around the corner and found herself in the town square. It was empty now. Completely desolate. She looked over her shoulder to see Jolly, and she paused to stare at him in bewilderment.

In the corner of her vision, she saw that flagpole swinging at her again, but she didn't have any time to react. It hit her side with a sickening *thud*, and she gasped in agony as she fell to the ground, clutching her stomach and struggling to breathe. She raised her head in a daze and managed to make out No-Face's shape leaning over her, reaching for her. Grabbing her, lifting her, dragging her.

Gabi winced in pain as she feebly fought back. The world was coming back to her now. She was in a building, being dragged up stairs. Her ribs were burning. "What are you doing?" she managed to gasp out.

No-Face looked back at her. "Getting rid of you."

Gabi shuddered when a cold draft blew over her. She looked up and spotted a half-destroyed balcony. She started twisting in an attempt to slip out of No-Face's grip, and No-Face let her fall to the floor.

"P-Please," she begged. "Please don't."

No-Face loomed over her. "Why not? Nobody will get it any other way." She kneeled to her level. "I'm Gabi." She put a hand on her own chest to enunciate her point.

Gabi gathered enough strength to crawl away and was quickly pressed up against a wall, letting out panicked breaths. "Please, stop lying to yourself. You're not me!"

No-Face stepped toward her before grabbing her by the shoulders. "I'm *Gabi*. Okay? Say it."

Gabi slowly shook her head. "Please. I can help you if you'd just let me...."

"Say it."

"Saying it won't help you. It'll only make things worse!"

No-Face paused. Then, her mouth broadened into an odd smile. "If you really want to help, I'll let you. But there's only one way you can." She kneeled down to Gabi's level. Then she wrapped her hands around Gabi's throat. "You can help me by dying."

Gabi's eyes filled with panic as she squirmed in No-Face's tightening grip.

No-Face started shaking her back and forth as she strangled her. "Die. *Die.* I'll be Gabi once you *die,*" she whispered.

Gabi tried to pry her fingers off but to no avail. She kicked and choked and writhed. Her lungs screamed in pain. Her ribs begged her to let them rest. Soon, her hands dropped to her sides as her head rolled back, her gasps growing faint.

No-Face's twisted smile grew. "I'm Gabi. Finally, I'll be *Gabi.*"

"Get off 'er!"

No-Face ducked, narrowly dodging a giant scissor blade swinging for her head and letting Gabi fall to the ground. She stumbled back and glanced at the blade's wielder, Calder. "You almost hurt me. Gabi."

Calder scowled and pointed the blade at her. "Yer nothin' like Gabs, *Liar.*"

No-Face cocked her head with a blank stare as Calder rushed to Gabi, who was still gasping for breath. He draped her arm over his shoulder as he helped her to her feet. "C'mon, Gabs," he urged her. "We gotta go."

There was a violent tremor from outside, and the three were swallowed up by a wave of dust that swept through the town. When it had settled, half of the building had been destroyed. Gabi looked around anxiously. "What was that?"

"It's Jolly. I dunno why he's 'ere, but he is."

She stiffened when she noticed Calder was on the verge of tears. "Are you okay? Where's Kearney?"

"I'm fine." He shook his head. "He's in Jolly."

"What's he doing in there—?"

"First Gabi," No-Face snapped, "I'm waiting."

They both looked at her. She took a step toward them and glared at Calder. "Go away. The grown-ups are talking."

He glared back with just as much ferocity. "I'm just as grown-up as you are, Liar."

Her face scrunched up with annoyance as she groaned. "None of you ever get it right. It's *Gabi*." Her gaze trailed to Gabi. "See? You're confusing him."

"Nobody's confused 'xcept you!" he retorted.

"Calder," Gabi urged, "go."

He looked up at her anxiously. "But—!"

"I'll be fine. Go make sure Kearney's safe."

He stared at her for another moment before lowering his head. "I'm not goin'." He gripped the scissor blade in his hands defensively.

Gabi looked away with a sigh. Calder couldn't tell, but she had the slightest ghost of a smile on her face. "Alright, then."

He smiled with relief, but his smile was immediately replaced with a look of dismay when Gabi shoved him down the stairs. She turned her attention back to No-Face as Calder tumbled his way down. That would only keep him away for a minute or so, but that was all the time she needed.

"This isn't going to make you happy."

"Well, gee. Thanks." No-Face frowned. "I'll be very happy when I return to being faceless now that I have your advice, won't I?"

"No-Face, listen—"

"You listen. I have your memories. I have your face!"

"But you're still not me. You never will be, no matter how hard you try." Gabi inched closer. "Your past, who you really are, will always be in the way of that."

No-Face shook her head. "It hurts too much to be me. You're easier."

"So, you just want to take the easy path? Is that what all this is? Killing me is the easy path?"

"Maybe it is. You can take the easy path, too, if you want. One that's nicer for you."

"Which is?"

"To give up. Your memories hurt a lot. That aside, I don't want to give them back. Do you really want them that badly?"

"None of that's going to stop me."

No-Face's eye narrowed as she studied her carefully. "Why do you want them so much?"

Gabi balled her fists with resolve. "Because out there, I have a sister, and I want to remember her."

No-Face scoffed. "You'll regret remembering."

They were standing only inches away from each other now. "I won't give up," Gabi promised.

"I won't either. Guess we're right back where we started," No-Face sneered.

Gabi wasn't feeling righteous anger anymore, only rage. "You don't have anything, No-Face!" she yelled. "I have parents waiting for me. I have a sister who needs my help. I'm tired of playing these stupid games. The only reason I'm still fighting is because I have something to fight for. What do *you* have?"

No-Face stiffened, taken aback by Gabi's sudden outburst. She stared at the floor. "I...I have...me."

"You don't even have that because you're too busy trying to be me."

She swallowed, her lips flattened in a white line. "I...I don't know, then." She looked upset that she didn't have a better answer.

Gabi's expression softened as she was hit by a pang of guilt. "I didn't mean to be harsh." She reluctantly reached for No-Face's hand. "I'm sorry. You *do* have you. That's reason enough to stop trying to be me. You're more than enough, No-Face."

No-Face slapped her hand away. "No, no. You're right. I have nothing. That's why I need your face." A hint of fury flashed in her eyes then faded, replaced with an immense sorrow. "It wouldn't be the same, would it?"

Gabi took a step back, unsure of what to make of No-Face's sudden shift.

"You have all those people who care for you. I'd just be alone," No-Face choked out. "I'm tired of being alone.... Maybe this isn't the easy way, after all. Maybe there is no way." Her eyes trailed up to meet Gabi's. "Are you sure you want them back?" she asked, utterly defeated.

"My memories?" Gabi was in disbelief. "I-I do."

No-Face's eyes fell again. She gave a small nod when she saw a string lying at their feet. She picked it up. "When you see this get pulled, grab it," she muttered. She walked through the balcony's tattered curtains without a word, disappearing from view with the string still in hand.

Gabi stared down at the string. *What's she doing?* "No-Face?" Horror took over as she realized what No-Face had in mind. She started running for the balcony. "No-Face, wait! There's a better way to do this! *Don't!*"

The sound of wood crashing and splintering came from outside. The curtains swayed slightly, entirely unaffected by what had happened beyond them. Gabi flinched back, letting out short, panicked breaths. With a shudder, she lowered her gaze to the string, which was now pulled taut. *Why didn't I stop her...?*

She stared at the string as it pulsed with red energy. She was too scared to move. Too scared to see what was left of No-Face. With a shaky hand, she reached out and touched the string, begging that doing this would solve all her problems and end this nightmare, even though she knew it wasn't that easy.

When her hand grazed the string, she screamed. It felt like her head had just been split in two and someone was dumping all of her missing memories into it like they were a vat of acid.

Red hair, teal eyes. Loved the library. Her legs crumpled beneath her as she fell to her knees, still holding the string. This was it. She was getting those memories back, and she didn't care how much it'd hurt to do it. *She'd go to the library after school.* She gripped her chest as her heart beat wildly out of control, and millions of emotions all fought for their place. *The library. Oh God, the library.* Her breaths grew short and shallow as her head swam. *I didn't make it. She's gone. The library.* The string slipped away, and she fell flat against the floor. She stared at the ceiling as images of her sister flooded her mind, and she struggled to breathe. *Anais went to the library.*

House Full of Strings

Chapter 26

The Tailor Talks About Committing Murder

Kearney shuddered as he coughed, breathing in more dust than air. Ignoring the soreness in his arms, he raised them to rub his eyes. He lay there in a haze, trying to remember what had happened before that point. *Jolly.* He groaned as he sat himself up. *Jolly's gone.* He swayed as he rose to his feet and looked around. He was still in Jolly. More like what was left of him.

Light started to seep through the thick clouds of dust filling the air, and he walked toward it. He stumbled into the light, only to be met by the ruins of Toy Town. He stared at it with wide eyes, hardly able to comprehend it. *But...Jolly's gone.* He started walking through the ruins. *What happened? Jolly's gone.*

A distant sob broke the haunting silence, and he gasped. *Gabi.* He started running. *Is she hurt? Where's Calder? Why's Toy Town ruined? Jolly's gone.* When he made it to the town square, he noticed a building—or, rather, half a building—with its door wide open. Gabi's sobs were louder now. He hurried into the building and raced up the stairs, and once he made it to the top, he spotted Calder hugging her as she kneeled on the ground.

"Gabi?" He raced to their side. "What's wrong?"

She didn't look up at him. All she did was shake her head as she cried. "I remember," she whispered. "She's dead. She's really dead."

Calder looked up at him, appearing just as confused and helpless as Kearney felt.

"What?" Kearney dropped to his knees to see her face. He gently held her hands and rubbed them as he tried to make sense of what she was saying. "Who's dead?"

"Anais." She still didn't look up, trapped in a world of her own grief. "My sister...my baby sister...she's dead. I came here because of that *stupid* dream." She kneeled over again, and Kearney was helpless to do anything to comfort her as she buried her face in her hands and continued sobbing. "That stupid dream...."

Dead? How? When? Kearney wrapped his arms around her, anxiously looking up at Calder for help, but he seemed to have no idea how to give any. Kearney continued his attempts to calm her, but they were all in vain, as her crying only worsened. "Gabi, please...." He wanted to be able to say the right thing more than anything, but the truth was, he was as big a mess as she was. "J-Just try to breathe." *Why would I say that? Of all the things I could've said, why that?*

"She's dead."

He struggled to steady his breathing as he hugged her. "Gabi—"

A loud *whizz* pierced the silence, and a needle pierced Calder's chest. Gabi yelped, and Kearney held her close as their attention snapped to the needle. Calder tried to pull it out, but he couldn't. He noticed the thread tethered to it. "What's all this about?"

"This is where our game ends, Calder," a voice echoed in reply.

While Calder appeared mildly annoyed at most, Kearney and Gabi were looking around in terror, and before they knew it, more of those needles were raining down on them. Kearney's ears were filling with whizzing chaos, and he quickly shielded Gabi and braced himself for what would be the last piercing pain he'd feel in his life, but it never came.

He slowly opened his eyes and looked at Gabi. She had her face in her hands, and she looked fairly alive. And he was pretty sure that he was alive, too. He looked up and saw nothing but needles in the ground and a prison of unyielding thread around them.

Gabi gasped. "What's happening?"

"I-I don't know."

The voice returned, "I told you I had a plan, remember? Well, it's time for you to play your part." The Tailor appeared on the floor above the pair, playing with a needle on her fingertips as she sauntered along. She glanced at Gabi. "I was betting on No-Face, but I suppose it's nice that you've come out on top."

Fresh tears poured down Gabi's face, and Kearney wiped them away and tried to console her.

He glared at The Tailor. "You're insane."

The Tailor smiled. "I prefer goal-oriented. After all, everything I do—everything I've ever done—has all been in pursuit of a single goal."

"And what goal is that? What could *possibly* be worth what you've done?"

"My dearest Phantasos, of course." She smiled. "Before there was any town or dolls or bright red doors, there was just him and me."

"You mean the *real* you," Kearney snapped.

Her eyes narrowed, and a heavy silence hung between them. "...Do you know why I call myself The Tailor?"

He did nothing but stare at her.

"It's because the memories I inherited were only fragments, and the 'real' me's name was never something I knew. Although such is normal for Liars, I suppose. As far as I'm concerned, these memories belong to me and me alone, and I'm no one but myself." She chuckled. "It's not like the real me needs the knowledge I possess anyway because, up until now, she was too busy trying to become Gabi."

"What's she talking about?" Gabi asked as her eyes darted between The Tailor and Kearney.

He continued to stare at her, only now in shock. "No-Face was...?"

"It's all in the past now, little friend. Unfortunately, I can't say that about everything." The Tailor glanced back at her needle. "Phantasos loved me very dearly. And how I loved him back! He told me that we were made for each other and that we'd be together forever and ever, and I gave up my very flesh and bone to be with him." Her eyes darkened, and a bitter look came across her face. "But then others came, and he threw me away. Like I was nothing." She dropped the needle and watched it fall to the floor. Then her gaze trailed back to Kearney and Gabi. "Do you think that pulling the strings of this town is an easy feat? If so, I'm afraid you're quite wrong. And a scheme of such magnitude as mine, I believe, my dearest will feel obligated to reward me for. Ergo, I return to being in his graces once I make it back to him." A twisted smile crept across her face. "His guard will be down, and that's when I'll do him in."

Calder tugged at the string in a vain attempt to get free. "You can't!"

"I will." The playful joy in her eyes vanished, and she leaned over the rails as she glared at him. "If only you understood the true depths of his lies. Of why this world even exists to begin with." Her grip on the rails tightened until she forced herself to relax. "Toy Town isn't needed anymore, and after he's dead, we'll all be free. Don't you want to be free?"

Calder stared at her as he stammered, his half-words filled with uncertainty.

"Free?" Kearney asked.

She tilted her head as she looked at him. "Free." She grinned. "And it looks like you'll play a grand part in his assassination, after all."

Gabi sniffed. "But why go through the trouble of the trials? Why lock us up?"

"Because getting past the dangers behind the Wall is no easy feat, and I wasn't about to pass up the ability to test two able-bodied youths." Her eyes fixed on Kearney. "One of which might even be able to help me control those dangers and use them in my favor."

"I don't plan on leaving Gabi here alone." Despite the certainty in his voice, his mind was in a panic. "And if you're really crazy enough to think I'd ever help you after what you did to Dakota, you're dead wrong."

The Tailor scoffed. "Dakota brought his downfall upon himself. And if you like having your little lover here alive, you'll come along."

Kearney froze in horror as he glanced at Gabi. He'd seen what The Tailor could do. She was insane enough to wipe out an entire town she'd built without batting an eye. Surely, hurting one girl would be far from the worst she'd done. He let out a shaky breath. "A-Alright."

Gabi hugged him tighter, as if doing that would keep him from going. "No, don't!" she sobbed.

"It's okay." *Nothing's okay.*

"No, it's not! I can't lose you, too—"

"And I can't lose *you*, Gabi." He desperately tried to keep his voice steady for her. "Just…get out of here as soon as you can, okay?"

"Please," she whispered desperately, on the verge of tears again. "*Please*, I'm not ready to lose you, too."

"Gabi," he stroked her cheek. "I'd never forgive myself if you got hurt."

"Why do you expect me to carry that guilt, then?"

"I...." He found himself at a loss for words. "I know how it hurts. But I want you to know that no matter what happens to me, I want you to be happy." He hugged her again, trying to stifle the pain rising in his throat. He'd never be able to hear those words himself, but he could still give them to her. He got to his feet as she watched helplessly, his fear gone as he glared at The Tailor. "Alright," he said again, his voice steadier.

The Tailor nodded with satisfaction. "Finally done wasting my time, are we?" With a snap of her fingers, the threads loosened, allowing him to walk out of the cage. Once he was out, the strings tightened once more, leaving Gabi trapped inside.

She didn't look at Kearney. Tears were sliding down her cheeks as she stared at the floor.

Kearney let out a shaky breath as he turned back to The Tailor, who was making her way down the stairs. She waltzed up to the door. "To the Wall."

"Freckles, wait!" Calder was still trying to yank the needle that had pinned him down out of his chest. "I'm comin' with you!"

"No, you're not," The Tailor hissed.

"Freckles needs me to keep 'im safe."

"He doesn't. That's the point of the trials."

He stopped thrashing and glared at her, his voice low. "D'kota would want it."

She glared back, her eyes unreadable. Then she looked away. "The only reason he came to me to begin with was because he was abandoned. Abandoned by you." She snapped her fingers, and the needle and string slipped out of Calder's chest. "If you think doing this will honor his memory, you'll come to find you're dead wrong," she scowled. She began to walk away.

Kearney looked back at Gabi, who was now watching him with a distant look on her face, seemingly accepting that she could do nothing but soak in this last moment they'd ever share. Kearney wanted more than anything to run back to her, to wrap his arms around her and kiss her, to tell her everything would be okay. But doing that would only make walking away harder. He squeezed his eyes shut as he followed The Tailor, fighting with all he could to not look back.

For the longest time, Kearney couldn't understand Toy Town's perpetual evening state, but as soon as he reached the Wall, he saw why. The Wall was massive, towering over him for what could've been miles, completely consuming him and all of Toy Town in its shadow. He probably would've noticed it sooner if he'd taken a good, hard look past Toy Town's gates. All this time, he'd mistaken the Wall for the sky.

There were hundreds of pencils and crayons scattered at his feet, and he could see that they had been used for all the writing scribbled across the Wall's gray surface in handwriting of various qualities. The thousands of words were all names, although he had no idea who had put them there and for whom.

He lowered his eyes to the tiny door in the Wall. It wasn't very impressive, being about half his height. The Tailor swung it open and glanced back at him and Calder, waiting patiently.

Kearney glanced back at Calder, who'd picked up a broken pencil and was writing a name on the Wall. *Dakota.*

He found a blue crayon and joined Calder. With a heavy sigh, he let the tip of the crayon touch the Wall's cold surface and wrote a name on it. *Levi.*

House Full of Strings

Chapter 27

The World's Scariest Ballerina Puts on a Show

Kearney struggled to keep his feet from dragging through the mud as he and Calder trailed behind The Tailor. It was quiet behind the Wall. Eerily so. It was the only place in the House he'd seen that had actual plant life, but it felt more dead than anywhere he'd been so far.

He scanned the area. It was too quiet. Noise was annoying; if there was a threat, it'd be harder to hear, making him less safe. But silence? Silence kept him in a state of constant anticipation, always tense and waiting for a sound that would never come.

He glanced at Calder. Ever since what had happened with Dakota, he'd been quietly staring at his feet with a dull look on his face.

The Tailor froze, as did the other two.

"What's wrong?" Kearney asked.

She stared at the metal gates in front of her. Her expression looked haunted. "Nothing." She turned to look at them. "We're about to enter Eye Stealer's den. While Eye Stealer's an integral part of the plan, it's also dangerous. So..." she cleared her throat and looked away, "watch out."

"W-Wait, who?" Kearney asked.

She let out a heavy groan. "Eye Stealer. It's a monster that lives here. Rumor has it that my dearest made Eye Stealer to keep anyone with ill intentions from reaching him. To be honest, it's been so long that I barely remember why he really made that thing to begin with." She gently pushed the gates, and they creaked open, making the trio wince in unison.

Kearney stared down the dark corridor then sucked in a big breath. *It's not like I have much of a choice anyway.*

They walked down the narrow passage in mostly darkness, and Kearney couldn't help but cringe as his shoes got even more soaked. It felt like he was in some kind of old, damp cellar. Every now and then, his feet would kick against something hard yet hollow, and he'd wince at the thought of what it could be. As they got closer to the other end of the passage, he was able to see the contents of the cellar better, although he wished he couldn't. There were doll husks everywhere, and they all had one thing in common: their eyes had been ripped out.

Calder lowered his gaze to his shoes, trying to keep himself from looking at the husks, while The Tailor continued on unabashedly with her head held high.

As Kearney's eyes trailed over the seemingly endless supply of husks, they fixed on one in particular. He jumped back, just as befuddled as he was alarmed.

The husk that stood out to him was horribly scratched, its face forever twisted in terror, and its wooden eyes ripped out of their sockets, not unlike the rest. But the unnerving thing was that the doll was The Tailor. He forced himself to look ahead at the other The Tailor, who was alive and well, walking ahead of him.

He noticed she'd also stopped briefly to look at the husk. *Now that I think about it, of course, she'd want to use something that's bested her before.* He wondered if the husk he was looking at had been The Tailor or No-Face.

The Tailor shifted slightly. "...Would you believe me if I told you that wasn't even the first time she'd had her eyes scratched out?"

He stared at her then back at the husk. *Oh.*

She cleared her throat, ready to move on. "Eye Stealer's blind, but do as much as breathe too loudly, and it'll shred you in a heartbeat. Not that *I'll* need to be quiet, but you two focus on getting to the other side and leave the talking to me."

Talking. The Tailor planned on talking to it. Kearney and Calder exchanged wary glances, and by the time they looked back at The Tailor, she was already gone.

Calder shifted uneasily and took Kearney's hand. "You better not tease me 'bout this," he muttered.

Kearney didn't reply. He kept walking without a word, his grip on Calder's hand tightening slightly.

The end of a cellar led to a giant ice rink. Kearney didn't know how, given the air was mildly chilly at worst, but the ice was perfectly solid and very slippery, too. His attention drifted to the giant metal puppet sitting in the center of the rink. Eye Stealer. Its body was limp and its head tilted back lifelessly, but Kearney couldn't shake the feeling that it was dangerous. *It looks like a ballerina.*

"I suggest you look up," The Tailor commented as she walked, not giving Eye Stealer as much as a glance, though it was evident she was nervous.

Kearney let his gaze trail to the ceiling and stiffened in fear. Hundreds of doll eyes dangled from the ceiling on strings as if they were the toys hanging off a baby's mobile. And they were all watching him. He looked away in panic and horror. Dangling from the ceiling like that, it didn't matter whether they were from a doll or a fleshy person; they were just eyes. "What's going on?" he demanded as quietly as he could.

She glanced over her shoulder at him. "Why do you think it steals other's sight?"

"So it...it can see us through the *eyes?*"

Watching Eye Stealer nervously, Calder hastily put Kearney between it and himself. Kearney glared at him.

He glared back. "It makes me n'rvous, that's all."

The three froze when Eye Stealer twitched. They stared in bewilderment as it lifted an arm as if trying to pull itself up through the air, but its arm fell back to its side in defeat. It raised another arm, this time scraping it against the ground as it sloppily pulled itself forward. It stumbled to its feet, teetering every which way as it gained its balance. After that, it stood in place, completely motionless.

Everyone stared at it, waiting for whatever was to come. Strings from overhead slithered their way down and wrapped themselves around its arms, trembling with excitement. Eye Stealer's legs clicked together as it straightened itself out, and with one gentle kick, it began to glide around the arena, its string-guided arms gracefully extended and every movement perfectly calculated.

Calder bawled in terror as he clutched Kearney's leg. "We gotta run!"

Kearney looked at The Tailor, whose eyes were wide in fear. "Walk faster," she whispered, her voice urgent. She started hurrying across the arena, her gaze skipping from Kearney to Calder to Eye Stealer, who was rapidly closing in on them.

It began gliding circles around them, cutting Calder and Kearney off from The Tailor. One of its legs lifted backward and in the air. Its needle-like edge glinted menacingly. Eye Stealer continued its performance as Kearney and Calder inched along, shaking at the thought of what it might do next. Kearney held Calder close as he glanced back at the dangling eyes overhead. They were all watching *him*.

Eye Stealer swayed its arms without a care in the world, and its clawed fingers trailed threateningly close to Kearney's head. They curled with sudden viciousness and a loud screech, aiming for his skull. With a gasp, he quickly jumped back and out of the way, pulling Calder with him. Eye Stealer stood perfectly still, its fist now clenched; it seemed to be struggling to comprehend the fact that he wasn't in its grip. With a swing of its arms, it skated back into motion, but now with aggression and purpose. The dangling eyes quivered as they watched

Kearney, who was now hurrying around the arena in a vain attempt to get away from Eye Stealer—but he was in its territory now.

He shoved Calder away and bolted for one end of the arena only to look back and see Eye Stealer gliding closely behind him. "Tailor!" he cried in panic. "Get it away from me!"

Despite Kearney's attempt to distance himself from Calder, Calder was running as quickly as he could to reach him, but running on ice didn't prove to be very effective. "Freckles, fight it!"

"That'll only make it worse!" The Tailor snapped. "We don't want to agitate it!"

"It looks agitat'd to me!"

It swung again, this time grazing Kearney's chin and sending him skidding back with a yelp of pain. It dove forward with a precise dash, caught him by the shirt, and lifted him off his feet. He kicked his legs wildly, but it hardly seemed to acknowledge his attempts to escape as it rested the sharpened tips of its fingers around his eye.

His heart pounded wildly. He shrank at the cold touch of the metal claws on his skin. He felt them tightening around his eye as if they were deciding whether to rip it clean out or slowly squeeze it out. "T-Tailor!"

The Tailor's brows went up. For the first time, she looked genuinely scared, which only terrified Kearney more. She started hurrying across the arena as she pulled out her needle, and all the dangling eyes fixed on her as they noticed her approach. Eye Stealer, now able to see only The Tailor, froze and waited patiently. As for The Tailor, her speed-walk turned into a saunter as she got closer. She seemed to relax, seeing Kearney was no longer in immediate danger.

"Eye Stealer," she began, "I have a proposition for you."

Calder's mouth gaped open. "You wanna *negotiate* with that thing?"

She ignored him. "I know you have a vendetta against Phantasos."

That name made Eye Stealer shift with curiosity.

"Coincidentally, so do I. I've come to enlist your help."

The eyes overhead looked at each other as if collectively thinking over this proposition. Then the strings latching onto Eye Stealer trembled again, and it slammed Kearney into the ground. He yelped in both shock and pain as he lay sprawled on the ice, and Eye Stealer spun to fight Calder, who looked ready to leave everyone behind and bolt to safety.

The Tailor scowled as she glared at the dangling eyes. "I was asking for *her* choice, not yours!" She rushed at Eye Stealer and, with a swift swing, slashed her needle at it again. Eye Stealer glided back before spinning at her, its metal tutu now a deadly sawblade.

Kearney was only just stumbling to his feet when Calder grabbed his hand and started racing for the exit. They rushed through the broken arch as The Tailor and Eye Stealer clashed behind them, and soon, they were perfectly safe. But the sounds of the clashing didn't cease. If anything, they only got more intense. But then, they went dead quiet.

Kearney and Calder waited in tense silence. Soon, they heard the sound of little footsteps running toward them followed by frantic shrieking.

"Run! Run!" The Tailor came speeding around the corner. "Forget the plan, just run!"

The three of them raced down the passage; the Eye Stealer's pointed feet scraped against the hard ground as it pursued them. They raced through another arch, and The Tailor quickly pulled the pair to the side. The three huddled behind a giant rock and listened fearfully as Eye Stealer glided closer to them. In front of the rock, it froze, its outstretched hand holding a single dangling eyeball that swiveled around in search of its prey. When it saw nothing, Eye Stealer glided on, disappearing down the path ahead. Kearney slowly let out the breath he'd been holding as he glanced at The Tailor. She looked nervous. And if she was nervous, that meant he should be terrified. He noticed the giant scratch on her back, leaving a tear in her ruffled white dress.

She glanced at him. "We'll be fine," she said curtly. "This is just a little bump in the plan, nothing more."

He nodded shakily, but Calder wasn't having it. "What happened back there?" he demanded in an irate whisper. "I thought you told us not to worry 'bout nothin'!"

"I said it was a small hiccup!" she hissed back. She rose to her feet, warily looking over her shoulder to ensure Eye Stealer wasn't there. She beckoned for the other two to stand as well. "We need to move. We can try ne-gotiating with it again up ahead."

"Why?" Kearney stayed in place with his brow knit. "What good will going somewhere else do? That thing will just try to kill us again."

"The point is to get her away from those eyes. They're both a blessing and a curse to her, providing her with sight but in return, controlling her."

"Her?" Calder asked as his green eyes narrowed.

"Yes, her." The Tailor walked ahead and peeked around the corner. "All clear. Follow me." She disap-peared around the bend.

Left without a choice, the other two headed after her.

It had been a while since they'd last seen Eye Stealer at this point, but Kearney still spent every moment waiting for it, or rather, her, to jump out of the hedges and tear them all to shreds. They weren't surrounded by rock walls anymore; instead, there were laurels. The Tailor stopped in her tracks with a soft gasp, and Kearney and Calder froze in response.

"What's goin' on?" Calder asked as his head swiveled in panic.

She'd paused in front of a statue of a man with ant-lers. Behind it was a wall of laurels. "Nothing serious."

A smug grin crept across her face as she looked at the statue. "Just a spitting image of my precious."

Kearney exchanged glances with Calder before reluctantly relaxing. "Well, now what?" he asked. "It's a dead end."

The Tailor studied the blank stone slab sitting at the statue's feet. "I remember this. He should give us instructions any time now." She stared at it patiently, her hands on her hips. Meanwhile, the other two sat down and watched her, leaving everyone staring at nothing in particular.

After a bit, Calder got to his feet. "This is dumb." He marched up to the slab and kicked it. "Come on, already!"

She gasped and pulled him away. "Are you insane?" she yelled. "Don't treat it like that! You, of all people, should know how easily he gets offended!"

"It's a *rock!*" he yelled back.

Kearney was watching the slab closely and almost jumped when words appeared on it. "There it is."

The Tailor and Calder stared at him before glancing at the slab.

The Tailor crossed her arms. "This is why I'm in charge." She studied words on the slab. "*Spin clockwise twice. Then counterclockwise three times.*"

Kearney got to his feet, not looking pleased at all. "I don't see how that would help. And why not just spin counterclockwise once? That would have the same effect." He hesitated momentarily before spinning around once and looking at the slab again. "See? It's nothing."

"This is our only option, little friend." The Tailor waved her finger with a condescending look. "Now, I order you to obey the slab's command."

Kearney rolled his eyes. Calder groaned. The three of them started spinning, counting as they finished each rotation.

"One, two—!" Calder wobbled into Kearney, who stumbled backward and stepped on The Tailor's foot, who just looked disappointed in them. She glared at Kearney. He quickly pulled his foot off hers, and they finished their spinning in awkward silence.

Once they were done, Calder looked around expectantly before crossing his arms. "All that did was make us look stupid."

The Tailor glanced back at the slab, which was now blank. "Well, something happened."

Calder kicked the statue. "Nothin' useful."

The statue then began rumbling as if attempting to retaliate. The laurels behind it quaked and split apart, revealing the stone path continuing through the maze.

Calder sputtered. "That was me, not the spinnin'!"

The Tailor suppressed a sigh as she brushed past him, doing everything in her power not to hit him over the head. She glanced back at the other two, who were still standing in place and staring at the newly opened path. "Are you coming, or shall I leave the two of you here?"

Kearney and Calder begrudgingly followed her through the maze, still trying to process what exactly was going on in this strange place. They walked and walked until they encountered a dead end with another statue. It was the same man, but now he was leaning down with an arm extended forward. He had a big grin on his face, as if offering something.

Another stone slab was laid out in front of the trio, and its command appeared: *"Green-haired one, slap the girl next to you."*

Calder grinned as he glanced at The Tailor. "I only see one girl 'ere."

Her face scrunched up with annoyance. "Just get it over with so I can repay you tenfold," she seethed with gritted teeth.

He joyfully sent the palm of his hand flying into her face, the sheer force of the hit so powerful that she fell back. She lay on the floor, dazed, before leaping back to her feet, her hand primed to hit him back.

But before she could repay him for his generosity, Kearney noticed another command on the slab: *"Slap her again."*

A few amusing minutes after that, they resumed walking down the path, only now, The Tailor had two scratch marks on her face while Calder had twenty. They soon encountered a third statue, this one standing upright and bearing a sterner expression. The shrubs behind it separated almost immediately, revealing three different paths, and the tablet in front of it spelled out the words, *"Split up."*

They stared at the slab and then at each other. Kearney frowned. "This is all weird enough as is. I don't think we should split ways."

The Tailor shook her head. "While I agree, my dearest must have a purpose for requesting such."

"Well, I'm not buyin' it!" Calder grabbed Kearney's hand. "*You* can go down that path alone if you want, but I'm takin' Freckles down this one."

Kearney nodded, and The Tailor watched as the two started wandering down one path together. After a peaceful minute of walking, the laurels began to rumble and rushed at the pair. They screamed hysterically and grabbed each other as if that would save them from the vines wrapping around them. They got dragged back to the fork in the road and were left sitting there, clutching each other and shaking.

"What was th-that?" Kearney stuttered.

"I-I think it r'lly wants us to split up," Calder gasped.

The two stumbled to their feet and nervously looked at each other before looking back at The Tailor, who was grinning with amusement. "What did I tell you?"

Calder frowned. "We get it already. Yer always right."

"If you get it, then you'll listen." She guided Kearney toward the path to the right. "You take that one, Calder will take the left, and I'll take the middle."

"No, wait." Calder anxiously jumped to his feet. "We can…climb over them hedges!" He ran up to a hedge and jumped excitedly. "Help me up, Freckles!"

Kearney sighed before reluctantly hoisting him up, which was fairly easy. Calder scrambled to the top and stuck his fist in the air in triumph, only to scream in terror while being sucked into the laurels and spat out moments later. He stared at the ground as he brushed leaves out of his hair.

"Fine, we'll do it yer way," he muttered. He looked up at Kearney. "What'll happen if you get lost?"

"Who's to say that *I'll* be the one to get lost?" Kearney mussed Calder's green hair and helped him to his feet. "I won't. Promise."

Calder lowered his head. "Alright."

The Tailor looked incredibly bored at this point. "Can we move on already, or are the two of you planning on making a blood pact while you're at it?"

The boys frowned. The moment was officially over. They looked down the three paths before exchanging glances in silence and parting ways, the laurels closing behind them.

It wasn't long before Kearney found himself in front of another statue, this one with a mocking smile on its face. Two separate paths appeared, and the stone tablet spelled out its command, though this time it was more like a riddle. *"The left path is the right way. Be sure to take the right path."*

He started walking down the left path before pausing. Now that he'd considered it, the tablet made less sense than he'd first thought. *I guess I'll keep going left be-*

cause it's right—or something like that, he decided. He continued to walk down the left path for a bit before finding another statue. This one was holding a hand to its face as though trying to keep itself from laughing at who was presented before it.

The words, *"You held him back,"* carved themselves out on the slab.

His brow furrowed as he read it. The laurels split behind the statue, revealing one path instead of two. He stared at the words for another minute before uneasily continuing down the path. Soon, a third statue appeared, now with a disgusted look on its face.

Kearney tensely stared up at it before looking down at the tablet, which said, *"You hurt him."* He scratched the back of his head anxiously as he felt his cheeks heat up, guilt worming its way into his chest. Another path was revealed, and he continued walking, now at a slower pace but still strangely anxious to know what the next statue would tell him.

The next soon came into view, with its back turned to him and its arms crossed and a tablet with the words, *"You took everything from him."*

Another path appeared, and he was now moving at a crawling pace. Yet another statue appeared, this one still with its back turned, but now it was looking over its shoulder with a repulsed look on its face.

"You never deserved him."

Another path and another slow and painful walk down it. He didn't feel like he was walking down the path to get to the end anymore, or even for Calder. He didn't know why he kept going; after all, there'd only be another cruel statue waiting for him. And there it was—this one facing him with an apathetic stare that seemed to pierce through him.

"You don't deserve anything."

One more path, and he walked down it. He didn't know why. He just did. As he kept walking, the silence weighed heavily on him, and he wished he could've heard the distant ringing of the payphone again. The truth was, he missed that voice, not because he was particularly fond of it but because he always had something to say. Even if he scared Kearney, at least he gave Kearney something to think about. Now, there was nothing.

Kearney reached the end of the path and passed through a broken stone arch. There, he saw nothing but cold, dark water that spread out before him like a vast ocean. Something in him told him that the statue, or rather, The Tailor's "dearest," believed he deserved to plunge into those waters and never come back up. What scared him more was that he shared some of those sentiments.

He sat down, staring at the lake. There were thousands of strings going into the dark abyss. He wondered what was at the bottom. He jumped when one of the strings beside him quivered and watched as it glowed red. Two voices started booming in his head. He scrambled back in shock, letting out a shaky breath as he stared at it. The more it glowed, the louder the two voices got. And the weird part was he knew the voices.

He slowly inched closer to the string, then let his thumb graze it.

He was pulled into a memory in a heartbeat. He was in Toy Town. A shinier version of Toy Town. One where all the rides were free of rust. One that felt more alive.

There was screaming. He spun in circles, only to see dolls running his way. They ran past him. *Through* him. It took him a second to realize that in this memory world, he was immaterial. He looked at one of the dolls running past him and nearly reeled back in shock.

It was Calder. He was wearing a tattered police uniform. His eyes were wide, and his breaths panicked. He was running away, just like the rest of the dolls were. Kearney stared at him, unable to move an inch as the doll ran right past him.

Then there was another scream. A bloodcurdling shriek.

Kearney felt his skin crawl. *I know that voice.* He glanced at Calder, who'd frozen in horror. Calder shook as he looked ahead at safety then back at the danger he was running from. Kearney stared at what was behind them. It seemed the place everyone had been running from had only just materialized in the dream. It was the Mirror House.

Calder bolted past him, racing for the Mirror House while trying to stifle sobs of fear. Kearney ran after him. He entered the Mirror House after Calder and began racing down the halls.

"D'kota!" Calder shrieked. "D'kota, I'm comin'!" He burst into a vast room; its walls were lined with shattered mirrors.

In the middle of that room was Dakota. His limbs were dangling limply. His black hair had been ripped out of his head, which was now split down the middle. His blue eyes were frozen with terror, and his mouth was gaping open in what once could've been a scream.

A purple-eyed monster was playing with his corpse.

Calder screamed.

Kearney recoiled, falling back in horror.

Thousands of voices screamed in his head.

"I'm scared, Calder! Come back! Caldeeeeeer!"

"D'kota, I'm sorry! I'm sorry!"

"Surprise, Kearney."

Chapter 28

Calder Gets Kidnapped by Dakota(s)

Kearney jumped awake with a scream. He shook as he wrapped his arms around himself. *No, no...Dakota...poor Dakota....* He buried his face in his knees. *Calder...that's what he meant by protecting him....* Those voices kept screaming in his mind, over and over. *And that last voice...it's him. I'm getting close to him. Too close.*

He gasped when something took his hand, flinching away and scrambling to his feet, only to realize—*Dakota!* He wrapped his arms around the little black-haired doll. "D-Dakota!"

The doll looked up at him and smiled. "Hi."

"You're here! How?" *Am I going insane, or is he really here?* Between the dream and now this, all he knew was that he was so happy Dakota was back. That Dakota was *safe.*

Dakota grinned as his hand squeezed Kearney's. "A box brought me here."

He'd barely finished his reply when Kearney had lifted him off his feet, still hugging him. "Calder's here, too! We should go to him." *He's going to be so happy to see you!*

Dakota grinned again but didn't say a word.

Kearney stiffened and set him back down. "Are you okay?"

"Hmm? Oh, yeah."

"Okay," he said. "You're just...it's okay if you're a little shaken from what happened. Nobody can blame you."

Dakota studied his face as if trying to decipher what he meant. "Alright," he finally replied. He opened his mouth to say something else, but Kearney could see that he was hesitating.

"Is something on your mind?"

Dakota cleared his throat. "...What happened before?"

Kearney stared at him, still puzzled. *Does he have...amnesia, maybe?* "Jolly crushed you," he slowly explained. "And before that, well...." *I have no clue when that monster hurt him. It could've been hundreds of years ago, for all I know.*

"Oh." Dakota paused for another second before opening his mouth to say something, but he wasn't able to say it because, in the blink of an eye, a giant needle had slashed through the upper half of his head, splitting it in two. His wooden body slumped to the ground, revealing The Tailor standing right behind him.

Kearney's mouth gaped open in horror as he stared at Dakota's husk. *Oh my God. He's gone again. She killed him.*

The Tailor glared at him. "What's wrong now?"

His face paled as he continued to stare at what was left of Dakota.

She groaned. "That was a Liar, not Dakota. Be honest with yourself. Was he really acting like himself there?"

His lips pressed together as he struggled to regain his composure. "Th-That was a Liar?"

"Yes." She straightened her cufflinks with a huff. "And a very confused one at that." Her expression shifted from one of annoyance to puzzlement. "Calder isn't here?"

Finally emerging from his haze, Kearney looked around and realized Calder was indeed not there. "Did he get lost?"

"Perhaps." She studied the Liar's husk carefully. "Or, he got mixed up with another Liar. Where there's one, there's many."

Kearney stared at the maze. "Do you think he's still in there?"

"Probably."

Without another word, he started heading toward the maze.

"What are you doing?" she asked. "We don't need him. Anyway, he'll be fine, no matter what happens to him in there."

Kearney shook his head as he kept walking. "I'm not like Henry."

After a moment, her eyes lowered to her boots, her expression unreadable, and her arms crossed. "Don't take too long, understood?"

Kearney nodded gratefully before taking off down the path. His walking quickly turned into running. His breaths were short and shallow as he raced down one passage before quickly hurrying down another. He passed the pond from before, which gave him comfort. He seemed to be on the right track. Soon, he came into a clearing and froze with a shudder.

Various pieces of Calder were sprawled out on the ground. There were a few fingers here and a leg there, but the rest of him wasn't anywhere to be seen. Kearney frantically looked around but froze when he heard something. A voice.

It was quiet, but he knew whose it was—Calder's. "D'kota," the voice called dreamily. "D'kota, yer okay...I won't leave again...won't let the monst'r hurt you...."

Kearney hurried in the direction of the voice, his heart pounding as the broken boxes around him hummed at his presence. Calder's voice was getting closer.

"...You won't be alone anymore...I'll be 'ere...."

Kearney stepped into a clearing and froze when he spotted Calder. At least, most of him was there—his head, torso, an arm and a leg, too—but he was horribly scratched and barely seemed to be awake; that must've been a consequence of being so close to the boxes. And he was surrounded by at least twenty Liars that all looked like Dakota. They were trying to wrap strings around Calder and failing miserably.

"I like his face. I want it."

"You can't want it. I'm taking it."

"No, you're not. *I* am."

Kearney watched the strange scene, eyes wide with bewilderment. He carefully stepped toward them, his foot brushing against a string when he did, and all of the Liars' heads snapped in his direction at once. They stared at him with their collective blue eyes, seemingly unsure what to make of him. Then, one of them returned to their attempt at wrapping Calder in strings, and the rest quickly followed. Kearney hurried at them and started brushing them all away as they complained, and he grabbed Calder the second he found him in the swarm of Dakotas. He pulled Calder away from them and gently cradled him in his arms.

"Calder, are you alright?"

Calder didn't reply. His eyes were open, but just barely. He looked like he was dreaming more than anything else. Kearney tensed as he fixed his attention on all the Dakotas grouping around him and doing little jumps as they reached for Calder. He gently kicked them away as he hurried off, and the Dakotas followed him. They didn't seem hostile, but they were very creepy.

As soon as the boxes were out of sight, Calder started waking up. "...D'kota?"

"No, Calder," Kearney explained. "He's not here. You were just dreaming, that's all. It's time to wake up, okay?"

"I don't wanna...don't wanna leave 'im again...."

"It's okay, Calder." *How can I say that? Nothing's okay. What happened was horrible.*

401

"It's not right." Calder's voice grew steadier as he kept muttering. "It's not right. He gave up ev'rythin' for me...gave up his par'nts...for me. An' then that monst'r.... I ran away."

Parents. That word pulled Kearney out of the cloud of horror his mind had been floating in. "Parents?"

"Yeah. Par'nts...all kids got 'em."

"But you're a doll."

The Dakotas, who were still trailing behind them, were hardly even a concern at this point.

"No...I...." Calder's eyes finally opened all the way, and he tried to look back at the Dakotas, but Kearney stopped him. He shook his head and groaned as if his memories were so painful they brought him physical discomfort. "I remember when I chose to stay...D'kota got so mad. But then, he went straight to the Mister an' asked to be turned into a doll, too...so I wouldn't be lonely." He looked up at Kearney as he came to his senses. "Then we got into a fight, an' I told him I never wanted to see 'im again. Even after that, he waited in Toy Town for me for so, so long. An' when I came back, it was only for a little while before that monst'r took 'im away again. 'Cause I ran away...." His grief-filled voice trailed off.

Turn into a doll? What...? Kearney remembered what The Tailor had said. About being free. He shook the thought away and hugged Calder tighter. "Dakota was so happy to have you back, Calder," he said between pants as he ran.

He didn't notice it, but the group of Dakotas behind him was gradually thinning.

Calder looked up at him. "He was?"

"He was. He got another chance to be your friend!"

The reason their pursuers were disappearing was that something was stalking them, picking them off one by one with silent and wicked slashes, sending heads and limbs flying everywhere in its wake, but its victims didn't cry out once.

"I think that he knew you were sorry, whether you said it or not."

A thoughtful look came into Calder's eyes. "R'lly?"

"Really." Kearney's smile faded. "...Calder?"

"Yeah?"

He couldn't help it. His mind kept coming back to it like a haunting nightmare. "What do you mean when you say you weren't always a doll?"

"I thought you knew."

"No."

"Oh. Well, ev'ry doll in the House used to be a fleshy person—me, D'kota, an' that ol' No-Face, too."

"*What?*" Kearney froze in his tracks. "How?"

"It's easy, r'lly." Calder stared at his one good leg, a hint of regret in his eyes. "You come to the House, an' you see all the cool stuff inside. You meet the Mister, an' things get even better. You can have whatever you want, an' all you gotta do to get it is be the Mister's friend forever. Or, that's what he always said...." His voice trailed off, as did his gaze.

"What happened then?" Kearney asked. "How come you're all stuck out here and not with him?"

The Dakotas were all gone now.

"The Mister gets bored pretty quick, an' he loves new toys a lot more than ol' ones. That's why we gotta work hard to make 'im happy. If you don't, he throws you into the Dark Place."

"The what?"

"The chasm between 'ere and the Mister's house." Calder lowered his head. "It's dark. That's all that matt'rs."

Kearney's eyes were fixed on the ground. He had no idea what to say next or what would even be appropriate. "Why did you choose to stay?"

Calder paused before chuckling, almost as if at himself. "The Mister made me feel like I had a papa again."

Kearney was overwhelmed by the horror that had overtaken him, but in a heartbeat, it was replaced with a different feeling. He shuddered, and his grip on Calder tightened.

There was something behind him, something huge looming over the two of them, its shadow swallowing them up. He turned his head slightly, just enough to be able to see what it was. Eye Stealer. One of her hands was holding up that eyeball on a string. It was watching him hungrily. Her other hand was hovering just above his head, waiting to crush it like a grape.

He felt the hairs on his neck stand on end. He could hardly breathe. He could hear the metal creaking as the monster's fingers prepared to coil. He couldn't move if it meant saving his life, which, unfortunately, it did.

Calder shook as he stared at Eye Stealer. "Freckles," he whispered. "Freckles, you gotta move."

I can't, was all Kearney could think. *I can't. I can't.* Eye Stealer was getting closer, and he still couldn't move. He didn't know why. Maybe it was the revelation that Calder had a life. Had a family. Maybe it was the realization that this monster was more than a monster. With a loud *whizz,* a giant needle soared through the air and struck the eyeball. It snapped off the string in Eye Stealer's hand and rolled to the floor. Eye Stealer froze, now completely blind.

"Eye Stealer!" The Tailor yelled. She was a few yards away. It seemed she could be threatening from any distance.

Eye Stealer wasn't fazed in the slightest. She rushed to where she knew Kearney was. Calder went flying out of Kearney's arms as he screamed. Eye Stealer slammed Kearney to the ground then raised a hand high over her head. That hand surged back down toward his face. On instinct, his hands flew up to block the attack.

The result was a cry of agony as his shaking hands struggled to keep the giant metal hand from sinking into his face. Eye Stealer's claws had gone clean through his palms. He could've sworn his left hand had one less finger than before. He shook in pain as he focused all his energy on forcing her back, but she pressed on relentlessly.

Calder joined in, managing to keep Eye Stealer off him just long enough for him to slip out of her way. He rolled onto his side, gasping for breath as he pressed his bloodied hands against his chest in the hopes of easing the pain. He started to feel lightheaded, barely aware of just how much blood he was losing. His hands were searing with pain. Blood oozed from them. It felt like they were dripping fire. He stumbled to his feet.

As soon as Eye Stealer heard him, her needle-like legs scraped against the ground as she surged forward. He stumbled back in a dazed attempt to escape but wasn't quick enough. With a sickening *squelch*, her claws slashed through his shoulders.

He gasped, a scream lodged in his throat as he crumpled to the ground. The pain searing in his shoulders was so great that the wet feeling of the blood soaking them was hardly noticeable.

Eye Stealer gently cocked her head, as if in mocking empathy.

Kearney struggled to open his eyes as he fought for breath, only to be met with a world blurred by tears. He saw a shadow lean over him and winced in pain as he felt himself being shaken.

He could only barely make out the words, *"Freckles, you gotta get up! Please!"*

The shadow gently lifted Kearney's head, and he only then realized how wet he was. He squeezed his eyes shut and shuddered in realization. *More blood.* He shriveled in pain as he felt himself being shaken again.

"Freckles!" The voice grew more distant. *"Kearney!"*

He vaguely became aware of the fact that Eye Stealer was looming over him and, in fact, had his arm in her grip. He winced as she dragged him across the cold floor, barely able to make out Calder's shape limping along, desperately trying to make Eye Stealer let go. She was using her free hand to feel around. Maybe she was looking for the eyeball. Maybe she had something else in mind.

Kearney grayed out, and when the world came back to him, he was staring down at darkness. *Is that the Dark Place?* He could still hear Calder's cries and feel Eye Stealer's cold grip, meaning he wasn't there yet. Then she threw him in with a swift and devastating swing.

Air rushed around him as he plummeted downward, and in seconds, any light that had followed him was swallowed up by blackness.

I'm going to die. I'm sorry, Gabi, I'm going to die. His eyes fluttered shut again as his thoughts grew muddled and his breathing faint. A coldness came over him and, with it, a strange peace. *Will I see Levi...?*

Eye Stealer held the eyeball close as she stared at the abyss she'd just tossed the boy into. Her gaze trailed to her hands, which were covered in something red—red and sticky. She clicked her fingers as she stared at the red substance, trying to comprehend what it was. It seemed vaguely familiar, but for the life of her, she couldn't remember.

"Congratulations," The Tailor praised as she clapped her hands. "You just killed a living boy. How do you feel about yourself?"

Eye Stealer didn't respond. She kept clacking her fingers as if still trying to comprehend that it really was blood staining them.

The Tailor watched, her face emotionless. "Everyone in this place has been lied to by Phantasos, so claiming that as common ground is a futile thing. Saying that in a world like this is saying that we should work together because we both breathe air. The way I see it, you and I have one thing in common." Her head hung low, and her narrowed eyes remained fixed on Eye Stealer. "We both want him dead."

Eye Stealer froze before tilting her head. Then she went back to clacking her fingers.

"You think yourself so tragic, don't you?" The Tailor scowled. "Because he lied to you."

Eye Stealer tilted her head again, intrigued. Her grip tightened around the eyeball. It was whispering to her. Telling her not to listen to the peach-haired doll.

"Well, he lied to me first." The Tailor shrugged apathetically. "He threw you away. He threw *me* away because he thought you were so special. You've been trapped in this barren world for more years than you can count. I've been here longer."

Eye Stealer rose to her feet. She dropped the eyeball.

"You think yourself so tragic. Well, get over it," The Tailor took a step toward her, "and help me write this world's final chapter."

House Full of Strings

Chapter 29

Henry Acts Somewhat Ungentlemanly

Levi groaned as he blinked awake, hugging his blanket. He pressed his face against his feather pillow as he tried to drift back to sleep, resulting in a half-awake state of comfy bliss. His scarf had somehow ended up at the foot of his bed. Given he wore it when he slept, it was fascinating that it could've traveled so far.

"Anais?" he asked, although it came out as more of a moan. "You up yet?"

She didn't reply.

"I won't bother you, then." He shoved his face so far into the pillow that it became hard to breathe. But eventually, nature's call overpowered his joy of being in bed, and he dragged himself to his feet and hurried to the bathroom, hoping to get back to his fluffy paradise as quickly as possible. As soon as he came back out, he looked at his nightstand, where he normally left Anais. She wasn't there. He stared at the nightstand for a solid three minutes before finally looking at what was sitting at its feet. A basket full of folded towels. His mouth gaped open in horror. *He didn't.* He tossed his coat and backpack on over his pajamas and wobbled out of the room. His ankle definitely felt better than before, but it still hurt plenty. *He wouldn't.* He hurried down the halls as he scanned them for Henry. *He would. He absolutely would.*

"Henry, stop!" Anais's voice echoed, and Levi froze. He waited for her to yell again to know which way to go. *When I get my hands on that little menace....*

"I said back off!" she shrieked again.

"Would you shut up already?" Henry snapped back.

That way. Levi spun around and bolted down the hall, reaching the fork at the far end of it in seconds. His ankle was begging him to slow down, but he refused to listen.

"Hey!" she screamed.

Now left. He darted down the left path and quickly spotted Henry in one of the open rooms. He had Anais in one hand and Annette's shiny black hair in the other, although she didn't seem to be complaining much.

"Hey, back off!" Levi yelled.

Henry spun to face him, eyes wide. He quickly stepped back, yanking Annette with him. "Don't get in the middle of this, snowflake," he warned.

"You don't get to call me that." He balled his fists threateningly. "I know what Phantasos told you, and I don't care what he says, I'm not letting you take Anais!"

"So you *did* eavesdrop." Henry's lip drew back as he snarled. "And that means you know what's going to happen, don't you? You know what's going to happen to me?"

Levi studied his face carefully. "...I don't."

"Really?" Henry cocked his head sideways, but the anger in his eyes didn't die. "I'll tell you then. I'll tell you because this is the only chance I'll ever get." He chuckled bitterly. "He's getting rid of me. He's choosing this little *good-for-nothing* over me." His last sentence ended in a sob as he yanked Annette again. He breathed shakily as he glared at her. His grip on her hair tightened. "Every day, I do all the work, but she gets all the love because she's nothing more than his little *pet!*"

For the first time, she genuinely looked upset. "I'm not his pet," she muttered.

"Then what are you?" he yelled into her ear, making her flinch. "What *are* you?"

"I'm...." Her green eyes searched the floor as if she'd find her answer there. "I'm *not* his pet." She sounded unsure.

"See? You don't deserve him. If you really loved Master, you'd let *him* decide what you are!" He pulled her hair again as he screamed, yanking her head back with it. He glanced at Levi before hiding Anais behind his back. "You've messed up my life enough as is. I'm taking Anais to him. At least I can do him one last favor before he throws me away again." His lip began to quiver, and he struggled to keep it still.

"We can figure this out, Henry." Levi took a step toward him, hardly able to believe that he was trying to negotiate. "I'll talk to Phantasos. He'll—"

"You think you know him so well, don't you? Well, *I* know him, not you. I love him more than anything, and that'll never change, no matter how many times he throws me away! As soon as you see how he is, you'll hate him, but *I'll* never—!"

"Henry." A coldness swept into the room, sending chills down Levi's spine.

The pain in Henry's face deepened. He slowly looked over his shoulder to see Phantasos.

Phantasos was watching him with that unreadable look in his eyes. "This is what you do when you're upset? Act like a child?"

Henry's legs began to buckle as he let Annette go. He looked over his shoulder again and stared at Levi with a look that shook Levi to the core. It was the look of desperation, like Henry's whole world was falling apart like a broken puzzle, and he was doing everything possible to hold it together.

"I-I did it all for you, Master," he explained.

"How very noble," Phantasos replied in a flat tone.

"You have to understand. I-I was *devastated*." He looked up at Phantasos as he fell to his knees. "I love you more than anything. You know that! I-I've worked harder than anyone else, and—"

"And you've grown to be more troublesome than you are helpful."

Henry froze, eyes wide in horror. "…You're lying." It sounded more like a plea than an accusation. "You're lying, Master."

Phantasos didn't reply. Instead, he shoved Henry to the side and grinned at Annette, who'd backed away nervously. "Come, Annette." He stretched out his hand toward her. "Let's enjoy the rest of our day without Henry's antics."

Annette's back was turned to Levi, and for once, he wished he could see her expression more than anything. But her tone said it all. "No."

Phantasos's eyes widened, and the fingers of his outstretched hand twitched. "No?"

"No," she repeated, her voice unwavering. "I don't want to."

That unreadable something flickered in his eyes again, and his smile started to fade. His voice was low, barely a whisper, as if to keep Levi from listening in. "Why don't you?"

"Because I don't like it."

"What's there not to like?" He sounded hurt. "Am I that unbearable?"

She was entirely unaffected by his demeanor. "Yes."

He grabbed her arm, and his eyes darted to Levi. "I-I'm so sorry, snowflake. Sometimes, Annette just doesn't seem to know what she wants! And Henry, well...." His gaze trailed to Henry. "His behavior will be addressed shortly. And I assure you, this will be the last time he troubles you." He chuckled as he began to lead them both away, trying to keep Annette still as she attempted to yank her arm free while Henry did nothing but stare at his shoes in shame. A strained smile crept across Phantasos's face as he kept his eyes fixed on Levi. "How's about we have tea in a bit? Help calm the nerves after this little spat?"

Levi nodded shakily, forcing a smile to keep himself calm.

After carefully studying Levi's expression for what seemed like forever, Phantasos turned around and led Henry and Annette away. He paused one more time, taking Anais out of Henry's hand. "And Levi?"

Levi stared at Anais in horror. "Y-Yeah?"

"How's about our friend joins us?" Phantasos smiled as he held her up. "It'll be nice to have her for tea again."

They left, and Levi stared at the floor in bewilderment. *Something is very, very wrong.*

In front of Levi was a little cup of tea. The cup was trembling. Levi sat across from Phantasos at the table, his sweaty hands digging into his pockets. Things were tense, and while Phantasos had tried to create a relaxed atmosphere, it shattered the moment Anais started talking.

"I'm going with Levi," she explained. "He's going to show me all kinds of cool things. Like the sky."

Levi winced. He could feel Phantasos's crimson eyes boring into him.

"Like the sky!" Phantasos threw his head back and laughed. "That's adorable, Anais, but you needn't stray so far from home to see something like that!"

She went quiet, and Phantasos's gaze fixed on Levi. His eyes grew darker again. "Are you really so intent on leaving now?" His voice was different—silkier but laced with venom all the same. "I've given you so much, and you're still unhappy here. Is there something more you want from me?"

Levi stiffened. "N-No. I just want to go for a bit." *Is a bit all I really want at this point?*

"Why's that? Homesick?" Phantasos chuckled light-heartedly. Looking away from his smile, Levi noticed Phantasos was violently cutting up the cake on his plate with a fork. The piece of cake seemed to be in a panic, desperately trying to drag itself away from the torrent of stabs it was being subjected to. "I'm sure you'll feel much better once that friend of yours comes. Speaking of which, where is he?"

Levi's cheeks burned with indignation as that cold, taunting tone sank its way into his mind.

"What if he never comes?" Phantasos continued. "Perhaps he's already left without you."

"He wouldn't."

Phantasos stared at him. "What makes you so sure?"

Levi felt chills run down his spine. "Because I know him."

Phantasos's gaze lowered to his plate, where his cake had been completely decimated. It seemed the cake had given up and accepted its fate. "With the way you're talking, it sounds like you trust him more than you do me. And now you're speaking of leaving." His eyes met Levi's again. "You're not planning on breaking your promise, are you?"

As Levi's anxiety froze his words before they could leave his mouth, Annette came bumbling into the room with a steaming teacup in hand. She started making her way toward him.

Phantasos watched her closely, his brows knit. "Annette, how did you manage to put your dress on *backward?* And your stockings are all wrinkled!" he exclaimed. "You really can't take care of yourself, can you?"

She didn't reply or even give him as much as a glance. She just stared at the cup of tea in her hands for a brief moment before dumping it on Levi's lap. He watched in confusion while Phantasos gasped in horror.

"Annette!" he exclaimed. "Are you *broken?*"

She grabbed a handful of napkins and dropped them in front of Levi. "Now clean up."

"*Annette!*" Phantasos jumped to his feet and grabbed her by the arm. He looked at Levi in a panic. "I-I'm so sorry, I have no idea what's gotten into her!" He glanced back at Annette. "Now, please excuse me while I deal with our unruly friend here." He hurried out of the room with her, leaving Levi and Anais completely befuddled.

Levi grabbed the napkins with a shaky hand and started wiping Annette's mess.

"What in the world was that? Is she okay?" Anais asked.

"I'm not sure." He'd soaked three napkins already and paused as he reached for the fourth, his eyes fixed on it. There were words on the napkin written in Annette's sloppy handwriting, and he could hardly read them. But when he finally managed to, he felt his breath catch in his throat.

Run away and do it fast.

He froze with his mouth gaped open in shock. He clenched his teeth and stared into the hallway Phantasos and Annette disappeared down.

That's it. That's. It. He grabbed Anais and went after them.

House Full of Strings

Chapter 30

Levi Goes Down the Stairs

It never occurred to Levi that it'd be so hard to be quiet with a sprained ankle. He did his best to tiptoe through the halls as silently as possible with Anais in hand. Anticipation and fear made him tremble out breaths. *Whatever's going on here, I'm sick of it. Or, I'm sick of not knowing what it is.* His eyes darted to a door that was swinging slightly, creaking as it did so. He peered through it and realized he was looking into Phantasos's workshop again. The table had been flipped over and tossed into a corner, the doll with the weird eyes that had been on the couch was now slumped over with a deep gash in its face, and the second uncompleted doll had disappeared entirely. There was a crimson door in the wall at the opposite end of the room.

Levi stiffened. "That wasn't there before," he mumbled.

"It wasn't. But that must be where they are." There was a chill in Anais's voice that made Levi shiver.

He walked through the workshop, timidly pushed open the red door, and found himself staring down a staircase that descended into a shroud of darkness. "This is the moment of truth, I guess." He took a deep breath, tightened his grip on Anais, and took his first step down. The pair slowly went down the steep staircase, and Levi flinched every time a crash sounded from the bottom. And there was screaming—a lot of screaming.

His ankle felt like it was on fire now. It was begging him to stop. Begging him to go back. Telling him that he didn't need to know what was waiting at the bottom of that staircase.

As they got farther down, they could make out words from what had previously sounded like incoherent madness: *"Oh, Annette, dear Annette, you little idiot!"*

There was a crash.

"Henry's childish outbursts were excusable at best. But you? You were always my good little girl! And now you stab me in the back like this? I knew it! I knew you were a liar, just like the rest of them! I knew it!"

Then came the sound of wood slamming against a table.

"He'll never leave, no matter what you tell him or how much Henry mocks! I won't let him!" That last sentence escalated into a scream, followed by the sound of wood scraping relentlessly against the ground.

Levi was at the bottom of the staircase now, face-to-face with a closed door. He knew it was Phantasos's voice shrieking on the other side of it. Trembling, he tentatively started picking the lock while listening carefully. He heard Phantasos's final words in the form of a low growl.

"You've told enough lies."

Finally, Annette spoke. *"Get over it."*

Levi flinched at the sound of the lock being successfully picked. He twisted the knob as quietly as he could and cracked the door open to peer into the room. He saw Phantasos open a closet and toss what was likely Annette's mangled body inside.

Indignation mixed with his horror, and Levi threw the door open without another thought. "How could you?" he yelled.

Phantasos spun around, his eyes wide with shock. After he spotted Levi, he shifted his posture to a more relaxed one. "H-How could I what?"

"Hurt Annette!"

"Why would I ever do that?" He let out a laugh and shrugged nonchalantly, but his eyes were narrowed. "Come now, snowflake, I wouldn't do that!" With the way he was standing, it was obvious he was hiding something behind him.

Shaking with anger, Levi looked behind Phantasos to see what was sitting on his bed. It was a doll, freshly finished, and it had the same white hair and blue eyes as he did. He stumbled back, holding Anais close to his chest as he suddenly realized the horrible error he'd made by barging in. But it was too late to back out.

"What's that?" he asked in a fearful whisper.

Phantasos's eyes flicked from the doll on the bed to Levi. "It's nothing." He started moving toward Levi, and Levi moved away, keeping an equal distance between them as Levi got closer to the doll on the bed and Phantasos got closer to the door, Levi's only way out.

"I'm not an idiot. Stop lying!" Levi's boldness started to shrink away. His next statement was filled with confidence mixed with fear. "I...think I was wrong about you."

"Why, I'm hurt, Levi. Whatever would cause you to think that way?" Phantasos's posture and voice gave the impression of despondency, but nothing could hide the emotion in his eyes.

Levi finally understood what it was: annoyance. He took a step toward the doll and grabbed it by its arm. "Because you've been lying! You lied about Anais and the dolls, and you're lying to me right now about this freaky wooden *me!*" He yanked it off the bed, sending it to the floor. With a yell, he slammed his foot down on its hollow head. It shattered.

There was a pause as Phantasos stared at the broken doll. "And to think I've been nothing but good to you." His voice was cold. He straightened his back and took a step forward, now towering above Levi and staring down at him like one would at a bug. "When you were in danger, I saved you. When you were hungry, I fed you. You were lonely and scared, and I was gracious enough to become your friend. And now you spit in my face like this."

Levi swallowed back his fear. "Y-You did save me, and feed me, and even became my friend. But now I know why."

"Can't one do something out of the goodness of one's heart?"

"Some can." Levi's eyes trailed to the doll, chills rippling down his spine. "But you're not like that, are you?"

Phantasos lowered his head in a half-nod. The cold wasn't a chilly breeze or a block of ice now. It was a whole blizzard. "A shame things had to end on such an...unpleasant note." He surged forward and snatched Anais out of Levi's hand.

"No!" Levi screamed. He rushed at Phantasos while reaching for her, only to be slammed to the ground. He lay shaken on the floor, staring up with wide eyes.

Phantasos opened the closet and tossed Anais inside, slamming it shut afterward. He glanced back at Levi with a glare. "I never wanted to hurt Annette or Henry, snowflake. But you've made things so hard for me. What choice do I have anymore?" He stepped forward, and Levi scrambled to his feet in an attempt to get away. Phantasos raised his hand and sent it flying at Levi, who cried in pain as the hit landed on his face.

Levi's now-red cheek screamed in pain, and he dazedly stumbled back as Phantasos grabbed his chin and shoved him up against the wall.

"After everything I've done for you, you still haven't given me anything in return. I think it's due time I got what I wanted," he hissed as he leaned close. "And what I *wanted* was you in that wooden body I worked so painstakingly hard on. But you just had to ruin that for me, didn't you?"

Terror screamed in Levi's mind as the realization of his helplessness set in. He started to writhe and kick but froze when Phantasos pressed his head even harder against the wall.

"I guess we'll just have to improvise, won't we?" Phantasos slammed him against the bed face-first and started rummaging through his backpack.

Levi started desperately clawing at the sheets in an attempt to get away, which only annoyed Phantasos more. He slammed Levi onto the floor, causing the contents of Levi's backpack to pour out as he yelped in pain.

Levi's eyes darted around, searching for something to fight back with, and once they fixed on his snow globe, he lunged for it. He swung it at Phantasos's face with all the strength he could muster, and with a violent crash, the snow globe shattered, sending glittery water flying everywhere. In the midst of the chaos, Phantasos gasped and pulled back, letting Levi collapse in exhaustion. He staggered to his feet and looked at Phantasos, who was leaning against the wall with a hand over the eye that had been hit.

Phantasos's mouth was gaped open in horror. "What…What have you done?"

Levi could only barely see what Phantasos's hand was hiding. Phantasos dropped to his knees, his wooden body twitching as red energy pulsed wildly through it. He scrambled for any piece of broken wood he could get his hands on in an attempt to fix his broken shell, but it was already too late. The cracks from his eye began snaking to the rest of his wooden body like a spider's web, and he stared at Levi one last time before he violently *burst*. But what was left when the dust settled wasn't wood chips. It was a horrendous black lump of a beast.

Levi's heart was beating so powerfully and wildly it nearly threw him off balance. He felt his knees buckling under his weight as he slowly swayed back and forth. He stared at the monster that had just erupted from Phantasos's wooden body. It was hideous. Terrifying. Like something that would chase you in a dream, but you'd never be able to understand once you'd fully woken up. Except in this case, that something was very, *very* real.

The monster stumbled to its feet, fixed its innumerable eyes on him, and spoke. "Great, *now* look what you've done."

Levi had never expected Phantasos's voice to come from something so ugly. He took a step back. He felt like his brain was going to break just from looking at this thing.

Phantasos's myriad of eyes twitched in unison as they darted around in search of something, and he wrenched the closet's door off its hinges and sent it flying into a wall. He hastily pulled Annette's body out and slammed her head against the floor, shattering it. He then dropped her decapitated remains, scooped up the broken wood left behind, and began molding it into something, his slim fingers twitching.

Levi screamed as he raced out of the room. He slammed the door shut behind him and hurried up the stairs as quickly as he could, his heart trying to force its way out of his chest as tears of horror streamed down his face like waterfalls. His ankle was screaming even more. He felt the steps under his feet trying to trip him and the walls slowly twisting around him, almost like they were reaching for him. But it wasn't the walls or the steps that were reaching. It was Phantasos. And the worst part was that it made sense. He remembered Phantasos's words, and they rang fear through him: *I see a lot more than you think.*

There was a violent crash at the bottom of the staircase, and Phantasos was racing after him moments later. He had strange little legs that were like a spider's, but he wasn't using those to move. Instead, he was using his giant, winding hands to drag himself up the stairs at a terrifying speed.

"I *knew* it!" he screeched. "I *knew* you were lying! Look at you run!"

Levi struggled to run up the steps and stare at Phantasos simultaneously. Phantasos had tried to build himself a shell from Annette's remains, but there was only enough wood to cover up the thousands of eyes from before, leaving a single slitted eye and the rest of his hideous black body completely exposed. On top of that, it looked like he'd scribbled a smiley face on his shell, likely in an attempt to make himself look less intimidating, but it only added to Levi's terror.

Phantasos lunged for Levi, successfully grabbing the tail of his coat. Levi shrieked as he stumbled to his knees and quickly shrugged off his coat to continue his escape. Soon, he reached the top of the stairs and was flying down the hall. His heart beat faster than he ever thought possible as realization after realization flooded over him.

Every little distraction he'd thought was just a coincidence could have been completely orchestrated. Because whether he was present or not, Phantasos saw and knew and *controlled* every little thing that happened in this place, meaning everything—even the scene upstairs that had made Levi laugh on the first night of his stay— might not have been as much of an accident as Levi had first thought. Everything could have been so perfectly fine-tuned to keep him distracted, to keep him happy, to keep him in the House forever. The only flaws in that plan were the two servants Phantasos couldn't control, and they'd been completely removed from the equation.

"So, you're scared of me now, is that how it is?" Phantasos's voice bellowed from an alarmingly close distance. "You know what? I'm tired of dealing with you and your *idiotic* antics. It's about time you learned your place!"

The carpet beneath Levi twisted and turned, causing him to lose his balance and fall every time he tried to scramble away. Before he could think of another way to escape, Phantasos's cold hands were pressing him against the floor.

"There we go. This is much better," Phantasos said with satisfaction before sweeping him off the ground. "Now, how shall you be rewarded for your behavior, hmm?" He tightened his grip around Levi's shoulders.

"Let me go!" Levi cried as he kicked wildly. "Let me go, please! *Let me go!*"

"I'm afraid that's not how it works, snowflake," he replied, his voice a purr. "You're staying here forever and ever. Just like you promised, remember?"

Levi sat in place, his hands balled into fists on his lap as he watched Phantasos, who was humming a song as he tried to hold the teacups as delicately as possible in his strange hands. He then skittered over to Levi, set a teacup down in front of him, and dangled the kettle from one of his lanky fingers as he filled it up. Swallowing back his fear, Levi pried his eyes from Phantasos and wrapped his clammy hands around his teacup.

Meanwhile, Phantasos attempted to sit in a chair, but his sheer size and strange shape caused the chair to break under his weight. "Would you like some sugar?" he asked.

Levi timidly shook his head.

Silence followed before Phantasos spoke again. "What's with the silent treatment, snowflake? How's about some cookies?"

Levi looked up and saw Phantasos towering over him. He shook his head again. "I-I'm not hungry."

Phantasos ignored him and dropped a plate of cookies in front of him. "Well, get over it. Eat up. Be lucky you're getting much of anything after your little scene earlier."

Levi felt tears threatening to pour out of his eyes and tried his hardest to stifle them. He had to be brave. He didn't know for whom, but he had to be. He grabbed a cookie with a shaky hand and took a bite out of it, and it made him feel sick.

Phantasos watched closely before nodding. "That's more like it."

Levi chewed on the cookie for what felt like forever before finally swallowing it. His gaze trailed to what was sitting beside Phantasos's plate. His broken snow globe. He mustered up the courage to speak and locked eyes with Phantasos. "...W-Why's that here?"

Phantasos tapped it with a bony finger. "It's for you. Why else?"

Levi felt his stomach drop. *No need for lies because there's no way out.* But he knew that was only half true. In actuality, there'd been no way out from the moment he'd stepped into the House. The only difference was that now he knew it.

House Full of Strings

Chapter 31

Kearney Walks Through a Dark Place

Kearney found himself floating in darkness—a very cold darkness, with only the pale blue light from overhead making his surroundings barely visible. Panic took hold of him. He remembered the white car. Out of the corner of his eye, he spotted the glint of the car's broken mirrors sitting on the floor of the riverbed and swam toward it.

Air was fighting its way out of his lungs, and he desperately tried to hold it in. He had to keep going. He had to do something. He reached for the car handle and latched onto it, floating in silence with his eyes squeezed shut. He wasn't ready to look in there. He knew what he'd see, and he didn't want to see it. Not again.

He slowly and reluctantly looked through the broken windows. Once again, of the three people in there, it was already too late for two. His gaze went to the broken window in the back, through which he saw a pair of blue eyes watching him. He desperately reached through the window, ready to feel a hand on the other side take his own like it always had. But this time, it didn't. Instead, the riverbed caved in on itself, and the white car sank into it. He watched helplessly as the blue eyes, trapped and scared, faded away.

He stared up at the pale light coming from the river's surface. A dull grief ached in his chest. It wasn't worth swimming back up. Nothing was worth anything anymore. He felt himself slowly sinking, and he looked down at the welcoming abyss. He froze.

A pair of glowing purple eyes stared back.

Kearney jumped awake with a scream. He let out a shuddering breath as he ran his hands over his face. *It was just a nightmare. A horrible, horrible nightmare.*

He looked around and found himself in darkness. Maybe the nightmare wasn't over after all. As the black faded from the corners of his vision, the world around him gradually came into focus, but it was still hard to see much of anything. Kearney was awake now, he knew that much. That meant this must've been the Dark Place. It was definitely dark.

He glanced down at his hands. Strangely enough, they were perfectly whole. His shoulders didn't hurt one bit, either. With a grunt, he tried to get up. The palm of his hand slipped and cut against something as he rose. He winced, glancing down at what had cut him, then stumbled back in shock. He looked around, hardly able to believe his eyes.

He was surrounded by doll remains—thousands upon thousands of broken heads, limbs, and torsos, some still twitching as their souls clung to their broken little bodies.

Briiiing!

Kearney flinched. *It's him.* He let out a shudder before shaking his head. He had no idea where the payphone was this time, but he had no intention of finding it.

Briiiing!

He cupped his hands over his ears. *Leave me alone. Please. Leave me here in this horrible place. I hate you. I hate myself. Just leave me alone.*

Briiiing! It was louder, as if it'd inched closer to him. He knew it must've been right at his side now.

Please. Just let me—

Briiiing!

With a growl, he opened his eyes and saw that he was surrounded by payphones. He grabbed the receiver closest to him and yelled into it. "Just let me die!"

"...Well, for someone who just fell a long way, you sound alive enough," the voice said. *"You're the toughest cookie I've ever stalked."*

He bit his lip as weariness washed away any anger he had left in him. "What do you want?" he asked in a defeated voice.

"Well, you're in a bit of a pickle, right?"

"Am I?"

"Yes, you are. And I'm going to get you out of it."

He rubbed his temples. "I don't want your help."

The voice paused. *"Did you hit your head on the way down?"* When Kearney didn't reply, the voice continued, *"Is this about your girlfriend—?"*

"It's about everything!" he cried. "Levi's gone, Gabi probably hates me. And even if she doesn't, chances are she thinks I'm dead! And now I'm here, so I pretty much am. A-And you—!"

"Stop being so dramatic. You can get out. Eventually."

Kearney let out a heavy exhale "That's not the point," he whispered as he stared dully at the lifeless husks around him. He remembered that night all those years ago. It had been dark like it was here. He remembered the things he did that night. The people who hurt him. The people he had hurt. "Maybe I'm meant to be here now. Maybe that's okay."

"You're being ridiculous, Kearney. Listen, I—"

He pulled out the cord, cutting off the call. Then he dropped the receiver and walked away. He suddenly froze, his hands shielding his eyes as purple light flooded the Dark Place. With a tremble, he dropped his hands to see a giant lighthouse, tilted sideways, sitting on top of a pile of doll corpses. A purple light shone from the top of it and pointed right at him.

The payphones around him screeched to life. "*Go on, Kearney.*"

He stared at the lighthouse. It was made of metal, which made it look alien in a place like this, and hundreds of payphones surrounded it. He lowered his gaze and saw that a path leading to the lighthouse had been sloppily burrowed through the wooden husks.

The voice is up there, isn't he? The helpful, unpredictable, terrifying voice.

As he made his way up the path, the payphones screamed all around him. *"And here he comes, folks! Nobody believed he'd make it this far, but he's beaten the odds!"*

He cupped his hands over his ears as he kept going, trying to silence the fear in his mind that was yelling at him to turn back before it was too late. But it already *was* too late. He found himself at the tower's door and, after a brief struggle, managed to shove it open. He was met with a staircase, one that continuously circled around the tower in its ascent to the top. He started making his way up it.

The payphones lying along the stairs continued to announce his presence as he climbed. *"Here he comes, ladies and gents! He's in the endgame now!"*

The anxiety in his mind continued to try to scream at him, but he refused to let it so much as whisper. *This is it,* he told himself. *There's nothing left for me. No Levi, no Gabi, nothing. If I die, I die.*

When he reached the top of the stairs, he was met with a small attic door. After a moment of hesitation, he shoved it open and lifted himself into the room. His breathing quickened when he realized where he was. It was the throne room in Jolly, only now, it was in complete ruins, and the mummy-like puppet on the throne had vanished. In its place was the doll that looked like Kearney, huddled up like a baby.

It was staring at the floor and talking to itself. *"I want to die."* It lifted its head and fixed its gaze on him.

Kearney looked over his shoulder, but the attic door was gone. There was no way out.

The clone stumbled off the throne, and Kearney took a step back. That thing had hated him before he'd beaten it to death. He could only imagine how it felt about him now.

The answer came when the clone pointed at him. *"You want to die. You deserve to die."*

He felt shivers run down his spine as the clone waved its finger. He knew what it meant. *That night on the bridge, I....* He sucked in a deep breath and balled his fists. *I'm not running anymore.*

The clone took a step toward him, and he did the same. Then it rushed at him, and Kearney's bravery was drowned by torrents of fear. He stiffened as his breathing quickened, and the primal instinct to stay alive took over. *No reason to run.*

He stepped back, dodging the clone's incoming fist, before sending his fist into its stomach. Only then did he realize punching a wooden doll in the gut would hurt him much more than it would hurt the doll. As he winced from the throbbing pain in his hand, the clone took the opportunity to slam him to the ground and get on top of him.

The memory of that night kept playing in his mind again and again. Levi would never have become an orphan if Kearney hadn't run away that night.

He quickly rolled to the side, giving himself the upper hand. He sent blow after blow into the clone's face, as it had done to him, but it hardly seemed fazed.

With one swift punch, it sent him reeling back. *"I want to die. You want to die. Let's die."*

He spotted a rock—a big rock. He rushed for it, reaching out to it, but the clone rammed into him just before he could grab it. He rolled back onto the ground, winded, and when he looked back at the rock, it was gone. It was gone because the clone was holding it. It struggled to carry the rock as it stumbled over to him. Then it lifted the rock high in the air, ready to send it slamming into Kearney's head.

Kearney froze, his eyes wide and horrified as he waited.

But the clone didn't move. It just stared and said, *"I want to die. You want to die."*

He trembled and choked. "I...I don't want to die." He didn't understand where those words were coming from. It felt like there was a little boy locked up deep inside him who was crying them out. "I-I don't want to die."

The clone kept staring.

"I just want to *live*." He lay in defeat as words poured out of him. "I want to kiss Gabi...I want to tell her how much I love her." Tears streamed down his face. "I want to see the stars with Levi...just one more time. I don't want to die. I just...I want a *reason* to live. I want *someone* to live for...." His chest jerked as he sobbed. "I just want a reason...."

The clone's expression softened, if only slightly. It opened its mouth. *"I want to die,"* it said in a strange voice.

Kearney looked up at it, confused.

"You don't." In an abrupt motion, the clone slammed its head into the rock and dropped to the floor in a heap.

Kearney flinched away, still shaking. He wiped the tears away from his eyes as he sat in silence, staring at the clone's lifeless husk yet again.

To his further bewilderment, the clone and the whole throne room seemed to dissolve out of existence, leaving him alone in a small attic. He let out panicked gasps as he tried to figure out what had happened. Then he noticed the broken payphones lying around him. Chills ran down his spine when he realized there were doll parts mixed in with them, too. He slowly rose to his feet, eyes studying the room until they landed on a single rocking chair, slowly swaying back and forth in the middle of the room. A wheeze broke the silence, and Kearney froze, his attention entirely on the chair.

It leaned back, and the silhouette sitting on it looked at him, his beady purple eyes watching Kearney excitedly—the same eyes from his nightmare. The silhouette lifted a skinny hand, and in that hand was an old microphone. He held it close to his mouth.

"Aaaand he's done it, folks!" the silhouette screeched, causing the payphones around him to scream out his message like a fanfare. Kearney winced as he covered his ears. At this point, his suspicions were confirmed: he'd found the voice.

The creature laughed giddily as he let the microphone drop to the ground. He spun his chair around to face Kearney. "Took you long enough, sucker!" His voice was just as grating in person as it had been over the phone. He leaned forward. "I still can't believe it, really. An actual, factual *human* guest. Who would've thought it'd finally happen again?"

"It's you." Kearney shook in anger.

The creature. The voice. The Purple-Eyed Monster. It didn't matter what he called this thing. The truth remained that he was horrible.

"Surprised?" The creature grinned, which was definitely scarier than his resting expression.

You hurt Dakota. Kearney's hands balled into fists. *You…. You….*

The creature's laughter abruptly stopped as his giddy expression shifted to a glare. "Oh, stop thinking like that," he snapped.

Kearney reeled back in shock. "H-How…?" He shook his head. *Focus, Kearney.* "How do you know my name?"

The creature snorted. "All you ever seem to do is ask, ask, **ask**. Don't you get tired of it?" He threw his head back and waved a hand. "Names hardly mean much in the grand scope of…well, everything. I know much more *interesting* things about you."

"Like what?"

The creature rose to his feet, and Kearney could make out his full shape. He was at least seven feet in height but was very skinny and made of wood. While the dolls were also wooden, they at least *looked* human, but this thing seemed to have no soul behind his cracked face and marionette-puppet jaw. On his head were two fat, bull-like horns. His purple eyes were mostly hidden by matted blonde hair, but they still seemed like they could pierce through Kearney and read his thoughts perfectly.

"Like the scars you try to cover up," the creature said. "Those nightmares you've been having? They were courtesy of yours truly."

"W-What? How?" Kearney's breath hitched. "And *why* would you want to remind me of that night?"

"Because then you'd see just how hopeless you are." A crooked smile crept across the wooden creature's face. "And that aside, it's fun to watch you squirm."

"You're...You're insane." The anger lacing Kearney's tone was hardly half of what he felt. "Even when you were just a voice in a phone, I knew better than to trust you."

"What, are you only just realizing I've got a few screws loose? I thought you were better than that!" He shook his head. "Anyway, you still came all the way here, didn't you? Funny, huh? Funny how this place breaks you down so quickly."

Kearney's eyes trailed to the creature's bony hands, which were holding something. He lurched back in revulsion. It was a doll head.

"The House might not seem like it, but it's a lonely place. It makes you desperate," the creature continued as he ran a finger along the head's scratched face. "Would you believe me if I told you this little guy chose to stick around?"

Kearney shook his head. "I'm not planning on it."

The creature threw his head back and laughed, although it sounded more like a vulture choking on a wet sponge than a sound any living being would make when amused. He started staggering toward Kearney. "And here I was thinking I had you all figured out! Looks like you still have a few surprises left in you, after all." He rested a bony hand on Kearney's shoulder.

Kearney felt chills ripple down his spine. He tried to take a step back, but the creature held him firmly in place. He stared into the monster's purple eyes, his heart pounding in his chest. *"What* are you? Why are you here?" he whispered. "And how have you been giving me those nightmares?"

"Curious, aren'tcha? I'll tell you in story form. How's that?" the creature chuckled. Then he spun around, shoving Kearney into the rocking chair. He leaned forward, towering over Kearney and pinning him to the seat as he began to tell his tale.

"A long, long time ago, my brothers and I had a mother. And what a scary mother she was. She loved having things, and in truth, that's what we were to her. Just things. One day, she made us leave home, and we traveled a long, long way to get here. She made a door and a little world behind it and turned her own sons into ugly cripples to keep them in the dark with her forever."

Kearney swallowed back his fear. He hardly dared to blink in case the creature did something. "W-What happened then?"

"One of my brothers was especially smart. Somehow, and I have no clue how, he managed to lure a girl into this place. A cute one with peach-colored hair. She was a bit on the chubby side, but she was a *vicious* little thing.

He used her to kill Mother and took over as soon as the old hag kicked the bucket. He had the support of his brothers, too. After all, he promised to set us free from our curse once Mother was gone." He snorted. "But instead, that backstabber made himself a new wooden body that was all cute and nice, and he left his own brethren to suffer. Eventually, he stuffed me down here. And then you came. The end."

"So, you're trapped up here?"

The creature's grip tightened. "Maybe."

Hearing that helped Kearney regain some bravery. "But why lead me here?"

The creature started pacing around the chair, rocking it back and forth. "A good reason would be because I crave the fear of a kid like you. It *nourishes* me, helps me *thrive.*" He was right behind Kearney now. He leaned the chair back so their eyes could meet. Kearney felt terribly helpless at that moment. "But that wasn't my reason. Not this time."

"What was your reason, then?" Kearney tried desperately to keep himself from shaking as he felt that previous bravery melt away like wax near a flame.

The creature giggled with pleasure, likely from Kearney's terror. He let the chair go, and it continued to swing and squeak in a repetitive motion that made Kearney sick. "That backstabber I told you about? He's the one holding everything together around here. And we're going to take him down."

"Why do you need me to do that?"

"Because I've been watching you, Kearney. You're tough stuff. Tougher than any other stuff that's made its way into this place."

Kearney didn't feel very tough at the moment. "What about The Tailor? She's trying to kill him, too."

"That girl doesn't know it yet, but she's at a big disadvantage. A doll can't kill my backstabber because he made them. He can break them just as easily."

Kearney lowered his head in thought. "So, you want me to find your brother...."

"And **break him**."

"B-Break him? Like a doll?"

"Like a doll. Just a little tougher." The creature shifted as he glanced to the side. "Never mind, a lot tougher. But I believe in us! And I should mention one more teeny tiny detail: this plan involves me living in your head. For good. And taking your body when you die."

"*What?*" Kearney's shoulders went rigid. His teeth gritted at the thought that this monster believed he was stupid enough to even consider that proposition. "Why would I *ever* want to help you? And that last part sounds horrible! That aside, there's no way I could do all of that. I'd just die trying!"

"What, you really hate the sound of my voice that much?" The creature kept his focus fixed on Kearney like a hawk with a mouse in its talons. "And weren't you fine with dying earlier?"

Kearney stiffened but didn't reply. Suddenly, he felt a strong ache in his tensed shoulders, which made him wince. But when he looked at them, they seemed completely intact.

"You'll be fine," the creature hissed. "It's not like the pain can really reach you here anyway."

"Pain? But...my shoulders aren't hurt."

"In the real world, you idiot," he sneered. "Remember Eye Stealer?"

Kearney's nails anxiously scratched at the old wooden armrests. "W-What do you mean by real world?"

"You're sleeping, kiddo. Your body's back where you first landed in the Dark Place. It really was quite a fall. Anyway, I put you in a little dream, and your soul made its way up here."

Kearney felt himself shiver. The creature almost made it sound like he was dead. "What are you that you have the power to do that?" he asked, his voice wavering.

The creature tilted his head. "Phobetor's my name. I'm known for my nasty nightmares and my love of snakes. Although people tend to know me more for the nightmares than the snakes, which I think is a real shame. As for what I *am*, I've been called many things, but you can call me a god."

A god? Kearney found himself pressing against the chair's back as he tried to keep himself as far away from "Phobetor" as possible. "So, the clone a few minutes ago? The throne room? That was you...controlling the nightmare."

"Bingo. And unless you agree to the terms and conditions, I won't wake you up. You'll stay asleep forever, which is a nicer way of saying you'll die. But, hey, at least you'll have me."

Kearney shook his head as he tried to keep his panic from clouding his thoughts, but Phobetor's cackle made it clear that it was too late for that. He stayed glued to the chair for what felt like hours, praying the nightmare would end without the monster's say. But it didn't. Ten minutes passed, and Phobetor was sitting on the floor and bowling using doll heads and limbs. He was insane, sure, but being kept in a prison like this for so long must've polished his patience.

Kearney stared into a corner. There was a broken hat rack there, and hanging off it was a tattered blue dress. Why Phobetor had a dress, Kearney had no clue. He didn't feel like asking, either, because the answer had an equal chance of being flat-out ridiculous as it did being vomit-inducingly horrific, and he didn't feel like taking his chances.

His eyes drifted back to Phobetor, and a question that had been buried in the depths of his mind finally resurfaced. *Calder, Dakota, and so many others...stuck here forever....* "Are the dolls really trapped in the House? There's no way out?"

"Yep," Phobetor answered. His beady eyes stayed on his toys. "As long as it exists, they'll always be here. Another reason to help out your new pal, don'tcha think?"

"How long has the House been around for?"

He paused his game to shoot Kearney a glance. "Long enough," he muttered.

Kearney shuddered as he remembered the wooden remains that surrounded them. The fact that Phobetor was so nonchalant about all of this scared him. The fact that Phobetor had taken advantage of the dolls to hurt them was sickening.

What would he do with my body if I died? What horrible things would he do with my face before I rotted down to bones? He balled his fists as beads of sweat formed on his forehead. He weighed his options, but then again, he'd hardly been given any to begin with. *Do it. Do it for them. Whether you live or die trying…no matter what he does when you die…it'll be worth it. Even if you have his stupid,* horrible *voice stuck in your head for the rest of your life, it'll be worth it. For them.* "I'll do it."

"Great!" Phobetor jumped to his feet and stretched out his hand before Kearney had even finished his sentence. "Now, let's have a little handshake to seal the deal."

"I have one more question." He eyed Phobetor carefully. "Why do you want to get into my head?"

Phobetor's fingers twitched. "Because," his voice had become a new kind of terrifying, like he was trying to sound calm but his anger couldn't help but leak through, "if you kill my backstabbing brother, this whole place goes down. And it just so happens that this place is the only thing keeping me tethered to the mortal world. And I like your world a lot more than my other options. So, if you let me into your head, I'll get to stay safe there even if this place *burns* to a *crisp.*" He leaned down, his face hovering inches away from Kearney's. His breath smelled like rotting wood. "If it brings you comfort, I'll be a little voice in your head as long as you're alive, nothing more. No possession crap or anything like that, just getting loud when I *really* want something."

Kearney paused, watching Phobetor's hand apprehensively, then grabbed it. Phobetor stared at their clasped hands for a long moment. Then his purple eyes trailed up to Kearney's face, stopping at his eyes. "Wanna hear a riddle?"

He struggled to suppress a groan. *Not this again.*

"...What's white at the tip, is very annoying, and is still alive?"

Kearney gasped. His eyes shot up, hope sparking in them. "Levi?"

Before Kearney could get an answer, Phobetor lifted his free hand and snapped his fingers. Everything faded to white.

Chapter 32

Kearney Talks to the Voice in His Head

Every part of Kearney ached. Now he remembered Eye Stealer perfectly. But it wasn't the pain he was focused on at the moment, although it made his world incredibly muddy. It was the two voices he was hearing. They were faint but steadily growing louder. He recognized them and was easily able to put a name to one—Calder. As for the other, he was pretty sure it was the voice that would be stuck in his head for the rest of his life.

Open your eyes, Phobetor's voice echoed.

He moaned as he fought to lift his heavy eyelids and could barely make out Calder hovering over him. He parted his lips in an attempt to say anything, but only a small stutter came out.

He heard a gasp. *"Yer awake!"*

He coughed as he struggled to adjust his position, but the rest of him refused to move. He felt a hand hold him down.

"Don't move, Freckles, yer hurt." Calder sounded like he was crying with joy. *"You'll be okay...."*

You sure as heck will be, Phobetor snapped.

Kearney's head rolled back as he groaned from the pain, but his mind felt perfectly clear now. Maybe that was also Phobetor. *You said Levi's alive.*

I did, Phobetor replied. *He's on the other side of the chasm. To make things even better, my beloved backstabber has him.*

Kearney squirmed nervously, which caused another jolt of pain to shoot through his shoulders. *Is Levi safe, at least?*

Not really. And we're not getting him back without a fight. My brother's very possessive about his things, you see. Not unlike your brother.

Kearney winced as he felt Calder sit him up and tend to his wounds. He finally managed to open his eyes all the way, and things gradually came into focus. He was able to make out where Calder's face was now, which was a good start.

"I'm glad you're alright," he said, his sentence ending with a gasp for breath.

"Glad I'm alright? We thought *you* were dead!" Calder laughed.

"We?" *Is Gabi here?*

"Becca an' Bens are 'ere. They got a lil' helicopt'r thing with 'em."

Kearney struggled to keep himself upright. "W-Where's Gabi?" He was able to see all of Calder now. He'd almost forgotten what had happened before, but he remembered the second he saw Calder's new arm and leg, which were both different colors from his normal skin tone.

He looks like he's holding up well.

Then he shrank back. It felt like a horrible betrayal, having Phobetor in his head while talking to Calder. It felt like Calder deserved to know that the Purple-Eyed Monster was so close, but Kearney had no intention of telling him. He had no intention of telling anyone about the demon in his head.

Calder frowned. "I dunno. Becca said some weird door appeared in front o' Gabs, an' she just...walked in."

"What?"

Ooooh, that sucks. Kearney could practically see Phobetor wincing in half-concern in some dark corner of his mind.

Calder looked over his shoulder. "You can ask Becca yerself. She's comin' right now."

She raced over to them. "Calder, I think the heli's strong enough to carry Kearney, too." Her eyes skipped to him, and she smiled. "You're up!"

"I-I am. What happened to Gabi?" He watched her keenly as he waited for an answer.

"I don't know." Becca fidgeted her thumbs. "She was just so sad after you left, and she wouldn't tell me why. She stopped talking completely, actually. Then a weird red door came out of thin air, and she went through it without a word."

Kearney felt himself begin to shake. "Calder, do you know anything about weird red doors?"

Calder shook his head. "Only the one that lets you into the House."

Maybe it was that one, then. Maybe she left, and she's safe. Kearney tried to console his racing mind, but the possibilities of what could've happened to her were endless.

Don't worry. If those kids say she went through a red door, then my brother probably has her, too. That means we're killing three birds with one stone when we get to his place. Pretty sweet, huh? Phobetor attempted to soothe him, although his efforts weren't very helpful.

How can I not worry? He's the one who turns kids into dolls.

Only when they let him.

The last I saw Gabi, she didn't look like she was in the best state of mind! Kearney only just became aware that the dolls had dragged him onto Becca's homemade helicopter, and they'd begun takeoff. "We have to go to the Mister's place," he barely managed to gasp through the pain that kept lapping at him.

Benny, who was sitting on Calder's lap, glanced at him. "You want to meet him?"

"He has Gabi and my brother, and I'm going to stop him."

"You don't *have* to stop him. Phantasos is—!"

"For good."

Everyone went dead quiet. It was clear they understood what he meant.

"You can't do that!" Becca cried in dismay. "The Mister's the best guy ever!"

"He lied to you, Becca. He lied to all of you, and you know it." Kearney felt desperation gnawing at his stomach. If Becca refused to take him, it'd all be over; there was no other way for him to get there on time, and they both knew it. "Please, I need to help them before it's too late."

Calder stared at his shoes. Kearney could tell he agreed, but he didn't look like he was about to verbalize it. Benny stared at Becca, whose face was scrunched up in anger. There was a small sliver of regret shining in her eyes as she tried to keep her attention on controlling the aircraft. She opened her mouth to say something but quickly bolted it shut.

Her green eyes were only barely visible as she glared over her shoulder. "Like how it's too late for us?" she muttered.

A heavy silence filled the air. Everyone felt it and quietly acknowledged its presence.

"...It's not too late, Becca." Kearney's eyes were fixed on the sky overhead, studying the pale light that was trailing down to meet them as they climbed higher. "I'll...I'll stop him. For good. I won't leave before I do that, I promise. I'll make sure you're all free."

She didn't look at him, but he could imagine how her face twisted when he heard her choked-up voice. "The Mister made promises, too."

"And I'll do everything in my power to keep mine." They continued their ascent.

You know, that girl reminds me of myself, Phobetor said. Kearney tilted his head. *Really?*

Kind of, yeah. He paused. *I loved Mother. Don't get me wrong, she was terrifying, but when I was young, I always felt I needed her. Like the world would fall apart if she left. It* was...*interesting when Phantasos killed her. Gave me some room to think.*

And how did that work out for you?

Still not sure. Phobetor paused again. *I don't know why I told you all that. I guess it just felt right. Don't judge me. This whole 'being in your head' thing is new to me, too.*

Soon, they made it over the cliffside. Kearney stumbled off the helicopter once it landed. He looked over his shoulder and saw Calder rushing to join him.

"You don't have to come."

Calder vehemently shook his head. "I'm not leavin' you, 'specially when yer limpin' 'round like that. Anyway, I wanna help Gabs, too."

He remembered what Phobetor had said. *He made them. He can break them just as easily.* "It's too dangerous for you. Just wait here for me."

"Dang'rous," Calder scoffed. "I'm a doll, Freckles."

"That's why I want you to stay."

He balled his fists. After a minute of thought, his expression softened a bit. "Take too long, and I'm comin' after you, got it?"

Kearney let out a small sigh of relief. "Got it, chief." He looked back at Becca and Benny, who'd already begun takeoff. *No going back.*

"Kearney!" Becca was looking over her shoulder at them as she and her brother flew away. "If you don't keep your promise, I'll make you pay for it!" she yelled.

He smiled while cupping his hand to his mouth. "Sounds good!" After that, he turned back to the giant gray mansion.

If it weren't for the circumstances, maybe the mansion would've looked less intimidating. Maybe even pleasant. But all he could think of as he walked up to its red doors was that there was a monster waiting behind it. A monster and his brother.

Chapter 33

Levi Finds a White Car

"Come on, Levi," a voice chuckled. *"You've gotta swim."*

Levi's eyes blinked open, and he couldn't breathe. He was floating in a pale blue void, and he couldn't breathe. And it was cold. So, so cold. He opened his mouth, but no sound came out, only a single bubble that floated away. But it wasn't panic that gripped him—it was grief.

The voice echoed again, *"You gotta kick your legs like this."*

He remembered that day. He was four when his parents took him to that beach.

"Come on, you can do it." The voice was gentle yet strong. It made him feel warm.

I can't. He felt his lip quiver. *I'm sorry.*

"Keep on trying…. Yeah, there you go!"

He reached a feeble hand upward in an attempt to swim. *I can't….*

He heard the sound of clapping. *"You're doing it!"*

He started scrabbling through the void, swimming in the direction he assumed was up. He tried to kick his legs, which seemed to help, but his lungs were screaming for air. Every part of him was begging him to give up.

"Come on, you're getting there!"

He remembered the image of his limbs flailing wildly as he tried to swim, the pair of floaties on his arms the only thing keeping him afloat as small waves slapped his back. And he remembered his dad's hands, eagerly outstretched and ready to catch him. *"You've got this, Levi!"*

Those words were the only thing he had to remind him of his dad's warmth. He kept pulling himself through the water, eyes fixed upward as he gathered all his strength to keep himself moving. Soon, he saw a piercing light and his dad's hands reaching for him. *"You're so close!"*

With a final push, his head broke the surface. Air and relief rushed into his thankful lungs.

"I did it! Did you see, Dad? I did it!" The young boy's excited voice echoed into oblivion.

Levi looked around excitedly, but everything was quiet now. There was only an ocean of coldness left. A small whimper slipped past his lips, and he kept spinning around in the water, hoping he'd find who he was looking for. But he was alone again.

A strange force started pulling his hair upwards, but when he looked up, nothing was there. His whole body was sucked out of the water, and he yelped in fear as he floated in midair, but then the invisible force dropped him. But now, the water had frozen over, so Levi slammed into solid ice. He winced as he pulled himself to his feet. He rubbed his arms in an attempt to warm himself, but that didn't help one bit. He looked around and saw nothing but the now-fog-shrouded ground beneath him, the pale blue void surrounding him, and the snow floating above him. He held out his hand and caught a few flakes before rubbing his fingers together. It wasn't snow at all. It dissolved in his hands like snow, but it didn't end up as water. It ended up as glitter. *I remember this place.* He stared at the void again as he pursed his blue lips. *So, that's what he meant.*

He shivered as cold mist rushed at him from behind and ran over his back. When it settled, he turned to see something big behind him. He stared at an old Toyota, its white paint peeling and headlights broken. Then he started walking away. *No. Not here, not now, not ever.* He kept walking, trying to keep the image of the car out of his mind. He started running, his heart gradually beating louder and louder against his will. He spotted something in the distance and focused on that—finally, something in this void to distract himself with. He got closer and closer until he could make out its shape. It was the old Toyota. He swallowed his anger and spun on his heel, taking off in the opposite direction. A minute later, it was there again. And again, and again.

He finally gave up and stared at the car. "What do you want from me?" he choked out.

It stood in place unapologetically and without reply. He took a step toward it and found the courage to take another after that one. Once beside it, he gripped the front door's handle and peered inside the window, which was cracked and clouded and provided no view of what he'd find once he opened the door.

Is there a chance that…? He yanked it open, and a river of water poured out, soaking his shoes and creeping onto the ground around him. He glanced inside, only to find the car empty. His grief swallowed him up again as he looked back at the blue void, a dull ache filling his chest. He got into the driver's seat and shut the door behind him.

He sat in silence as if waiting for some sound—no, not just a sound, a voice. *Voices.* But he was alone, and he felt himself accepting it. *They're gone. I'm never going to hear them again, never going to feel their warmth again….* He choked back tears as the silence drowned out the voices in his mind. He couldn't escape the car or the past or the truth. *I can't run from it. The cold is all that's left.*

House Full of Strings

Chapter 34

Kearney Fights Literature

Kearney winced every time the floorboards creaked beneath him. The house was so empty, so quiet. As tempting as it was to call out for Levi, he didn't dare to. He kept glancing at the swaying crimson curtains, each time thinking something was there and having to reassure himself there wasn't.

Phobetor wasn't helping. *My brother's probably waiting around that corner. I bet he is.*

Kearney struggled to keep himself calm, but it was hard to do that when his heart was beating so quickly it felt like he was having a panic attack. Every inch of him was tense, which made his shoulders ache more. He did his best to ignore the pain, but that, paired with the stinging in his hands and Phobetor's ramblings, was driving him insane.

Don't you dare lower your guard, Phobetor continued. *We'll both die if you do that. He'll kill you the first chance he — The curtains are moving! False alarm. Nothing there.*

Kearney groaned although he was too scared even to do that loudly. *Would you just shut up already?*

I'm helping.

You're not. What happened to the Phobetor from before, anyway? He didn't seem half as anxious as you are.

Like you're any better. After that, he went quiet.

Kearney sighed with relief. His eyes snapped to a red door to his right. It was the first door he'd seen so far that was open. He tiptoed over to it and peered inside, ready for the worst. Instead, he saw a staircase going down. *That looks ominous.*

Too ominous. I bet the stairs turn into a slide, leading to a trap of spikes coated with poison. And the walls close in on you for good measure.

Or Levi's there. He took a step down the stairs, then another.

Why are you so adventurous all of a sudden?

He kept making his way down. *I'm not adventurous. I just know he needs me. Anyway, I have a hunch.*

So, you just magically cease to be scared whenever he "needs you"?

I'm terrified. But I guess having a reason to be brave helps, that's all.

You really like reasons, don't you? A reason to not be a chicken, a reason to not give up on your pitiful existence. Reasons, reasons, reasons.

Maybe you wouldn't be half as miserable as you are if you had one.

The idea of having Phobetor stuck in his head for the rest of his life sounded even more horrible to Kearney now, given how tired he already was of him.

Step by step, he got farther down until he was in almost complete darkness. He kept his hands pressed against the walls in the hopes he'd be able to catch himself in case he tripped in his blindness, but that didn't happen; he began to see a soft light waiting at the bottom of the staircase. And soon, he saw a doorframe but no door where one should've been. Instead, there was splintered wood scattered at his feet and scratch marks on the walls.

He gulped. *What could've left those here?*

I think we both know, kiddo.

He took a step forward and peered inside. *Everything's a mess, but there doesn't seem to be anything threatening here....* A gasp of horror came out of the silence, and Kearney could hardly believe it had come out of his own mouth.

At his feet was an old pink scarf. It was torn, but he still recognized it in a heartbeat. His gaze trailed to the center of the room, where there was a chair, and tied to that chair was a boy, and wrapped around that boy's neck was a single silver string that went up and into the ceiling.

"Levi!" Kearney scooped the scarf up and rushed forward.

Levi's eyes were wide open and brimming with tears, staring at nothing. The rest of him was twitching as he muttered incoherently, occasionally making a small choking sound. Kearney could see the marks the string had left on his throat, but no matter how much he tried to loosen the string, it only got tighter.

"Levi, wake up!" Kearney quickly untied Levi's bonds and started shaking him, but that didn't change anything, either.

Get rid of that string! Phobetor snapped.

Kearney searched for something sharp, and once he'd found a broken piece of ceramic, he started relentlessly slashing at the string, but it wouldn't tear.

Desperation was gnawing at him. "Let him go!" He didn't know who he was yelling at or if they would even have the pity to listen. All he knew was that he was getting Levi back. In the midst of his fury, he missed his target, and the back of his hand brushed against the string instead. And when his hand touched it, thousands of thoughts poured into his mind. Thousands of voices, all crying. All Levi's.

He stared at the string in shock and reached out with a nervous hand. He brushed against the string again, and those voices returned.

The string must be moving his mind somewhere.... Phobetor's voice was quiet. *The receiving end of the string tends to be weaker. Find it and cut it off there.*

Kearney tugged the string, watching the ceiling closely and almost jumping with excitement at the sight of dust falling. He tugged it again, and more dust, all in a line, came floating down. He knew where it was going.

Kearney set the scarf on Levi's lap and gave him one last longing glance before hurrying out of the room and back up the steps. Then he raced down the hall in the string's direction, and his suspicions were confirmed when he found a string that was hanging from the ceiling and snaking through the passageway.

He touched it and heard Levi's voice again. *This is the one!*

Keep in mind, it might be a trap. I bet my backstabber's waiting for you at the end.

Kearney ignored him as he ran along the string down every twist and turn. The trail was soon cut short, leaving him staring at a door the string went under. Without any fear, he grabbed the handle and shoved the door open, only to be met by a room blanketed in darkness. But a pale light glowed at the center, beckoning him like a flame would a moth.

Oh, this is definitely *a trap. Watch yourself. Or don't go in at all. Personally, I'd prefer if—*

He headed inside without hesitation and made his way through the inky blackness, the light getting brighter only slightly as he got closer. Suddenly, he heard the sound of paper rustling. He stopped and looked around, which didn't help since he was still in complete darkness. He waited patiently for another rustle. Instead, he was met by a rush of wind in his face as some invisible enemy relentlessly slashed at him. He stumbled back with a yelp, desperately trying to get a hold of his assailant. Then there was another slash, and another, and before he knew it, he was being attacked by a swarm of unseen enemies.

Slap them, kill them! Phobetor screamed wildly as if they were being assaulted by wasps. *Kill them, kill them, kill them!*

Kearney's hands seared with pain as he wildly flailed his arms around, panic fueling his screams. Suddenly, he felt one of his attackers firmly in his grasp, and he dropped to the ground, slamming it against the floor as the rest of its companions flapped aggressively over-head. He held it down as it squirmed, feeling it and try-ing to figure out what it was. But all he felt were pages. His curiosity mixed with confusion as he patted it down. It was a book.

He felt the scars on his face. *Papercuts.*

My backstabber loves using stuff like this. He's close, Phobetor said shakily.

Kearney slithered along the ground, his head held low but gaze still on the faint glow. The books dove overhead, searching for him, but they didn't find their target. Once the table was in front of him, he stood up, leaning close to study what was before him. His eyes widened in shock.

Levi's snow globe? He leaned closer. It wasn't broken like it used to be; instead of a miniature city inside, there was a single figure—a boy with white hair. He reached out with a shaking hand to touch the snow globe but froze. He froze because he felt a bony hand on his shoul-der. "W-Who's there?" He trembled as the stranger leaned closer.

"A new friend, perhaps. You look a little lost, boy."

Run, run, Phobetor began to shriek. ***Run!***

Then came the sound of a clap, and the room lit up. Kearney's eyes darted to all the books that had just dropped dead on the floor; he was too scared to look over his shoulder. His legs trembled as the stranger spoke again in a playful tone.

"Whatever's the matter? Got cold feet?"

He breathed in shakily, trying to gain whatever courage he could. The snow globe was right there. All he had to do was grab it.

Get it, get it, Phobetor hissed. *Don't just stand here all fish-mouthed, you idiot.*

"Awfully quiet, aren't you? It's not my looks, is it?" The stranger leaned over Kearney's shoulder and into his line of sight, giving Kearney a good look at whatever it was that had taken Levi. But he had no idea what he was looking at. The best his fear-frozen brain could come up with was 'tar monster with antlers and a noodle neck,' but even that was hardly sufficient.

The creature chuckled. "I assure you, I'm nicer than I look!" He walked around him to face Kearney directly.

Kearney glanced down at the creature's lower half.

Antlers, noodle neck, spider legs, Phobetor commented nervously. *He's had better days, that's for sure.*

"Forgive me, my home is a mess quite unfit for a guest like you!" The creature chuckled lightheartedly. "You've caught me in the middle of spring cleaning. I'm normally more of a neat freak, but this special time is my exception." He leaned in close again, giving Kearney a good look at his strange doodled-on smiley face and single red eye. "Now, what's your name, friend?"

"M-My name...." He found himself struggling to speak. "Kearney."

"You look like a Kearney." He laughed, his chest heaving unnaturally. "As for me, I go by Phantasos."

"You...look like a Phantasos!" Kearney gave a forced laugh as he screamed inside. *Why did I say that?*

I don't know. Why did you? Phobetor hissed back.

"Do I now? I haven't heard that one before." Phantasos cocked his head sideways with amusement. "Tell me, how'd you wind up here?"

"I just got a little lost, that's all."

Liars can see through lies pretty easily.

Shut it. His eyes darted between Phantasos and the snow globe, which Phantasos quickly caught wind of.

"Quite a sight, isn't it?" He turned his giant head to look at it.

"Yeah. I can hardly look away!" Kearney reached out with a hand to touch the snow globe, freezing the second he saw Phantasos tense. "M-May I?"

"I'm terribly sorry." Phantasos put a hand on his shoulder and gently led him away. "But I'm afraid I'd never get your prints off if you did that! It's quite a rare variety of glass, you see."

"Sorry, my bad." Kearney was completely focused on it now.

Get it, get it.

Shut up already.

"It's quite alright," Phantasos replied with a chuckle. "Now, you look positively famished and" he paused when he noticed Kearney's shirt was torn at the shoulders and stained with blood, "look like you've been in quite a few skirmishes."

"That was before I came," Kearney hastily replied.

"I see." Phantasos continued to lead him away from the snow globe. "Well then, let's get that checked."

To Phantasos's confusion, Kearney stopped, frozen in place and still staring at the snow globe. *It's so close.* He's *so close. I have to get him now.*

Yes, get him!

He rushed past Phantasos, hands reaching as far ahead as humanly possible to grab it. But once his finger touched it, his whole hand felt numb, and the rest of his body quickly followed suit. He screamed in a panic as the room around him peeled out of existence, and all that was left was a blue void. He stumbled forward before spinning around, but nothing was behind him anymore. The slight tremble in his legs turned into a quake that shook his whole body. *I'm dead for sure.*

Chapter 35

Levi Learns to Drive

Kearney ran through the void, screaming into the uncaring silence and desperately waiting for a reply, but none came. He screamed for Levi and even Phobetor, but he was only met by more silence.

Phobetor, where did you go? He continued hurrying through the pale blue void. *Where am I? What is this place...?* He paused. There was something in the distance. Something white. He ran for it, his heart pounding in his chest as he got closer and closer. He knew what it was, and as much as he hated it, it was the only tangible thing in this place. He slowed down as he got closer until he'd completely stopped.

It was the white car. The white car that had flown off the bridge on that horrible night. That horrible night that had given Kearney the best thing ever to happen to him. Levi.

He stared at the car briefly before taking a step forward. He let out a shaky breath as he warily opened the front door.

He gasped, choking back tears. "L-Levi?"

Levi was sobbing in the driver's seat with his face in his hands. He slowly lifted his face and looked up. His mouth gaped open. "Kearney?" He wiped the tear stains off his cheeks as a smile of disbelief grew across his face. "Y-You found me! You really found me!"

Kearney rushed forward and hugged him, tears pouring down his face. "You're okay!" It was one thing to be told Levi was alive; it was another entirely to have Levi back in his arms, to feel that Levi was alive, to hear his voice. Everything before this point had felt like a hopeful fantasy. Now, Kearney had stepped into reality.

Levi hugged back and spoke between sniffles. "I-I am!"

"I can't believe I ever thought you died!"

"Died?" Levi stared at him with wide eyes, still crying with joy but now looking stunned as well. "You thought I *died?*"

"Well, you're not the best swimmer," Kearney said with a laugh. His smile faded as he remembered how he'd felt those mornings following their separation. That grief and emptiness felt miles away now, but part of him still remembered it. "But you're okay." He hugged Levi even tighter, running his hands through Levi's hair as he smoothed it down. "I'm so, *so* glad you're safe!"

Levi leaned his head against Kearney's chest without a reply. His sniffling gradually ceased, and soon, Kearney's warmth was all he knew. He let out a heavy sigh. "The truth is, I'm not safe." He hugged Kearney even tighter, almost like he was too scared to let go. "I made some big mistakes, so I kind of had it coming. There was a man...he made me happy."

Kearney studied his expression. "Phantasos?"

Levi nodded, ashamed. "He reminded me of my parents. I just...really wanted them back. Even though I could tell something was wrong, I was too scared to let him go." He shoved his face into Kearney's shirt, hoping that would keep him from bursting into tears all over again. "A-And you were always so strong, but I could tell just how tired I was making you. I didn't want to be your burden anymore—"

"You were never a burden, Levi. Never." Kearney felt the guilt of that night gnawing away at him. *I'm the reason he feels like this. I'm the reason they're gone.* He wanted to pour his heart out more than anything but shoved the idea down. He raised his hands and gently held Levi's face, his thumbs stroking Levi's cheeks. "You're the strongest, bravest kid I know. I've just been too scared of letting you go to admit it."

Levi's eyes met his. "Letting me go?"

He nodded. "I was worried if I let you spread your wings, you'd get hurt. Or...." his voice trailed off.

"Or what?" Levi watched him intently.

Kearney cleared his throat. "I-I mean, the truth is, you have your whole life ahead of you! And as soon as you step into the world, you're going to meet so many new people. You'll build a new life for yourself, maybe even start a family one day!"

"You think I'm going to leave you behind, don't you?"

Kearney looked down, trying to hide the shame that had overcome him. "Or hate me," he muttered. "All this time, you could've had a normal life if it weren't for me. I messed up too much."

"Everyone messes up sometimes." Levi smiled reassuringly. "Think of all the good things you've done. I'm *alive* thanks to you!"

Kearney stiffened. "That's not what I meant, Levi."

"What is it, then?"

"I've...." He let out a shaky sigh, ready to finally say it. To confess. "I've ruined your life."

Levi furrowed his brow. "How can you say something like that? You didn't ruin anything—!"

"I'm the reason they're dead, Levi."

Those words pierced through Levi like bits of shrapnel, and he stared at Kearney in bewilderment. A heavy silence hung over them before he finally gained the courage to ask, "What do you mean?"

Regret flickered in Kearney's eyes. He sucked in a deep breath, but his voice was still as shaky as before. "The night it happened...I was running away, and I ran onto the road." He couldn't bring himself to look at Levi anymore. "A-And I didn't mean to, but I ran in front of your car. Your parents drove off the bridge to avoid hitting *me*."

Levi stared at him, mouth hanging open, completely speechless. Tears welled in his eyes.

"I-I wanted to tell you from the moment we met, but I just...I couldn't bring myself to do it." Kearney shrank in his seat. His trembling hands pulled away from Levi's face. "I felt so guilty...I just wanted to blurt it all out, but I *couldn't*...."

"Why couldn't you?" Levi choked out.

Kearney opened his mouth to answer, but no words came out. He shrank and turned away, his back facing Levi as he buried his face into his hands and struggled to stifle his sobs. *Don't cry,* he begged himself. *Please, don't cry. Not here. Not now. Please....*

Levi stared at him in utter bewilderment. He remembered that night, standing on the river's shore and seeing Kearney on his knees, screaming, *I'm sorry,* over and over. That made sense now. "K-Kearney," he fought back tears, "it wasn't your fault."

Kearney's only reply was a small head shake as he kept his face hidden in his hands. He only found the courage to look up once Levi had wrapped his arms around him.

"You didn't mean to, Kearney!" Levi hugged even tighter as he choked out the words. "It wasn't your fault! Don't say it was your fault!" He kept crying as he held Kearney's hands in an attempt to console him, but he only started crying more as he realized how bloodied and torn they were, not to mention that one of them was missing an index finger. "I-I told you to k-keep an eye on them," he said, half crying, half laughing. "H-How are you going to fix my scarf for me now...?"

Kearney gently wiped his tears away. "I'll fix it just fine," he whispered as he let out a shaky breath. "I p-promise I'll keep an eye on the rest. I promise."

"You'd better!"

Kearney pulled him close in a hug, and Levi rested his head on his shoulder as he struggled to stifle his tears.

"I'm so sorry," Kearney choked out. "So, so sorry."

Levi sniffled again. "Is that what you thought all this time? That you're a murderer?"

Kearney bit his lip.

"You're not a murderer, Kearney. You're the best person I know. You're not a murderer."

"Levi, I—"

"I don't want you to ever say or even *think* that again. I forgive you, okay? It wasn't your fault. I forgive you!"

Kearney hugged him tighter. "Okay." But deep down, he knew *okay* would never be enough. Would Levi ever truly forgive him for what he'd done?

"And I want you to forgive yourself, too."

He froze. "I-I don't know if I can."

"I want you to, Kearney." Levi looked up at him, his brows knit in resolve. "Please. Do it for me, at least."

Kearney kept quivering as memories of that night overtook him. Running away. The bridge. The car. Getting carried down the freezing river. Meeting Levi. His throat grew sore as his memories played on repeat in his head. He thought of the clone. What it had said to him. What he had said to it. "I-I can't...."

"*Please.*"

The memories of that night faded, as did the car, and Kearney was left standing in the void of his mind. In front of him was that clone, only smaller. It looked to be the same age as he'd been on that night. It was staring up at him with a dull look on its face, eyes filled with grief and self-loathing. After a moment of silence, Kearney kneeled down. He and his younger self stared at each other, too afraid to touch, hug, or even speak. It felt like all they could do was quietly acknowledge what had happened to them. The things he'd told Levi and the things he hadn't. It didn't feel right to forgive himself. After all, he'd spent his whole life doing just the opposite.

He blinked and was back in that car with Levi. He hugged Levi tighter without a word.

Levi sighed. "I understand." His eyes met Kearney's. "Just…remember that *I* forgive you, okay? I love you, Kearney."

He gave Levi a small, grateful smile. "I love you, too."

"And don't give up yet. Keep trying. You'll forgive yourself one day."

Maybe.

They hugged in silence a little longer.

Kearney felt calm. He felt at peace. He let his eyes flutter shut as he quietly reminded himself that Levi was back. That they were hugging, that this was real, that they were together again. That despite everything, Levi loved him. He glanced down at Levi. It was strange, but Levi had never hugged him this tightly before. Maybe the feeling was more mutual than he thought. He gently kissed Levi's forehead, and Levi gave him an affectionate squeeze in return.

Soon, Levi cleared his throat and pulled away from him, their hug officially ended. "We should get out of here."

Kearney chuckled. "We should."

They looked through the windshield and stared out at the void. Levi glanced at the car's pedals below his seat. That mischievous smile was back. He slammed his foot on the gas, and the car jerked forward in response. He flinched and quickly hit the brakes. "Th-That was a lot freakier than I thought!" he exclaimed.

Kearney rubbed his head, which had just slammed into the dashboard thanks to Levi's prowess. "Warn me next time," he muttered as he slid onto the passenger seat and put on his seatbelt.

"Sorry."

He sighed. "Just take it slow, okay?" He reached out and put a hand on the wheel. "Does this help?"

Levi smiled shakily. "Yeah."

"Now, let's try again."

Levi nodded, his brow knit with newfound determination. "Alright!"

"B-But buckle up first!" Kearney scrambled to say as Levi's foot dove a second time for the gas pedal.

After Levi had aggressively buckled himself, he gently pressed on the gas, sending the car into a slow roll. He glanced at Kearney's hand, which was still firmly on the wheel, and it gave him courage. He pressed harder, and the car went faster. His eyes shone with excitement.

"I'm doing it. Kearney, I'm *doing* it!"

"You are!"

In seconds, the ground was gone from beneath them, and the car was soaring through the endless blue sky. Kearney could see the dream begin fading away, and it seemed Levi could, too.

"I'll see you soon!" Levi said with a grin, his voice an echo.

He and the car faded out of Kearney's sight, and Kearney was left hurtling through darkness. He didn't scream although, at the speed he was going, screaming would've been a perfectly natural reaction. He could see something in the distance. It looked like light, and it was approaching *very* quickly. Soon, he could make out that the light was actually a room, a little gray block of space existing in the void. He flailed his limbs in the air as it got closer. Panic overtook him, but he could do nothing to stop himself from slamming into the room. He didn't feel any pain when he rammed headfirst into one of the room's walls, which only startled him more. Not to mention the wall had a Kearney-shaped dent in it now.

He stumbled to his feet and looked around. The room he was in was largely empty, with one doorway being the only way forward. After a brief moment, he walked through it and looked around. A graveyard of damaged books lay at his feet, and decrepit shelves towered above him, leaning forward and making the tiny room feel even smaller. He guessed he was in a library. A very scary one, at that. His gaze trailed to the middle of the room, where he saw two chairs sitting side by side. In one of them was a brown-haired girl with her back to him.

Gabi! He ran toward her.

She didn't turn at the sound of his approaching foot-steps. As a matter of fact, she was so still that he won-dered if she was a statue. He walked the last few steps up to her and leaned down to see her face. At that point, he had no doubt that he was standing next to the real Gabi. The only thing he couldn't understand was why she was crying.

"Gabi?" He put a hand on her shoulder. "I'm here now. Are you okay?"

She didn't lift her head. Her voice was barely a whis-per. "She's dead. This is where she died."

He stiffened as he lifted his eyes to search the room, but he didn't see anyone or anything other than them. He looked back at Gabi. "...Her name was Anais?"

She nodded. After a minute, she forced a small smile, although it didn't seem to bring her much comfort. She sucked in a shaky breath. "She loved reading corny ro-mances. I told her they were dumb, but even then, I'd always find her here after school."

"What happened?" he asked quietly.

"Some sick guy got his hands on a gun, and...I didn't make it on time." She shrugged as tears slid down her cheeks. "I had a hard time believing she was really gone. I guess that monster knew it, and that's why he started giving me those dreams. Dreams that she was stuck here and that all I had to do to get her back was come and save her...." Her voice trailed off.

He sat down and wrapped his arms around her in the biggest hug he could give. He knew how horrible the feeling was, but at least he had the comfort of having Levi back. Gabi never would, and he only wished there was something he could say to make it hurt a little less.

"...I'm here now, Gabi. I'm here."

She started sobbing again, grabbing his shirt as she pressed her face against his shoulder.

He sighed as he hugged her tighter. He gently rocked back and forth with her. "I'm here. I'm here."

She choked and sniffed, her lips pressed in a white line as she struggled to stifle her sobs. Those sobs were the only sound that filled the quiet library for a while until she was finally calm enough to speak again. "How did it feel? When you lost your brother."

She doesn't know. "It felt like nothing." He lowered his eyes. "Where he used to be, there was nothing. No voice, no him...I couldn't even think of him, really. And whenever I did feel something, it was either sadness or anger."

"Anger?"

He let out a heavy sigh. "We were in Jolly, and he threw us out. We fell into a river, and when Calder only pulled me out, I assumed that meant Levi was dead."

She let out a shaky sigh. "At least...at least you never had to see it."

"The thing is, he's alive."

She gasped and looked up at him. "He is?"

She looks so excited. She doesn't even know him. "He's in the mansion, too."

"You have to go get him then," she said urgently.

"We," he corrected as he rose to his feet and offered her his hand. "I'm not leaving you here."

The light in her eyes quickly died. "I'm fine here."

He grabbed her hands fervently. "You're not, Gabi. Listen, what happened to your sister wasn't your fault."

Her hands slid out of his and fell onto her lap. After a moment, she sighed. "I thought you were done with me."

What? "Of course, I'm not!"

"You left me on the Ferris wheel. Then you left again with The Tailor."

"Neither of those were because of you!"

"That's why you could do it again."

His cheeks were hot with shame as he sat back down in defeat. "Th-Things were different then. I—"

"I'm not ready to lose you, too." Her hands curled into fists on her lap, and her lip quivered as she struggled to keep it still. She bent over as sobs overtook her again.

He hugged her again. "I'm so, *so* sorry I left. I won't ever again, I promise."

Her eyes brimmed with tears as they searched his. "You'd better not break that promise, Kearney," she sniffed.

"I won't." He gently cupped her cheek and nodded with resolve. "I'll keep it until the day I die. And if I don't, feel free to be the reason the day I die comes a little quicker."

She gave a small chuckle and let her cheek rest in his palm. "That's a big responsibility. I'm not the Grim

Reaper, you know." The sorrow in her eyes began to fade, slowly replaced with a humorous look. "How about I coat you in honey and toss you on an anthill?"

"Fire ants?"

"That one can be your choice," she said with a laugh. "I'll let you have that much."

He struggled to suppress a giggle as he imagined how ridiculous a scene like that would look. But no matter how hard he tried to keep a straight face, Gabi's laughter was too contagious, and before he knew it, he was laughing with her. Soon, their laughter died down, and his gaze lowered to her lips.

"I'm glad you're safe," he whispered.

She smiled. "Of course I'm safe. I have you, don't I?"

"Right." He gazed contentedly into her eyes, remembering the time he'd kissed her cheek—how soft her skin had been, how warm she'd felt, how he'd panicked when he'd first realized how precious she was to him. Now, he didn't feel any panic. After all, why would he?

After a hesitant moment, he leaned a bit closer.

She watched him quizzically. When she understood, she closed her eyes and leaned in a little, too. He tilted her head toward his and kissed her.

In a way, he could hardly believe it. He was kissing Gabi. There was a time when he hadn't thought it'd be possible, yet here they were. He was astounded, but he didn't stop, and she didn't push him away. Instead, she wrapped her arms around him and leaned into him as she kissed back. She leaned so far that he almost fell back in his seat. Tears flowed freely down her face, and he wiped them away, but even after her cheeks had gone dry, he continued to stroke them. His hand trailed from her cheek to her ear, and he gently ran his fingers through her hair as he brushed it away.

They pressed into each other, savoring each other's warmth, and after what felt like hours, he pulled himself away just far enough to look her in the eye. He opened his mouth to say something, but she spoke first.

"What's going to happen when we leave the House? Where will you go?"

He paused, pursing his lips in thought. "Well, I promised I wouldn't leave you. So, I guess I'd go with you."

"Go with me, as in home?"

"Yeah. Home."

She chuckled. "That almost sounds too good to be true. Home, but with you." She rested a hand on the nape of his neck. "I guess all of this proves it, huh? It's too hard not to love you." She pulled him close and kissed him again.

Chapter 36

Gabi Meets Her Sister (and an Annoying White-Haired Brat)

Air rushed into Levi's lungs as the world snapped into focus. The car was gone. He was back in Phantasos's room. He leaned forward in his seat, wincing from the ache in his lungs. He glanced down at the dead string hanging from his neck and carefully freed himself from it. He rubbed his neck, his fingers going over the indentations the string had left on his skin. Then he gasped. *My scarf!* His panic ebbed away when he realized it was resting safely on his lap.

He glanced to the side and saw Annette's headless body lying where Phantasos had left it. He forced himself to look away and shuddered. *Annette...I'm sorry. I'm so sorry.*

His gaze snapped to the disheveled closest, and he slowly got to his feet. He peeked inside, eyes darting every which way in search of Anais. Instead, he saw Henry, who was lying with his mangled body bent in ways no living person would be able to endure.

"H-Henry?"

Henry's expression was dull. "What do you want now?"

"What *happened* to you?"

He grinned from ear to ear with joy, although it was just as likely to have been madness. "Master didn't get rid of me, after all," he whispered giddily.

"Where's Anais?" Levi demanded, unaffected by Henry's euphoric state.

"Master probably took her," Henry said. "For his plan."

Levi felt himself shaking with anger as he tried to keep himself from looking over his shoulder at what was left of Annette. "I'm not letting him hurt her, too," he growled.

Henry's ecstasy vanished, and he shook his head with sudden alarm. "Please don't hurt him," he quietly begged.

"Why would you want that? After what he's done?"

"I *need* him." His voice was low but fierce. "I'm nothing without him. You can't!"

He's well beyond helping. "I will!" Levi yelled before stopping himself. *He's shaking.* His eyes trailed to the pillow lying at Henry's side. It had its insides torn out and spread everywhere. "Is…that your pillow?"

Henry forced himself to stare at the wall at his side. "It was."

"What happened?"

"I'm not supposed to touch her." His voice wavered as he tried to keep his face from twisting in grief. "It's one of Master's tests, that's all."

"What?" Levi shook his head in astonishment. "But—!"

"I promised Master I wouldn't love her ever again!" His voice was as shaky as he was. "N-Never again."

Levi froze in bewilderment. "Is she...meant to be someone you knew?"

"What if she was?"

Levi stiffened, ashamed of how he'd treated that pillow before. "I'm sure she misses you, you know."

Henry paused before choking out the words, "I broke her heart. I was all she had, and I broke her heart." He hugged his knees as the light in his eyes faded. "...She'd never love me again. Master's...all I have. All I am...." His broken body went limp and slumped to the side.

Levi stared at what was left of the little butler, hardly able to wrap his head around the fact that he'd never hear his voice again. He stared at the grief that would forever be in those eyes, and his chest tightened with anger. He lifted his gaze to the ceiling, the only place in that room that didn't cause him pain to look at. Then he marched out of the room, determination swelling in his chest.

This won't happen to any doll ever again. I'll make sure of that.

Gabi rubbed her temples, exhaling with a groan as she roused herself from sleep. When she opened her eyes, the first thing she saw was her own face, only horribly scratched. She reached out and touched it, and her fingers rubbed against smooth wood.

"No-Face?"

The wooden version of her didn't reply or move in the slightest. It lay staring at her with that giant smile. A very fake smile. Kind of stupid-looking, too.

She stared at it before apprehensively shoving it. It rolled off the couch and rag-dolled to the floor. She sat up to get a good look at where it was now, thoroughly convinced that thing wasn't No-Face. But why would a random wooden version of her be lying around? Her gaze lowered to the string on the doll's wrist, and she quickly realized it was tethered to her own. She yanked it off, and the string glowed red in protest before fading back to its original shiny white. She shook her head, trying to process whether or not she was really awake. When she stood up from the couch, she stepped on something soft. She glanced down and saw a red-haired fleece puppet lying under her shoe. It had the same teal eyes and red hair as her sister.

After she had been dazedly studying its features for a quiet minute, it spoke. "Can you get off me?"

She jumped back in shock. "Sorry, sorry! I didn't realize you're alive!"

"That seems to be a recurring theme," it muttered.

She paused awkwardly before picking up the puppet and gently brushing dust off it, muttering another sorry as she did. "I'm Gabi. What about you?"

There was a brief silence. "…I'm not really anybody," the puppet replied. "I was made to be someone, but only for a little while. Now, I'm pretty much worthless."

"I don't think you're worthless."

"It's not like you know anything. You just met me."

"Well, maybe you can help me understand." Gabi smiled. "You said you were…made to be someone? Who?"

"Some chick named Anais," the puppet replied quietly.

"Anais?" Gabi felt her gasp get caught in her throat.

"You sound like you know her."

"I.…" She lowered her head. "I did."

"Something happened to her?"

"Yeah."

"Oh." The puppet paused for a moment, seemingly searching for words to say. "Sorry to hear that." She sounded disappointed. "I guess I was made for you, then."

"I thought you were made to be Anais."

"Yeah, and that was probably because Phantasos wanted to bring you here," the puppet began. "When he first made me, I felt a tug deep inside. A really small one, but it felt important. I bet you had the same thing, and that's what motivated you to get here."

Gabi nodded, her lips pursed as she processed those words. "And now that tug is gone—"

"Because we're finally together. And that means I'm worthless."

"You're *not* worthless," she repeated more emphatically.

"I've *outlived* my worth."

"Well, maybe you shouldn't base your worth on dumb things like that!"

"What do I base it on, then?"

Her grip on the puppet tightened but stayed gentle all the same. "On those who really care about you. The things that matter to you and what you believe. Not things that pass by so quickly."

"What if I don't know what all of those are yet?"

"Well, you never run out of time to figure them out," Gabi said. "I'm going to be leaving this place soon with some friends. If you want, you can come!"

"Why? Because you need a new Anais?" The puppet's voice was cold.

Gabi flinched as those words stabbed her heart. Hearing this puppet speak just like her sister had was messing with her. She wanted to spill all of that pent-up love she had for Anais onto a perfect stranger. It almost felt wrong not to, really. "I do miss her, but you're not her. I know that."

"What's with the mushy invite, then?"

Gabi sighed. "Because it doesn't feel right to leave anyone here, really. If you choose to come, I promise I'll try my hardest to help you figure things out and show you how beautiful life is. We can even be friends if you want." Friends. It felt so strange to be saying that to the puppet with her sister's face.

"Show me stuff about life?" The puppet's voice was quiet, but she sounded curious. "Like a sky?"

"More than the sky! Like...Like wrapping up in a cozy blanket to watch a movie or walking early in the morning while the sun warms everything up!"

"Were those the kinds of things you'd do with your sister?"

"Some of them. But if you want, I'll do all of them with you!"

"That sounds...interesting." She paused. "I have one more question."

"Yeah?"

"Do you think I could be a Wendy?"

Gabi's grin turned into a small, thoughtful smile. She was having a hard time adjusting to the puppet's appearance and voice. A different name would definitely help. "It's pretty cute, just like you."

"You think I'm cute?" The puppet went quiet for a few seconds, likely deep in thought. "Alright, I'll do it. As Wendy. I'm Wendy now. Don't forget that."

Gabi held 'Wendy' close in a hug. "You're a great Wendy already."

Their joy was interrupted by the sound of someone stomping upstairs behind them. They both turned to look at where the noise was coming from, and a boy with white hair soon appeared, although at that point, he was crawling, as he hadn't realized how energy-consuming stomping up a staircase could be.

His blue eyes fixed on Wendy. "Anais, you're okay!" he gasped.

"Yeah. By the way, I'm Wendy now. And this chick is my friend."

The boy seemed to be fully aware of Gabi's presence at this point, as he was now trying to hide the excitement in his eyes and act more nonchalantly. "Cool, cool."

Gabi glanced at Wendy. "Who's this?" *And how the heck is his hair so white?*

"I'm Levi," the boy explained with a wave of his hand. "But what's in a name, right?"

Levi. "Hang on, you're Kearney's little brother!"

Levi blushed. "Yeah," he replied. She could see his eyes fill with warmth at the mention of Kearney. "A-Anyway, I have to find him before Phantasos does."

Gabi felt panic set in. "He's not with you?"

"No, and I can tell he's not with *you*." He ambled past her and out the door, trying not to put too much weight on his left ankle, which seemed to be sprained. "And that means I need to hurry up!"

"That means *we* need to hurry up!" she corrected.

He glared at her, clearly mad his authority was being questioned. "*Me*."

House Full of Strings

Chapter 37

Everyone Falls Through the Floor

Wake up. Please, wake up. We're going to die unless you **wake up**....

Kearney opened his eyes. He was in Phantasos's library again, sprawled out on the ground and staring up at the ceiling. His hands were sore, and he didn't want to know how it'd feel to move his shoulders. He squeezed his eyes shut.

Can't lie here all day. He tensed every muscle in his body as he tried to get up but quickly realized he couldn't. Fear pricked down his spine as he glanced at his hands. There were little holes in his palms left by Eye Stealer, crusted with blood. And there were strings running through them, rubbing his skin raw every time he moved, keeping him pinned to the floor.

His eyes started wildly darting around. *All* of him was tied down. His heart leaped in his chest as his breath quickened. *I'm in a web.*

I know. Now, get out of it. Phobetor was back, which brought Kearney some comfort. Not a lot, but some.

He squirmed. *It's not that easy!*

Something shifted in the corner of Kearney's vision, and his focus was on it in a heartbeat. It was Phantasos.

He cocked his head slightly. "I didn't think you'd wake up so soon. No matter." He crept over to Kearney, his red eye fixed on him keenly.

Get away! Get away from him! Phobetor's shrieks rang in Kearney's ears.

"I was hoping we could've been friends, but it seems that you came into my home with ill intentions." Phantasos was looming over him now.

"Ill intentions," Kearney spat as he tugged against the strings with courage he didn't know he had. His hands started burning again. "I'm getting my brother away from you. Those are my intentions!"

"Away from me?" Phantasos looked offended. "Levi's quite happy here, mind you. I gave him the freedom you were too afraid to."

"Freedom? He didn't look free to me!"

"It's better than what he had with you. The poor boy told me all about your tyrannical nature—the ways you gatekept him, how all he wanted was to get away!" He leaned in close. "It's a real shame. He once seemed so fond of you, but as soon as I brought some critical thinking to the table, he grew to despise you."

Liar. Anger billowed in Kearney's chest. "I just talked to him, and he seemed to like me just fine."

"You what?" Phantasos reeled back. "Talked to him? You're bluffing." Then, seeming to understand what Kearney meant, he stiffened. "I designed the snow globe to put you in a dream when you touched it, but to fall into *his* dream...." His eye widened as he put a bony finger on Kearney's forehead. "How ever did you do it?"

Kearney shrank at Phantasos's touch. "I-I didn't do anything. Levi needed me, that's all."

"Interesting," Phantasos murmured. "Yes, that's very interesting. You're quite exceptional, aren't you?" That last sentence was different from the rest, filled with warmth, and it caught Kearney off-guard.

"Exceptional?"

"Yes, exceptional! To come all this way, through all sorts of trials and tribulations, you truly are a talented boy, aren't you?"

"What are you doing?"

"Telling you how amazing you are! After all," Phantasos leaned in again, but this time closer and more intimately, "you never had anyone to tell you these things, have you? To have someone tell you you're smart or strong...or even congratulate you on overcoming that nasty stutter all on your own when you were young." His voice was a silky purr. "And in that dark closet, no less."

Kearney stared in bewilderment. "Even Levi doesn't know about that. How do you?"

"*I* know, Kearney." Phantasos gently strummed a string beside him. "I made these strings. I can read the memories in them in a heartbeat. Stay, Kearney." He stroked his forehead again, warmth glowing in his red eye like fire in a hearth. "Stay, and I'll tell you how exceptional you are every day."

Anger crept into Kearney's chest. Those words would've been tempting if they hadn't been said by a proven kidnapper. "No."

The warmth vanished in an instant, and Phantasos's finger curled with anger, its fingernail scraping down Kearney's forehead. "*Why not?*"

Kearney shuddered as he felt blood slide down his face. "B-Because I know better."

Phantasos stared down at him with an unreadable look. Then he grabbed Kearney's face, his hand nearly covering all of it as his fingers arched with irritation. "A shame you're clouded by such prejudice." His hand surged down, ripping the web under Kearney as he slammed Kearney's head into the floor. "You know, from the moment you stepped into the House, I never cared for you."

Kearney's thoughts swam as he tried to make sense of the world around him, but he didn't have time to do so before Phantasos slammed his head down again. He grabbed Phantasos's hand, desperately trying to wrench it off his face. His shoulders were burning again. Fresh blood flowed from his hands and stained Phantasos's bony, black wrist.

"The only reason you're even remotely a threat now is because you have *him* in your head. And you'll come to realize he's nothing but a pathetic coward. That's why he's so quiet now that I'm here. He only chose you to begin with because he's *desperate.*"

Phantasos slammed him down again, and Kearney could do nothing as the world around him grew fuzzy.

Phantasos' voice was a distant echo now. "*After all, what's there to care for? A little rat whose own parents didn't love him?*"

Kearney was vaguely aware that Phantasos wasn't slamming his head down anymore. He realized he was dangling in the air with Phantasos's hand still firmly gripping his face. He heard a fuzzy voice.

"What are you doing?" the voice screamed.

"Taking out the trash, that's all. You don't need him, snowflake."

"Put him down right now!"

Kearney felt his body slump to the ground, and he could finally breathe again.

Get up, kiddo. Get up!

Please…shut up.

His vision slowly came into focus, and he saw Phantasos hovering just inches away from Levi, who was glaring at him with balled fists.

Kearney struggled to his feet. "Don't touch him!" he tried to yell, but his words came out slurred.

Phantasos didn't glance back, and Levi only looked at Kearney briefly before shifting his attention back to the monster. Kearney noticed Gabi was there, too. She was hurrying to his side and helping him to his feet as the terrifying exchange between Levi and Phantasos continued.

"Kearney, you—!" Her smile faded. She ran a hand over his forehead, then the back of his head, and felt blood. "You're bleeding." She lifted him to his feet. Then she noticed his shoulders. "A-And you're bleeding some more…." She held his hand, which was sticky with crusted blood. Her eyes were huge. "And you're *also* bleeding there.... Just stay with me, alright? We'll be out of here soon enough."

He half-nodded in reply, struggling to focus his attention on Levi and Phantasos.

"...I'm leaving." Levi's voice was shaky but determined. "And I'm taking Anais—*Wendy* with me," he said as he held the little fleece puppet in his hand defensively.

"Is that so?" Phantasos's voice was a low growl as he glared at Levi. Suddenly, he threw his head back and laughed. It was a scary laugh, playful yet menacing. "It doesn't matter if she and the girl are with you in this room or not. If you're so insistent on abandoning me, you're taking your *rat* and nothing more. And I'm so generous, I'll even give you a head start. Ten seconds." After that, he did nothing but stare, and they realized the countdown had begun.

They raced into the hall as Phantasos watched hungrily. The only sound in the mansion was the sound of their footsteps thumping against the carpet and their panting. Kearney hardly had any sense of time anymore. The only thing he seemed to be able to concentrate on was the sound of footsteps, and even that was distant. Everything hurt. He felt like he was about to fall over. He wanted to take a nap and wake up from this nightmare. At times, he was barely even aware that he was moving, and he doubted he would have been moving at all if not for Gabi guiding him.

The ten seconds ended just as quickly as they'd started, and the four kept hurrying, waiting in tense silence for what was to come. But Phantasos didn't come racing into the hall after them.

Instead, the walls around them started rumbling and caving in on them.

Everyone screamed as they ran faster, although they had no idea where they could go to escape the towering walls that hunched over them and rapidly drew closer, like a pair of hands ready to clap a mosquito dead.

Kearney's head buzzed with pain. He skidded to a halt, pressing a hand over his eyes as his head screamed for respite. He could feel Gabi tugging his other hand, making his shoulder jerk and hurt.

"Kearney, move! Move!"

There's a door!

In a shift so violent it made Kearney feel like his skull was splitting open, he snapped back to reality. All the pain seemed to melt away and become a distant memory. His senses felt heightened, although he wasn't sure if that was due to Phobetor or his concussion-caused delusions. He scanned the area. *What? Where?*

Straight ahead. Go!

His eyes skipped from Gabi, who was screaming at him, to Levi, who was screaming at nothing in particular, to the door at the other end of the hall. The door didn't seem to be screaming.

"This way!" he yelled as he raced toward it.

The others seemed shocked he'd come back around so quickly but followed without hesitation. He was running so fast he slammed into the door in a heartbeat, but horror set in once again when he realized it was locked.

Levi hurriedly reached for a pick in his pocket and started working at the lock, and Kearney pressed his back against the wall behind him, kicked his feet up against the wall opposite him, and strained with all his might to keep either of them from closing in any farther. Gabi followed suit, but given the walls were so close that each one was already touching Levi's shoulders, they hardly had seconds left. Kearney struggled as he felt the walls squeezing his body, unfazed by his attempts to keep them apart. He glanced at Levi, who was still frantically picking the lock.

"Hurry up!" the fleece puppet in Levi's hand shrieked, which thoroughly freaked out Kearney. He couldn't tell if his concussion had made him hallucinate that shriek or if it was real.

"I'm trying!" Levi yelled back.

Kearney could see the beads of sweat rolling down Levi's face as his shaky hands kept working. Finally, salvation came with a tiny *click*, and Levi shoved the door open. He grabbed the others and pulled them through moments before the walls clapped shut behind them, sending dust and debris flying everywhere. They lay dazed on the floor, gasping for breath for only a moment before Kearney wiped his brow and got to his feet. He grabbed the other two and helped them up, spotting another door. They began warily walking toward it, eyes scanning every corner of the room, fearing something might jump out at them. It didn't seem like a stretch to assume that the fancy candles might commit suicide and plunge off their stands just to start a fire or that the giant piano in the corner might jump to life and crush them.

Soon, they were in the middle of the room, at which point they all realized the only place they hadn't been intensely staring at was the floor. The floorboards rippled and split, and they all fell into the freshly made hole.

Kearney landed on his back, gasping for breath once he hit the ground. He stared up at the floorboards above him as they closed back up, leaving them in darkness.

Oh no. We fell right into his trap, Phobetor's voice rattled.

This whole place is under his control. You could've said that about anything!

Gabi was on her knees, feeling around for something in the darkness. "Levi, do you have Wendy?" she asked. When he didn't reply, she groaned in frustration. "You dropped her, didn't you?"

"I *fell!*" he retorted.

"I'm fine," a third voice said tersely. Kearney concluded the third voice was that of the sentient puppet, also known as Wendy. It seemed she wasn't a hallucination after all. He'd make note of that.

Levi was brushing splinters off his shoulders, one hand firmly holding onto Kearney's hand in the darkness. "Well, now what?"

Kearney opened his mouth to reply, but then the boards around them rumbled again. They split before the four of them, revealing a dimly lit passage.

Kearney stiffened as he stared at it. He exchanged glances with the others. "We don't have much of a choice, do we?"

Levi squeezed Kearney's hand a little tighter and huffed, likely in an attempt to hide his nervousness. "Guess we don't."

They headed toward it.

What are you doing? Don't you have any sense of self-preservation? Phobetor screeched.

Even you can tell there's no other way.

The light ahead of them slowly faded as they got closer to it, which was strange and worrying, to say the least. And things were quiet, too, with their footsteps and an occasional cough being the only sounds to fill the tense silence.

Kearney could barely make out Levi's figure in the darkness, but he could see him moving awkwardly. *How did I not notice sooner?* "Are you hurt?"

Levi shook his head. "I'm fine."

"Is it your leg?"

"I said I'm fine," he snapped.

Kearney let out a sigh. "If you insist." After a minute, he felt Gabi's hand slip into his own and squeezed it.

"Are you feeling alright?" she asked. "How's your head? And don't lie to me about it."

"It's better."

"You sure?"

"I am." He leaned toward her. "Everything will be alright."

He felt her kiss his cheek. "I know it will be."

Levi jabbed him with his elbow. "Of course, it will be. We've got each other now."

Wendy groaned. "You're so dense."

Kearney could hardly suppress his chuckle.

They resumed walking in darkness. It was beginning to feel like the tunnel would never end. Kearney furrowed his brow. "Is it even possible for this thing to be so long?"

"I don't know." Levi bit his lip as he looked around. "Maybe it's a liminal space."

"A what?"

"It's kind of like a portal—"

Everyone froze at the sound of footsteps overhead. Kearney felt his skin crawl as he tried to figure out who they belonged to. It couldn't have been Phantasos; they were too light and quick.

"Freckles!" a voice called.

Levi's eyes narrowed. "...Is that vomit-hair?"

Oh, no. Kearney's heart was racing. *No, no, no.*

Gabi was squeezing his arm in a panic. "You brought him *here?*"

"I told him to wait outside!"

"What made you think he'd listen?"

"Freckles! Gabs! Where are ya'll?"

Then came a second pair of footsteps. Or, rather, three sets of footsteps in one. They were heavy yet incredibly quick, like a spider's. It seemed a certain monster had heard Calder as well.

Kearney and Gabi were running now. Levi didn't understand why they cared so much about the little brat, but he sped up to keep pace with them.

"*Freckles!*" Calder's footsteps stopped. Then he screamed.

They were flying down the tunnel at this point.

Calder was shrieking wildly. "*No, don't touch me! G-Get away! Freckles! Freckles—!*" His cries were cut off.

The light was getting brighter now. Kearney could feel Gabi's grip tighten in his hand as they hurried toward it.

They made it to the end of the passage, which was, more or less, a giant hole in the wall. They warily walked through it, struggling not to breathe in the sawdust drifting around them. Once they were on the other side, they were bathed in the room's soft yellow glow.

Kearney scanned the yawning room. *Where's Calder?* He stiffened. They were in the library again.

Levi's eyes darted every which way. "H-He led us back here?" He started backing away, tugging Kearney with him. "We have to go!" His back hit the wall. The tunnel had closed up.

Gabi squeaked in terror. "He's got Calder."

Kearney started spinning around, trying to find Phantasos. He realized Gabi was looking up and slowly raised his head. To his horror, the antlered noodle-neck spider monster was on the ceiling, his giant arms wrapped around an utterly terrified Calder. How he'd gotten up there, Kearney had no clue.

Kearney quickly brushed Levi and Gabi behind him and started backing away. "S-Stay back!"

Phantasos dropped from the ceiling, shaking the room with a loud *thud* as he landed and slamming Kearney to the ground. He threw Calder at Gabi with one hand while sending Levi flying into a bookshelf with the other.

Kearney writhed and kicked, his shoulders burning with pain, but Phantasos had him pinned down with his pointed legs, which were threatening to stab through his chest.

Levi winced as he struggled to stand. He finally gave in to the pain in his ankle and collapsed under the avalanche of books that had come down on him.

Gabi and Calder quickly got to their feet, but the threat of Phantasos killing Kearney right then and there made them too terrified to move.

Phantasos picked up Wendy and dangled her by her tiny arm as she cried out. His red eye flickered with delight that he'd won. And so easily, too.

That delight faded in an instant when he turned his head to look at something overhead. Kearney struggled to look past Phantasos's bulky frame but couldn't pry his eyes away when he spotted the giant metal ballerina.

Everyone froze and stared at her. She stood high above them on the guardrails of the second floor, perfectly still and poised. With a click of her needle-like legs, she hopped off the guardrail and descended, landing in a gracious bow. Her arms extended toward Phantasos as if inviting him to dance.

Phantasos stepped back, dropping Wendy and freeing Kearney. Gabi quickly scooped up Wendy and shifted closer to Kearney as she continued studying the metal dancer. Levi finally managed to drag himself out of the pile of books and limped to their sides. Kearney slung one of Levi's arms over his shoulder to support him. Levi shot Calder a sneer for good measure. Calder sneered back.

"What's that?" Wendy asked in awe. "It's pretty."

Kearney shuddered as his mind went back to his bloody shoulders. *Pretty* was the last word he'd use to describe that creature. "Eye Stealer."

Phantasos's head jerked back upward, and he fixed his gaze on someone standing on the balcony Eye Stealer had just descended from. "Oh. It's you," he spat. "Petty revenge? Is that what this is?"

"Call it whatever you like, dearest," the person sang in reply as she played with the needle in her hand. "Regardless, you hardly look in a state to indulge her in that dance she's been waiting for." Her eyes locked with Kearney's as if to say, *Good to see you're still in one piece.*

He looked away, his fists clenched in anger. He had no intention of forgiving The Tailor for leaving him to die. When her stare persisted, he glanced back.

She had something else to say. *You've done enough.*

Kearney beckoned for Levi and Gabi to start backing away, but Phantasos quickly noticed. He took a step toward them, closing the distance between him and them while still keeping his gaze on Eye Stealer.

"Forward," The Tailor said.

With one swift kick, Eye Stealer bolted ahead, her claws reaching for Phantasos. He shrieked and skittered out of the way, but as soon as The Tailor said, "Left," Eye Stealer was lunging at him again, this time successfully grabbing him by the throat, flipping him over her head, and slamming him to the ground.

"Go!" Kearney grabbed the others and raced away as Phantasos's wild screams thundered behind them. They raced into the hall and under a chandelier, which slammed into the ground and immediately used its winding appendages as legs to chase after them.

It bounded after them through the halls, sending its dangling crystals flying everywhere as its targets screamed in terror. If they'd stopped screaming for as much as a second, they'd have realized that the chandelier was barking at them.

Punch it, Phobetor hissed. *Punch it! What are you waiting for?*

Kearney didn't hesitate. He spun around with a jump and sent his fist flying into the chandelier. It immediately shattered at the contact, leaving only golden dust in its wake. Everyone slowed to a halt and stared at Kearney, who found a window, threw it open, and pulled them through before they could say a word. They landed outside and hurried away from the mansion.

Kearney's eyes darted around frantically. *What do I do now?*

You hit the ground as hard as you can, Phobetor said.

Kearney froze in his tracks, still in a haze from the strange amount of power that had overtaken him, and slammed his fist into the ground, which only made it sting a little. The others stared at him like he was insane. Kearney kept wildly hitting the ground again and again.

Harder.

He kept punching, but it still did nothing. *Why's it not working?*

Harder.

Strength pulsed through him, and with one last surge, he slammed a fist into the ground. The ground quivered in response. Small cracks snaked from where the blow had landed, and pale purple light seeped from the cracks, which continued to slither across the ground and around Phantasos's house. With another surge of energy, they split open, sending the mansion menacingly close to falling into the Dark Place.

Now on his knees from exhaustion, Kearney stared at his shaking hands in awe. Then his teeth gritted with annoyance. *I thought you said you'd just be a voice.*

So long as we're in the House, that won't be true. But in a minute, you'll sure be glad for that.

How so?

Hit the ground one more time, and you'll see.

Levi reeled back with confusion when Kearney slammed his fists into the ground yet again. But it wasn't the slamming that scared him. It was the cracks in the ground that were spreading everywhere and the purple light coming out of them. It was like Kearney had superpowers or something.

Levi watched as the cracks surrounded the manor. All his memories of Phantasos came rushing back, and Levi was suddenly terrified that the mansion was in danger and that he'd never feel Phantasos's warmth again. That fear was replaced with a very different one when he saw Phantasos, his shell horribly scratched and half-broken, rushing out of the manor. Levi could just barely see bits of metal and doll limbs sprawled out behind Phantasos. That was a nice wake-up call.

As the manor fell into the abyss behind it, Phantasos's eyes met Levi's. He slammed his head into the ground, shattering his already brittle shell and allowing his thousands of eyes to pour out of it. His vaguely human form sped forward with a screech as his winding arms reached for Levi, practically flooding Levi's vision in a haze of blackness dotted with red eyes.

Levi shrieked as he buried his face in his hands. Time seemed to slow as he let the darkness from his hands become his whole world. He could hear Kearney screaming for him to run, but he was frozen in terror. The eyes, Phantasos *himself*, had shaken Levi to his core. He knew freezing up was the worst thing he could be doing, but for the life of him, he couldn't think of how else to react.

Moments before Phantasos would've had his target, he froze.

Levi lowered his hands and saw Phantasos staring at him. He saw Phantasos's bony arms scraping against the ground as if being pulled back by some invisible force. Then he saw it. The string around Phantasos's neck. The string that kept him bound to the mansion that had just gone over the cliff.

With an animalistic shriek, Phantasos was yanked back, his claws leaving trails in the dirt as he fought back helplessly. He reached for Levi, clawing wildly. "Don't leave me, please!" he screeched with desperation. "I want you! I want you! *Just stay with me!*"

The string continued to tug mercilessly, and he was soon dangling over the cliff's edge, begging for dear life as the cracks in the abyss's cliffsides started glowing purple. With a rumble, the cliffs slowly began to move closer to each other.

"Please, *please!*"

Levi watched Phantasos cry out, barely aware that the world itself was bending toward Phantasos as if this was his last attempt to save himself. Phantasos was yanked back again until all Levi could see was a single hand reaching upward. "Snowflake! L-Levi! After everything I've done for you, *please—!*" he shrieked one last time before the cliffs clapped shut, crushing him and leaving his one hand reaching in desperation.

After a moment of perfect stillness, the hand twitched and went limp, and then it began to dissolve. A ripple echoed from where Phantasos had been crushed, and the world began to shrivel in response. More and more crimson particles swirled into the air like sparks from a bonfire.

Kearney was breathless as he watched the little red specs scatter into the air. There was something so beautiful yet so haunting in the image that he couldn't describe, but it gave him goosebumps. His eyes flicked to Levi, then to Gabi, then to Calder, who was staring vacantly at the ground.

"Calder?" he asked. "What's wrong?"

Calder started swaying back and forth, Kearney rushed to catch him just as he was about to fall.

Calder shuddered as red energy struggled and flickered all over his body. "Th-The Mister's gone...that means it's all over." He wrapped his arms around Kearney in a hug. "P-Promise me you'll take good care o' Gabs, okay?"

Kearney hugged him back, eyes wide, unsure what he could do. He looked at Gabi in a desperate search for help.

She shook as she glanced at Wendy. "Where's the way out of here? We'll take Calder, too!"

"If I'm right, then a door should appear any time now," she quietly replied.

Kearney forced a grin. "See? You'll be okay!"

A door materialized just behind them. It was small and looked brand new. It was glowing. Beckoning them. Kearney tried to carry Calder to it, but Calder refused to move.

"I don't want to go, Freckles. I'm tired. I miss D'kota." His face was pressed against Kearney's shoulder. "Just promise me."

Kearney let out a shuddering breath as he stared in disbelief. "I-I can't...." Then he hugged him back. "I promise," he choked out.

Gabi stared at Calder, her eyes glassy with tears. "You...you *can't* stay...you...." She shook her head then backed away with a sob, holding Wendy against her cheek.

"I'm gonna miss you so much, Freckles," Calder continued, "but I get to see my mama an' papa again. So, thank you. Thank you more than anythin' in the whole wide world."

Kearney fought back tears as he hugged Calder with all the love he could muster. "I'm just...happy you get to be happy." He gently let him go and rubbed his shoulders. "Will we ever see you again?"

Calder watched the sky thoughtfully. "I think so. One day."

Even though he didn't fully understand what that answer meant, it brought Kearney peace. He forced a smile as he mussed Calder's hair. "Tell your parents and Dakota that I said hi, okay?"

Calder grinned. "I'll tell 'em more than that!" He laughed weakly. His eyes then trailed to the glowing door behind Kearney, and his smile faded. "You gotta go," he said in a quiet voice.

Kearney glanced over his shoulder. "I do, don't I?" He fought back tears as he got to his feet. He glanced back at Calder one last time and forced a smile, and Calder smiled back, which made it harder to fight the pain tugging at his throat.

Kearney glanced at the door that would give him his freedom back. It was strange to think that once, he had been willing to give anything to see a door like that, but now, he just stared at it, hesitating.

Hurry up, kiddo. Phobetor was quieter now. Kinder. *There's not much time left.*

I know. He felt Levi take his hand.

"You okay?" Levi asked.

He flattened his lips into a white line as he nodded.

Levi gave him a sympathetic smile. "Let's go?"

He let out a shaky sigh. "Yeah." He looked up and saw Gabi waiting at the door, her eyes fixed unwaveringly on Wendy. She looked like she was struggling not to cry, probably because she knew she'd never see Calder again. But what hurt Kearney most was seeing that she was too scared of the grief to say one last goodbye.

He wrapped his arms around her and kissed her on the cheek. "Let's go home."

She nodded. "Yeah."

Kearney glanced at Levi again, who seemed confused as to why he'd just kissed a girl, given they were famous for having cooties. They all faced the glowing door together. It was wide open now, with golden light pouring out of it. One at a time, holding each other's hands, they passed through it. Kearney was the last in line, and he got to look back at Phantasos's dying world one last time and whisper "Goodbye" to the friends he'd made there.

Chapter 38

There Once Was a House Full of Strings

Levi was lying on cold concrete. He didn't know exactly how he'd ended up there, only that passing through that tiny door had been more chaotic than riding a rollercoaster in desperate need of maintenance. He sat up and brushed his hair out of his face. He glanced at the little house and its carved red doors, which had started this entire journey. The doors were different now. They'd lost that unnatural vibrancy and alluring presence he'd first known them for. A small smile bent along his lips as he got to his feet. That house would never trick another soul again.

Suddenly, he realized how light he felt. It didn't feel right for his back to not bend under the heavy weight of his backpack. He gasped. *My backpack!* He dropped to his knees again, shaking in utter grief. *Nooooo! All my cool stuff is gone!* A bright glint to his right caught his eye. It was his snow globe. He reached for it, brushing away the broken shards of glass, and held it close. He let out a heavy sigh. *I'm glad I still have you.*

He glanced at Kearney, who was hugging Gabi again. She had her face pressed against his shoulder, her chest jerking from tears. He kissed her forehead as he comforted her. For a brief second, Levi thought they looked romantic.

That's ridiculous. Kearney would never. He walked up to them. "Everything alright?"

Kearney nodded. "Yeah." He glanced back at Gabi for a brief moment. "Levi, I have something to tell you. It's important."

"What is it?"

"I'm going to stay with Gabi. I-I didn't know if you'd have a problem with that or not, but I didn't have any time to bring it up before. So—"

"So, what? I don't hate girls *that* much. Of course, I'm coming with you!" He squinted. "Unless you were planning on ditching me."

"Never in a million years," Kearney chuckled.

Gabi lifted her tear-soaked face. She smiled at Levi as she rubbed her eyes then glanced down at Wendy, who was still firmly in her hands. "I wanted to say thanks for taking care of Wendy. She really loves you."

"It was nothing, really," he replied with a shrug. Deep down, he felt warmth. *Really loves me, huh?*

After that, they all went quiet, seemingly unsure of what to do next.

"Hey, Kearney," Levi asked.

"Yeah?"

"What was going on earlier? With that weird purple light and stuff?"

Gabi joined in. "Yeah. How did you do that?"

Kearney forced a smile. His eyes were wide with panic. "Just a coincidence."

Nobody was satisfied with that. "What kind of coincidence is that?" Levi demanded.

"The coincidental kind." Kearney began leading them out of the alley, hoping they'd let it go. They didn't. Luckily, they forgot all about it when they got to the chain-link fence. Sunlight poured through it, which was a shock to them.

Wendy gasped. "Is that blue thing the *sky?*" she screamed at an extremely high volume, making everyone flinch.

"It is!" Gabi exclaimed.

"And what's the giant orb thing?"

"That's the sun. It gives us light in the day."

"Woah. That's so *weird.*"

Once they'd all gathered their bearings, they began climbing over the fence. First Levi, then Gabi, then Kearney.

"Hey, Kearney," Gabi called as Kearney climbed over the fence.

"Yeah?" he replied.

"I know why I felt funny when Calder called me 'Gabs.'"

"Really?" He landed beside her, grinning. "What is it?"

"It's my dad's nickname for me!" She giggled. "It feels so great to remember him and Mom again. I can't wait to tell them all about that weird house!"

Kearney was still smiling, but he became aware that his legs were beginning to shake. He'd hardly thought about her parents. What would they be like? *No turning back. Anyway, it'll be fine...right? Isma's nice. At least, I think she's nice. But what's Gabi's dad like?* Thinking about that only made Kearney more nervous. He forced a laugh as if that would help him calm down. Then he took Gabi's and Levi's hands and led them down the street. *I made Gabi a promise.* He took a right and stepped into Rob's store with a grin. *And I made Isma one, too.*

His grin faded instantly when he saw that there were two other people, a man and a woman, talking with Rob. Whatever they were doing before, Kearney had completely captured their attention now. He recognized the woman as Isma, but the man caused him to take a shaky step back.

That's the dad, isn't it? "M-Maybe this was a bad time to come in. Let's wait until—"

"Mom?" Gabi's hand dropped out of his. Her eyes were welling with tears. "Dad?"

Isma's lip quivered as she smiled, leaning against the man as if to steady herself. The man stared at Gabi in shock and joy and a bit of disbelief.

"Gabi?" they asked in unison.

She rushed forward and threw her arms around them. "I-I'm so sorry! I love you guys *so* much!" she sobbed. "I didn't mean to scare you or anything—"

"It's okay, honey," Isma soothed her as she wiped away her own tears. "It's okay...b-because you're back! You're back...." She started sobbing with Gabi.

Their crying turned into laughter when Gabi's dad wrapped his arms around them in a big hug.

Kearney stared at them in a haze, unsure if his mind was muddled because of the pain in his shoulders that was slowly overtaking him or because he'd never seen anyone act like this before. He figured it must've been a mix of the two, but a second later, he was teetering back and forth, feeling incredibly lightheaded as his head buzzed. Definitely a result of the pain rather than the fascination. He fell over.

Levi screamed as he caught him, his eyes frantically darting between him and Gabi. "He's bleeding everywhere! He's going to die!"

Gabi raced back to them with a shriek. Kearney shook his head, which made him even more dizzy. "I'm fine."

"Yeah, guys. He's fine," Wendy snapped. "Chill out!"

Isma started spinning when she heard Wendy's voice, unsure of where it'd come from. Her husband continued watching the strange scene before him in perplexity. It was obvious to Kearney that this was a terrible first impression.

Levi was shaking. "He's lost too much blood!"

Gabi was beginning to cry again. "You'll be okay, I promise! Just hold on for a little longer!"

"You guys are embarrassing!" Wendy hissed.

"I'm fine. It's nothing serious, really," Kearney quietly protested. He felt the world start to slip away from him again. He'd almost forgotten about getting his head slammed into the ground twenty consecutive times. He wished Phobetor would give him that weird superstrength again, just to be able to stand with some dignity.

Gabi ran to her parents and grabbed each by the arm. She was still holding Wendy, who was now getting smushed in her grip. "We have to get him to a hospital!"

Isma went back to staring at Kearney in shock. "How did that even *happen* to him...?" She looked at her husband helplessly.

"*What* even happened to him?" he asked, his red brows knit in a line.

"Can we drive him to a hospital, Rowan?"

"It'd probably be a crime if we didn't," he muttered.

Kearney struggled to console Levi, who could only blubber at this point. He glanced at Gabi, who seemed to be anxiously explaining to her parents what "Jolly" and "Phantasos" were, probably in an attempt to explain how he'd gotten so beaten up.

Isma stared at her, looking utterly confused, while Rowan slowly nodded with a serious look on his face as if that would somehow help him understand better. It didn't.

Kearney watched them, his wariness slowly fading. He was familiar enough with Isma not to be afraid of her, but he was terrified of Rowan. But he'd made Gabi a promise, and promises were a sacred covenant. And he had Levi, too. So, whatever was to come, he knew they'd all get through it together. Deep down, he had a feeling everything would be okay. He glanced back at Isma and Rowan, and he felt a little less afraid than before.

I don't like them, Phobetor muttered. *Not one bit. I bet they're serial killers.*

Kearney frowned. He had Phobetor, too.

House Full of Strings

Extras

The pages that follow are filled with lies and mysteries
and secrets and tragedies.

The Leash

Phantasos and Levi were in the tea room on the little red couch. They'd just finished a riveting game of petteia, and now, Levi had his eyes closed as he slumped beside Phantasos, his head resting on Phantasos's arm.

It was always fascinating to Phantasos how humans had a sense of time, even without the presence of a clock. As an experiment of sorts, he'd ensured visitors of the House had no means of knowing what the time was, and his theory always proved true. Humans just knew. How else could Levi have some idea that it was time for bed? He gently brushed Levi's mussed hair out of his face and, at that point, realized the boy was fast asleep.

He smiled. *You're just the sweetest thing, aren't you, snowflake?* His smile slowly flickered away, and he stared at Levi with a new emotion. A more primal one. Wanting.

After all, it didn't feel right for Levi to belong to that "Kearney" fellow. If he should belong to anyone, it should be to Phantasos.

Phantasos smiled again, now at the thought of sitting little Levi down and tying a string around the boy's neck. The thought that Levi would be his and only his was magical. It always was.

It's funny, snowflake. You think of yourself as a brave little lion, don't you? Prancing around and doing whatever you like, being friends with whoever you like. Acting as if they're so lucky to have you.

One of his hands inched closer to Levi's throat.

Little do you know, you're no lion. What you really are is a puppy. Sulking around with a leash in your mouth, whining and begging for someone to be gracious enough to take it and guide you. It seems, little Levi, that you've handed that leash to me.

He wanted to wrap a string around Levi's neck at that very moment. To choke the boy out as he slept and have him wake up in a pristine body of wood.

After a moment, he pulled his hand away. *But don't fret. I'm a good and gracious master.*

The Lullaby

"Three kings are sleeping,
Each in his bed.
Three kings are sleeping,
Mother tucked them in.
Three kings are dreaming.
The first dreams of dreams,
The second dreams of monsters,
The third dreams of strings."

The mummy on the throne quivered as he sang. It was an old song. Mother had sung it to him when he was little. He only barely remembered Mother. Mother had a beautiful voice.

When the mummy sang that song, he thought of—or rather, *remembered*—two names. The first name was Phobetor. That name made him laugh. When he thought of that name, he thought of a weak little boy hiding in a corner, crying because Mother had scared him again. He thought of an ugly little boy with ugly little hobbies. How that boy was ever Mother's child was beyond the mummy.

The second name he thought of was Phantasos. That name made him mad. It made him mad because he hated liars. Phantasos was a liar, so the mummy hated him. But, for the life of him, he couldn't remember what Phantasos had lied about.

The mummy paused, leaning back and staring at the high ceiling. Although he didn't want to admit it, a third name came to mind when he sang that song. It was buried deep in his mind as if it was playing hide-and-seek with him. Taunting him. It deeply upset him that he couldn't remember it. He knew only one thing about that name: he thought of it whenever he sang a special part of Mother's song. *"The first dreams of dreams."*

Maybe that part was about him.

The mummy quivered again. Why couldn't he remember? He looked down at his bony hand, which was wrapped in strings. He couldn't lift as much as a finger.

Why am I here?

Was that third name mine?

Mother was scary.

He paused and shook his head. Mother wasn't scary. He was Mother's favorite. But as he stared off into the nothingness around him, he remembered more of Mother. He was Mother's favorite. Mother's favorite toy. Mother wasn't very gentle with her toys. Perhaps she'd broken him. He couldn't remember.

The giant door to the throne room slowly rolled open, and the people who'd opened it were two boys.

The mummy was pulled out of his thoughts and watched them. They hadn't knocked, which made him mad. Very mad. So he treated them how Mother would've.

The Grief

Gabi's head hurt. That happened when she cried a lot. Her head hurt all the time after Anais died.

She was on her knees, looking up at Kearney pleadingly. He was leaving. He was going with The Tailor to the Wall. He'd probably die there.

She wanted to cry and scream, but she didn't. She sat and watched as he disappeared. He didn't look back once. Even when he was long gone, she kept watching, thinking maybe he'd come back for her. He didn't.

There was a rumble, and she looked over her shoulder. A red door was waiting for her. It swung open, and inside was a room. In that room was a couch, and on that couch was a little fleece puppet that looked just like Anais. But it wasn't Anais. Anais was dead. Gabi went through the door, anyway.

When she was on the other side, she realized there was a monster there with her. He looked like a monster but didn't sound like one. He wrapped his arms around her in a hug, and she didn't protest. Even though he was cold, the hug was warm. She wished he would've hugged her for longer.

He asked her to stay with him. He said he'd always be there for her. He said he would make sure her heart was never broken again. He said the new Anais would always be there for her, too. The new Anais wouldn't die on her like the old one had.

Gabi thought of her parents. She'd been gone for months. They'd probably given up already. She thought of Kearney, but he wasn't coming back. It hurt to think of him. She thought of No-Face. She'd told No-Face she had things to live for. People to live for. Was that a lie?

Gabi said yes to the monster.

House Full of Strings

The Dance

There was a woman who was born without sight. She wanted to dance and sway her arms in rhythm with the music that graced her ears. It was music that made her heart soar out of its darkness. She was pained to know she could never truly dance, for she stumbled each time she tried.

One day, that woman had a dream, and in that dream, she saw. She saw a man, tall and kind. He held her hand and kissed it. "Find me," said he, "and we will dance until the stars themselves go out."

So, the blind woman searched. For years, she searched, fueled by that dream and her love's voice, sweeter than honey. One day, she found a house and went inside. There, her love caught her up in his arms and kissed her. And they danced. For days, they danced and laughed and drank merry drinks. Not once did the woman leave his home; not once did she think of returning to her own.

Days turned into weeks and weeks into years, and before the woman knew it, she was old and frail while her love stayed young and jovial. She was soon too weak to dance, so he held her. He promised her death wouldn't end their story and that they surely would dance until the stars went out. Those words brought her peace, and she died in his arms. A new darkness had overtaken her world.

Shortly after, she woke from what should've been eternal slumber. She woke in a cold body of steel and in another world of darkness. Her love was nowhere to be found, and she had no mouth to cry out his name. She sat in utter silence, knowing she would dance with him no more.

-An excerpt from The Tailor's journal

The Friend

Dear Diary,
Calder didn't come to school again. I keep telling him to
come, and he always says he will, but then he doesn't. He's
been acting so weird ever since his dad left to go fighting. It
should make him sad, but he doesn't really look sad. He looks
distracted. I'm going to ask him why.

Dear Diary,
Calder came over today, and I asked him why he was missing
school. He said he made a new friend. I told him that he and
his friend need to stop missing school, but he laughed at me.
He said his friend is a grown-up. I got scared when he said
that. Mama tells me not to trust really nice grown-ups be-
cause they might be kidnappers. I told Calder that, and he
laughed at me again. I asked Calder if I could meet his friend.
He said no, and now I'm even more scared. What if his friend
is a really bad guy?

Dear Diary,
I skipped school and waited outside Calder's house so I could
follow him. When he left, he started walking down the street,
and I followed him. I was so quiet he didn't even notice. He

went between two buildings, and there was a little house in there. He knocked on the doors, and they opened for him. He went inside, but they closed before I could follow him.

Mama got mad that I wasn't at school today, so she made me go to my room. I cried because I'm always the good kid, but I know I have to be bad right now for Calder.

Dear Diary,
I followed Calder again. I got inside the house this time, and I saw a statue of a man with deer horns. But there were even weirder things, like a candy world and also an amusement park. It looked really fun, but it was kind of scary because everywhere I went, there were wooden kids. I followed Calder through the amusement park, and I saw a man there. The man had deer horns, just like the statue, and he was talking to Calder. I think he's the grown-up friend. I decided to be brave and go to them, and I shook the man's hand. Calder looked really mad at me for following him, but I didn't care. The man said his name is Fantasus. He was a lot of fun, but I have a bad feeling about him.

My mouth is bleeding, and I think I lost a tooth. When Calder and I left the house, I told him I think Fantasus is a bad guy. I said he's too nice and that everything in that house is weird, but Calder just got mad. We started fighting, and he punched me. I don't want Mama to see me when I get home. I don't want her to worry. I'm crying right now, so as soon as I'm done, I'll go home and hide in the bathroom.

Dear Diary,
Calder was at school today, but he kept ignoring me. It made
me sad, but I'm also happy he's safe.

Dear Diary,
Calder didn't come to school today. I went to his house, and
his mom said she didn't see him all day. I'm getting scared
again.

Dear Diary,
Calder never came home.

Dear Diary,
I went to the police station and told them about Fantasus,
but they didn't believe me. I tried to show them the house,
but when I took them there, the doors wouldn't open. They
probably think I'm a liar now.

Dear Diary,
Calder still didn't come home. I think I have to go save him
by myself. I'm scared, but I have to stop crying and be brave
for him.

Dear Mama,
This is my diary. I don't know if I'll come back, so I'm leaving it on my bed so you'll read it. I want you to know about the weird man, and I also want you to know that I love you. I'm not a bad kid, promise.
Love, Dakota

House Full of Strings

Kearney and Levi's story continues in

No Strings Attached

About the Author

Emmi lives in Snohomish, Washington, where the frequent rainy weather gives her an excuse to indulge in many, many hot cups of tea because "the weather just feels right." And when she isn't drinking tea (which is a task in and of itself), she's reading fantasy, duking it out with video game bosses, or watching terrible movies to get a good laugh out of it.

As of now, Emmi is probably tucked away in her room, sipping even more tea while fanatically writing whatever story piques her interest.